BENEATH THE SNOW

When Lisa McCall, a young and brilliant scientist, disappears from the small Alaskan town of Lake's Edge in the middle of a snowstorm, her estranged sister, Abby, flies out from England to join the rescue team. As soon as she arrives Abby knows there is something wrong – Lisa's cabin has been ransacked and her research material is missing. It emerges that as well as influential friends, Lisa has powerful enemies who will stop at nothing to protect their interest, so Abby embarks on the dangerous task of locating Lisa before someone else gets to her first.

BENEATH THE SNOW

BENEATH THE SNOW

by

Caroline Carver

Magna Large Print Books
Long Preston, North Yorkshire,
BD23 4ND, England.

British Library Cataloguing in Publication Data.

Carver, Caroline
    Beneath the snow.

    A catalogue record of this book is
    available from the British Library

    ISBN 0-7505-2583-5
    ISBN 978-0-7505-2583-1

First published in Great Britain 2005 by Orion,
an imprint of the Orion Publishing Group Ltd.

Published in Large Print 2006 by arrangement with
Orion Publishing Group

Magna Large Print is an imprint of Library Magna Books Ltd.

Printed and bound in Great Britain by
T.J. (International) Ltd., Cornwall, PL28 8RW

For Christina and Patrick.
One day maybe you'll actually get to
read the book.

Many thanks to Sue Acquistapace Redding, retired Alaskan State Trooper, for her extensive knowledge and goodwill.

Special thanks to Dr Janet Seed for creative thinking.

To Sara O'Keefe for her guidance.

Many thanks to Shirley Liss for introducing me to her huskies, Dr Mary Albanese for advice on all things Alaskan, Rachel Leyshon for her expertise and friendship.

Special thanks to Dominic Cole.

Thanks to Juliet Ewers, Jenny Page, Jane Wood, and the team that is Orion.

As always, all mistakes are mine.

One

It was just past midnight and Lisa was exhausted. She'd been on the run for five hours and the storm was still blowing hard, the temperature dropping. Recently even twenty below fahrenheit had become a rarity in Alaska, but this storm was from the old days and she reckoned it had to be at least minus thirty with the wind chill. Her attempts to keep warm no longer seemed to be working. Her feet and fingers were obstinately cold and if she didn't find shelter soon, she knew what would happen: she and her dogs would die.

Through the roaring wind she could hear the rattle of snow flakes on the hood of her parka, the dogs' harnesses creaking, her skis rustling on snow. She couldn't hear any engines, but she didn't doubt her pursuers were close behind. They'd have radioed for snow machines, walkie-talkies and guns. Lots of guns.

She could still hear the crack of the .45 calibre semi-automatic echoing in her mind, see the white-winter camouflaged figure swinging the pistol her way, seeking her out. If it hadn't been for her huskies, Roscoe and Moke, she'd already be dead.

Don't think about it. Push it aside and keep running. A snow machine can only go so far on a tank of gas, but my dogs can go much further. And when we're safe, then I can think about what I'm going to

13

do. Once we're safe.

They came to a frozen river. Immediately she urged the huskies across, checking ahead for dark, tell-tale cracks. Break-up had started last week when the much anticipated forty-degree mark had been reached, and she could barely believe the river felt as solid as bitumen beneath her skis. One day the countryside had been drip-dripping as it gently thawed itself in the sunshine, the next it had been thrown straight back into the deep freeze.

She had just started to turn towards Wildwood Ridge when the world closed in on her. The horizon vanished between the snow clouds and the endless white line of the Imuruk Hills. There were no shadows or edges and she could no longer tell whether there was a dip or bend ahead.

She lost the trail.

It was a whiteout, and there was no point in retracing her tracks because they were already covered. On one hand this was good, because it meant her pursuers would lose her spoor, but on the other, she might never find her way to safety.

Soon the dogs were up to their shoulders in soft snow and having to porpoise. A chill crept deep into her bones. She knew she was losing heat faster than she could produce it. Already her face was numb, and her feet and hands had become frozen. It became more difficult to push each ski forward and the desire to lie down and sleep was almost overwhelming. She had nothing left to draw on but sheer will, but she would not let them win. She'd rather perish with her dogs than give up.

The wind was now nearly head-on, picking up clumps of snow and ice pellets, and pounding her. They were all struggling, having to fight for every inch, when the terrain shifted, forcing them to climb. Roscoe and Moke stopped briefly and looked over their shoulders at her. Their expressions were puzzled and faintly hurt, telling her they were tired, and wanted to rest. Out of nowhere, Lisa wished Abby was with them. She'd have them sprinting to the top of the hill in no time.

And there she was. Her sister. Standing right in front of her. She'd forgotten how broad Abby's shoulders were, how statuesque her figure. She looked like a Nordic athlete and Lisa felt a rush of admiration.

A memory of Abby grinning down at her in her pram; playing hide and seek; extracting little green caterpillars from cauliflowers picked from the garden and throwing them at each other; water fights; painting each other's toenails: Abby walking out of Lisa's cabin four years ago, the air bitter as acid between them.

Abby seemed oblivious of the storm and was smiling. Lisa was so relieved she'd been forgiven she wanted to weep, but she couldn't. Her tear ducts were frozen. She wanted to tell Abby how tired she was, but she couldn't form the words. She felt disembodied, buried up to her thighs in snow, wind and ice whirling and shrieking around her. Slowly, she fell to her knees. A mantle of snow started to cover her, and it was strangely comforting, as though Abby was tucking her under the duvet at night. A great tranquillity suffused her. Snow clogged her eyelashes, blanketing her vision, but Abby was still there, smiling.

15

Lisa didn't see her two huskies standing over her, didn't feel their anxious faces pushing against her.

All she could see was her sister. Abby.

Two

Abby loped down Cowley Road, ignoring rush-hour stares. Her suit was drenched, her hair plastered against her scalp, but the bliss of wet pavement against her stockinged feet was exquisite. No amount of money would make her wear high heels again.

It had been raining for most of the day, a steady grey drizzle that England was so famous for, but it hadn't deterred the tourists. Her office looked east, towards Magdalen College, and the High street had been clustered with umbrellas for most of the day. But that was Oxford for you, a flourishing commercial city filled with meadows and ancient colleges that rarely took a day off.

Ducking into The Golden Dragon she inhaled the steamy aroma of frying onions and garlic, trying her best not to drool while she ordered. She could eat a whole duck she was so hungry. Lunch, a minuscule plate of politely sliced sandwiches with their crusts cut off, had been six hours ago. Shoes in one hand, briefcase in the other, Abby dripped on to the lino while Tony filled her order. Crispy duck for two, pancakes, hoisin sauce, cucumber and spring onions. A guy she hadn't

16

seen before took her money and passed her the carrier bag. He looked her up and down.

'You tall woman,' he stated.

'Not just in inches,' she responded, mentally rolling her eyes at his stating the obvious.

'Strong too, huh?' He appeared to be assessing her for a slave market. Abby left before he could start feeling her biceps and checking her teeth.

Head down, she strode for home. She couldn't wait to get out of her soaked suit and slide into something warm and comfortable. Damn Hugh. She never normally dressed up to impress clients, but this time her boss had insisted she forgo her usual uniform of jeans and workman's boots for something more businesslike, more feminine. How women could wear high heels all day defeated her. You couldn't walk properly and they were hell on your back. Abby felt as though she'd been weightlifting for half the day instead of presenting restoration plans for a nineteenth-century garden.

Dumping her briefcase in the hallway, she padded into the house. 'I'm home!' she called.

Her mother's voice floated down the corridor. 'See you when you're ready!'

Abby ducked the beam above the kitchen door and unwrapped the takeaway, popping it in the Aga's simmering oven to keep warm. She took her shoes to the bin, then hesitated. She may not want to wear them again, but what if she needed them in the future? Dithering briefly, she decided to be prudent and put them by the Aga to dry out.

The phone started to ring, but she ignored it. Her first priority was to get changed. Besides, her

17

mother always had a phone within reach; if it was for her, she would yell. Or she could press the little button on a chain around her neck that would emit a polite buzz throughout the house, but that was only used for emergencies.

To her relief there was no yell, no polite buzz, just the sound of rain rattling on the windows, the splash of traffic outside and, way in the distance, an ambulance siren. Heading upstairs she breathed in the faint odour of wood smoke and beeswax, looking forward to stretching out in front of the TV in an oversized fleece and sweat pants. She couldn't understand people who didn't go home at the end of their working day. Why risk being uncomfortable in some pub when you could have all the comforts of home?

Abby had just hung her sodden jacket in the airing cupboard when the house gave a polite burr. The emergency button.

She piled down the stairs, shouting, 'I'm coming!' Her mother had only pressed her emergency button twice in the last month: once when she had fallen out of bed and couldn't get up, the other time after she'd accidentally dropped a lit match into the bin and it had gone up in flames.

She'd suffered from MS, multiple sclerosis, since Abby was a child, stoically enduring her progressive physical decline, even accepting she could no longer drive and had to use a scooter with phlegmatic aplomb. Although she had been forced to give up her biology sciences tutorial post at Christ Church College, Professor Julia McCall had no intention of retiring and was researching four academic papers, one scheduled

18

to appear later in the year, launching a scathing attack on creationism and firmly rebutting the re-emergence of 'intelligent design'.

Abby rocketed into Julia's room to see her sitting up in bed, computer glowing on her lap, pencils and reference books everywhere. For a second she thought it was a false alarm until she saw how pale her mother was, and that the vibrant light in her eyes had been extinguished.

She tightened inside. The last time she'd seen Julia looking as shell-shocked was when she and Lisa had returned from school to discover their father was abandoning them for another woman. He'd gone to Australia on a business trip – he'd just been promoted to export director of a major publishing house – and returned not only in love with an Australian fitness instructor, but with her sun-drenched lifestyle too. There had been a lot of rows and tears and bitterness, and when he eventually left, even the house seemed to heave a sigh of relief. Julia had tried to encourage her daughters to stay in touch with their father but it had been difficult. Not just because the sisters were desperately hurt and angry, but because he didn't seem to be that enthusiastic. It was as though he didn't want reminding of his old life, and it didn't take long before contact shrank to birthdays and Christmas. None of them, as far as Abby knew, had heard from Dad since the Millennium.

'What is it?' Abby said. 'What's wrong?'

'It's Lisa. She needs your help.'

Abby stared at Julia, astonished. She hadn't spoken to her sister for four years and it took a

19

moment for her to convince herself that she wasn't imagining things. Her mother was doing it again, trying to patch things between them.

Abby was about to walk out when her mother added in a whisper, 'A policewoman just called. From Alaska. She says Lisa's missing.'

Belatedly Abby saw Julia was trembling, her mouth working to stop herself from crying. Her heart squeezed. Mum never cried. Not even when the nerves in her mouth played up, making her feel as though she had drills spinning in each of her teeth.

'Oh, Mum.' Abby sat on the edge of her bed. 'You know what Lisa's like. She'll turn up within the next few hours, guaranteed.'

Julia shook her head and tried to speak, but a sob choked the words. One shaking hand rose to her mouth, then covered her eyes.

'You remember when she vanished from the yacht we rented in Croatia?' Abby prompted gently. 'She had us all convinced she'd drowned, when all she'd done was swim ashore to meet a waiter she'd taken a fancy to.'

And four weeks later when a group of them were having a meal at Brown's, Lisa had disappeared again. She'd found someone more interesting to talk to but hadn't thought to let the others know she was joining them in the pub just down the road.

God, Abby, stop panicking, Lisa would say. *You're such a fusspot.*

Abby would lecture her sister about consideration for others and Lisa would nod contritely, but nothing ever changed. Lisa would have to have had a personality bypass for her to believe this wasn't another of her almighty cock-ups.

Tears fell from behind Julia's hand and on to a computer printout. Abby reached across and gently took her mother's hand from her eyes. It was cold and thin. She brought it up to her cheek and pressed it there to warm it. Julia gave her a watery smile, and with a monumental effort took several deep breaths and finally steadied herself.

'She went skijoring,' she managed, 'with her dogs. She got caught in a storm up in the mountains. A really bad one. She's been out there for four days.'

Abby's eyes widened. 'You're kidding.'

Julia shook her head.

'Sorry.' Abby rubbed the space between her brows and sighed. 'It's just that I've got a ghastly sense of déjà vu.'

'She was meant to show up at a friend's place on Saturday,' Julia said, 'but she didn't. He's a ranger, apparently. He waited a couple of hours, then went to her cabin. He found equipment gone from her shed, along with her dogs...'

'I bet she's tucked up in a bar somewhere, along with her equipment and her dogs. Anything's possible with Lisa.'

'Abby, I know you don't have any patience for your sister ... but this time I need you to listen.'

Abby ducked her head.

'The ranger reported her missing. The police-woman said something about Lisa using a lodge, her getting into trouble in between two points, but I couldn't concentrate...'

Abby refused to believe Lisa wasn't safely snug

21

in the arms of an illicit lover. 'Are they *sure* it's Lisa who's missing?'

Julia didn't answer. She didn't have to; Abby knew she was being insensitive but she couldn't help herself. Lisa was always getting into trouble, and getting herself out of it.

'They've got people looking for her,' Julia continued. 'It sounds as though they're doing everything they can, Abby, but I'm not so sure. I'm really worried they're not telling me everything.'

Julia looked away for an instant, then back. 'I want you to go over there. Liaise with the police in Lake's Edge and keep tabs on how the search is progressing.'

Abby felt as though her parachute had just failed to open. 'Lake's Edge?' Her voice was a notch higher. 'I thought she was moving back to Fairbanks to live with Greg.'

Julia looked away. 'She and Greg split up. She stayed.'

'You want me to go to *Lake's Edge?*'

Julia wouldn't meet her eyes. Abby's brain was clogged with disbelief. Why hadn't Lisa gone missing someplace else? They sat in silence for what felt like an hour, but was probably only a couple of minutes, until curiosity got the better of Abby. 'What about Thomas?' She was referring to Lisa's boss at the UAF, University of Alaska, Fairbanks. 'Doesn't he mind she's still living in the back of beyond?'

'No.' Julia pulled a tissue from the box on her bedside table and blew her nose. 'Lake's Edge is in the middle of some powerful magnetic field, which is what they've been researching. She goes to Fairbanks every month, and he puts her up while she's there. It's worked pretty well ... so far. You know how she loves the wilderness, and it's not like she has to be at the lab full time. She does the majority of her work via computer, after all.'

Julia scrunched up the tissue. She was still pale, her eyes rimmed red, but she had regained her composure. 'Darling, I know you don't want to go back there, but maybe this isn't such a bad thing. Perhaps it will do something to bring you back together. Please go, Abby.'

A small, angry child's wail started up inside her: *But I don't want to!*

'Ralph will take care of me.'

An army colonel, widowed and recently retired, Ralph lived at the end of their street and had been part of Abby's life ever since she could remember. He organised street parties, hosted bonfire night for the kids in his back garden and, at some point after her father had left, he'd asked Julia out on a date but Julia had turned him down flat, scathingly informing a startled Abby he wasn't intelligent enough and that he reminded her of a dishwasher; functional but dull. He hadn't seemed to have been offended, and cheerfully offered to look after the girls while Julia went on a conference to Venice. Secretly Abby had been thrilled when Julia agreed. She adored Ralph, and without realising it, over the next few years allowed him to take on the role of part-time surrogate father.

Whenever Abby thought of Ralph, she thought of long country walks, pints of Speckled Hen and the way the froth would cling to his neatly trimmed moustache. It was a shame Lisa never bonded to Ralph like Abby had, but at least she'd eventually found her own surrogate father when she moved to Alaska. If it hadn't been for Thomas, Abby doubted Lisa would have dug in her roots as firmly as she had.

'I thought Ralph was going to France on some reunion thing.'

'That's not the point.' Julia took a shaky breath. 'Darling, this is not the time to be stubborn.'

'I'm not being stubborn! I'm just not sure if my going over there will change anything.'

'She's your sister, Abby. She needs your help.'

Abby looked around Julia's cosy room, the antique standard lamps casting a soft glow over the watercolour paintings, the heavy amber-coloured drapes and rows of leather-bound books lining the walls. She thought about the local council who were screaming for the landscaping plans for their riverside park, the Sunshine Community Gardens in their critical stage of development, and her favourite clients, Jon and Ali Price, desperate to get their Italianate garden planted before the summer.

Then she looked at her mother, the anxiety already etched into lines around her eyes and mouth, and she knew she didn't have a choice. If she didn't go, Julia's health would plummet and she would, inevitably, end up in hospital.

'All right.' Her voice was quiet. 'I'll go.'

Julia's eyes filled with tears. She gripped Abby's hand. 'Darling, thank you.'

Abby bit her lip.

'The trooper left me this number.' Julia passed across a computer printout, where she'd scribbled in one corner. 'We should let them know you're coming.'

Abby took it, reached for the phone, and dialled. The line crackled and hissed for several seconds until it began ringing. A woman picked up on the third ring, barked, 'Demarco.'

Abby introduced herself, and immediately the trooper's tone softened. 'Ma'am. I spoke with your mother earlier. I'm sorry to have called with such bad news.' The trooper's voice was warm and mellow and sounded as though she was speaking around a lump of toffee. 'Your mother has told you the situation?'

'She says you're searching for my sister.'

'Yes, ma'am. Started the second we heard from the ranger. The RCC, the Rescue Coordination Centre enlisted CAP, the Civil Air Patrol, who've provided pilots and aircraft for the search. Plus our helicopter from Fairbanks. We're searching as best we can, ma'am. Rest assured, we're searching, but...' She cleared her throat. 'It's not looking too good for Lisa. She's been out there a long while. We're not sure what state she's going to be in. Which is why we called you – her next of kin.'

Abby's skin contracted. Jesus. The trooper thought Lisa was dead. No wonder Julia wanted her out there.

'Are you sure she's missing? I mean, this isn't the first time something like this has happened.'

'I don't know about that, ma'am. All I can say is that we don't kick off a full-blown search like this unless we've got hard evidence someone's in trouble. The ranger checked the trail she usually takes. Found she'd used one wilderness lodge, but not the next. He believes she got into trouble somewhere in between. He picked up a harness tangled in some trees.'

'Couldn't someone else have used the lodge?'

'No, ma'am. We've a serious situation here. One of her dogs chewed through its harness to get back home. It's got frostbite on its ears and around the genital area. That dog had been on the mountain a long time.'

'Maybe the dog was lost?' She expected the trooper to lose patience with her, but hats off to Demarco, she maintained her poise.

'No, ma'am. That dog knows the mountains inside and out. Been trotting those trails since it was a pup.' She cleared her throat noisily. 'You may not appreciate this, Miss McCall, but over here dogs are not just pets. They can be real heroes, and are known for saving the lives of many men over the years. What that dog did was bring a message home that things weren't right on the mountain. We respect that.'

There was a long pause while Abby digested this information. Then it was her turn to clear her throat.

'We've decided...' She flicked a glance at Julia who gave her an encouraging nod. 'I'm coming over.'

'There's no need for that, ma'am.' Demarco's voice was firm. 'We'll find her soon enough, and let you know.'

'I want to liaise with the rescue services. And yourself. Then I can keep my mother informed on what's happening.'

'Ma'am, it would be better for all of us if you

stayed at home. Coming out here isn't going to do anyone any good, least of all your sister. We're professionals. We know what we're doing.'

'I won't interfere, I promise.'

Silence rang, telling Abby the trooper didn't believe her, but she refused to let it deflect her.

'You can expect me the day after tomorrow,' Abby said briskly and, before the trooper could protest any further, hung up.

Three

Abby shivered and stamped her feet, trying to bring them to life. She had a queasy feeling in the pit of her stomach and she swallowed several times in an attempt to prevent it rising. She breathed into her gloves, pulled her turtleneck up to her chin. Now she could see why the guy loading the plane wore a pair of ear muffs; her ears were aching with cold. The wind sliced through her paltry layers of sweater and waterproof jacket, and she wished she was snug inside a fur-lined parka like everyone else.

It was April, and she'd expected the country to be melting into spring, but a series of late-winter storms had altered the season dramatically. She didn't think she'd felt such cold before and put it down to having spent all her life in a temperate climate that rarely suffered temperatures below thirty fahrenheit.

The queasy feeling intensified as she surveyed

27

the battered, rusting ski plane. She was more worried about the next leg of her journey than the fact her sister had gone missing up some mountain; the skis were tiny, and looked as though the lumpy runway of frozen lake would rip them apart the second they commenced their take-off. The whole aircraft looked as though a gust of wind would reduce it to scrap metal, and she bet it didn't have heating. Not like Wright's Air, with its nice big Camel airplane parked outside their offices, but Wright's Air weren't flying to Lake's Edge until the end of the week.

'Try Mac,' a girl with black braids had told her cheerfully. 'He's flying a friend up near Lake's Edge later today. He'll drop you off, I'm sure. Oh ... and he's real experienced, Mac. You'll be in good hands.'

Abby prayed the girl was right. She hated flying. It didn't matter if she was in a 747, first class or baggage, as far as she was concerned human beings weren't supposed to be in the air. They were meant to have their feet planted firmly on the earth, and should they ever reach heights over 10,000 feet, it was because they'd climbed a mountain. She had wanted to hire a car, but since the road north was shut due to the storm, she was trapped. Bush flying may be a way of life in a state twice the size of Texas with a few thousand miles of highway and just one railroad, but no way was it for her.

Not like Lisa, who loved not only to fly, but to glide, parachute and even skydive. The closest Abby got to adventure in the UK was hill walking in Wales.

She stamped her feet again, looking at the mountains in the distance, their white fangs gouging the sky. Was Lisa *really* lost up there somewhere? She wasn't sure if she was in denial or just finding it difficult to believe, even with her mother's insistence. After suffering countless emergencies over the years, she'd stepped off the aircraft in Fairbanks automatically looking for an apologetic official of some sort cringing over the absurd mix-up, and when they hadn't appeared, she had sighed and gone to collect her bag. She didn't doubt someone would turn up at some point with an explanation for Lisa's disappearance. She just hoped it would be sooner rather than later, and preferably before she got to Lake's Edge.

Pulling up her scarf to cover her nose and mouth, she lugged her single bag to Mac, a broad bear of a man with a haystack of blond hair and a moustache thick and bristly as a scrubbing brush. He took her bag, hefted it briefly as though gauging its weight, then dropped it to the ground.

'Just three of us today,' he said. 'Glad you travel light. Not like my other passenger.' He nodded to a pile of gear: shovels, axes, skis, snowshoes, rifles, boxes of ammunition, a tarpaulin, a case of bananas and another of flares, and a variety of unmarked crates that could have contained gelignite or loo paper for all she knew.

She was wondering if she was sharing the flight with an arctic explorer when the passenger turned up, shotgun in hand. He had a fur cap with ear flaps, blue padded trousers tucked into wide-legged rubber boots, and a red padded jacket. His scruffy dusting of grey stubble seemed incongruous against the neatly cropped iron-grey hair and military set of his shoulders.

'What are you staring at?' His tone was aggressive.

'Nothing. Sorry.'

A pair of shrewd eyes raked her up and down. 'Christ,' he growled, and spat on the ground. 'I had no idea.'

Bristling at his belligerence, Abby was working up to bite something back but the man had switched his attention to her bag. He was scowling at it as though it was a sack of snakes.

He said, 'Hope we don't come down out there cos you're going to be a real liability, aren't you?'

'You're assuming we'll get airborne with all your clobber on board,' she replied, stung. 'Do you *really* need three crates of Alaskan Amber?'

'Six,' he corrected. 'I'll squeeze 'em in once Mac's cleared his reserve fuel out.'

Abby thought it was his idea of a joke, but to her horror ten minutes later Mac removed his reserve drums and in their places went the beer. Mouth dry, she seriously considered cancelling the flight and waiting until the roads cleared.

'Not scared of flying, are you?' he asked. He gave a cough but it didn't hide what she took to be a snigger.

She stuck her chin in the air. 'Not at all. I was just concerned what would happen if we're forced to land off-course, or something, and need to refuel.'

'We'll have to walk,' was the laconic response.

She glanced at the forbidding, snow-laden

30

mountains and couldn't prevent a shiver. What if the trooper was right? She may not like Lisa much, but she didn't want her to have perished up there.

'You wouldn't last three seconds, would you?'

'No,' she admitted.

He cocked his head and studied her briefly. 'Not like your sister, are you?'

She felt as though he'd punched her in the midriff. 'My *sister?*'

'You're Abigail McCall, right?'

'How on earth–'

'Saw the flight plan. Abigail McCall flying to Lake's Edge, where Lisa McCall's gotten herself in trouble.' He gave a little sneer. 'Don't have to be a detective to put two and two together.'

He was looking at her as though she was something foul he'd just trodden in. Jeez, what had she done to him in a previous life? Her mind gave a little hop. Maybe it wasn't her, but something Lisa had done in Lake's Edge?

'Yo, Victor!' Mac called out, thankfully drawing his attention away. 'You really need that canoe? We can strap it below, but it's gonna play hell once we're up.'

Canoe jettisoned and everything securely roped down, Mac wedged her firmly behind Victor, who was in the co-pilot's seat, and passed her a headset before running through a speedy preflight check. Palms damp, she looked desperately outside, but there was no official running towards them, no trooper about to offer an apology for wasting her time. She was going to Lake's Edge and there was nothing she could do about it.

The next she knew they were skittering down

31

the ice-packed lake with the throttles wide open, and she readied herself for the swoop as they lifted into the air, but the plane remained firmly lake-bound. She was beginning to panic, a scream building in her throat as the end of the lake began to approach with alarming speed, and at the last minute Mac said, 'She's a bit heavy, but we *should* be okay,' and at the same moment the aircraft reluctantly lumbered skywards.

Abby sat rigid as a board, concentrating on slow, steady breaths. She wondered if she could distract her terror by picking out landmarks she might recognise. Teeth gritted, she braced herself and glanced out of the window. Almost immediately, she got her bearings by identifying the Mitchell Expressway and Airport Way. The traffic was light on both roads and cruising slowly through brown slushy snow.

'Abby?'

She started as Mac's voice came through her headset. She twisted the mouthpiece round, closer to her mouth and said, 'Yes?' Her voice was hoarse with fear, but he didn't seem to notice.

'Victor tells me you've been here before?'

Suddenly she forgot she was suspended hundreds of feet in the air. How the hell did Victor know that? A jet of panic rocketed through her veins. Would everyone in Lake's Edge remember her? What had Julia said before she left?

Darling, you can't lose your past any more than you can lose your shadow. Isn't it time you made amends?

Unless the entire population of Lake's Edge suffered amnesia, they'd remember her, all right.

'Conservationist or some such?' Mac prompted.

32

'I came out to do a feasibility study four years ago.'

She didn't like dwelling on her memories of that summer, but sometimes, if she caught the waft of a particularly strong insect repellent, or smelled barbecued steak, she'd be transported back to the Brooks Range and its gaunt mountain peaks glowing in the long rays of summer's midnight sun.

For two months, July and August, she had joined a group of scientists and researchers in one of the world's last, great unspoiled wildernesses, that stretched across the entire breadth of Alaska. Their chartered helicopter had flown them from Lake's Edge right into the heart of the range, where they set up camp. Each morning thereafter, the chopper would fly them to a different area, and they'd spend the day sketching and mapping, packing samples of plants, and taking notes of wildlife. In the evening, the chopper would fly them back to the campsite, where supper would be cooking on the camp barbecue. Despite her loathing of the helicopter, Abby had loved every minute, and when she returned to Lake's Edge she didn't think she'd been happier. Not only had she been sun-browned and fit, but she'd been in love.

Abby flushed as she remembered those two months with Cal. He'd been the group's profess-ional hunter and wilderness guide, teaching them about the web of life in the Arctic, and making sure they didn't get too close to any bears. What a cliché, falling for the guide. She still felt so *stupid*.

Mac twisted in his seat to look at her briefly. 'A feeza-what?'

'Background research in the field. Looking at

tundra and its context to see if we could duplicate it back in England for the general public to look at.'

Mac snorted. 'They want to look at tundra, they may as well come out here.'

Which was exactly what the Eden Project in Cornwall had decided in the end. Not only was human habitation minimal in the Arctic, they said, but the plants weren't exactly sexy to the average punter. Abby had talked about the textural qualities of tundra and its tactile beauty, the joy of running your hands over lichens and mosses that were wet, hairy, silky and spongy, but they'd decided to go for the more appealing aspect of cacti and cave dwellings in the desert instead.

Steeling herself once more, she peered outside to see they were heading north over the Chena river, which resembled a dirty white rope flung between squat buildings. The plane gave a little bump, then resumed its smooth ride. It wasn't warm in the plane but she was sweating buckets.

He's an experienced pilot, she lectured herself. *Wright's Air said so. You're in good hands.*

'Keep a look-out,' Mac told her as he banked north-west, the city starting to fall behind them. 'You might get to see a bear or two. It was warm enough last week to get them moving. Hibernation's over.'

Abby gazed down but couldn't see anything, thanks to an opaque grey cloud. They droned on for another two hours. She tried to doze, but each time the plane lurched, she'd bolt upright, clutching her armrest, convinced they were about to crash.

How she wished she was more like her dauntless sister. Not for the first time, Abby wondered at their differences. Lisa was a physicist and mathematician whose research was as impenetrable to Abby as the theory of relativity. Unlike Lisa, she'd never been dominated by mental goals, nor particularly interested in delving into abstractions or intricate ideologies. Her thinking was solid and practical, her feet planted on terra firma. Which was why she'd always been happy to leave Lisa poring over her calculations while she gathered huge bunches of pussy willow and meadowsweet and got intoxicated by the feeling of soil between her fingers.

Her eyes snapped open when Mac suddenly put the aircraft into a steep dive.

'Going down now!' Mac yelled. 'Victor's dropping-off point. Destination nowhere!'

Abby bolted upright.

They emerged under the cloud and she gave a muffled yelp. Holy cow, they were barely a hundred feet above the gleaming surface of a lake covered in viscous ice. Mac inched down further and kept cruising. Abruptly, he pulled the nose up.

'Nope.'

'Come on, Mac!' Victor protested. 'You've landed on worse.'

'Soft ice ain't safe.'

'It's frozen solid as my front drive.'

'So what are those cracks at the edges? Native art?'

'For Chrissakes, at least let's have another look.'

There was a brief pause as Mac turned his head

to look at Victor.

'You that desperate to get away you want the cost of hauling this thing from the bottom of the lake?'

'Yup.'

'Jesus.'

The wing dipped and they were turning, scooping low again, skimming over the ice. She could see the sinister black fissures Mac had mentioned and was waiting for him to abandon all pretence of landing when he throttled back. Abby couldn't believe it. All her worst nightmares were coming true. They were about to land.

A yell stuck in her throat and a handful of seconds later they were bouncing and sliding across the surface until the aircraft lost speed, finally coming to rest beside a scooped area beneath a tall cliff cloaked with ancient pines.

It looked as though it might be a beach in summertime but right now the whole area was frozen beneath a cape of snow. Stark cloud-topped mountains were hemmed by stretches of treeless tundra. There was a tiny log cabin with snow up to its windows tucked beneath the cliff but there was no other form of human habitation, or an animal, come to that. No birds in the sky or fluttering between the trees. It was a bleak desert of cold and Abby couldn't think what Victor was doing all the way out here.

Mac didn't cut the engines. 'Better get a move on! Not long till dark!'

Abby sprang into life at the realisation that the sooner they got rid of Victor and his equipment, the larger the window of safety she'd have on the

36

next leg of the journey. Hauling a crowbar and pickaxe from the back of the plane, she edged her way on to the creaking ice and to shore, feeling the cold biting her neck, her wrists and face. Her feet were already numb, and on her next relay, she stamped, and felt the ice shudder slightly under her booted feet.

'See ya,' Mac told Victor with a clap on the back. 'Watch out for the grizzlies.'

Victor patted his rifle, and without even glancing at Abby, crunched away. Abby scowled. If she never saw Victor again it would be too soon.

'Next stop, Lake's Edge,' shouted Mac. 'Let's go!'

Four

They flew west for another ten minutes before Mac pointed out Lake's Edge. The queasy feeling returned as Abby looked down at the remote outpost clinging to the side of a lake. Set in a deep valley between two mountains, if she hadn't known where to look, she'd have never spotted it.

Mac began to drop altitude and as they approached she recognised the same hardy spruce trees, the same main street, the same spiderweb of trails connecting the various dwellings.

'You want a certificate?' Mac asked her.

'A what?'

'We crossed the Arctic Circle a while back. Most people who come this far north like a memento.'

'Thanks, Mac, but I've already got one.' She couldn't remember where she'd put it, though. No doubt she'd burned it with all her other Alaskan memorabilia. Abby leaned forward a little further as she continued peering outside. At the southern end of town she spotted a dirt runway cleared of snow.

'Since when did Lake's Edge get that?' she asked, pointing down.

'Couple of years back.'

She looked across at him. 'Don't you have a plane with wheels?'

'Sure, but it wouldn't have got Victor to his cabin.'

'The ice on this lake isn't soft?'

'Nah. We're higher up here and don't you worry, I got the go-ahead before we flew. Couldn't do that for Victor with no one being there to check, but he was that desperate...' He trailed off as the lake began to approach. Abby held her breath as he set the aircraft down, gently as a feather, but she didn't unclench her fingers until he'd cruised to a firm stop beside a pontoon.

Abby reckoned she was coping pretty well with being hauled unceremoniously from her cosy life in Oxford and forced to endure a terrifying bush flight, but when she saw the vast expanses of snow and ice reaching as far as the eye could see, the snow pluming off the tops of the mountains, jagged rubbles of rocks forming landslides on their flanks, she felt as though her mind was going to implode.

If the trooper was right, Lisa has gone missing up there somewhere. People are looking for her.

They've trackers and airplanes and dogs, and the trooper believes she's dead. Whether I like it or not, this is for real.

Abby clambered out of the aircraft. Hands tucked beneath her armpits, breath steaming in the freezing air, she looked around. Buildings, sheds and trees were all slumped under a coating of fresh snow. There were no cars or snow machines or people. The place looked deserted.

Engine still running, Mac jumped out with her bag and dropped it on the pontoon. Abby was surprised at the dismay she felt when he held out his hand for a shake. 'You're not staying?'

'Got to get to Glacier for a job first thing tomorrow.'

Abby looked at the light bleeding out of the sky. 'I didn't think pilots out here flew in the dark.'

He grinned, his scrubbing-brush moustache lifting to reveal a set of startlingly white teeth. 'It's only a short hop,' he told her. 'It'll still be light when I get there.'

'If I need to get back, shall I call you?'

'I'm sure someone'll give you a lift. Fairbanks isn't that far, you can make it in a day.'

'Aren't all the roads closed?'

'Only because of this last storm. The haul road'll be clear pretty soon.'

He was about to go, when she stopped him.

'I don't suppose you know where the police station is?'

'There isn't one. Nearest is Coldfoot.' Mac jerked his chin towards the village. 'You needn't worry, Demarco's on the way.' She was about to turn to look for the trooper when he added,

39

'Hope you find your sister.'

'Me too,' she murmured.

Mac clapped her on the back before heading for his plane, calling, 'Good luck!' over his shoulder.

Engine bellowing, he slipped to the end of the lake and turned, accelerating until the air was under his wings and he lifted off. Gradually the engine's roar was coated with a dense, almost jelly-like silence that made her ears ring.

'Miss McCall?'

The voice was threaded with confusion and Abby felt the familiar surge of irritation that the trooper had assumed she and Lisa would look alike. As a kid she was convinced she'd been swapped in the hospital for another baby she was so different from her family. With their compact bodies, curly dark hair and wild gestures that would knock vases and magazines off table tops, Abby always felt washed-out and emotionally pale in comparison.

Her mother had called her 'my little changeling' and Abby never forgot the feeling of bewilderment when she'd looked it up in the dictionary – *a child believed to have been exchanged by fairies for the parents' true child*. It wasn't until she was thirteen and Julia was having a clear-out one wet weekend, when she'd fallen on a yellowing photograph of her great-grandmother. And there she was, right down to the slightly tilted, intense blue eyes and tiny birthmark at the corner of her mouth. If she hadn't known it was Marijka Schikora, Norwegian bride to Dewitt McCall, she'd have thought it was a picture of herself.

'Yes,' she said now, 'I'm Abby McCall.'

40

Abby looked down at the uniformed trooper. Dark blue trousers with gold stripes down the sides, matching blue thickly padded parka with lots of pockets. Pistol on one hip, walkie-talkie on the other. Curly brown hair peeking from beneath a hat made of long beaver fur. Intelligent brown eyes. Warm beige lipstick. She was staring at her hair and Abby felt like saying no, it wasn't dyed, and that yes, she liked it short-cropped and spiky like a bleached-white hedgehog; she rarely had to drag a comb through it and never had to use a hair dryer.

'Ma'am,' she said, finally giving up her hair inspection, 'I'm Trooper Demarco.'

'Hi.'

'Hope the trip was okay.' The trooper kept her intelligent eyes on Abby's. 'It's a long way to come.'

Abby knew full well this was the coded version of *you could have saved yourself the trouble if you'd listened to me and stayed at home,* and refused to drop her gaze.

Demarco smiled, as though she'd heard Abby's thoughts. 'I've a car,' she said, all amiability. 'I'm from Fairbanks, flew up in the heli when the ranger called me, but folk are generous around here and I've been loaned a vehicle.'

They crunched their way along the pontoon for the car Demarco had pointed out. 'I'll take you to the school and fill you in. As a temporary measure we're using one of the teachers' rooms. We don't have a trooper post here, you see. Just a VPSO. A village public safety officer.'

With the heater on full blast, the trooper

41

bounced her loaned Ford Explorer from pothole to pothole, crunching on muddy ice and fresh snow, making Abby feel as though she was riding in a cement mixer. A snow plough had gone through recently, piling banks of snow five feet high on either side, but there were no other vehicles.

'I understand you've been here before,' Demarco said.

Abby nodded but didn't say anything. She didn't want the past dragged up. Turning her attention outside, she wondered where everyone was. It was like a ghost town. Log cabins with pitched roofs and wooden decks were covered in snow, their walls decorated with caribou antlers, saws and gold pans, but there was nobody about. Not even a dog.

They passed a row of souvenir shops, snow-crusted signs for B&Bs, pizza pies and salmon steaks, and the Moose bar with its neon-pink sign flashing, *hot coffee, all-day breakfast, Budweiser, B&B*. It was all terribly familiar but also strangely alien, as though she was watching a movie. The only indication of any change she could see was that the small visitor centre offering hiking, canoeing and fishing had expanded to take over the shop next door. Every storefront was closed up and sealed with wooden shutters; the tourist season didn't kick off in full force until the end of May.

Finally the trooper made a right, then slowed to a stop outside an industrial-looking single-storey building that looked more like a prison camp than a school. Abby unbuckled and stepped into the icy air, following the trooper up a set of concrete steps and through some double doors. The corridor smelled of disinfectant. Walls were covered in crayon drawings of bears, whales and flowers, and she could hear children chattering, their voices bright and happy, infusing Abby with a sudden sense of normality. But where were the parents? Why did the town appear to have been abandoned?

At the end of the corridor Demarco pushed open a door and ushered Abby into a stuffy, over-heated square box with whitewashed concrete walls. She could see four plastic chairs, an aluminium desk piled with paper, and a filing cabinet that looked as though it had been dropped from a roof. Beneath the windows was a small side table over-flowing with paper cups and dirty mugs, packs of sugar and teabags. Aside from the teaching schedule pinned to the back of the door, Abby couldn't see any evidence that it was a teacher's office. They'd obviously moved out lock, stock and barrel.

Demarco went to the coffee machine and poured them both cups. She offered Abby a chair, which she declined. She'd been travelling non-stop for twenty-four hours and if she sat down in the heat of this room, she knew she'd fall asleep.

The trooper settled behind the desk and reached for a green folder. Ran a finger down the front page as though gathering the facts, then looked up at Abby with a sombre expression. Abby put her coffee on the windowsill and leaned a hand against the wall, concentrating on the warmed concrete against her skin, a long dried worm where the paint had run. 'You've found her?' Her voice was hoarse.

Demarco shook her head. 'Not yet. Everyone's out there at the moment. Looking.'

Abby swung to the window and glanced down the empty street. 'Everyone?'

'Pretty much. Folk from Wiseman and Coldfoot are chipping in too. We've dogs on the ground, and Ron and Lou... I mean Mr and Mrs Walmsley, are scouting in their airplane.' Demarco glanced at the phone sitting on the desk, then away. 'They'll be back after dark.'

'Where are they?'

The trooper reached down to the floor and pulled up a crumpled map, spread it across her desk. Abby was immediately reminded of her ex-boyfriend, Robert. Newly divorced and charming, Robert had been a cartographer who'd taken her to the Lake District and taught her how to orienteer. Unfortunately, when he'd asked her to move in with him, she'd just about had a heart attack.

Commitment isn't a dirty word, Abby, he'd sighed. *Not all men are bastards. Some of us are quite nice if you'd give us a chance.*

When he'd given her the ultimatum – move in or we're finished – she'd taken the latter option. She hadn't trusted him not to get back together with his ex-wife, to whom he spoke just about every other day. She found it hard to trust men after Cal. She hadn't been out with anyone since.

'We're here.' Demarco showed her where Lake's Edge was, and then swept her finger south-west. 'And we're searching here.' She pointed to an area marked with big black letters: WILDERNESS.

Abby studied the swathes of areas shaded in green, white and brown, denoting glaciers, glacial moraines, crevasses and springs, woodland, waterfalls, and mile upon mile of cramped contour lines rising to various mountain tops. Only a handful of the rivers were named, and aside from the really big peaks, the mountains were also nameless. They just had a small dot with the height etched beside it. 4,492, 5,318.

'Your sister was supposed to meet Joe Chenega at the weekend. Joe's a forest ranger. He's also a friend of your sister's. They go fishing from time to time. He taught her about the wilderness, survival skills, that sort of stuff. She was supposed to collect a dog sled he was fixing up for her. When she didn't turn up, he went and checked her place. From the equipment missing in her shed, he was of the opinion she'd gone skijoring.'

'Skijoring?' Abby repeated. Julia had mentioned something about skis, but she hadn't taken it in.

'Skiing behind a couple of dogs, with supplies either on her back or tied to a small sled. She's known for taking off like that from time to time, but it's the first time she's been in trouble.'

Abby's jaw tightened. *No it's not. She's been a magnet for trouble since the day she was born.*

'You know my sister?' she asked.

'Never met,' the trooper admitted. 'But she's well known around here...' She reached into one of her zippered pockets and withdrew a tissue, briefly blew her nose. 'I told you about the dog. He's got frostbite, I think I told you, and he's still pretty weak after his ordeal on the mountain...'

The trooper was still talking but Abby's mind had frozen on the vision of Lisa crawling through the snow, her elfin face blackening with frostbite, blood staining her mouth.

'Ma'am?'

She swallowed drily, forcing herself to push the picture away. Lisa was a survivor. Just because her dog had broken free didn't mean Lisa was dead. She might be walking back down the mountain right as rain for all they knew.

'Joe knows the score when someone goes missing. He did a recon when the storm cleared.' The trooper pushed her finger at a small black square on the map. Abby checked the legend. *Structure, ruins.* 'He ascertained someone stayed here recently ... it's a wilderness cabin. Your sister likes M & Ms, right? Smokes Marlboro?'

Yes and yes, Abby replied silently, but a stubborn cynicism made her say, 'My sister can't be the only person in the world who smokes that particular brand of cigarette and eats chocolate-coated peanuts.'

The trooper reached into the desk drawer and pulled out a small, clear plastic bag and passed it over. 'We found this too.'

For a second, Abby thought she was seeing things. It was her necklace, the one she'd bought with Granny Rose's money for her sixteenth birthday. A slender silver chain with a turquoise drop. Lisa used to drive her mad, borrowing it without asking, and it appeared she'd done the same again. She hadn't worn it for years and had had no idea it was missing. When in the world

46

had Lisa pinched it? When they were kids? Or had it been later?

'It's Lisa's, right?' The trooper was watching her closely.

'Actually, it's mine.' Abby gave a tight smile. 'But I guess it means the same thing as far as you're concerned.'

The trooper gave a nod and popped the necklace back inside the drawer. Abby was going to ask if she could have it, but realised Demarco wouldn't know for sure that it was hers, and would have to wait for Lisa's corroboration before handing it over.

'This is where she'd be headed next, but it looks like she never made it.' Demarco had returned to the map. 'It's been untouched all winter, still is.'

Abby traced the route. It was fifty miles from one place to the next across valleys and lakes, through forests and up cliffs. 'She couldn't do this in one day, surely.'

'She'd camp out.'

Abby must have looked incredulous, because the trooper added, 'There's an old trail linking the cabins. See, it makes a nice loop back to Lake's Edge. It's an easy three or four days. I gather she'd always aim out there if she'd been away, especially after a trip to Fairbanks. Joe says she liked to clear her head.'

Nothing had changed, obviously. Abby could remember Lisa coming home from school, dumping her bags in the kitchen and disappearing into the garden – usually inside the tree house if it wasn't too cold – for at least half an hour before

47

she'd talk to anyone. Abby called Lisa weird, her father called her baffling, her mother, unique.

'Joe says Lisa got back from town late on Friday, so it makes sense she left Saturday morning. She obviously forgot she was supposed to be meeting up with Joe later the same day.'

Walking to the window Abby looked down the street. She wondered if it looked so colourless because night was falling, and whether the place would brighten up in the morning when all the people searching for Lisa returned. She flinched when the phone rang.

Demarco picked it up. Listened briefly. 'Yup. Loud and clear... You've found *what?* Jesus...' She tucked the phone between her ear and shoulder and pulled the map across. 'But that's miles away.'

Long silence.

'Yup. Yup, okay. Will do.'

Demarco dropped the receiver back into the cradle and bent over the map, studying it with a frown.

'What is it?' Abby asked. 'Is it Lisa?'

The trooper raised her head and looked at Abby straight. 'They've found something... But it's nowhere near where your sister went missing. I'm sorry.'

'What have they found?'

The trooper had started re-folding the map and said again, 'I'm sorry.'

Not liking her evasiveness, Abby picked up her mug of coffee, realised it was cold, put it back down again.

'Miss McCall–'

'Abby, please.'

'Abby. I was thinking maybe you could stay at your sister's for the night. It's not far, I'll drive you, okay? Then we can meet tomorrow when you've rested up.'

Abby followed Demarco outside and into the still, cold silence. The trooper's steps were light in the snow, her spine erect. Something close to a smile tugged the corners of her mouth and her eyes were over bright. With a shiver Abby recognised what it was: adrenalin.

Five

Lisa's cabin wasn't a prefab like some of the other homes in Lake's Edge, but a traditionally built log cabin with solar collectors on the snow-covered roof. A dozen black dishes the size of dinner plates nestled alongside, faces turned to the sky. They hadn't been there when Abby last visited here, and she couldn't think what their purpose might be.

The trooper handed Abby a door key with a miniature stuffed moose attached to the key ring. 'Most people don't lock their doors out here, but your sister was the exception. Diane keeps a spare.' Demarco sent her a sharp look. 'She's a friend of Lisa's. The owner of the Moose. You remember her?'

'Not really,' said Abby, cringing. 'I only stayed there a couple of nights.' She turned away to hide her flush at the sudden memory of Diane, fresh

49

sheets in hand, catching her and Cal lounging in bed one morning. The expedition had returned from the mountains the night before and although Cal was meant to be staying with friends, he'd snuck into her room past midnight. Diane had taken one look at them, hair awry and sleepy from sex, and thrown the sheets on the floor and stalked outside, slamming the door behind her.

'You'll be okay?' the trooper asked, and stuck the gear into drive.

Abby got the hint and climbed outside into the freezing air, pulled the door shut. Spraying snow, Demarco rocketed her Explorer back down the trail at three times the speed she'd driven Abby.

The sky still held a little light and it was clear and cold. Stars edged the horizon. Abby picked up her bag and crunched over to the broad deck at the front of the cabin. To one side of the front door there was a bench and a small circular table, and on the table was a rusting gold pan filled with grey-coloured sand studded with cigarette butts. Lisa's makeshift ashtray. Abby's head buzzed, her vision wavering. Lisa had wanted so badly to give up the last time they saw each other.

It was as if time crumpled, as if the last four years' silence had never been. Abby could feel the shape of Lisa's small, strong body when they'd hugged on her arrival at Fairbanks airport, and smell the orange shampoo in her hair. Her laughter was bright and infectious, and people looked at them, smiling as they always did, unable to help themselves, and Abby was basking in her sister's sunlight and laughing too.

A deep, dragging ache started in her heart, as if

50

a giant hand was squeezing it. She couldn't believe it, she really couldn't. Lisa was too ebullient, too full of life. She was indestructible. She must cling on to that, or she'd splinter, crack like an ice cube being ground slowly beneath a boot heel.

She unlocked the front door and gently pushed it open. The silence pressed on her ears and in an effort to dispel it, she knocked her boots against the doorstep to shake off the snow. She stepped inside. The air was dense and freezing. It felt as though the wood stove hadn't been fired up for months. She fumbled until she found the light switch and flipped it up. A single low-watt light at the far end of the room came on.

The first thing she saw was a huge length of platinum fur crouched in front of the wood stove. Wolf! her instincts screamed and she leaped back, but it didn't move. It wasn't alive. It was, in fact, extremely dead.

'Jesus,' she said, heart still pounding. What Lisa was doing with a dead wolf in her home she didn't know. There was some guy's stuff hanging on a clothes stand next to the stove as though drying out – a down coat, fur cap and gloves – and she wondered who he was and how often he visited.

She scanned the open-plan room. As usual, the place was a mess. There were piles of washing up, packets of cereal spilling flakes all over the counters, toast crumbs, open jars of jam. Drawers were open, magazines and papers tossed on the floor. Her skin tightened as she looked around. Oh, God, she thought. It's not just a mess. *It's been ransacked.*

51

A gust of cold air reached her from the stairway ahead. Abby trotted down the stairs to find the mud-room door was wide open. Then she saw that the lock was broken, the wood around it splintered where it had been forced. Cautiously she stepped outside, but there were no fresh footprints in the snow. Just a snowy pile of what appeared to be an old fire set away from the cabin to her left. She was about to pull the door shut when she gave it a second look. Why on earth had Lisa built a bonfire at this time of year? If she wanted to burn anything, wouldn't she have used her wood stove?

Crunching over, Abby kicked some snow aside to find a charred mess of computer discs and ring binders, their metal twisted and melted into blackened shards. What the hell...? Abby stared, astonished, then hurried inside to check the cabin. One bedroom, ransacked. Another bedroom-cum-office, also ransacked. No notebooks littered the desk beneath the window, no files sat in the cabinets, no papers in the desk drawers, no computer or computer discs.

She could feel her heart pumping as she looked at the broken lock on the mud-room door. A burglar had definitely been in here. There was no reason for Lisa to rip the coats from their hooks or leave the freezer door open. But why had Lisa's work been burned? Had she done it herself, or had it been the burglar? Why? And what about Lisa's boss? Did her beloved Thomas know?

Shivering in the icy air, Abby headed upstairs for the phone. Cell and mobile phones didn't work out here, which is why she'd left hers at home. And as for radios, it was strictly line-of-sight communication, where if you could see the person or aircraft you're talking to, then you could talk to it, otherwise you may just as well try and shout your message. Even land-line telephones were scratchy and not always reliable, which was why a lot of people in rural areas had ham radios.

Hunting around the living room she eventually unearthed the phone, sitting beneath the dining table with piles of scientific magazines and journals. She flicked through the White Pages until she found Lake's Edge. Just twenty-two phone listings, including a Tribal Council number, an Alcoholics Anonymous listing, USA post office, school and National Park Service, but no number for the police. She wondered whether to dial 911 or not, and then remembered what Trooper Demarco had said.

We don't have a trooper post here ... just a village public safety officer.

Abby dialled the VPSO number and a woman came on the line. When she explained who she was and what had happened, the woman's tone turned brisk.

'I'll radio Demarco. Hang on a sec.'

Abby heard the woman talking, but the only words she could make out were her and Lisa's names. There was a clatter and then the woman returned. 'She says she'll be with you as soon as she's free.'

Demarco stayed barely half an hour. She checked the broken lock, made a handful of notes in her notebook, and told Abby break-ins were highly unusual in places like this, but not unknown.

As the trooper headed for the front door, Abby said, 'Aren't you going to get someone to dust for prints?'

'Unfortunately I don't have the resources.' Her tone was dry. 'It's just me up here, Abby. If I feel it's warranted, I'll bring the Crime Lab folks in, but do you really think it's worth it?'

Abby got the point. She shook her head.

'I'll be getting on then.'

She watched the trooper leave, boots crunching in the snow. Demarco hadn't made much of the bonfire of discs and files, but Abby knew better than to take the trooper's lack of reaction as an opinion. She'd already learned Demarco didn't like giving anything away.

After she had fixed a sliding bolt to the mud-room door, she decided to take a shower. Lisa's bathrobe lay on the floor like a pool of spilled yellow paint. Lisa loved bright colours. Green, orange and purple and red, some days all in one outfit, and uncaring if they matched or not. She could hear her sister's voice almost as if she spoke right next to her: *You try wearing hot pink and being miserable. It's just not possible.*

Abby's heart became a stone, tumbling down a ravine. Her throat tightened. Lisa had to be all right. Anything else was inconceivable.

Hair still wet, she pulled on a man's blue robe slung over the towel rail and went and heated up a can of tomato soup. She ate staring at the blank screen of the TV, her mind as blank, her body sluggish, as though the blood in her veins was pumping at half speed.

She didn't want to ring her mother when she

barely had the energy to raise the fork to her mouth, but she knew she had to. Julia would be going mad with worry. Checking her watch, she counted back eight hours, making it two p.m. English time.

'Mum? It's me.'

'Where is she? Is she with you?'

Deep breath. 'They're still looking.'

Abby hadn't expected Julia to break down, but when her voice remained calm, even if a bit wobbly, she felt a rush of relief.

'And you, Abby? How are you?'

'Tired. Weird.' She rested her head on her hand and closed her eyes as she described her bush flight, then her meeting with Trooper Demarco. She didn't mention Lisa burning her files, or the burglar. Julia was worried enough about Lisa without adding to it.

'I saw this map, Mum, where they reckon she went. Skijoring, they call it–'

'She loves those dogs,' Julia said. 'But Roscoe's her favourite. I've a picture of him here. Darling...' Her mother's voice turned uncharacteristically hesitant.

'What is it?'

'I just want you to know how glad I am you're there. You know that if I could have gone–'

'I know. And I'm glad I'm here too,' she lied and hurriedly changed the subject. 'How's Ralph?'

'Driving me mad with his appalling jokes.'

Abby felt a rush of love for Ralph. He had dropped everything to help out. He knew as well as Abby did that if left to her own devices Julia would forget to care for herself. That was the reason why, after she'd graduated with her land-scape architect's degree from Leeds Uni, Abby had found a job in Oxford and moved in with Julia, and if she was honest she'd done it more for herself than for her mother. She worried far less knowing she'd be at home at the end of each day to check up on her.

Abby spoke with Ralph for a while, then hung up. Feeling unsettled and restless, she busied herself washing up the piles of dishes, and then she tackled the mess the burglar had made. As she tidied, she tried to get a sense of her sister, but it was like being in a stranger's home. On Lisa's bedside cabinet stood a glass lamp in the shape of a leaping orca and a soft-backed beige book, well thumbed and filthy with charcoal and dirt smudges.

Abby picked it up. Published by the Army in 1970, it appeared to cover everything from orient-ation, scouting and patrolling to fire making and cooking. There were countless diagrams and hand-drawn sketches of traps and snares, tree pits and animal carcasses, how to build the perfect shelter in a snowstorm. *Survival in the Arctic.* Not her type of bedtime reading, but typically Lisa's. She'd been fascinated by survival ever since Abby could remember, which in turn had led to her concern for the environment. Or was it the other way round? Abby put the book aside.

Sliding open the top drawer, she was expecting to see tissues, maybe even a packet of condoms, but what she saw made the oxygen rush out of her blood cells.

Her own handwriting looked up at her.

Abby shut the drawer. Stared at it as though it was a precipice she was about to fall into.

Steeling herself, she pulled open the drawer and took out a stack of letters tied with ribbon. She untied the ribbon. Some letters were on lined paper torn from school books and covered in childish drawings, others neatly penned on thick vellum. There were postcards she'd sent from Wales, Normandy and Paris; every postcard she had ever sent Lisa appeared to be there.

Her fingers spasmed on a doodle she'd made when she'd obviously been on the phone. Something she'd chuck away without thinking, but Lisa had kept.

She sank on to the bed feeling dizzy. She hadn't kept any of Lisa's letters. She'd ceremoniously lit a fire and burned every last one the night she'd returned from Alaska. Her fingers felt detached, almost numb, when she opened the next drawer down.

It was full of photographs of the two of them: riding bicycles and ponies, camping in the garden, opening Christmas presents, having lunch at The George. There was one of them playing in a paddling pool, sprays of water arcing in the sunshine, their bodies brown, faces split with toothy grins. Her mind echoed with their happy shrieks.

She had loved her little sister so much, she was suddenly baffled how they had become estranged. Tears welled in her eyes and she brushed them angrily away. Jet-lag was making her tired and emotional. She must get some sleep, and then she'd regain her usual equanimity. Pushing the childhood memorabilia back into the cabinet she wriggled under the covers and turned out the light.

Abby awoke to the sound of hammering on wood. She thought she heard her name being called. Her eyes snapped open to see pale arrows of sunlight falling coldly through the window.

Pulling the robe tight around her, Abby blearily checked the VCR clock as she stumbled through the living area. Ten a.m.! She couldn't remember when she'd last slept in that long. Yawning, eyes watering and feeling every one of her thirty-one years, she peered through the window to see Trooper Demarco stamping her feet on the porch, vapour pouring from her nostrils and mouth.

Shit. Abby groaned aloud. She'd arranged to meet Demarco at the Moose for breakfast at nine.

Abby opened the door and made an involuntary sound, something between a yelp and a moan. Christ, it was cold. She was about to urge Demarco inside and offer her a coffee when she took in the trooper's expression. Her heart faltered.

Demarco took off her beaver hat and held it formally in front of her. She cleared her throat, held Abby's eyes.

Oh, God, please no. Please don't let Lisa be dead. She's my past, my history, she knows everything about me. Please God, she can't be dead.

'I'm sorry, Abby. We've found the body of a woman in the mountains.'

Six

Abby sat in the rear of the thundering helicopter, looking down at the icy tundra dotted with spruce. She felt slightly sick, her limbs fragile and weak. It was, she recognised dimly, not dissimilar to how she'd felt in her teens, when the Blackpool roller-coaster car finally came to a halt. Where Lisa was bounding about, screaming delightedly at conquering the highest, fastest, scariest roller-coaster in the world, Abby had to force herself to open her eyes, unclench her jaw, and try and stop herself from throwing up.

Their mother, she remembered, had taken one look at Abby's ashen face and rushed them off for ice-cream, the usual family cure for anything upsetting. Oh, God. How on earth was she going to tell Julia that Lisa was dead?

Abby took a deep breath and tried to quell a rising tide of panic. She forced herself to focus on the map Trooper Demarco had passed her earlier.

There was a pencilled X where she assumed the body had been found, at the junction of Fox and McDoe creeks, and at the base of an unnamed mountain topping 5,875 feet. Abby looked for the winter trail Demarco had shown her the previous day, but couldn't find it. Unfolding the map to the next section, she searched for the two black boxes denoting ruins but the contours began to waver, making her dizzy. She pushed the map away.

The helicopter swooped to the right and began to descend. Demarco turned around, a sympathetic grimace around her mouth.

'Nearly there,' she called.

Abby peered outside to see a stand of leafless cottonwoods and a ghostly white creek with a frozen waterfall. As the aircraft drifted down, she tightened the strap across her thighs as hard as she could. Craning her neck left and right she couldn't see any vehicles or police or yellow tape, and in the next few seconds she couldn't see anything at all as the rotors whipped up the snow into a thick white storm. It was like landing in the bottom of a noisy milk bottle.

Lisa would have loved it.

Abby closed her eyes briefly, biting her lip to stop the whimper fluttering in her throat. She wanted to raise her head and scream, let herself howl, but she couldn't yet. She'd have to wait until she was alone.

The engines wound down to a high-pitched whine as the snow fell away and resettled. Doors were opened, people jumped out. The pilot turned in his seat.

'Sure am sorry about this,' he said. His eyes were kind.

Abby nodded. Unbuckled her seat belt with stiff fingers. As she stepped outside on to the soft snow, she felt the tissue in her throat contract at the change in temperature. Wrapping a scarf around her face, she let Demarco lead her along the creek and past the frozen waterfall. The only sound now was their footsteps crunching.

The cold gnawed through her jeans and boots,

numbing her legs and feet almost immediately. The down jacket she'd grabbed from Lisa's cabin seemed as effective as a cotton sheet. Her whole body was freezing up.

Around the corner was an AST – Alaska State Troopers – helicopter, its doors open. Inside she could see parcels of yellow. There were a couple of snow machines parked near by, and dozens of ski tracks leading to and from the chopper vanished along the creek.

Breath clouding the air, two men stood beside a bright yellow plastic hump lying on the ground. It was a body bag. Abby stumbled, nearly falling to her knees. Demarco had her elbow and was making soothing noises as she helped her upright and walked her towards the men standing silently beside the bundle.

Abby had never seen a dead body before, and for a panicky instant wondered how she'd react. Would she vomit? Scream, or faint? She'd been told not to touch the body under any circumstances and had thought she might be tempted to press a kiss to her sister's face, but now she felt like turning tail and fleeing. She swallowed hard. Her legs trembled but she eased herself away from Demarco. She would do this alone and with dignity, and not fall apart.

Slowly, her boots crunched through the snow. One man took a step back but the second raised his head and although he was watching her, she didn't look at him. She was looking at a snow-sprinkled cap of short dark hair. The zip of the body bag had been lowered down her chest and Abby took in the red skinny-rib shirt, the single chunky gold earring in her left ear, and the gold cross nestled at the base of her throat.

One of the men murmured something, and crunched a few slow steps away. She heard a click, and then smelled a waft of cigarette smoke.

Abby studied her face. The eyes were closed, eyelashes frosted with ice crystals. The skin was a mottled blue, the lips cracked and black, and more ice crystals edged the brown, almost black hair, like a fairy crown.

Abby's mind was perfectly blank as she stared at the corpse that wasn't her sister.

Seven

When Lisa came round, she thought she was in a tomb.

She blinked and blinked, but she couldn't see anything. It was pitch dark and the air cold and bitter as dried ice. She could hear the storm was still raging, the wind roaring and howling, but she couldn't feel a single breeze on her face, or her body.

She couldn't feel any pain or discomfort.

She must be dying.

She had heard death by hypothermia was relatively painless, that it began with a wandering mind, walking in circles, and then apathy would set in, followed by a desperate desire to sleep. Eventually the blood would stop pumping to the extremities as the core temperature continued to drop. The breathing rate would slow, the pulse weaken, and gradually the limbs would grow rigid. Men had been found sitting on a sled or with their backs against a tree, frozen solid in the act of trying to light a fire.

It was death by freezing.

Not such a bad way to go if she had nothing to live for. But she hadn't finished yet. She had something important to complete.

Lisa tried to move to check her sled, to look for her research, but her body refused to respond. She had no heat in her core to spare. She was nothing but a lump of slowly freezing meat. Despite her best efforts, she had failed.

Distantly, she wondered when Abby would hear of her disappearance and whether she'd fly out. She doubted it, not after last time. But then she remembered a row they'd had one Christmas – she couldn't recall what it was over – after which Abby had refused to speak to her ever again. She'd had a burst appendix six weeks later and been rushed to hospital, and to her astonishment when she'd come round from the anaesthetic, the first person she saw was Abby.

I thought you never wanted to see me again, Lisa said.

I couldn't give up the opportunity to talk to you without you butting in, she'd answered. *It's nice when you're quiet.*

Lisa closed her eyes. Her breathing started to slow. She made a last, final effort, and sent a prayer to the heavens. She asked for Abby to keep hating her. Keep her anger burning bright so she wouldn't want to come and help her.

Eight

'We were just following procedure.' Demarco was scowling.

'You must have some idea who she is,' Abby said. 'Hasn't anyone reported her missing?'

They were in the trooper's Explorer, skidding and slewing down the road back to Lisa's cabin while the woman's body was being flown to Anchorage, and an autopsy.

Demarco gave a noncommittal grunt, tapping the steering wheel with her blunt-edged fingers but Abby got the impression she'd rather be banging it. She obviously wasn't happy the body wasn't Lisa's. Her workload had just doubled.

'Was she alone?' Abby asked. 'Was there any sign of anyone else?'

The trooper braked for a corner and didn't reply.

'What was she doing up there, do you think?'

Demarco shrugged.

'She wasn't wearing outdoor clothing,' Abby persisted. 'Or was she? Did you find a parka or anything?'

Demarco's chin jutted forward and for a moment Abby thought she was going to respond, but then she gave another shrug.

'Maybe she drove there,' Abby suggested. 'Maybe she broke down and had to walk...'

Abby turned her attention back to the map on her lap, to see there was a track leading to Wolver-

64

ine Creek. There were no houses, no ruins, nothing except snow, glaciers and frozen lakes and rivers. Abby judged the distance between where Lisa had gone missing and where the body was found. There had to be forty miles between the two and she pointed this out to Demarco. The trooper kept her gaze dead ahead and didn't say a word.

'Two women have gone missing in the mountains,' Abby said. 'It can't be a coincidence, surely?'

The trooper veered around a pothole, making the rear wheels slide briefly. She said, 'We'll be holding a public meeting at the Moose in half an hour or so. Shall I drop you at your sister's place so you can freshen up?'

'Do you know who broke into Lisa's cabin yet?'

'Then I'll take you to the Search and Rescue command post,' Demarco added as if she hadn't spoken. 'See how the search for Lisa's going.'

'Sure,' said Abby, caving in against the trooper's immovability. Some days, like today, she wished she was more like her sister. Lisa wouldn't have let Demarco stonewall her, she would have been firing questions at the trooper, wearing her down with her innate persistence until she'd got the answers she wanted. Abby sighed. Compared to Lisa she had the influence of a shower curtain.

As soon as Abby was back inside Lisa's cabin, she called home. She was still talking fifteen minutes later, winding the cord round and round her fingers before loosening it and winding it all over again.

'Yes, I'm fine, Mum, I promise–'

'They don't know who this woman is?' Julia asked for the umpteenth time.

'Not yet, no. Look, Mum, I've got to go.'

'Darling, I'm sorry.' Julia was close to tears.

'You'll be okay?'

'Ralph's here. He's being very kind. Love you.'

Abby hurriedly hung up and, grabbing her day pack, raced outside. She didn't want to be late for the public meeting. How long would it take her if she jogged? Ten minutes? Twenty? She glanced at the snow-topped vehicles parked in Lisa's driveway, one red, one beige, and went back inside and started hunting for keys. Eventually she found a set on top of the microwave. Grabbing a scraper from the deck she went to the red SUV. No way would Lisa drive a beige car.

Abby cleared the driver's door to see it was unlocked. Breath steaming, she hopped inside. She tried to push the key into the ignition but it didn't fit. Hell. Wrong keys.

She was about to belt back inside the cabin and do another search when she considered the beige car. Crunching over, she cleared the door to find it was locked, the lock frozen solid.

Refusing to give up, Abby searched through the red car until she unearthed a can of WD40 from behind the driver's seat. She sprayed it over and into the lock until the ice melted then pushed in the key like a hot knife through butter.

She saw it the instant she made to climb inside. Lying on the passenger seat was a single chunky gold earring.

'Shit,' she said.

Carefully, she picked it up and turned it from side to side. It was identical to the one the dead woman had worn in her left ear. If it had belonged to her, what was it doing here?

She looked around and saw a rental-car tag dangling from the rear-view mirror. Putting the earring back on the seat she opened the glove box and pulled out a flimsy white sheet of paper. The rental agreement. Made to a Marie Guillemote, from Virginia.

She considered Demarco's shrugs to her questions earlier and bit the inside of her lip. She'd never been one to flout the rules, preferring to keep her head below the parapet, but she didn't think she could ignore the earring, not with the woman dead and Lisa in trouble.

She walked back into the cabin and picked up the phone. Hesitated. Then she firmed her resolve. Clearing her throat, she dialled the Fairbanks number at the top of the rental agreement. A woman answered.

'Hi,' Abby said. 'I'd like a Chevy Blazer like my friend rented...' She checked the date. 'On Saturday, third of April. Do you remember her? Her car?'

'Nah, sorry. Curtis was on that morning.'

'Is Curtis around?' Abby asked.

The phone was thumped down and she heard the woman bellowing, 'Curtis, you lazy piece of shit! Phone for ya!'

When a man came on the phone, Abby repeated what she'd said to the woman.

'Everything all right?' he asked. 'She's okay, isn't she?'

Abby pushed her other hand between her thighs. Her skin was suddenly clammy. 'Oh, sure. She says good things about you.'

'Nice lady, your friend.' He sounded pleased.

Abby tried to work out how to start the Alaskan flow of gossip that, once released, would avalanche out of control.

'Can I hire a similar car to hers up here?' Abby asked.

'Where you at?'

'Lake's Edge.'

'You scared of flying too?' He chuckled.

'You bet I am,' she said feelingly. Her flight in Mac's rusting Super Cub had taken at least ten years off her life.

'Never seen anyone so petrified as your friend. She was gonna fly with Todd, he's a real good pilot, but she took one look at his Piper and turned tail and the next we knew, she was in here booking her car. Beige. Real pretty too.' He cleared his throat. 'Your friend. Not the car.'

'Are we talking about the same person?' Abby asked, purposely doubtful. 'Tallish, a redhead?'

'God, no. She was real little, with short dark hair.'

Abby hung up feeling shaky but euphoric. She now knew the dead woman's name – Marie Guillemote – and that she'd rented the SUV outside her sister's cabin. Taking action was scary, but it felt good.

She hoped Demarco wouldn't be angry when she informed her of her findings.

Like the village itself, the Moose hadn't changed.

It still looked more like a hunting lodge than a bar with its trophies of moose, Dall sheep and salmon displayed on the log walls. The same colossal stuffed bear stood just inside the door with its coat the colour of dirty straw and claws the length of her hand. High ceilings stretched over the same wooden boards and the chimney fireplace in its centre continued to throw out heat like a volcano. Even the sign behind the counter was the same: *Firearms not permitted in this area.*

The place was empty aside from a big Native guy at the counter, drinking coffee. His fur-trimmed parka hung from the back of his chair and he'd kicked off his bunny boots, which lay by the door. Bunny boots, Abby faintly recalled, was a generic term for the big, white rubber boots that most of the locals favoured.

'Trooper Demarco?' Abby asked him. 'She's gone?'

The big guy turned and peered at her from beneath a broad forehead and a pair of bushy black eyebrows. It was like being scrutinised by a buffalo. He didn't say a word.

'Where is she?' Abby shifted from foot to foot. 'Can I catch her up?'

'She asked me to take you to the campground. The Search and Rescue command post.' He raised his mug, which she took meant he'd like to finish his coffee first.

'Won't we be late?'

He fixed a steady dark gaze on her, face impassive. 'I'm Joe Chenega,' he said, and stuck out a paw the size of a frying-pan. 'Most folk around here call me Big Joe.'

Abby blinked. 'You're the guy Lisa was meant to meet up with at the weekend?'

He nodded.

Abby shook Big Joe's hand. It was strong and warm as creased leather. Most Natives were small, but he'd broken the mould. The man was built like an oak tree. His nickname suited him, but since Bigjoe was a fairly common surname in Native culture out here, she wondered if it didn't cause some confusion.

Big Joe leaned along the counter and pulled a pot of coffee over. He poured her a mug and gestured to the stool next to him. She remained standing, looking through the window at the frozen length of lake.

Lisa, Lisa, Lisa. The name was running through her mind like a mantra. Please God, let Lisa be all right.

Big Joe downed the last of his coffee in three swift swallows and got to his feet. 'I'll fetch the car,' he said. 'You wait here.'

'Demarco's at the campground, isn't she? I've got something important to tell her.'

He gave a nod before turning on his heel.

A gust of fog blurred her senses as he strode away. Jet-lag kicking in, reminding her it was five a.m. back home. Blinking away tears of fatigue, Abby watched a woman arrive in a rush, carrying a tray of glasses. She was small and strong looking, and wore a pink and white teatowel at her waist. She took one look at Abby and nearly dropped the tray.

'What the...?' she said. From her expression it appeared she was fighting an internal struggle, as if a ball of acid was burning her throat.

'Diane,' said Abby cautiously.

'Abby.' The woman's dark, tilted eyes were appraising her warily. 'You want some coffee?'

Grateful for the peace offering, Abby said, 'Sure.'

Diane glanced away, then back. She was biting her lip. 'Go sit by the fire. I'll bring it over.'

Grateful for the woman's relative equanimity, Abby dropped her day pack to the floor, shrugged off her parka and settled into one of the leather armchairs placed around the fire, their arms rubbed to a greasy shine. To her left hung a moose head the size of a fridge. Its glass eyes seemed to be staring directly at her with the same steady complacency of Big Joe. She looked away.

Diane brought her coffee over and looked as though she was about to say something, then changed her mind and gave her a tight smile instead.

'Rest up all you want. You look like you need it.'

'Diane, I ... thank you.'

Without saying anything further the woman walked off, her shiny black plait twisting at her waist.

She was amazed Diane hadn't thrown the coffee in her lap. Did this mean the Native woman had forgiven her? Diane had been apoplectic with rage when she'd caught her and Cal in bed that morning, but Abby hadn't understood the reason for it back then. She'd snuggled back beneath the covers without a second thought for the bad-tempered maid with an armload of fresh towels.

Abby leaned back in the leather chair and closed

71

her eyes. The Moose smelled the same as it had when she'd been here with Cal; wood smoke, coffee and fried bacon. After Diane had slammed the door behind her, she could remember Cal flinging back the bedclothes and muttering something about coffee. She had watched him head for his clothes at the end of the bed, broad shoulders sloping to a narrow waist, nice legs, terrifically firm and rounded behind that always made her want to bite it, like she would an apple. It was indecent how good he looked naked.

While he left to get coffee and muffins, Abby went and showered. He was away for nearly an hour, and it was only later that she realised he must have been talking with Diane. When he returned they had breakfast on the balcony of their room overlooking the glassy blue lake. Abby talked over the expedition, what the others might be doing now, but Cal was distant and distracted. Eventually he'd got up, and said he had to go.

'Meet me for supper tonight?' she asked.

A cloud passed over his face.

'What's wrong?'

'I, er...' He ran a hand over his head and down his face. 'There's something I have to do.'

'What is it?'

He looked away, biting his lip. 'Nothing. I just need ... a bit of time. I'll see you tomorrow, okay?'

She didn't make anything of it because he came over and pulled her close, pressing a kiss against her mouth. As she watched him walk down the street, she replayed the conversation they'd had on the expedition, talking about the possibility of his coming to see her in England. She felt exuberant, more alive than she could remember, and an hour later, when she bounded into Lisa's cabin, she embraced her sister like she hadn't in ages.

'Blimey,' Lisa said, looking her up and down. 'What happened to you?'

'I met a man,' Abby blurted.

Lisa grinned. 'And he's obviously giving you an endless supply of happy pills.' She dragged Abby into the kitchen and opened the fridge, brought out a bottle of wine. 'From the way your tail's wagging, this is cause for celebration.'

Wine uncorked even though it was barely eleven a.m., the sisters sat at the table – then a piece of plywood on top of four tree stumps that tilted wildly if you leaned an elbow too hard on one side – and Abby flooded Lisa with how she'd never thought she'd feel like this, how he was thinking of coming to England, and Lisa told her to slow down, and start at the beginning.

So Abby did. She'd only uttered a couple of sentences when Lisa said, 'What? Did I get his name right? Did you say *Cal?*'

'He was our guide. He's setting up an insurance company in Fairbanks, but he used to guide hunters–'

'Oh, shit.' Lisa was staring at her in open horror. 'You've got to be kidding. You're *in love with Cal Pegati?*'

Abby blinked. 'Why? What's wrong with that?'

'Jesus H. Christ, why *him*, for God's sake?' She flung up her hands in despair. 'Weren't there any other guys willing to fuck you on your expedition?'

'Hey, hang on a minute! It wasn't like that!'

'Oh, sure it wasn't. I don't fucking believe this.

73

You sitting smug as can be, carrying on like Saffron doesn't exist.' Lisa got slowly to her feet, eyes glittering. 'One of the nicest, most beautiful women around and she's tossed aside in a moment.'

The name rang a bell but Abby shook her head. 'Who's Saffron?'

'Just my best friend in the whole wide world.'

Abby looked blank and Lisa flung up her hands again. 'She was the first person to make me really welcome up here. Helped me find a cabin to rent, introduced me to everyone. We used to go picking berries, fishing together–'

'What has Saffron got to do with me and Cal?'

'Oh, just a small issue, like she's been Cal's wife for the past eight years.'

'He's *married?*'

'Oh, drop the bullshit, Abby. Married men stick out a mile, so don't pull that on me, it won't wash.'

'But I honestly didn't know!'

'You'd better pray this doesn't get out.' Lisa clenched her fists. 'Saffron will *die* if she hears about this. Cal's her whole world, her whole reason for being. They were childhood sweethearts, for Chrissakes! And along you come, happy as a fucking clam, talking about taking him to bloody England!'

'Lisa, just wait a moment–'

'Couldn't you keep your sodding hands off him? I know he's a bit of all right, but to go all out and break up his marriage? I thought you were better than that.'

Abby scrambled to her feet, face burning. 'How

dare you judge me. You're the one who whips off her knickers at a moment's notice. You're the slut here, not me. You've broken up more marriages than I've had hot dinners.'

'And you're a bossy, controlling cow who thinks she's so fucking perfect looking after Mummy she can get away with anything.'

'You *bitch*.' Abby was stunned.

'You're the bitch here.' Lisa's tone was like acid. 'The *in-heat* bitch who's fucking my best friend's husband... Saffron doesn't deserve this, and if I think you've done it on purpose to get back at me–'

'You self-centred little snake. This hasn't got anything to do with being upset over Saffron, it's *you* that's the issue here, isn't it? *You* that's got to be the centre of attention, *you* who's never cared about anyone else, let alone your sister–'

'Too fucking right. You're my sister but Saffron's a friend.' She ran a hand over her face. 'Why do you think I left England? To advance my career?'

A hot wave of horror rolled up Abby's spine. 'You left because of *me?*'

'Don't say you didn't break open the champagne the second you heard I was going.'

'I was *pleased* for you. I thought it was what you wanted.'

'That's what you always say. That you're *pleased* for me. I'm sick of it. I want you to leave. I can't bear the sight of you.'

A strange sense of calm descended over Abby as she looked at Lisa. She studied the raggedy home-cut hair, the little scar on her forehead, the sinewy strength in her arms from chopping logs, and then she got to her feet and walked to the door.

'Goodbye,' she said.

By three o'clock that afternoon, Abby was on a plane and flying out of Alaska.

Nine

Abby was dreaming of the dead woman. The blue of her skin, the ice crystals on her eyelashes and in her hair. Her skinny-rib shirt, red as hot coals, red as the flames dancing across her eyelids.

'Joe. Dammit, Joe!'

The voice made her jump and drop her mug to the floor. Abby blinked blearily at it lying on the rug, glad she'd drained it dry. She wondered how long she'd been asleep. It felt about two minutes.

'Joe!' Another protest.

Big Joe was approaching, Demarco hot on his heels, looking like an angry horsefly.

Abby clambered to her feet.

'She's got something to tell you,' Big Joe said, looking at Demarco. 'And if she doesn't, I will.'

Demarco was staring at Big Joe as though he'd grown horns and a tail.

'The trooper isn't used to Natives being forward like this.' He was speaking to Abby, but he didn't move his steady gaze from Demarco. 'Usually we stay in the background and don't say or do any more than necessary. Conflict avoidance is our culture. But not today.'

Demarco gave Big Joe a long, final look, then said, 'Let's have a seat.'

'You've found Lisa?' Abby asked.

Demarco shook her head as she took the armchair next to Abby. Big Joe stood to one side of the fire, arms folded, snow melting from his bunny boots and forming a puddle on the hearth.

'I didn't tell you before,' Demarco started, 'because it ... well, it wasn't entirely necessary. Not then, anyway. When you saw the body wasn't your sister's.'

The trooper glanced at Big Joe then away.

'But things are moving fast. We're now pretty sure who the woman is, and that she was visiting your sister.'

'Marie Guillemote,' Abby said.

'You know her?' Demarco asked, excited, expectant.

'No. I just found out she rented the car that's parked outside Lisa's cabin.'

Twin spots of red appeared on Demarco's cheeks. There was a small pause while Abby watched the trooper trying to hold on to her composure. 'As I was saying... I didn't say anything before. But I guess you should know that the woman you saw on the mountain had been shot. There is no question she was murdered.'

A chill raced across the back of her neck. 'Murdered?' Abby repeated. 'Marie Guillemote was *murdered*?'

'Shot twice in the chest at close range.'

Abby stared at the trooper, unable to think of anything to say.

'If it wasn't for wild animals,' Demarco continued, 'the body might never have been discovered. It was well hidden beneath the snow, wedged in a crevasse, but a wolf, maybe a wolverine, managed to free a section of the body. Someone with Search and Rescue found part of an arm, and after an extensive search of the area, we eventually found the rest of the remains.

'Her indoor clothing and ultimate lack of blood at the scene immediately suggested murder. The lividity confirmed this. We could see instantly that the body had been in more than one position post-mortem. She wasn't killed on the mountain, but moved there from the scene of the crime.'

Demarco held Abby's gaze. 'The tags on the Chevy Blazer match up with the car Marie Guillemote rented from Fairbanks. We're in the process of getting a search warrant for your sister's cabin.'

Abby forced herself to speak and when it came out, it was a croak. 'You don't think Lisa's been shot too, do you?'

'We can't say. Which is why we need to check her place out. See if we can put together what's going on. Meantime, we would appreciate it if you didn't return to the cabin for the moment.'

'What about my stuff?'

'We'll let you have it when we're finished. Meantime, we'd prefer it if you wouldn't mind finding alternative accommodation.'

The Trooper got to her feet and, with a nod to Big Joe, walked outside.

Abby folded into the armchair. She picked up her mug and set it upright on the floor. Her hands were trembling. She heard Big Joe talking

78

to Diane, but not what he said. Her ears felt as though they were filled with water.

She looked up when Big Joe came and squatted in front of her, holding out a glass of what looked like whiskey. Abby downed it in one swallow, feeling it burn all the way down her throat. Joe retrieved the glass and put it next to the mug.

'Lisa's not dead,' he said.

Abby stared into his unfathomable eyes. 'How do you know?'

'I just do.'

The calm passivity of his gaze gave her an inordinate rush of relief. Big Joe gave a nod almost in recognition and rose to his feet. 'Let's go get your gear.'

'But Demarco said–'

'She doesn't have the search warrant yet. Let's get there before she does.'

Abby picked up her day pack and walked after him, feeling peculiarly light-headed. Lisa is alive, Big Joe said so. She chanted this under her breath as she followed him out to a half-shovelled car park. *Lisa is alive, Big Joe said so.* A trickle of hope seeped inside her, and with it, her senses and thoughts began to sharpen.

There were only four cars in the car park and right off she knew which one was Joe's. Big guy, big car. The white Dodge Ram pickup could have fitted the entire contents of her and Julia's home inside.

'Nice wheels,' she said.

He gave a shrug.

When they got to Lisa's cabin, Abby saw Demarco had called for back-up. A uniformed trooper was stationed outside. He looked about sixteen. He introduced himself as Trooper Weiding and was polite but firm. He couldn't let them inside. Orders, he said, sorry.

With Abby cursing under her breath, Big Joe turned his Dodge around. At the bottom of the trail, Abby asked him to stop next to a row of mailboxes. Fifteen of them, but she knew exactly which one was Lisa's because she'd painted it yellow and given it a red roof. Door keys in hand, she crunched over but she didn't need them. The box was unlocked. Abby took the stack of mail and stuffed it in her day pack. Big Joe didn't say a word, just headed south for his place, where he said he had something important to do.

'Once it's sorted,' he told her, 'we'll join the search.'

Abby had a quick check through her day pack, glad she hadn't left it in Lisa's cabin for Demarco to confiscate. 'Could we stop at the supermarket first?' she asked. 'I need supplies.'

While Big Joe waited in his car, Abby hurriedly bought the basics: toothbrush and paste, undies, shampoo and soap, deodorant. She hoped Diane wouldn't mind if she stayed at the Moose. Nowhere else was open. At the checkout, she asked for two packs of Marlboro Lights and a lighter. She'd given up well over five years ago, but ever since she'd heard about Lisa going missing she'd battled against the urge to sit down and smoke a whole pack.

Back in the Dodge she held up her cigarettes and asked if Joe minded, and when he shook his head, she cranked open the window and lit up.

The cigarette tasted of burned rubber and ash and chemicals, and the fact it tasted so disgusting made her feel fractionally better, like she was punishing herself.

Big Joe lived just outside town, and Abby spent the five-mile journey gazing outside and trying to ignore the fear building inside her. Why had Marie been murdered? Who had hidden her body on the mountain? Had Lisa been shot, and hidden too? And what about the burned discs and files in Lisa's yard? Had Lisa burned them, or someone else?

Grinding her cigarette out in the ashtray, Abby pushed her hands between her thighs. They were like ice and she couldn't stop them trembling.

The car lurched heavily to one side, then the other, making Abby feel as though she was on a boat. Global warming had begun to thaw the permafrost, buckling the road into mounds and hollows, even making houses tilt, but Big Joe's place didn't seem to have been affected. A small cabin that looked as sturdy and strong as Big Joe himself had been extended over the years into a sprawling mass of haphazard buildings. A caribou carcass hung from a meat hook beneath an awning. He didn't invite her in, just dropped the tailgate and vanished.

Abby climbed outside into the cold air and stood listening to nothing. Her stomach growled, reminding her she hadn't eaten, so she lit another cigarette. Dragged the smoke deep into her lungs and exhaled a cloud of smoke that hovered in the stillness.

She stamped out her cigarette when Big Joe

returned, hefting a bundle of blankets spilling fur, which he shifted carefully into the back. For a brief moment she thought it was a dead animal, but then she saw a bright blue eye wink at her. It was the piercing colour of blue glacier ice and rimmed with black, as though it had been painted with eyeliner.

'Same colour,' said Joe, watching her.

'I'm sorry?'

'You and Moke. Same eyes.'

'This is Lisa's dog? The one that came back with its harness chewed through?'

'Yup.'

'Hey there,' she said to the dog. A faint thump of metal told her it was wagging its tail. 'You did good, you know.'

'You normally talk to dogs?'

'No. Of course not. I just wanted to, er... Never mind.'

Joe snapped the tailgate shut, his face unreadable, but she got the uneasy feeling he was laughing inside.

Four doors down from the Moose, Big Joe parked outside a little log cabin with red curtains in the windows and snow swept from the porch.

'All yours,' he said, tilting his chin at the cabin. 'It's been shut all winter so it'll take a while to warm up, just keep the wood stove burning and you'll be okay.'

Abby stared at him in astonishment.

'It belongs to a friend of Lisa's. Michael Flint. He said you can stay as long as you like.'

'Who's Michael Flint?'

'I just said. He's a friend.'

'What sort of friend? Boyfriend? An old lover of hers? A new lover? What?'

Big Joe's jaw flexed briefly and then he climbed out of the car. Abby joined him on the board-walk; a raised plank path that was designed to keep pedestrians clear of the tumultuous spring melt. She reckoned she'd have more chance of extracting a diamond from an icicle than getting Big Joe to reply when he didn't want to.

'What about rent?'

'You can figure it out when you see him.'

The cabin consisted of a single room with a tall ceiling that made it appear bigger than it was. There were colourful Native rugs on wooden boards, a comfy-looking sofa, and a kitchenette with stools. In one corner was a shelf with a double mattress. It was clean and bright and she was so relieved to have somewhere nice to stay she could barely speak.

'Bathroom's out the back,' he said. 'Can't miss it.'

He strode outside. Abby hurried after him.

'I'll pick you up in twenty minutes,' he told her. 'Take you to where Search and Rescue have set up. They'll tell us where they want us looking.'

'Joe, I can't tell you how grateful I am.'

He gave her one of his nods and she leaned over the tailgate and stroked the thick fur over Moke's head and ears. The dog closed his eyes and started making a rattling sound deep in his throat. It was, she realised, a rather sick-sounding doggy purr.

'Where are you taking him?'

'Vet.'

'He'll fix him up?'

'With a lethal injection.'

She could feel the horror on her face. 'You can't do that!'

'It's just another dog to feed. A useless one at that.'

She hadn't taken Big Joe to be heartless, but out here she guessed that was the way things were. If an animal couldn't pay its way then it was deemed worthless. Moke was nuzzling her hand, asking for more attention and her throat immediately clogged up.

'Can't we, er...' Abby bit her lip. 'I mean, won't Lisa be upset when she discovers you've destroyed her dog?'

Big Joe raised his eyebrows. 'You want him?'

'I'm not sure about that. I've never owned a dog and wouldn't have a clue how to–'

She swallowed her words when he snapped open the tailgate and hefted Moke in his arms and carried him into the cabin, easing him down on what looked suspiciously like a dog bed already prepared in the kitchenette.

'All yours,' he said.

'But Michael Flint might not want–'

'Mike said it was fine.' He passed her a tube of ointment and a pack of pills, then gestured at a sack sitting on the counter. 'Dog food. Make sure he's got lots of water. When he's better he'll prefer to sleep outside. Gets too hot indoors.' He flicked his gaze to her feet. 'And get yourself some decent gear for the mountain. Sports store's open down the road. Your boots are rubbish.'

With that Joe walked back to his car, leaving

Abby staring at the dog, mouth open.

The Search and Rescue command post was a motor home parked on the edge of a ploughed expanse of dead grass and ice. Knee-high wooden rails surrounded the campground, forest crawling along one side, a frozen creek on the other. Waves of mountain peaks rose through a thick white layer of clouds, like islands in an ocean, and the air was clear and cold.

Come June it would be packed with hikers and their tents, but right now it was littered with an assortment of four-wheel drives – the Alaskan version of a quad bike or all-terrain-vehicle – and snow machines. No wonder she hadn't seen any vehicles in town, they were all here.

Big Joe gave her new boots the once-over. Her Sorrels felt good. Warm and strong, with flexible lug soles for traction, medium-height leather uppers and, if the tag was to be believed, completely waterproof up to her ankles. 'Good choice,' he said and nodded approvingly, making her feel like a kid who'd been given a gold star for a maths test. She was terrible at maths. Not like Lisa who was a walking calculator.

'Let's see where they want us,' said Joe and he marched for the motor home.

Abby followed, feeling snug in her new gear. She was wearing padded trousers, deliciously warm, a parka with fur trim around the hood and wrists, a thick soft hat that covered her ears, as well as some gloves and a pair of mittens to go over the top.

People were eating sandwiches and drinking

from thermoses, voices ringing in the icy air as they compared their morning sorties. Occasionally someone would catch her eye, but they never looked away. They'd either give her a nod or lift a hand in a faint salute, to show they recognised who she was, but didn't want to encroach on her emotions.

She felt a rush of warmth for these people she didn't know. People who had come from miles away, people who had never met Lisa, but who knew what it would be like to be out there in the cold and all alone.

Two guys with *Paramedic* stitched across their chests were sitting on the motor-home steps, eating donuts and sipping from steaming Styrofoam cups. They moved aside to let Abby squeeze past, raising their cups and greeting Big Joe who gave them a nod in return.

Inside it was hot and stuffy and chaotic. Maps were stuck on walls and thrown across tables; hats, gloves and down jackets stacked in piles everywhere; cups and ashtrays on every surface. People were talking, radios and walkie-talkies crackling, and from somewhere came the faint twanging of country and western music.

Abby's eyes snagged on a guy at the far end talking into a radio, and for a second, her heart nearly stopped. Taking a deep breath, she told herself to stop being so paranoid, and she was about to relax when the man glanced around.

This time her heart did stop.

It was Cal Pegati.

And he looked as though he couldn't believe his eyes either.

Abby jerked her gaze away, her heart kicking back into action at triple-rate and her skin springing with sweat. What the hell was he doing here? He'd said he was giving up guiding, that he was sick of the hunters who only wanted the trophy and would – if they could get away with it – leave the meat to rot. He said he was exchanging his gun for a computer, and had even shown her pictures of the offices he was leasing in Fairbanks.

Out of the corner of her eye Abby saw Cal put down his radio and get to his feet. She hurriedly busied herself, pretending to study a map on the wall. Stay calm, she told herself. Don't let him see how much he gets to you.

'Abby.'

'Hello, Cal.' She fought to keep outwardly calm. 'How are you?'

'Like everyone else.' He nudged his chin at the team who appeared to be filling Big Joe in on what was happening. 'Concerned about your sister.'

'Good of you to chip in,' she said. 'Especially all the way from Fairbanks. You are still based in Fairbanks, I take it?'

'Yes, I am.' Cal ran a hand over his head and back, making his hair stick up in tufts. He hadn't shaved for a couple of days and she could see speckles of white dotting his stubble that hadn't been there before.

'Look, Abby, there's something you need to know. I'm here in an official capacity.'

'You didn't set up your business?'

'Sure I did, but I've taken on some other stuff – which involves Lisa.'

He took a step towards her, and he was so close

she could smell the scent of wood smoke rising from his parka, reminding her of the last time she'd slept with him, the way he'd kissed the base of her spine, barely brushing it with his lips so all the hairs stood erect and a rush of heat suffused her body.

Abby scooted sideways in order to put some distance between them.

'Okay.' Cal held up his hands. 'Let's do this outside.'

The icy air had little effect on her nerves but she maintained her casual air by leaning against the flank of the motor home and crossing one boot over the other. 'You went into the insurance business?' she asked, pleased with her tone; politely interested.

'Yup.'

'It's a long way from walking the wilds with the earth beneath your feet and the sky on your shoulders.'

'That's what weekends are for.' His expression turned rueful. 'Besides, the thought had crossed my mind that when I'm old and grey, I might not be as nippy around a grizzly.'

She knew a lot of Alaskans had two jobs, like the postman she'd met who doubled as a Search and Rescue crew member, but she was having trouble believing this. A tough professional hunter and tracker, who could navigate by the stars and build a bear pit with one hand, turning into a white collar worker? He had to be kidding.

'What about Wright's Air? Weren't they advertising for more pilots?'

'I wanted to work for myself, Abby. And believe

it or not, in the aircraft industry there's less risk being an insurance broker than hocking myself up to my eyeballs renting an aircraft and lugging equipment around the state.'

There was a silence broken by the roar of a snow machine. A radio crackled.

Her mouth was dry but she forced herself to keep going. 'You said you're here officially?'

Cal folded his arms. 'I'm acting as Insurance Investigator. For one of the big firms, Falcon Union. They've used me before. Several times. We have a good relationship.'

'Hope they pay you well.'

'Oh, yes. Money's not a problem.' Cal unfolded his arms and dragged his hand back and forth over his head again. It was, she remembered, a gesture that meant he was uncomfortable, even embarrassed, and she'd never mentioned it to him, finding it a useful indicator of his emotions.

'So?' she said.

More head dragging, then a big sigh. 'I've been retained to investigate your sister.'

For a second she just stared at him. She was having trouble assimilating his words into something logical. 'You've *what?*'

'It's just that she took out a life insurance policy six months ago.' Another drag of the head. 'A big one. And Falcon Union are concerned that maybe ... everything is not what it seems.'

Abby narrowed her eyes. 'And what does that mean?'

'There's a lot at stake. Two point four million dollars to be precise.'

Belatedly the penny dropped. 'You think Lisa

took out a life policy and that she's disappeared *on purpose?*'

Cal shuffled his feet and looked away.

Fury suddenly met her nervous jitters in a head-on collision. She could almost hear the crash reverberating around the mountains. She stopped worrying about her own vulnerability and without hesitation walked right up to Cal and thrust her fingers against his chest, prodding as hard as she could.

'How dare you even think it? Lisa may be a bit wild sometimes, but she's not a criminal! Sure, she's buggered off occasionally without telling anyone where she's going, but that's only because she doesn't *think.* Sure, she can be selfish and self-centred enough to drive us all nuts but trying to rip off an insurance company by pretending she's died on some mountain? Give me a *break.*'

Cal took a step back but Abby kept with him, fingers still stabbing.

'You may think everyone's a blood-sucking con artist, but that's only because it takes one to know one. So why don't you bugger off back to your *retainers* and tell them to stick it where the sun doesn't shine?'

'Some people would do a lot for that sort of money.'

'Oh, come on, Cal. Listen to yourself, will you? Lisa is not *some people.*'

'The guy who sold Lisa the insurance told me she said that when her beneficiary got their hands on the money she'd rise from the dead to share it with them.'

'For God's sakes, it was a *joke!* You know how

irreverent she is! Besides,' Abby shot him a look, 'if she really wanted to rip off the insurance company, she'd never say anything like that. She may be a bit mad sometimes, but she's not stupid.'

'That had occurred to me,' he said stiffly.

'Oh, good!' She beamed at him, sarcasm dripping. 'So you're looking at both sides of the coin. That makes a change.'

He glanced down at her fingers resting on his fleece, then back at her. 'Finished?'

Abby snatched her hand back. 'So you'll return to Fairbanks? Tell them it's not a scam?'

'No. I've a job to do – and I'm going to do it, whether you like it or not.'

Silence fell. Abby was trying to think of a way she could persuade Cal to go home when he did the head-hand thing again.

'Abby? Can we talk about when you were last here?'

She spun on her heel and stalked away, speaking over her shoulder. 'What's to talk about? You conned me and I fell for it. End of story.'

Ten

Abby felt emotionally and physically wrecked the next morning. Her muscles were stiff and aching from floundering through deep snow alongside Big Joe and two other guys all afternoon, only stopping to peer through a set of binoculars from time to time, desperately trying to see a trace of

91

anything man-made that might lead them to Lisa. No one had found anything.

Moke stood by the door, looking hopeful. Struggling up, she pushed him outside, then put a pan of milk on the stove and hunted through the cupboards until she found a sachet of chocolate. She needed something rich and soothing and sweet against the previous day.

She fed some kindling into the wood stove, then read the instructions on the tube and packet of pills Big Joe had left her. Letting Moke back in, she smoothed Silver Sulfa Diazine over his frostbite, and put his pills in a piece of bread to make sure he swallowed them. She made some buttered toast, but the instant she bit into it her appetite vanished. To Moke's delight, she chucked both slices into his bowl. Lighting a cigarette, she smoked it while she looked out over the cold white length of lake.

Where are you, Lisa? Where the hell are you?

Lighting another cigarette, she fetched the mail she'd swiped from Lisa's mailbox and settled herself on the sofa. There was a lot of junk mail, offering deals on everything from colouring your log home beautiful to reversing baldness, but only a handful of bills, which she put to one side. There was one personal item.

Written and printed by computer, it was from someone called Tessa who'd signed off with *lots of love* and pressed the X key to produce a line of kisses. It was headed in capitals: DON'T LET THE BASTARD GET YOU DOWN.

Abby scanned the letter, but it didn't make much sense.

No one cares about the past out here, you should know that by now. Half our upstanding citizens moved here because they were running from something, and if there was a law against it we wouldn't have a single politician in Alaska.

It went on in the same vein for a while, and ended by saying:

It was only a minor offence, remember, so don't panic and blow it out of all proportion. We all love you. Who cares what happened some other place, some other time? We certainly don't.

Abby turned the paper over then back, but there was no address or telephone number. Frustrated, she checked the envelope, and her spirits lifted. Dated the second of April, it had been franked by a company called Peak Adventure in Fairbanks. She grabbed the phone and dialled.

'Peak Adventure,' a woman said brightly.

'Hi, can I speak to Tessa?'

'She's not in today. Can I take a message?'

Abby introduced herself and the woman immediately said, 'Oh, heavens. Have you found Lisa?'

'Not yet.'

'Dear Lord, I hope you do. We've been missing her like crazy here ... we're all just so fond of her. Look, give Tessa a ring at home. She's not flying this week. She'll be glad to speak to you.'

Abby lit another cigarette before she redialled. Tessa picked up on the second ring, and when she heard who Abby was and that Lisa was still missing, launched into a tirade of anxiety. Abby smoked while the woman ranted, and eventually managed to interject some questions, learning that Tessa and Lisa had struck up a friendship through Peak Adventure, where Tessa flew clients in the company helicopter to various peaks and glaciers around the country for mountain climbing and hiking.

'She did Denali last year,' Tessa was saying. 'If she can do Denali, she can survive some tin-pot mountain. She knows her stuff, your sister. I can't believe she won't be walking out of there.'

Abby made a neutral sound, then braved herself to confess she'd read Tessa's letter. Tessa didn't sound annoyed as much as puzzled.

'How's that going to help?'

Abby stubbed out her cigarette and told her about the murder of Marie Guillemote. There was an appalled silence, which Abby hurriedly filled. 'Which is why I need to know some stuff. Like did you know Marie?'

There was a long silence.

'Hello? Tessa?' Abby wondered if she'd been cut off.

'Yeah, yeah. I'm here. Shit, I can't believe this.'

Abby let Tessa shake herself down before prompting her about Marie.

'Never heard of her before.'

'Okay. And what's this about the past? "Don't let the bastards get you down"?'

'Bastard. Just the one.' Tessa sighed. 'Peter Santoni. He used to work with Lisa. They've never liked each other, and she likes him even less now he's found out about her court case.'

'What court case?'

'She told me not to tell anyone... Oh, shit. I guess you'd better know, hadn't you? Where to start…? Well, six years ago, your sister was summoned to the US District Court to face charges made by a professor at her university. Professor Crowe.'

Six years ago Lisa would have been twenty-three and in the middle of the Ph.D. she never finished in Washington DC. And Crowe? Well, Crowe had been a highly respected professor at Lisa's university.

'What charges?'

'Professor Crowe took Lisa to court to get a restraining order against her.'

Abby stared at the cigarette smoking in the ashtray in disbelief. Bloody hell.

'What was the outcome?'

'The professor won. Lisa couldn't come within a hundred yards of Crowe without risking a jail sentence.'

'What on earth was Lisa doing?'

'She accused Crowe of murder.'

Gobsmacked, Abby couldn't think of a word to say and let Tessa continue.

'We're talking fifteen years ago, right? A student called Jared – can't remember his surname – died in a climbing accident. He was brilliant, apparently, one of those geniuses that are light years ahead of everyone else, but he died before his Ph.D. thesis could be submitted. Nobody knew what happened to it… Anyway, his buddy at the time, who also shared a tutor with Jared, was Crowe. And the thing is, Lisa unearthed a copy of Jared's thesis, don't ask me how, and it bore an uncanny resemblance to the one Crowe submitted just after Jared died. When Lisa heard

Crowe had gone climbing with Jared the day he fell to his death, she went nuts. She immediately accused Crowe of pushing Jared off the mountain and stealing his thesis.'

By the time the conversation was winding up, Abby had smoked five cigarettes and was in a state of shock. If what Tessa said was true, both Lisa and the professor had been forced to leave the university.

'Who else knows about this?'

'Nobody as far as I know. Santoni was using it as something to bait her with – keep him feeling superior.'

Eventually Abby hung up, and began to pace the room, Moke's vivid blue eyes following. Lisa had lied to her and Julia. She hadn't been offered a dream job in Alaska, she'd been *thrown out of uni.*

She paused to look through the window at the ice-coated landscape. Where the hell was she going to go from here?

Hands cosy in her mittens, Abby walked to Lisa's cabin. The trail was filled with vehicles pulled hard against the snowdrifts, the last in line being a black Dodge Ram, identical to Joe's aside from the colour. Lines of bright yellow tape were strung between slim metal poles stuck in the snow, forming a tenuous fence around the property. It wasn't the flimsy plastic that stopped her but the continuous mantra: *Police Line Do Not Cross Police Line Do Not Cross.*

Trooper Weiding appeared, beaver hat crammed low on his forehead. She asked if Demarco was around. He trotted off. Abby surveyed the view beyond Lisa's cabin, stretching past outlines of spruce trees and across the white sheen of the lake to the cliffs opposite. There wasn't a breath of wind. She could see why Lisa had bought a place out here. She wouldn't have felt hemmed in or pressured, she would have revelled in the space. Lisa needed a lot of space.

To Abby's dismay, the trooper returned with Cal.

'Where's Demarco?' she asked.

'Busy.'

'Why are you allowed in? You're not a policeman.'

'I'm considered part of the investigative team. This doesn't mean I get to tramp all over the crime scene, but hang well back and out of the way.'

'Crime scene?' The words came out high-pitched with anxiety.

Cal studied her at length. 'I'll let you know what's happening, but only if you have a drink with me.'

Abby rallied enough strength to say, 'Blackmail. How come that doesn't surprise me?'

'Call it what you will, but the cops aren't going to share much with you. Not until they know what's going on.'

'Oh all right,' she snapped. 'So long as you're paying.'

'I've been paying for the past four years,' he said, his voice low and hard.

There was silence for a handful of seconds. Abby couldn't think of a single thing to say.

'You got a car?' Cal asked. 'Or would you like a lift?'

Abby checked her watch. Nine a.m. 'I thought you said a drink, not a cup of coffee.'

'You can have a bottle of whiskey for all I care. Now, are you coming with me or not?'

Abby glanced at the trooper who didn't seem to be taking any notice of them. He was looking at the mountains on the other side of the lake with a serene expression on his face, as though he was meditating.

'Where were you thinking of going?'

'There's only one place open.'

'All right then,' she said with a sigh.

Feeling mulish, Abby told the lanky guy serving at the Moose that she'd like a bottle of whiskey, please. Preferably something top shelf, like Glenmorangie or Macallan.

'Wild Turkey do?'

'Nicely, thank you. And a hot chocolate, please.'

Bottle of whiskey labelled with her name and put behind the bar, Abby took her mug of chocolate to one of the leather chairs by the fire. Two guys in workshirts and jeans were eating breakfast at a table to one side. Both looked up and appeared to be about to say hi, when they froze, staring first at her, then at Cal.

Abby felt her cheeks flame but she didn't look away. She glared at them, anger rising at their assumption. Immediately they dropped their gazes.

Still flushed, Abby took a seat and busied herself, stirring the cream into her chocolate.

'Look, Abby,' Cal leaned forward, cradling his coffee mug in both hands, 'I really wanted to talk to you about Lisa's insurance policy–'

'She isn't scamming you, Cal,' Abby said wearily. 'She'd never disrupt all these people's lives like that. Lisa can be thoughtless, but she's not un-kind.'

'I know that, but when she took it out–'

'Please,' she held up a hand, 'I don't want to hear your accusations. I want to know what you think is going on here.'

Cal bit down on his lip.

'That's why I'm having a drink with you,' she reminded him. 'So you can tell me what's happening with the crime scene.'

He picked up his mug, put it down again, glanced at her, then fixed his gaze on the dead moose. When he spoke, it was to the moose.

'Well,' he cleared his throat, 'first up, the cops have found a bullet lodged in the wall of Lisa's cabin. From a .45 calibre semi-automatic weapon. They've sent it to ballistics to see if it matches the one that killed the woman on the mountain. Marie Guilemote.'

Abby was glad she was sitting down because she reckoned she might have fallen if she'd been standing. 'Marie was shot in Lisa's cabin?'

'They found some blood. It's gone to the lab for analysis to see if it's Marie's … or Lisa's.'

She had to struggle to get the words out. 'I didn't see any blood.'

'Luminol,' Cal replied. 'You spray it on an area, shine a blacklight, and it reappears.'

Abby looked blank.

'A blacklight's like a fluorescent tube,' Cal explained. 'When you switch it on it glows deep purple, and body fluids – or blood – fluoresce back at you.'

Her mind became a desperate whirl. What if the blood was Lisa's? Had she been killed too? But what if it was Marie's? What would that mean? Had the two women fought over something?

'How did Marie know Lisa?'

'We're not sure, but it looks like she was a friend. We found her bag tucked behind the couch.'

'But how did they know each other? I mean, Marie lives in Virginia. It's hardly around the corner.'

'Through work, maybe at a conference. They're both into science in a big way.'

Abby thought of the burned mess of computer discs and files in Lisa's yard and her mind turned to Lisa's boss. 'Does Thomas know Marie?'

'I don't know.'

Abby resolved to talk to Thomas later that day. He was a nice man and, like Lisa, addicted to M & Ms. Wherever you went, the institute was always littered with their multi-coloured wrappings. He might have some idea why Lisa's work had been destroyed.

They sat in silence a long while. Abby could hear the other men talking in low voices, the clatter of their knives and forks, a piece of wood hissing on the fire.

'What about the guy's stuff in her cabin?' Abby eventually asked.

'They're not sure. After Lisa split with Greg, she went out with Jack Molvar. She dumped Jack over a year ago. Apparently she hasn't been seeing anyone since.'

Abby found that hard to believe. Lisa always had a man on the go, sometimes *more* than one.

'Jack says they had a blazing row and that Lisa threw him outside without his bunny boots.' Cal gave a wry smile. 'He thought he'd have to walk through the snow barefoot, but apparently Lisa threw his boots out after him.'

Abby heard her voice repeating what she'd said to Cal just minutes ago. *Lisa can be thoughtless, but she's not unkind.*

Suddenly she was ambushed by a memory of playing hide and seek with the Bedley boys down the street, and Lisa persuading her to hide in the trunk of the Bedleys' car. Lisa was only six, Abby eight, but Abby was already used to deferring to her smarter younger sister and unhesitatingly climbed inside.

The second the trunk lid slammed, Abby's body tightened with fear. She couldn't see anything in the sudden darkness, not even her hand in front of her face. The air was cloying with the sweet, soft smell of oil and she couldn't hear a thing. Not the Bedley boys yelling to each other as they searched, not even the sound of any traffic.

She started to shiver, and she wanted to bang on the lid and get let out but she knew Lisa would never forgive her if she gave herself away. Abby lay there a long while, sobbing softly, tears streaking her face and running into her mouth, until finally, she gave in to the exhaustion of weeping and fell asleep.

When she awoke, she panicked. She thumped on the metal lid, the sides of the boot with her fists and feet, but nobody heard her, nobody came. It was, Abby later learned, three hours before Lisa confessed to their father where she was. When he unpopped the lid and lifted her into the cool, damp air, he took one look at her face, swollen and battered with tears, and immediately rounded on Lisa, yelling so hard his cheeks and forehead swelled and turned red.

Lisa was banished to her room for the rest of the week, only allowed out for meals and bath time, but she managed to sneak to Abby's room the first night when their parents were asleep. She'd brought her favourite toy, a stuffed yellow horse called Butterpat that Abby was never allowed to touch, and gave it to her. Her narrow face was screwed up and she was crying so hard she was almost unable to speak.

'Daddy says … I'm very very bad and that I must never ever do anything like that again, but I knew they'd never find you, not right under their noses… I didn't mean to hurt you, I didn't mean it, I promise I didn't mean to make you cry…'

She found herself filled with sadness at the memory. Lisa should have had a brother, a tough little guy who could have taken all those knocks with aplomb rather than sufferance.

'Abby.'

She jerked back into the present to see Cal leaning forward, expression wary.

'About Lisa's insurance policy.'

'Oh, for God's sakes, Cal–'

'Her beneficiary,' he went on quietly, 'is you.'

Eleven

Cal insisted on walking her to her cabin, as though she was some sort of invalid. She didn't have the strength to object. Her limbs were loose and rubbery and her ears felt as though they'd been stuffed with cloth.

If she had taken out a recent life insurance policy, would she have made Lisa her beneficiary? The answer was a resounding no. She'd have left it to her mother. Or Hugh, her boss. Even Holly, their receptionist, but she'd never have left a penny to her sister.

Demarco's Explorer was parked outside her front door. Trooper Weiding climbed out as they approached. Apparently the ABI – Alaska's Bureau of Investigation – wanted a word, would Abby mind accompanying him to the briefing room? They'd set one up at the school and he'd be happy to drive her. Demarco and a Sergeant from Fairbanks were waiting for her there.

'Give me a second,' she told the trooper. 'I just need to give the dog a quick walk.'

He gave a nod, and hopped back into the warmth of the car.

'Are you sure you'll be okay?' Cal hovered. 'You look awfully pale.'

'I'm always pale, remember?'

'If you're sure...'

Abby opened the door, utterly unprepared for

103

the blur of snarling fur and teeth that pushed her aside and flew straight for Cal.

'No! Moke, No!' she yelled.

The dog stopped inches short of Cal's legs, stiff-legged, ruff standing high, and growling deep in his throat.

'Jesus Christ!' Cal stared at the dog.

Abby put a hand on Moke's neck. 'Leave, boy,' she told him. 'Leave.'

Moke's hackles dropped and he stepped around Cal's legs, sniffing his ankles and knees, the backs of his thighs. Then he sauntered two paces and, still looking at Cal, lifted his leg against a shrub and proceeded to kick back chunks of snow with his hind feet. Abby couldn't help the snort of laughter that escaped.

'You think it's funny?' Cal said. 'Setting your dog on me and nearly giving me a heart attack?'

'Sorry,' she said. 'I didn't know he was going to do that. So far he's been a great big softie, but I guess he's feeling better. I'll be a bit more careful in future.'

'That would be wise,' Cal said drily. 'I wouldn't want you up under the dangerous dogs act.'

He was smiling, his eyes crinkling at the corners, and she felt a swoop in her lower belly. She had to look away.

'See you later?' he said.

'Sure.'

Still smiling, he stepped warily around Moke, and strode down the boardwalk.

Abby watched him go. Her heart felt as though it was crumbling all over again. Tears tightened her throat. She could remember the last time they'd slept together as if it were yesterday, how they fitted together snug as spoons, whichever way they lay.

'Miss McCall?'

She started to see Trooper Weiding leaning out of the car and looking hopeful.

'You ready to join me?'

Abby nodded. She went and fetched Moke and, much to his disgust, shoved him back inside the cabin.

When they arrived at the school, she was surprised that it was so quiet. Maybe she'd watched too much television, but she'd expected the place to be bustling with teams of detectives discussing various theories, making phone calls, drinking coffee, chewing gum and smoking as they collated evidence to track down Marie's murderer. And find her sister. Please God, let them find her soon.

'Where is everyone?' she asked.

'This here's the, ah … briefing room.'

He ushered her inside the same whitewashed teacher's office. The only evidence it was now a briefing room was a single portable white board that was hurriedly being turned around. She just managed to catch the headings of three columns before it faced the wall. *Scenario: one, two* and *three*.

Three scenarios and just two cops. She was unsure what she thought of this, aside from the fact Alaska obviously didn't have the resources of Miami Vice or Scotland Yard.

Demarco dropped her hands from the white board and swung to face her, looking at her colleague then back at Abby, suddenly uncertain.

105

Abby tightened up inside as she stared at Demarco's colleague. The last time she'd seen him he'd had a couple of days' worth of grey stubble, a shotgun in one hand and antagonism at the back of his eyes, but now he was a clean-shaven, brisk-looking man in neatly pressed trousers and a thick fleece the colour of slate.

'Victor?' she said hesitantly.

He gave a grunt and came over to shake her hand in a grip that could have juiced an apple. 'Sergeant Pegati.'

A distant bell rang as she stared at Victor. Cal hadn't talked about his parents much, but she could remember his mother was half Athabaskan and that when he was born his father had swapped his army fatigues for a policeman's uniform.

'You're Cal's *father?*'

He gave a curt nod. 'Trooper Demarco's helping me with the investigation.'

Demarco gave her a half-smile, which she supposed was to put her at ease, and took up position by the window, arms crossed.

Victor took a seat behind the metal desk and indicated she take the one opposite. Abby didn't move. He leaned back and steepled his fingers in front of his face.

'We'd like to ask you a few informal questions.'

She repressed the urge to ask him if she needed a lawyer – God, she felt as though she needed one with him glowering at her – and nodded, studying him and his change of persona. It wasn't just the uniform; he even spoke differently.

'Let's start with this: why did your sister have

106

one hundred and twenty-three thousand dollars in her account?'

'What?' Abby was astonished. Lisa couldn't possibly have that much money. She was always broke.

Victor stonily repeated the question.

'God knows,' Abby shrugged. 'I haven't spoken to her for four years.'

'Ah, yes. I heard about that.' He raised his eyebrows in expectation. 'You had a disagreement, I gather?'

Abby could feel the heat rise to her cheeks. She risked a quick glance at Demarco, but she appeared to be engrossed in the teaching schedule tin-tacked to the back of the door.

'It was years ago,' she said dismissively.

'Years ago, or yesterday, I want to hear what happened.'

'Sibling row,' she said. 'We always had them. This time I'd had enough.'

'What was it over?'

'Nothing much.'

'That's not what my son tells me.'

The heat turned into a burn. Hoping to diffuse it, Abby went and sat down, concentrating on crossing her legs, picking several clumps of dog hair from her knees.

'If your son had worn a wedding ring, then we'd all be one happy family, wouldn't we?' She fixed him with as arctic a gaze as she could manage with her cheeks flaming bright red. 'Personally, I'd like to see men like that branded with the word "married" on their foreheads. It'd make life so much easier for us single women.'

'I see,' he said, and for the first time his voice lost its certainty.

'I doubt you do.' Her voice was cold.

He watched her closely for a few seconds, then cleared his throat noisily. 'Right,' he said and, still holding her gaze, gave a couple of nods and launched right back at her. 'How do you plan to spend the money?'

She blinked at him, confusion standing between her and comprehension.

'Two point four million is quite a lot to get through.'

Abby's blood pressure started to rise. 'For heaven's sake, I've already told Cal it's a load of rubbish that Lisa planned to fake her own death. Besides which,' she added cunningly, 'the insurance company won't pay out unless a body's found.'

'In this kind of case, there are exceptions to the rules. Like when a legitimate accident occurs.'

Abby digested this at length. 'So, if someone's kayaking out at sea and everyone knows this, has waved them off, say … and then their kayak is found empty, the insurance company will assume they've drowned and pay out even if there's no body?'

'Yes.'

Now Abby could see why Falcon Union had retained Cal. They expected her to grab the insurance money and head to the hills where Lisa would be waiting for her.

'But that isn't what's happened here. Lisa's not *like* that.'

'What is she like?'

Abby narrowed her eyes. Was he trying to trip her up? 'I thought you knew my sister,' she said.

'I'd like your opinion.'

'She can be difficult, demanding, solitary or social, depending on her mood. Obsessive, neurotic, vivacious.' She was struck by a memory of Lisa at a party, head flung back and laughing, attracting people in droves. The effort required to be popular had never appealed to Abby. If people wanted to talk to her, they could come over and introduce themselves.

'And you?'

'We're very different.'

'Hmm. And your sister's attitude to money?'

'Careless.'

'And yours?'

Wary now, she said, 'Not so careless.'

'Do you enter the lottery much?'

'Once in a while.'

'So you'd welcome a couple of million bucks.'

She knew where this was going and shot him a poisonous look. He returned it with such bland equanimity she could have slapped him.

'How can you possibly think I'm in cahoots with Lisa when we haven't even spoken for–'

'What I find interesting,' Victor cut in smoothly, 'is how people envision spending their windfall.' He made a show of riffling through some papers, pulled a piece of paper out. 'A converted Dutch barn in Somerset with country-style gardens comes to a million dollars.' He scanned down the page. 'Oh, sorry. The one you want to restore has fifteen acres of woodland and costs nearly two million. I like the nature walk

109

idea for the local kids.'

He tossed the piece of paper across so she could see it. She recognised the sketch immediately. It had been ripped out of her sketch book. She never travelled without one and, inspired by an advert in *House and Garden* on the flight over, she'd stuck it in her book. She'd spent the next two hours designing the perfect garden for the barn, including a walled vegetable garden, a tree house for adults as well as children, a flight pond for ducks, and a planting plan filled with giant plants that was totally mad and totally, wonderfully unobtainable.

Astonishment was overcome by a wave of anger that her belongings at Lisa's were being pored through. 'That's personal,' she snapped.

'Nothing's personal in a murder investigation.'

Abby snatched the sketch, folded it into four, and stuck it in her pocket. She waited for him to object, but he didn't. No doubt he'd copied it in triplicate earlier.

'Quite ambitious, aren't you?'

'Dreaming isn't a crime. Don't you have dreams, Sergeant? Aspirations?'

'Not of ripping off an insurance company for two point four million.'

'Oh, come on, you can't be serious.'

His eyes swivelled away from her, over the aluminium desk and battered filing cabinet.

'Tell me, did Lisa have any enemies that you know of?'

'Everyone loves Lisa,' she said automatically, and then remembered the professor at her sister's university. 'Well, there is someone...'

Abby trailed off. She couldn't see that Lisa's old professor had anything to do with this.

'An enemy, you say?' Victor's interest quickened.

'Well, it got pretty acrimonious. The police even got involved at one point. They slapped a restraining order on my sister.'

Victor's eyebrows shot up.

'Lisa accused a professor at her university of murdering a fellow student over a decade ago – when the professor was also student, that is – and then stealing his Ph.D. thesis.'

Eyebrows still standing to attention, he motioned her to go on, and Abby re-told the story she'd heard from Lisa's friend, Tessa.

'And the name of the professor?'

'Crowe. I don't know the Christian name, sorry.'

Victor made a note. 'Should be pretty easy to follow up. Anything else?'

'Not really,' she said vaguely. Her thoughts were on her sister, and her uncompromising stance once she'd got an idea in her head. She could still hardly believe Lisa had accused someone of murder.

She flinched when the phone rang. Victor snatched it up and listened briefly, then rose to his feet and gave a nod to Demarco. 'Carry on.' He left the room.

The trooper shed her jacket and put it over the back of Victor's chair. 'Wish it were as warm outside,' she said affably. 'I'd like to see the back of winter. Eight months is a stretch.'

Abby's lips were numb and she had to work her mouth to get any feeling back. 'You know Victor well? I mean … the sergeant.'

'We've worked together before.' Demarco came and sat next to her, hip propped on the corner of the desk.

'Is this the good-cop scene?' Abby wanted to smile but couldn't.

Demarco chuckled. 'He's not a bad guy once you get to know him, and he's got a good record for solving crimes.'

Feeling claustrophobic, Abby pushed back her chair and walked to the window. She leaned her forehead against the window, letting her breath cloud the glass. 'I can't make any sense of it. Lisa was reported missing up a mountain, but you find Marie Guillemote murdered instead... I don't know what's going on. I feel like I've stepped into a nightmare.'

'We'll get to the bottom of it,' Demarco said in a professionally reassuring tone.

'I can't believe Victor thinks I'm working with Lisa to rip off her insurance company.'

'Don't let it trouble you,' Demarco said drily. 'He just likes rattling people's cages.'

She snapped her head round. Gave the trooper a startled look.

'That doesn't mean we're not curious about the policy,' Demarco added carefully. 'It'd be nice to know your sister's mindset when she took it out.'

Had Lisa known she was going to die? She couldn't believe Lisa had organised any of this, she honestly couldn't. Lisa didn't plan as much as *react* to life.

'Abby, didn't you resent Lisa going to college in Washington DC – leaving you behind to care for your mother?'

'No,' she said, which was true. She was a home body who loved luxuriating under her own roof amid familiar surroundings.

'You've borne a load of emotional burdens,' Demarco observed. 'Your loyalty to your family would break the back of anyone else.'

Abby blinked. 'I'm nothing special. There are loads of people out there who do much more than I do.'

The trooper drummed her fingers on her thigh, looking thoughtful.

'Tell me about Lisa's friends,' Demarco said. 'Old ones at university that you remember. Would they help her if she turned up on the doorstep?'

Startled, Abby said, 'You think she's left Alaska?'

'Not that we know of,' she admitted. 'We've covered the airports, but she might be able to bribe a private pilot to fly her out – she's got the money. Or she could try and drive across the border.' Demarco reached into her pocket and pulled out a card. 'You hear anything, call me, would you?' She scribbled a number on the back, gesturing at the phone on the desk. 'That's this number. My cell doesn't work too well up here.'

Abby pocketed the card. Both of them turned when the door banged open. Victor beckoned Demarco outside. The door closed with a little click behind them. Abby could hear their voices but not what they were saying. She walked over to the door and pressed her ear against it, but the plasterboard absorbed the sound and she couldn't make out any words.

Their footsteps gave a brief clatter and she man-

113

aged to scoot into her chair as the door opened and both cops came inside. Demarco whipped her jacket free just before Victor sat down. Shuffling some papers, he cleared his throat.

'Do you know what Lisa was working on?'

'No,' she said.

'Do you know who Meg is?'

Abby shook her head.

'Has Lisa ever mentioned the name to you?'

'Not that I remember. Why? Did she kill Marie Guillemote?'

Victor leaned forward, put his hands on the table. Abby pushed her hands beneath her thighs.

'You know that we found some blood in your sister's cabin,' he stated.

Thanks to Cal. Who'd obviously reported the fact he'd told her straight to his father. She gave Victor a nod.

'It belongs to Marie Guillemote. The bullet we found lodged in your sister's cabin belongs to the .45 semi-automatic that killed her.'

Abby felt the blood draining from her head.

'We've issued a warrant for your sister's arrest in connection with Marie Guillemote's murder.'

Twelve

Lisa walked the slope with grim-faced determination, Roscoe padding at her side. She concentrated on putting one foot in front of the other, emptying her mind of the punishing grade,

114

fighting the waves of dizziness brought on from exhaustion and hunger.

The area they were crossing was a mind-numbing series of never-ending mountains, valleys and creeks, of climbing up one ridge and heading down the other side, hour upon hour. The only consolation was that she hadn't seen anyone behind her yet.

That didn't mean they weren't trying to follow. Her enemy was determined and ruthless, they would stop at nothing. They had already proven themselves by killing Marie. However, it appeared they didn't know much about the bush. They may be dressed in white-winter cam-ouflaged snowsuits, but she hadn't seen any sign of the three men since she'd fled her cabin. But then she had the advantage of knowing the area. She knew which direction the rivers flowed, the direction in which mountains and ridges ran, and how to navigate using landmarks. She could determine her position from the sun, and guide herself by the stars. All the men had were her footprints, and sometimes not even that when she cut across a glacier, forcing them to search far and wide for her spoor.

Her heart gave a squeeze when Roscoe paused to glance over his shoulder with a mournful expression. He was looking for Moke.

'He's gone home, boy.' She tried to comfort him. 'Sorry.'

It was thanks to Moke that she hadn't frozen where she'd fallen. Through the storm her numbed senses had registered something tugging at her waistline, and she'd looked down to see the dog trying to chew through his harness. Moke appeared to believe she'd reached the end and was determined not to die alongside his new mistress. His condemnation had forced her to act.

She dragged herself on until, amazingly, Roscoe led her to a fissure in a rock face. There was just enough room for her to squeeze inside and, as soon as she was out of the wind, the temperature seemed to soar twenty degrees.

Lisa forced her frozen muscles to haul herself deeper inside the mountain where it would be warmer. She never let go of her sled. If she was going to die, she'd die with it, along with her laptop and handfuls of disc recorders.

She wanted to light a fire but as she made to pull her sled towards her, her body shut down at the effort. She had no final memory. No image imprinted on her eyelids as she lost consciousness.

Lisa didn't wake until dawn and for a second she thought the cave had collapsed. Her ribs were being crushed. She could barely breathe. When she tried to roll on to her back, the cave parted and looked down at her. She could barely believe it. She'd been wedged in a doggy sandwich for most of the night. The dogs had saved her life with their body heat.

It took her a long time to get her numbed hands to release her emergency pack and light a fire. She warmed snow in her tin pan and drank it as hot as she could to warm her core. Knowing the dehydrating effects of subzero temperatures, she pinched the skin on each dog's neck to check if they needed fluids. To her relief, both pinches fell quickly back to their normal positions, but she still melted more snow for the huskies. Ate some chocolate. She didn't share her food, even though their eyes pleaded. Outside, the storm continued to howl.

Her cheeks began to burn. Searing hot, her skin felt as though it was going to melt from her bones. She had frost nip, but there was little she could do aside from protecting it from the cold. She kept her cheeks covered whenever possible, wrapping her face in her scarf, and took comfort in the fact it wouldn't kill her.

Gradually her brain began to function. She thought of her pursuers and how to divert them. Bringing Moke close she studied his harness, where he'd tried to chew it through. Using her knife she finished the job, and then chewed the end vigorously before studying it at length. It wouldn't fool Joe Chenega, but it might convince everyone else.

Twenty minutes later, she took Moke to the cave's entrance and pushed him outside.

'Home, boy,' she commanded, and pointed back the way they'd come.

Eyes squinting against the driving snow, Moke refused to move. Lisa picked up some loose rocks and the instant she made to throw them at him, he bolted.

Huddled against Roscoe on the frozen cave floor she prayed Moke would make it. She hadn't had him long, but he seemed fit enough, with strong hairy pads that didn't need booties and a coat thick enough to insulate him should he be forced to curl up and rest. She knew he had nowhere else to go, and that he would return to Lake's Edge.

117

Some people would say she was being cruel, but they didn't know what was at stake.

When she came to a forest, Lisa held her course by lining up two trees forward of her position and in the direction she was headed. As soon as she passed the first one, she lined up another beyond the second. Usually she'd mark her route by cutting or bending vegetation in case she was forced to backtrack, but should it snow and cover her tracks, she couldn't risk their discovery.

She moved slowly and steadily, stopping periodically to listen and take her bearings, careful not to disturb any birds or animals that might reveal her position. Here and there squirrels and rabbits had left their retreats to forage for food, and coyotes, lynx and wolverines added their trails to those of deer and moose.

She stopped when a shadow padded like smoke between the trees ahead. From behind a snow-covered boulder crept another dark grey object. She looked over her shoulder to see four creeping up behind her.

Lisa grabbed her rifle from the sled. Loaded it. Chambered a round. Her fingers were stiff with cold but her heart was hammering.

Roscoe was growling and snarling, hackles stiff as the wolves slunk forward. They were thin after a hard winter, their shoulder blades and hipbones jutting through bush-torn coats. She didn't fear an attack. Most wolves knew a great deal about mankind and would be too wary to try that, even if they were starving. Roscoe was the intended victim.

Slowly Lisa raised her rifle to her shoulder. She didn't want to fire in case someone heard the shot, but she had no choice. Without Roscoe, her survival statistics would halve. And she mustn't waste ammunition. She had to make every shot count. Carefully she chose a big iron-grey female as her target. If she could scare the leader away, the others would follow.

Her finger was tightening on the trigger when the scene changed. Another wolf walked quietly between the pack and stood a little distance from Lisa, watching. A great creature the colour of platinum with a chest as broad as a mastiff's. One ear was slit, and there were old wound-marks on his neck and shoulders.

Lisa lowered her rifle a fraction.

'Hello, King.'

His fierce yellow eyes locked on hers.

'Joe's told me a lot about you. He's quite a fan of yours, you know. He's sorry he shot your father, but he was creating hell down in the town. You know better, don't you?'

The wolf didn't look away.

'Big Joe wouldn't want me to shoot you. So how about you find a nice caribou or a moose to satisfy your family's appetite? Roscoe's not up for grabs. Sorry.'

King stared at her, unblinking, as though he was reading her mind.

Lisa didn't lower her rifle. King had ruled for over twelve years and was as wise as they came. She hoped he'd be wise enough to leave her and Roscoe alone.

The minutes ticked past.

Stand-off, Lisa thought. A goddamn stand-off. If the pack moved in one wave, Roscoe wouldn't stand a chance.

Suddenly King gave a single bark, and trotted away in the opposite direction. The rest of the pack followed.

Her hands were trembling as she strapped her rifle back on to the sled. Roscoe's tongue was lolling and he was panting hard and fast. She talked to him in a steady monotone, trying to settle him down.

'You may be big, but deep down you're a scaredy-cat,' she told him. 'If I'd let you loose, I bet you'd have run a mile.'

Her mind flipped to Abby, who nobody ever challenged in the school yard. Abby was big, was she a scaredy-cat too? She tried to remember a time when Abby had been brave, but couldn't come up with anything. Abby was just *there*, always had been. A rock at her back. Someone who would say she hated her one instant, and be hugging her the next.

She hadn't walked far when her eyes snagged on something symmetrical, a right-angle joint of wood that jarred at her. Lisa crept forward and peered at it from around the trunk of a jack pine. To her astonishment, the forest revealed a cabin. It had a tatty spruce thatch for a roof and no windows, just a front door, and moss grew between the logs making it resemble a rotting tree stump. A wisp of smoke rose from a chimney made from a length of rusting pipe.

She'd heard of this place, heard the rumours of Mad Malone, but she'd never met the guy. She wasn't sure she wanted to either. Apparently Mad Malone hadn't been with a woman for twenty years, and local gossip said if he found one, he'd keep them chained and naked inside his cabin as his plaything.

Mad Malone was a trapper. He didn't have any running water or electricity, didn't believe in the finer things in life like cutting his hair or bathing, but he had an intriguing hobby, if Big Joe was to be believed. And this hobby might just save her life, if it existed.

Lisa eyed the cabin cautiously, weighing up the pros and cons.

'Stay,' she told Roscoe in a low voice.

Kicking off her skis, Lisa quickly extracted her laptop and discs from the sled and buried them in the snow. They were well wrapped in plastic and oilskin and wouldn't suffer. She scuffed the area and laid a twig where they lay, in case she had to dig them out in a hurry. She had every intention of winning this battle. It was the least she could do after Marie's support. She could only hope Marie's family would find it a comfort when their goal was accomplished.

Picking up her rifle, she crept to the front of the cabin and looked around. Fresh prints led from the door and into the forest. She couldn't see any indicating Mad Malone had returned recently.

Lisa rapped on the door. Silence. There was no lock in the door, no bolts, just a battered wooden handle. It turned with a heavy *clunk*. Pulse rocketing, she slowly stepped inside.

It was dark and fetid so she left the door ajar, waiting for her eyes to adjust to the gloom. Her

121

breathing was shallow, her heart tripping fast. Carefully she moved around the single room, boots thudding softly. There was a waist-high stack of hides and pelts to her left, and something bloody lay on the floor in front of the wood stove. A freshly skinned rabbit. She'd swipe that on her way out for Roscoe.

She let her eyes run over a wooden counter, scanned the tools and knives, and as she looked further right, there it was in its full glory of dials and switches. A ham radio.

It took her a while to find the frequency she wanted and even then she had to pause to gather her thoughts. People might be listening in. She'd have to be careful.

Pitching her voice higher than normal, she tried to cover her English accent by drawling a parody of broad American.

'Bravo, Jericho, you read? This is King.'

She prayed Big Joe would pick up the reference and realise it was her. He had told her he'd given the wolf its name on their last trip into the Brooks Range, adding that she reminded him of a wolf with her untamed ways and love of the wilderness. Pray God he'd remember.

Silence.

Lisa kept trying, until finally the radio crackled. 'King? As in the King who hates anchovies on their pizza?'

Lisa sagged with relief. Not only did she recognise his voice, but he'd referred to anchovies as an easy test that it was really her.

'You know I love 'em, stop poking fun because I ate all yours.'

'You okay?'

'Sure, why shouldn't I be?'

'Been missing you.'

'Yeah, well. Tough titty to ya. So whass'appenin' your end?'

'Got a surprise waiting for you here.' Brief pause, then he added, 'a bitch called Alpha. Big sister of the pack.'

'Alpha?' Her voice was hoarse. Oh, dear God. Was he referring to Abby?

'Yup. She got here a couple of days ago. She'd do anything to see you.'

A rush of emotion rocked Lisa, and she was unsure whether to laugh or cry. Abby was in Alaska, looking for her.

'How is she?'

Before Big Joe could answer, she heard a soft crunch of snow. She spun round.

'Quiet, Joe,' she told him. The radio fell silent.

She listened hard and then she heard another soft crunch.

Her breathing jammed in her windpipe. Please God let it be Roscoe disobeying my order. I don't want to meet Mad Malone.

Picking up her rifle she tiptoed to the door. The stock felt warm and reassuring in her hands as she poked the barrel cautiously outside.

Everything was still and silent.

Blood thudded in her ears as she inched the door a couple of inches wider and suddenly a hand whipped out and grabbed the barrel, yanked the rifle from her hands and she was falling forward, losing her balance, sprawling face down in the snow, and then she felt the rifle ram into the back of her neck so hard she thought her skin had split.

A rancid odour wafted over her, making her choke.

'Well, well, well.' His voice was hoarse, rusty from not having spoken for a long time. 'If all my Christmases ain't come at once.'

Thirteen

Abby finally gathered the courage to ring her mother. Beside herself with worry, Julia kept repeating herself and Abby knew the stress was affecting her health, but she kept reassuring her that Lisa was bound to be okay, and that they had to concentrate on that and let the police unravel the rest.

'Do you know what Lisa was working on?' Abby eventually asked. 'The police asked me, but I haven't a clue.'

'Oh, darling, you know what she was like, we may have shared things when she was smaller, but when she grew up she became impossibly possessive.' Abby heard Julia sigh. 'She gets it from me, I'm afraid. Until I'm published I find it inconceivable to let anyone even glance at my work, and your sister obviously feels the same way.'

There was a short pause while Abby tried to think what else she could ask, when Julia said, 'Have you asked Meg?'

'Meg?' Abby repeated.

'She was part of their team. Lisa would phone when she was in one of her moods, you know, either about to slit her wrists or screaming with excitement, and she'd always refer to Meg, praising her to the heavens or cursing her to hell and back. I must say she sounded a very awkward type of person to work with. Impossible one day and a delight the next.'

Meg sounded as though she could be Lisa's twin sister, and Abby almost smiled at the thought of Lisa having to experience some of her own medicine. Good on Meg, she thought. Go girl.

'Mum, do you know Meg's surname?'

'Lisa never mentioned it.'

They chatted a little more about Lisa's obsessive secrecy, then Abby changed the subject. 'Did Lisa ever mention a Professor Crowe at her uni?'

'Oh, yes. Best of friends at the start, I remember that. They worked closely for, oh, around a year or so, then they had a falling-out. Lisa never told me what it was over, probably a difference of opinion about her work. You know she's not great on criticism, your sister.'

'Did she mention anything about going to court?'

'Court?' Julia repeated, sounding alarmed.

'Oh, it's nothing,' Abby said hastily. 'If you haven't heard about it, then it's not what I thought it was. I'm just trying to fill in some blanks.'

Obviously Lisa hadn't told their mother about her accusing Professor Crowe of murder, or the resulting restraining order. Her sister could be secretive not only about her work, but about her personal and public life too.

'How's Ralph?' Abby asked.

'He's just about moved in, but I don't mind. His fish pie is really rather good.'

Abby blinked. Julia was letting Ralph cook for her? Talk about a turn-up for the books. 'Is he there?'

'No. He's gone to buy a newspaper. You know how he likes nothing more than catching up with the gossip in the corner shop.'

Eternally grateful to Ralph for stepping into the breach, Abby hung up and, once again, delved into the White Pages and flicked to Fairbanks. She dialled the number for UAF and asked for Meg.

'Meg who? Which department?'

'Sorry, I can't remember her surname. Maybe try the Sir John Ross Institute?'

There was a short silence while the woman checked and Abby considered the institute where Lisa worked. Terrible parking, she remembered that, but the building had been filled with natural light, the labs busy with people who always seemed ready to stop and chat. The institute was named after Sir John Ross, who had discovered the magnetic pole in the 1930s. He was another of Lisa's heroes, after Telsa and Whittle, that was.

'Sorry,' the woman came back on the line, 'I can't find a Meg... Wait up... We've a Megan Wilson in the Geophysical Institute? Shall I put you through?'

Lisa didn't work in geophysics, but she said, 'Yes, please.'

There was a click, and the sound of a phone ringing. Nobody picked up. Abby waited until it cut off. She'd try the woman later.

126

Meantime, she'd call Thomas, Lisa's boss, friend and mentor, but the UAF receptionist told her he was on vacation and not due back for three days. Before she could ask anything further, the woman hung up.

After doing a quick shop at the local super-market – cigarettes, wine, bread, jam and some canned food – she was about to try Meg again when Moke started barking at the top of his voice. A big, deep *WOOF!* that had her dropping the phone receiver, hair standing on end, her heart hammering.

'Jesus, Moke! What a racket!'

Grabbing his ruff she told him to be quiet. Diane stood outside in the sunshine in jeans and shirt-sleeves. Obviously the temperature had rocketed, even if Abby couldn't feel it. Diane was holding a piece of paper in her hand, looking uncertain.

Moke peeled back his lips into a snarl.

'Stop it,' Abby told the dog. Immediately he stopped growling, and looked up at her as if to confirm he'd got the command right.

'Well, that's a first,' said Diane, staring at the dog. 'I've known him since he was a pup and he's never growled. Not once. Must feel protective of you or something.'

'Or something,' said Abby ruefully. 'Personally, I think giving him buttered toast for breakfast might have had an effect.'

She eyed Diane cautiously, but couldn't see anything to alarm her. Diane was one of Saffron's oldest friends – they'd known each other since pre-school – but it was only when she'd discovered this that Abby understood why the Native woman had

127

been so rude and unfriendly to her. Nobody had said anything to her face about sleeping with Cal, just given her the finger behind her back.

'You want a coffee?' she ventured, waving the same olive branch Diane had yesterday.

'No... But thanks. Appreciate the offer.' She gave Abby a thin little smile but it didn't reach her eyes.

'Diane, did you know Marie Guillemote?'

The woman shook her head.

'Did Lisa mention her at all?'

'Never heard the name until her body was found. Sorry.' She shoved the piece of paper out. 'I just came to bring this over.'

Torn from a notebook, it was folded into four, and the instant Abby opened it, her trachea closed down. The air couldn't get to her lungs.

Meet me at Mad Malone's. Everyone knows where he lives. Don't tell anyone. I'll look after you, promise. Love you. Lisa.

She'd drawn a heart around the words 'love you' and surrounded them with kisses, just as she used to when they passed messages to each other during prep.

Her breathing returned with a rush, making her head spin. Sweet mother of everything that was holy.

Lisa was alive.

'Where did you get this?' Abby pulled Diane inside and shut the door. Her hands were trembling.

'My uncle.' Diane was looking at the floor.

'Malone Fischer. Known as Mad Malone around here. He's a trapper. Lives in the mountains. He doesn't like people much. People don't like him much either, so it's good he lives out there. Only comes into town two or three times a year for supplies. He came in late last night. He was in a bit of a state. Babbling more than usual...' Diane fiddled with her plait, swallowed audibly. 'He wanted help with "women's things".

'When I asked him what women's things, he said I should know, because I was a woman... I teased him back, asking if he had a girlfriend hidden in his cabin and he just about had a heart attack. He made me swear not to tell anyone, especially not the cops...'

'You've read this?' Abby demanded.

'She's my friend too.'

'How do I find your uncle?'

Diane squinted at Abby. 'You're not going to tell the police, are you?'

Abby's mind was whirling. She ought to, she knew, but not only had Lisa told her not to tell anyone, but her sister was up for murder. The instant the cops saw her they'd throw her in a cell. She'd much rather see Lisa on her own and find out what was going on before setting the police on her.

'Er...' She dithered, wondering what the hell to do.

'Malone will kill me if the cops turn up at his place.' Diane was biting on a fingernail. 'He's likely to shoot one and I don't want him slung in jail. Can't you go alone like she wants? I've got a snow machine you can use.'

129

'Won't you get into trouble?'

'Not if you don't tell nobody. Come on. Let's go.'

Abby took one look at the map and quailed. No way was she going out there on her own, no matter what danger Lisa might be in.

'Diane, you've got to come with me.'

'I can't.'

'I'll get lost. I don't know the mountains. Finding a single snow-covered cabin out there will be like looking for a needle in a haystack as far as I'm concerned.' And what about bears? her mind yelled. Wolves and crevasses and weak ice? Lisa was asking too much.

'The bar won't run itself,' Diane said. 'Not until tomorrow when my cousin can take over.'

They were standing at the back of the Moose in the half-shovelled car park. The sun was warm on the back of her neck and she could hear ice drip-dripping from the roof. Abby looked at the map again. Malone's cabin was forty miles north-west of Lake's Edge, and on the lower reaches of an unnamed mountain 6,088 feet high. Diane reckoned it would take her a couple of hours to get there by snow machine, but Abby had visions of it taking much longer, especially if she lost her way or got the machine stuck in a drift.

'She's your *friend*,' Abby pleaded.

'She asked you to go alone,' Diane said, shuffling her feet.

Abby looked at the snow machine and realised she didn't even know how to start the damn thing, let alone drive it. And what if another late-winter storm blew in? She could hear Victor's voice echoing in her head. *You wouldn't last three seconds, would you?*

Not for the first time Abby wished she was more like her sister. Lisa wouldn't hesitate to climb on a snow machine and roar up a mountain in search of her, but she wasn't like Lisa. She wasn't at all brave.

Abby pointed at a symbol on the map, a U inside a circle, around ten miles from Malone's cabin. 'What's this?'

'Unverified landing area.' Diane peered closer. 'Looks like it belongs to Flint's hunting lodge, I remember him hiring earth movers after he bought the place a few years back. It's probably in good shape now.'

'Michael Flint?' Abby asked. 'The guy who owns my cabin?'

Diane nodded.

'Big Joe said he was a friend of Lisa's. Is he local?'

'He's well known around here. Bases himself between Anchorage and his lodge. He's got his own aircraft – makes it easy to flit in and out when he pleases.'

'What does he do?'

'Oh, lots of different things. He's into mining in a big way. Zinc and gold. He even owns a couple of hotels and guesthouses, and a canning company.'

'Fingers in all sorts of pies,' Abby mused.

'You got it.' Diane was looking at the symbol, a small smile playing on her lips. 'I remember Lisa staying there once. She did it for kicks...' The smile vanished as she went on, 'They didn't see eye to eye, you see. Poor guy had no idea. She ate his cupboards bare, slept in his bed. She left a note saying, "Thanks, from the three bears." He didn't find it very funny. But that was back then. Before they, er ... became friends.'

How typically Lisa, acting as though she was nine years old instead of twenty-nine.

'He's got some wilderness cabins through the forest. She uses them like they're hers...' Diane's smile suddenly broadened into a grin. 'Hell, if I haven't had an idea.'

'What?' Abby demanded. 'What is it?'

'Goddammit, why didn't I think of him before? Flint knows the area real well, and since Malone thinks the sun shines out of his proverbials ever since he turned a blind eye to Malone taking a moose out of season last year, he might not shoot him.'

'I can trust Flint?' Suddenly Abby was full of doubts. 'Won't he call the police?'

'Nah. He'll do what's right for Lisa. I'll go and call him now.'

Michael Flint had a pair of Sorrels like herself, padded trousers and a blue and yellow parka. Tall, dark-haired and freshly shaved, he would have been handsome if it weren't for his red-eyed and haggard appearance. The man looked as though he hadn't slept in a week.

Shaking her hand briefly, he said it was nice to meet her, brushed aside her thanks for his cabin, ignored her offer to pay rent, and got right down to it.

'Diane tells me Lisa sent you a note.'

'You're not going to tell the cops, are you?'

He shook his head.

'Why not?' She was curious.

'They'll arrest her.'

'What about Marie Guillemote?' Abby pressed further. 'Did you know her?'

'No.'

'Do you think Lisa killed her?'

'Of course not. Look, can we do the twenty questions later? I'd like to get going.'

Flint double-checked Diane's snow machine – oil, plugs, belts, track and fuel – and prepared a pack of emergency supplies. A knife and a flare, shotgun and shells, flashlight, dried twigs, and in his pocket, a waterproof container with matches and fire starters. He showed Abby how to use his handheld GPS – Global Positioning System – which, he told her, he never travelled without.

If she'd had one of those, she scowled, she could have gone alone after all. It pinpointed your position anywhere on the globe within a hundred yards. But then if she'd got stuck or, God forbid, hit a snow storm, it wouldn't matter if she knew where she was; compared to Lisa she had the survival skills of a terracotta tile.

Snow machine ready, Flint studied the map at length. 'I don't like it.' He frowned. 'Malone's miles from where we've been searching.'

Abby peered to see he was right. The wilderness trail and the cabin littered with M & Ms was way south of Lake's Edge and Big Joe's place, but Malone lived in the opposite direction.

'Lisa couldn't have made it to Malone's,' Flint

added. 'It's impossible, unless she grew wings and flew.'

They all stared at the map in silence. Then Diane ran a tentative finger between Lisa's cabin and Malone's. 'Maybe she wasn't skijoring after all,' she suggested. 'Maybe she *wanted* to get to Malone.'

More silence while everyone digested this.

'But what about the dog harness on the wilderness trail?' Abby said. 'The nylon traces they found?'

'What if someone's trying to put us off her scent?' Flint said. His eyes were narrowed, his mouth a hard line.

Abby stared at him, apprehension crawling up her spine.

'Like who?'

He didn't answer, just refolded the map and stuck it in his parka pocket. 'We should be back this evening,' he told Diane. 'If we don't show up by tomorrow midday, come and get us.'

'Take care of Moke for me?' Abby asked Diane, and when she nodded, quickly ran over his medication routine.

Flint looked startled. 'You've Lisa's dog?'

'I thought you knew.'

'I knew you had a dog, but not *which* dog in particular.'

'It's just that Big Joe was going to put him down ... and I ...' Abby trailed off.

His pinched expression vanished beneath a smile. 'And you believed him?'

She knew it; she'd been duped. Still amused, shaking his head at her naivety, Flint mounted

134

the machine and started it up with a clattering roar. Abby climbed behind him, and the instant she was settled they took off, skidding and sliding across the icy car park until they reached a snowy trail leading away from the main street.

Flint accelerated past an old Chevy and a listing tractor with one tyre, flaking oil drums and bare engine blocks, and then they were snaking between log cabins and trees and soon the town fell away and they were in a world of glittering white. High above the endless spires of snow-clad spruce, the sky was a deep clear blue and the sun looked as white as the snow they were traversing.

They headed directly up the hill until it steepened, forcing Flint to zigzag. When they reached the top, he paused and looked back over his shoulder at the view. It was worth looking at. She could have been in Mac's airplane, studying the spiderweb of trails connecting everyone's homes, the frozen river feeding into the lake and flowing out at the southern end. The entire landscape was jaw-droppingly majestic, but she knew if she'd been on her own she wouldn't have been able to appreciate its beauty; she'd have been petrified.

'Okay?' Flint asked her.

'Okay.'

'If it gets rough, put your arms around me. I don't want you thrown off.'

He didn't wait for her to reply but launched the machine over the crest of the mountain and hurtled down the slope. She nearly came off when he ducked around a tussock the height of her thighs, and hurriedly decided to drop her

English reserve and put her arms around his middle. It felt strange hugging a stranger, oddly intimate, and she was glad when she felt him pat her mitten briefly in approval or she might have taken her arms away.

The miles flew past in a noisy blur of ice and snow. Everything, as far as the eye could see, sparkled in a shimmering display of light. Ice crystals shone blue and pink and yellow as they raced past, reflecting the colour from the snow machine. The air was cold and sweet and she found herself smiling for the first time since she'd arrived in Alaska, exhilarated and impossibly intoxicated by her surroundings, the speed they were doing.

Eventually Flint slowed and began winding through a forest. Spruce branches whipped past, and Abby turned her head aside and ducked low to rest her cheek against the back of Flint's parka. She didn't want to break her nose, or lose an eye.

Soon he stopped the snow machine and switched off the engine. The sudden silence closed in on Abby. Climbing off the machine she had to steady herself against the seat. Her muscles were weak and soft as over-boiled pasta.

'I'm going to do a re-con first.' Flint picked up his shotgun, loaded it and snapped it shut. He pushed the safety catch to ON with a tiny click. 'Make sure the coast is clear.'

'Clear of what?' Abby asked.

'You stay here.'

He started creeping to the left, between two spruce trees, and then he vanished. She listened for his boots crunching on snow, but couldn't hear anything. It was still and silent. She shivered. She didn't want to follow Flint in case it was dangerous but she didn't want to be alone either. And what about Lisa? Chilled and uncertain, she began following Flint's tracks.

She stopped when she thought she heard something behind her. She swung around, eyes staring. Jesus. What if it was a bear? Hibernation was over and they'd be out and about foraging, hungry after their long winter.

Her heart hopping, Abby backed up against a tree trunk. She listened to the tiny drips of ice melting on to the snow, the faintest rustle of pine leaves in the higher branches.

She caught a waft of something rancid and foul and turned her head, wondering if it was a dead animal. She nearly screamed when she saw the man standing right next to her.

Fourteen

He was dressed head to toe in animal skins and had what appeared to be a dead rabbit sitting on his head. The look in his eyes was hungry, like a man who hadn't seen food for days.

'Shhh.' He had a finger to his lips and a shotgun at his side.

'What the…? Who are you?'

'Where is he?'

'Are you Malone?' Her voice quavered.

'He gone to my cabin?'

'Where's Lisa?'

'He's come for her, hasn't he? I'll deal with him. Scum.'

Eyeing his gun, Abby thought it best to try and befriend him. 'I'm a friend of Diane's. Your niece? She gave me Lisa's note. I'm Lisa's sister.'

Malone studied Abby carefully, letting his eyes travel from her boots right up to the top of her head. 'Don't look much alike,' he remarked.

'No,' she managed. 'We don't.'

'Stay here. I'll be back.' He turned and began to follow Flint's tracks.

'Malone, wait. Where's Lisa?'

He crunched away without responding. Sweat springing, Abby stood there briefly, and then she followed, quietly as she could. Somehow, she had to warn Michael Flint, but unless she shouted – which would bring Malone to her as well as Flint – she couldn't think how to do it. And where was Lisa? In Malone's cabin? Or was she also creeping about with a gun in her hand?

Somewhere above, a raven cawed. Abby crept around a rock glistening with ice to see a shabby-looking log cabin nestling in a clearing. She couldn't see Malone anywhere, but she could see Flint.

He was walking to the cabin, arms wide and hands raised, like a man under arrest. He no longer had his gun.

'Flint,' she hissed, but she was too far away for him to hear.

The raven cawed again.

'Malone?' Flint called. 'You there?'

'Flint!' she called and he swung round, startled,

at the same time that Malone appeared between the trees, shotgun steady and pointed directly at him.

'Malone, put that thing down, will you? It's me, Mike.'

Malone didn't move.

'We're looking for Lisa McCall.' Flint's voice was steady and conversational, seemingly unperturbed that the man was aiming his gun at him. 'She went missing recently. The note you gave to Diane told us she was here.'

Abby watched Malone approach until he stuck the barrels of his shotgun into the front of Flint's parka. Her mouth dried up. What if he shot Flint? Oh, God, what the hell was she supposed to do?

'We just want to know if Lisa's okay,' Flint continued in the same steady tone. 'It was a rough storm and we've been worried for her.'

'Rough all right,' Malone rasped, but he didn't lower the gun.

'We won't trouble you any further if you could tell us if Lisa survived the storm. Everyone thinks she perished up here, you see.'

'Not dead,' he said, and lowered the gun a fraction. 'At least, not the last time I saw her.'

Abby didn't feel any sense of relief at the information, her attention was riveted to the shotgun. It was now pointed at Flint's groin.

'When was that, Malone?'

'Yesterday. When I left for town.'

'You went to get things for her. Diane told us. That was good of you.'

'She's all right, for a woman,' Malone said.

'So is Abby.' Flint turned and beckoned her

139

over but she remained where she was. She had no intention of getting any closer until Malone had disarmed.

'Yeah.' Malone flicked a look at her. 'Good lookin' pair, all right.'

At last he broke the shotgun and hooked it over his left elbow. He stuck out a hand and Abby crunched over to shake. His hand was dark brown and engrained with dirt, his fingernails rimmed black. The same foul stench wafted from his clothes as they shook and she tried not to recoil, unsure whether the stink came from him or the animal skins he wore, stitched together with twine and hanging off him like grisly trophies.

'Sorry she left,' he said. 'You sister was tired as hell, but it didn't stop her telling me a couple of good jokes.'

'Where did she go?' asked Flint.

Malone squinted into the sky then around the clearing. 'God knows. It snowed some last night. Covered everything.'

'But *why* isn't she here?' Abby wailed. 'Why didn't she wait for me?'

'Dunno.' Malone shuffled his feet. 'I only got back yesterday and she was long gone by then.'

'Did anyone else see this note?' Abby brought out the scrap of paper and waved it at him. 'Did you tell anyone, aside from Diane, that Lisa was here?'

More shuffling of his battered boots. 'Malone, please.'

'Well, I was in the Moose, havin' a beer, haven't had one in that long, see, and I bumped into Hank and Billy-Bob, then Big Joe, and I knew how worried Big Joe would be... And then this woman got talkin' to me... Not bad looking either. I'd have bought her a drink 'cept she said no before I even asked.' Malone looked wistful. 'Next time, maybe.'

Abby looked at him in horror. 'All these people knew Lisa was here?'

'No, no.' Malone shook his head so hard she was surprised the rabbit didn't fly off. 'Just Big Joe. He's her friend.'

Abby wasn't sure about that. For all she knew Malone had got wildly drunk on his first beer in a year and spilled the beans to the lot of them, which was why Lisa wasn't here. Someone else had got here first. Had Lisa managed to get away, or had she been shot, like Marie?

'How was she when you left?' Abby asked anxiously. 'Was she okay?'

'Bit of frost nip here and there. Not surprising really. Took her a while till she got her strength back. She was pretty weak.'

'What was she doing here?' Abby asked. 'We've been looking for her miles away.'

Malone looked down at his misshapen boots, suddenly uncomfortable. 'She told me not to tell anyone. She made me promise.'

'Why?'

'It's of a personal nature.'

'Malone, she's in trouble,' Abby pleaded. 'She needs our help. A woman's been murdered. And Lisa is involved somehow.'

Malone looked up, surprise in his eyes. 'Who killed the woman? You know?'

'Not yet.'

'Bet it was him, then.'

141

'Who?'

Malone shuffled his feet. 'The man she was running from.'

'What man?'

'Her husband.'

Flint reared back in surprise as Abby blurted, 'Her *what?*'

'You hard of hearing?' Malone said.

'She's *married?*' Abby was stunned.

Malone gave her a sly look. 'Wonder why she didn't tell ya. Must'a had her reasons.'

'Who?' Abby demanded. 'Who's she married to?'

'Never said his name.'

'How long has she been married?'

Malone raised his head to the sky as he gave the question some thought, then shook his head. 'Didn't say.'

'Is he local? American? English?' She could see Flint shaking his head but she ignored him. 'Come on, Malone, she must have let *something* slip.'

Malone thought some more, then said, 'He's a pilot.'

'Who isn't?' said Flint drily.

'Of what?' Abby asked. 'Commercial or private? Airplanes or helicopters? Or both?' Maybe she could run a register of pilots and track him down that way.

'Mind if I have a look around?' Flint asked Malone. 'See if I can see which way she went?'

'I already did that.' Malone looked insulted, but Flint appeared oblivious and moved away without rancour.

'Can I see where she stayed?' Abby looked

longingly at Malone's cabin.

'It's private.' Malone shuffled his feet.

'Please?'

'She's not chained up inside, if that's what you're thinking.' His tone turned hostile.

'God, Malone, I didn't mean...'

'Shit.' He spat on the ground. 'You live your own life and people think you're crazy. Come on then. But don't touch nothing.'

Malone opened the door and allowed her a peek, hovering over her shoulder as though she might steal something. What she would steal she couldn't think. The row of animal skulls lined up on a shelf, perhaps? Or the filthy pair of moccasins the size of battleships by his rocking chair?

Trying to breathe shallowly against the odour of unwashed clothes and drying animal skins, she moved inside. It was gloomy without any windows, and dusty, but it was surprisingly warm.

'Where did she sleep?'

A filthy forefinger pointed at a sleeping shelf in the corner, piled with pelts and blankets. He blinked several times as though clearing his vision of an elfin woman curled up in his bed. He cleared his throat noisily and ducked his head. 'I took the chair.'

Abby moved her eyes around the room until they stalled on a radio. A big black box with a multitude of dials. A ham radio.

'Did Lisa call anyone?'

'She might have. But not when I was around.'

Malone started to edge her back to the door. He was still holding his shotgun. 'Keeps me sane, that thing. Talk to all sorts of people, you know.

143

Even spoke to the King of Jordan once. Before he died that is. It's good in winter. Good company.'

Abby was still scanning the single room, the bare boards and the pile of animal skins. 'Did she leave anything behind?'

Malone had a hand between her shoulder blades and was ushering her outside as though unable to bear her inspection of his home any longer. He dropped his hand as soon as they stepped into the hard, bright air.

'Pretty much left with what she came with. Oh, she swiped an old shotgun of mine. Some ammo and stuff. But she left a note saying she'd pay me back.'

'Shotgun?'

'Better for small game. Ptarmigan and the like. Rifle's good for distance, though.' He nodded approvingly. 'She's got it together well enough to live off the land a while.'

Abby continued to question Malone but the only other thing she gleaned was that Roscoe was partial to fresh rabbit and having the base of his tail scratched. She was desperately trying to think of another question to point her to Lisa or her husband, when Flint returned. He put out a hand to Malone, which Malone took and pumped up and down.

'Wait,' Abby said. She didn't want to go yet, didn't want to lose the closest contact she'd had with her sister in years.

Flint put a hand on her arm. 'She's not here, Abby.'

'I know, but...' Her heart felt as though it was splintering.

144

'We've got to get back.' His tone was gentle.

Tears pricked at the back of her eyes. She went and gave Malone a peck on the cheek. 'Thanks for looking after her.'

He put his hand where she'd kissed him, as though it burned.

Fifteen

Abby spent the journey back to Lake's Edge with her mind spinning over everything Malone had said, the jokes Lisa had told him, the wolves she'd met, but it inevitably circled back to a shocked explosion of amazement and relief: Lisa was *alive*. And not just alive, but *married*.

But where had she gone? She couldn't have travelled far, with just one dog, especially since Malone had said she was weak. Abby considered the ham radio in Malone's cabin, and wondered if Lisa had called someone for help, and who they might be. And why had Lisa left before she got there? She'd sent her a note, dammit. Had something caused her to move on? Maybe the cops... Out of nowhere she recalled Flint's hardened expression as he'd studied the map in the car park.

She batted his shoulders with her mitten until he stopped the snow machine. He turned his head, his forehead creased.

'What did you mean when you said someone might be trying to put us off her scent?'

'Nothing,' he said, his tone studiedly careless. 'Call it paranoia.'

With that, he set off again, leaving Abby staring at the back of his parka. Why had he lied? She closed her eyes against the chill wind biting her cheeks and chin. Big Joe and Diane said Flint was Lisa's friend, but could she really trust their word? Trust him?

By the time they arrived at Lake's Edge the sky still held a little light and the snowy trails glowed blue from the frosty clear sky. Houses and cabins were lit with tiny Christmas lights, transforming shadows of shrubs and frosted trees into diamonds in the snow. How much nicer, she thought, to look out of your window in the long winter darkness and see snow sculptures rather than an endless, miserable black.

Numb with cold and completely exhausted, she hesitated when Flint suggested they could do with a drink.

'I won't bite.' His teeth flashed white in the darkening gloom.

She knew she should go with him and learn more about his friendship with Lisa, but she was so tired, so desperate to be inside her own four warm walls with the comfort of her own – albeit meagre – belongings, she could weep.

'Another time,' she said between chattering teeth. 'Thanks for the ride.' Unclamping her un-feeling legs from the machine, she struggled off.

'What's next for you?' he asked.

'Try to find Lisa's husband.'

'Alaska has nearly eleven thousand registered

pilots,' Flint warned her. 'That's one for every fifty residents. Good luck.'

Abby rubbed her mittens together, suddenly depressed.

'Get in and have a hot bath,' he told her. 'While you do that, I'm going to see Sergeant Pegati. Tell him we know Lisa's alive.'

An automatic protest formed on her lips.

'Look, Search and Rescue's still scouring the mountains. People from all around are being inconvenienced for nothing, and besides that,' he gave a quick grin, 'she's long gone from Malone's. They'll never find her. She's far too good.'

'Really?'

'Yes, really. Could you give me the note? I'll need it.'

Abby took it out and smoothed it between her mittens. She looked at the heart surrounded with crosses, denoting kisses. Her heart wrenched.

'I'm sorry, Abby.'

She didn't want to, but she passed it over.

'Thanks.'

The snow machine's engine lifted but she stopped him.

'Do you happen to know Meg? The woman Lisa worked with?'

There was a flash of something at the back of his eyes; horror, anger, she couldn't be sure because the shutters came down so fast.

'Meg?' he repeated in a strangled tone. 'Why? Who's been asking?'

'The police.'

He was looking straight at her but he didn't seem to be seeing her. The seconds ticked past.

147

Gradually the focus returned.

'Abby,' he said. His tone turned gentle. 'If there's one piece of advice I can give you, it is to be extremely careful who you say that name to.'

'Why? Who is she? What does she—'

'Promise me you won't say that name again.' His expression turned fierce. 'Not ever.'

'But—'

'I like you, Abby. I don't want you to get hurt.'

The engine rose, drowning out her words, and before she could stop him, he roared away, leaving her standing in a cloud of exhaust.

Abby lay in an achingly hot bath in the outhouse, which – along with the handbasin and loo – had been built separately from the cabin and stood ten yards from the back door. Moke was sprawled on the bathmat, watching her. He hadn't been impressed at being left behind, and wanted to supervise her every move in case she tried to leave him again.

Closing her eyes, she luxuriated in the velvety heat. She'd forgotten how well set up rural villages out here could be.

There was a water storage tank buried out the back that gave the cabin running water, which would no doubt be delivered regularly by truck. And she had a flush loo, which meant a septic system. She appreciated these amenities big time right now.

She also appreciated the return of her bag from Lisa's cabin, which she'd found dumped on her sleeping shelf. No note, no apology for the messy state everything was in, having been pored through by Demarco and Victor, but she was inordinately glad to have it back. Aside from the sketch Victor had swiped, nothing appeared to be missing.

Eventually the bath water cooled, and she pulled the plug and climbed out. Clipping her nails, she doused herself with moisturiser, wrapped a towel around her and, Moke at her side, dashed back through the melting snow into the cabin. Her feet stung with cold and her skin puckered tight, springing with goose bumps, and she was yelping as they shot inside. Jesus, she wouldn't want to do that in midwinter.

She'd fed Moke and built up the wood stove, and was brushing the husky head-to-toe when she realised she was prevaricating. It didn't help that she knew the fact, because it still took her another hour before she worked up the courage to ring her mother.

She had rehearsed what she was going to say, and she was curled up on the sofa, wrapped in her favourite oversized cashmere sweater, a pair of thick socks and tracksuit pants, a bottle of wine and pack of cigarettes to hand, as ready as she could be for a talk that might stretch past midnight.

She'd barely said hello, when Julia butted in.

'Darling, I don't want you to worry, but I've had a man here. He's been asking about Lisa's work colleague, Meg.'

Immediately alarmed, Abby said, 'What man? Did he threaten you? Are you all right?'

'Abby, *calm down.*'

She sounded just like Lisa when she used that

149

tone of voice and Abby bristled. 'I am calm.'

'Good.' Julia's voice was brisk. 'I wasn't going to trouble you with it, but Ralph insisted. He says you should be kept informed of anything to do with Lisa, no matter how small, since you're trying to find her...'

'And?'

'He said he was a friend of Lisa's, but I've never heard of him. I thought I knew all Lisa's friends. Those she likes, those that she doesn't.' Julia gave a chuckle. 'I even know the name of Thomas's cleaner as well as his cat, but I've never heard of Matthew Evans. Not once.'

'What did he look like?'

'Quite a big man. Brown hair, brown eyes. Mid-forties. Receding hairline. No distinguishing features, if that's what you're asking, but he did wear a pair of designer glasses. Tinted too, which struck me as odd, given it was overcast.'

'Was he British?'

'Oh, no. American. West Coast, Ralph thought, but he couldn't be sure.'

'Not Alaskan?'

She heard Julia ask the question and realised Ralph was in the room with her. The feeling of security it gave was immeasurable.

'He doesn't know,' Julia came back on the line. 'He's never met an Alaskan. Anyway, this Matthew was very insistent about wanting to know where Meg was. He also wanted to know what Lisa and I talked about the last time we spoke, whether she'd sent me anything... He knew an awful lot about her – things only someone who knew her well would know. Like the name of her

150

old teddy bear. I mean when was Fuzzy last mentioned in this house? It was very disconcerting.'

'Maybe he's a guy she had an affair with and kept quiet?'

Julia gave a snort. 'Lisa's never been attracted to couch potatoes. Matthew Evans looked as though he'd expire on a walk to the local shops. Oh, and he chain smoked. The house reeked for days afterwards.'

Abby glanced at her cigarette stub on the saucer and then away. What her mum didn't know... God, she felt as though she was fourteen all over again and that she'd be found out.

'This Matthew, what was he like?'

'He was very personable, quite charming, I suppose, but there was something ... not quite *right*.'

For Julia, who had the intuition of a turnip, to admit that, was like setting off a dozen distress flares.

'Jesus,' said Abby, then on the same breath, 'Mum, look. Before we go any further, I've got to tell you that Lisa's alive. Really, *truly* alive. She made it through the storm. As far as I know, she's okay. A bit of frost nip here and there, apparently, but she's okay.'

'She's all right?' Julia sounded dazed. 'My baby's all right?'

By the time Abby had finished filling Julia in on Malone, and answered all her questions, she'd drunk two glasses of wine and smoked five cigarettes.

'Mum, did Lisa ever get married?'

'Goodness, Abby, do you really think I wouldn't tell you if she did? Of course she's not married.' A note of doubt crept into her voice. 'Well, not unless she'd done something completely mad that she regretted. Like falling for some man in Las Vegas and marrying him on the spot.'

'I don't think that happened,' Abby reassured her. 'I just wondered, that's all.'

When she finally hung up, she felt as though she'd been through an intelligence debriefing. She was exhausted.

'Not normal,' she told Moke, who'd had his head planted in her lap during the entire conversation. She hadn't even realised she'd been stroking him. Talk about subliminal actions. 'My family,' she told him, 'are not normal.' Moke opened his arctic-blue eyes and blinked at her as if to say, 'Whose are?'

She massaged his ears gently. Big Joe had told her Moke used to be owned by a guy who looked after Michael Flint's hunting lodge during the summer months, but when he'd lost a leg to a chain saw last autumn, his dogs had been rehomed.

'He wasn't too particular about their welfare,' Big Joe said. 'Three of them had to be put down. Didn't get on with people.'

'And Moke?'

He surveyed the dog a long while. 'Nice enough, but he never bonded with Lisa. If he had, she could have set fire to him and he wouldn't have left her. Instead, he came back to town, looking for his mates.'

Abby wondered what had gone through Moke's mind as he made his desperate journey home, wanting to be with his doggy friends rather than die with his new owner in a snow storm.

She downed another glass of wine to try and anaesthetise her worry, then she let Moke out briefly, topped up his water bowl, and crept into bed. She lay with her hand resting on the thick fur of the husky's belly as she stared into the darkness. A tear escaped and trickled down her cheek. Abby wiped it away. She didn't want to cry.

Sixteen

'Abby? Abby McCall?'

Hand on Moke's ruff – he was growling lowly at what he considered to be an intruder – Abby opened her cabin door to an overweight figure with a bonfire of auburn curls. A multitude of scarves hung from the woman's shoulders like prayer flags in the still, cool air.

'Yes. I'm Abby.'

'Oh, thank God I've found you. I'm Connie, a friend of Lisa's. Connie Bauchmann.' The woman was clutching an enormous bag that appeared to be made out of carpet and she dropped it to the ground, stretching out her arms. Abby allowed her to grasp her hands and give them a little shake. 'How are you bearing up? I have to say you look remarkably good, considering, it must be all the fresh air, I know it makes my complexion positively *glow*.'

'Hi.'

'Look, I know you're probably going through

hell and back, but I just wanted to hook up with you and see if there's anything I can do. It's all gone crazy, hasn't it? I can still barely make sense of it all, and I dread to think how you're feeling.'

'A bit peculiar,' Abby admitted, instinctively liking the woman, her face round and jolly as a candlelit pumpkin.

'I've been going quite mad with worry, ringing everyone I can think of who Lisa might have gone to, I know she's liable to do a disappearing act from time to time, but this is ridiculous.' The woman gave a slightly hysterical laugh. 'Nobody seems to know *anything*. I just wanted to let you know I'll do everything I can to help you find Lisa, although I'm not sure what we can do aside from sending a balloon up over the mountains with *Lisa, come home* on it...'

Abby desperately wanted to ask the woman if she knew Meg, but after what Flint had said, she held her tongue.

'I could *strangle* your rotten sister for putting me through this, I really could. Alaska is such a backwater, I can barely endure it.'

'I'd ask you in for coffee,' said Abby, 'but maybe later. There's someone I've got to see.'

'If you mean either of those two pathetic excuses for investigators you may as well stay where you are. They flew out in their helicopter first thing this morning.'

Abby looked up at the sky as though she might see the aircraft.

'Pegati and Demarco,' Connie added for good measure. 'They've gone to talk to some recluse in the mountains.'

Malone, Abby thought. They'd gone to question the trapper about Lisa hiding out with him.

Connie was now looking at her hopefully.

'Come inside,' Abby relented.

She was immediately rewarded with a happy beam from Connie who, as she crossed the threshold, bent over and retrieved a mitten from the floor. 'Yours, I assume?'

'Whoops, yes. Thanks.'

'Sweet,' Connie said, referring to the wrist decoration: a line of dancing wolves with bows around their necks. 'But they're not so sweet themselves, are they? I've heard some terrible tales about wolves...'

Connie dumped her carpetbag by the sofa, unwinding her scarves and pulling off her knee-length down jacket, wrists clanking with bracelets.

'And the bears! Quite terrifying. Lisa told me about a friend of hers spending a winter outside Fairbanks in a wilderness cabin, and one day a bear tore the door off. Can you imagine! She spent the next two weeks with just a blanket hammered in its place... Oooh, don't they look good?' Connie's eyes brightened when Abby brought some muffins out of the fridge.

Abby poured the coffee and put out a plate of blueberry muffins before settling with Connie on the sofa. Sun streamed through the windows, lighting the Native rugs into jewels of blue and red, and suddenly it felt so like home that for a moment she found it hard to picture her room in Oxford. It seemed terribly grey and bland in comparison.

'So,' Abby decided to plunge right in, 'how do

155

you know Lisa? From the UK? You sound English.'

'Do I?' Connie blinked several times. 'Good heavens. I haven't been back there since I was a child. I thought I'd lost my accent.'

'It's more your language patterns.'

Connie gave a rueful smile. 'I guess it's hard to shake off your past.'

As if Abby didn't know. Before Connie could begin to fill her in on her English connection, she said again, 'How do you know my sister?'

'I've been working with her for the last six months. And Thomas.' Connie toyed with her muffin briefly. 'You haven't heard from Thomas, have you? I really want to see him, but he's not answering his phone.'

'He's on vacation.'

'I don't even know if he's heard about Lisa's disappearance,' Connie said. 'He'll be devastated when he finds out. They're so close those two. Like two peas in pod. Well, not peas, exactly, but you know what I mean.'

He's like the father I should have had, Abby remembered Lisa saying. *He understands me.*

'I'm worried about him,' Connie took a bite of muffin. 'I'm worried about Meg too.'

Abby reared back, startled. 'Meg?'

'Don't tell me you haven't heard the name.' Her eyes were sharp.

'No. I mean, well, yes, I have.' Abby was flustered.

'Look,' said Connie, 'I'd love to fill you in completely, I really would, but I made a promise to Thomas–'

'Who's Meg?' Abby interrupted.

'I'm sorry, Abby,' Connie sighed, 'but a promise is a promise. If I didn't keep my word in this business, I'd be flat broke by the end of the week.'

'As Lisa's sister, I have a right to know.' Her tone was hard.

Connie shifted in her seat.

'A man went to my mother's home yesterday wanting to know about Meg. She felt threatened. *I have to know what's going on.*'

Connie hesitated. She saw it. And Connie knew she'd seen it and looked away. 'Abby, just *knowing* about Meg puts you in danger. Both Thomas and Lisa know this.'

Abby felt a creeping sensation. Michael Flint knew this too.

Connie took a deep breath. 'Okay then. Since you insist... It's just that Meg is top secret. And if I hear you've breathed a word, Thomas and I, *and your sister,* will have your guts for garters. Understood?'

Abby sketched a cross over her heart and tried not to think of Sergeant Pegati and Trooper Demarco.

'Good. Because we can't have anyone, and I mean *anyone,* getting wind of Meg, or we'll be up the proverbial creek without a single paddle.' Connie leaned close as though she might be overheard. 'You see, Meg's not a who but a *what.* It heralds the Mega Engine Generation. MEG.

'Thomas and Peter – that's Peter Santoni – had been working on it for years, so long, in fact, they'd just about made themselves a laughing stock. Santoni showed it to me once, but the technology was so shaky I couldn't see how they'd be able to make anything of it.'

Peter Santoni was the guy Tessa had referred to in her letter to Lisa. Santoni knew about Professor Crowe taking Lisa to court, and for the first time Abby wondered how he'd found out about it. By chance? Or had someone told him? She hurriedly switched her attention back to Connie when she realised she wasn't listening.

'...Lisa joined them, she brought something fresh to the project, a new pair of eyes, whatever, but personally I believe it's the way she can think so amazingly *laterally*, being totally unorthodox and making wild leaps no normal person would dream of. She's never been strong on convention, your sister, and... Oh, dear, she had a terrible row with Santoni.

'Which isn't surprising when you think of it. Santoni's methodical, deliberate and meticulous with his data, whereas Lisa ... well, you know what Lisa's like. She used to call him Santoni Craponi. It drove him mad.'

Connie reached across and took another bite of muffin. She ate surprisingly daintily, with quick, catlike movements.

'Santoni wanted Lisa off the project, but Thomas didn't want to lose her. He told Santoni that if he was that unhappy with the situation he could leave. There was a huge fight, lots of slamming of doors and shouting, but Thomas didn't give in. In the end, Santoni did.'

Abby looked across as Moke went to his water bowl and had a drink.

'Thomas and Lisa shut Santoni out. They put

158

locks on the door of their lab, locked their offices behind them whenever they left ... poor old Santoni went from being an integral part of the team to a pariah. He's still unbelievably bitter about it all.' She dabbed her mouth briefly with her fingers, licking them of crumbs. 'I can't say I blame him.'

Abby didn't either. She could see why he'd treasure a piece of nasty gossip about Lisa.

'What does MEG do?'

'You know what she was obsessed with, your sister?'

'Flight,' Abby answered promptly. 'Telsa was her hero, but she admired the pants off Whittle. He invented the jet engine...'

Out of nowhere came Lisa's voice, clear as day. *All we're doing now is building variations on a theme. We need another Whittle to take us forward, so we can fly London to Sydney in two hours rather than twenty-four. Preferably without using fossil fuels.*

Connie's eyes were intent on hers. They were large and tawny and made Abby feel as though she was holding the gaze of a very large, very fat, lioness.

There was a huge silence.

A slow smile spread across Connie's face.

Abby's eyes widened. 'They've invented a new jet engine?'

Folds of flesh almost obscured Connie's eyes as she beamed. 'A jet engine with no moving parts whatsoever.'

'You're kidding.'

Connie shook her head. She was still beaming. 'Aren't they brilliant?'

159

Abby had never felt so lost for words. Brilliant wasn't the word, gobsmacking was more like it. Her mad, crazy sister had actually helped invent something *useful*? Well, more than useful, she thought, as her mind began to take it in. If what Connie said was true, MEG was going to change the entire aeronautical industry.

'Abby?' Connie looked at her anxiously. 'Are you all right?'

'Um, I'm just a bit surprised.'

Connie laughed, a big deep laugh from low in her belly. 'Aren't you excited?'

'Oh, yes,' Abby said hastily, but a knot of fear had lodged itself beneath her breastbone. 'Connie, do you know about Marie Guillemote? What happened to her?'

'But of course!' Connie looked shocked. 'Why do you think I'm here? The second I heard I was on a plane flying out of San Francisco! I was terrified all my money had gone!'

'Money?' repeated Abby.

'Dearest, I'm their business investor.'

Seventeen

Abby looked out over the frozen lake as she and Connie drank more coffee. It felt good having an ally to join forces with. A cheerful ally at that, who appeared just as determined as Abby to find Lisa and get to the bottom of what was going on. Connie headed the research department for

Brightlite Utilities, a forward-thinking electricity company who invested in ideas for future energy.

'But she's invented an airplane engine,' Abby said, confused. 'What has that to do with electricity?'

'We believe MEG could herald a new age of energy, for domestic needs as well.'

At least Abby now knew where Lisa's $123,000 had come from. Good old Brightlite Utilities had stumped up the money three months ago, with another $100,000 promised the following year. It seemed like a bargain considering what they were getting in return.

Abby knew, however, that Connie wasn't as concerned for Lisa as for her company's money and, of course, MEG. Apparently not only was the prototype missing, but MEG's lab books, which, Connie informed her glumly, were almost as important as the actual prototype when it came to patenting the machine. If anyone contested MEG, they'd need the lab books to prove they created the engine first. Without them, they'd be stymied, and Connie was petrified both prototype and lab books had got into the wrong hands and that someone was patenting MEG themselves right that instant.

'It isn't patented?' Abby was horrified.

Connie groaned and pushed her head in her hands. 'Thomas wouldn't do it. Lisa begged him, but he was paranoid someone would pinch their idea before they'd completed it. He kept going on about Bell and Gray, do you know the story?'

Abby didn't, and Connie told her how both men had filed patent applications for the telephone on the same day and with the same clerk, but days later an extra paragraph appeared on Bell's application that hadn't been there before. It was almost identical to Gray's design. The patent clerk later admitted that he had sold Gray's ideas to Bell's lawyers. Gray tried to sue but was unsuccessful. Bell died fabulously wealthy, leaving a vast business empire today known as AT&T, Gray died unknown and unrecognised.

'I told him time and again that the USTPO, that's the United States Trade and Patent Office to you and me, changed their regulations recently but he wouldn't budge. You see, it's not who files the *application* first for an invention any more, but who has the *idea* first. Which is why the lab books are so valuable – they show Thomas's work since its inception thirty-two years ago.'

Abby gazed through the windows. It was a stunningly beautiful day, with ice glazing every twig, turning rocks and gravel into shining crystals, but she couldn't appreciate it. She was still trying to absorb the implications of MEG.

'And Marie Guillemote? Who's she?'

'A woman from the patent office in Arlington, Virginia.'

Abby's jaw softened. 'Shit,' she said.

'Exactly.' Connie's tone was arid.

'Who killed Marie?' Abby asked. 'Do you have any idea?'

Connie shook her head. 'All I know for sure is that Lisa approached the USTPO a year ago, and when Thomas balked about filing an application, Lisa and Marie struck up a friendship. They've kept in touch over the Internet ever since.'

162

Had Marie tried to steal MEG? Abby wondered. Could Lisa have shot her? Would she?

'Do the USTPO know about MEG?' Abby said.

'No, thank God. Just Marie.' Connie put her hand on her heart and raised her eyes to the ceiling briefly. 'Marie was even more paranoid than Thomas, if it's possible. I spoke to her colleagues before I flew here, and from piecing together various conversations, it's my theory that she came over to see the prototype, maybe persuade Lisa to take the first step in patenting the technology.'

'Why didn't Lisa meet Marie in Fairbanks? Wouldn't it have been easier rather than have Marie rent a car and come all the way up here?'

'I'd like to get to the bottom of that too,' Connie said.

Moke was by the door, looking at her expectantly, so Abby opened it for him. While she watched him find something interesting to pee on, Connie said, 'One more thing you need to know, dearest.'

Abby turned to see Connie fiddling with her bangles. 'I've told the police I'm Lisa's business investor, but nothing else. I haven't dared breathe a word about MEG.'

Abby was shocked. 'Shouldn't we tell them?'

Connie strode over, expression fierce. 'If we tell the police it'll be out all over town, spread across all the papers, and your sister will be in even more danger than she already is!' She gripped Abby's wrist so hard, it hurt. 'She and Thomas have dreamed of this for *so long*. If Lisa finds out you've thrown all their work away for nothing,

163

then God help you.'

Abby shook her wrist free, and rubbed it. She didn't want to withhold information from the police, but nor did she want to destroy her sister's dream. 'But if the cops know you're their investor, how can they not know about MEG?'

'Brightlite's learned over the years how to keep a secret. So I flummoxed them with science. Told them we invested in EVals. That's capital EV, in case you need to know...' Connie suddenly grinned. 'You should have seen that dim little trooper's face when I asked her how to get 100 billion electrons to huddle together. She hadn't a clue what I was talking about.'

Abby called Moke back inside and gave him a dog biscuit. He swallowed it in one gulp.

'Connie, who else knows about MEG?'

'No one as far as I know,' she said, openly crossing her fingers.

A charge of apprehension tightened Abby's skin as she thought of Michael Flint. How did he know about MEG if it was so secret? She paused in the kitchenette, thinking hard. Even though she could see Connie's point of view in all this, she couldn't not tell Victor and Demarco about MEG. Could she? She screwed up her face, racked with indecision. She had to speak to Thomas first, she realised. MEG was his invention, and he may well shed some light on how the hell Flint knew so much.

'Connie, I'm going to call Thomas.'

'Good idea. Tell him I want to see him, would you?'

'Sure.'

Connie started to get to her feet. 'Shall I leave you?'

'No, no. Stay.' Abby looked up his number and dialled. An answer machine kicked in.

'Hi, you've reached Thomas...'

Abby left a message asking him to call her urgently. Then she rang the UAF switchboard, who told her Thomas was still on personal leave. She wouldn't say where.

'Oh. I thought he was due back today.'

'One minute...' She heard the operator shuffling in the background. 'Ah, here it is... He'll be in tomorrow.'

When she hung up, she saw Connie was looking alarmed.

'Oh, dear Lord. He's still on vacation?' She briefly covered her mouth with her hand. 'He can't know about Lisa yet, or he'd be back by now. I bet he's staying with those friends of his in the mountains. No TV or radio, let alone newspapers. A complete rest, he calls it. More like solitary confinement if you ask me.'

Abby's heart sank. She didn't relish breaking the news to Thomas that his beloved protégée had gone missing.

'Dearest, shall I drive us to Fairbanks? It's not something I feel we can do on the phone. Then we can tell him together.'

Abby shook her head. Much as she felt for Thomas, she didn't want to leave the area. Lisa might send her another message. 'I'll call him.'

'That's all very well, but you do realise he will refuse point blank to discuss anything about his research over the phone. He's paranoid about

165

security, remember? The only way to find out what's going on is to have a face-to-face meeting with him. He won't say diddly otherwise. He won't discuss it via email either, as I've learned to my cost.'

Connie got to her feet and began gathering her belongings. 'I'll go down tomorrow. If seeing him is the only way we're going to get to the bottom of all this...'

Abby dithered. She knew she could ask Connie to ring and tell her what Thomas had said, but it wasn't the same as talking to him. She remembered Connie's reluctance to tell her about MEG, and wondered if she'd hide anything from her. If she met Thomas, she'd hear it from him straight, and know exactly what to do next. She could even see MEG. Without realising it, her mind had been made up.

'I'll join you.'

'Oh, that is terrific,' said Connie. 'Let's meet after breakfast in the morning.'

After Connie had left, Abby pulled out Demarco's card and rang her. 'Just so you know where I am,' she told the trooper.

'I appreciate it.'

The temperature had risen a little so Abby settled herself on the deck with a cup of coffee. Moke's head lay in her lap. She gazed across the cold, white length of the lake, her spirits enervated, crushed beneath a block of anxiety.

When she finished her coffee, she made another mugful and returned to sit in the sunshine. She knew she should be doing something to help Lisa, but she couldn't think what. Asking ques-

166

tions about Michael Flint, maybe. Or checking exactly who Malone had spoken to about Lisa when he was in town.

Abby stayed around the cabin for the rest of the day, waiting by the phone in case Thomas rang, but deep down she knew she was making excuses. She was more scared than she wanted to admit.

It was bright the next morning and even Abby could feel how much warmer it was. Not that it was T-shirt weather at thirty-five degrees, but to the locals it must have felt like a heat wave: everyone was in shirtsleeves. Snow was melting fast and the main road out of town was slushy, spraying mud and wet snow up the flanks of the car and, when they hit a pothole – which was frequently with Connie's somewhat haphazard driving – over the windscreen.

'Hey, take it easy,' Abby said after Connie had hurtled into another blind corner without lessening her speed. 'There might be a moose standing in the way next time.'

Connie didn't take any notice and Abby nervously double-checked her seat belt, grateful she had an air bag in front of her. She leaned forward to peer into her wing mirror, hoping nobody was behind them in case Connie was forced to do an emergency stop. A white SUV was following, but luckily it was well behind.

'How's your mum taking all this?' asked Connie.

'Hard.'

'Must be tough with her MS, you looking after her the way you do.'

Wanting to distract herself from Connie's driving, Abby studied the emptiness around them.

'Is that why you and Lisa fell out?' asked Connie. 'Because she never came home to give you a break?'

Abby sighed. She and Lisa were two such different creatures, it was a miracle they'd ever talked at all. It was only being out here, trying to untangle what the hell was going on, that she realised how fundamentally disparate they were. Trying to work out what Lisa was doing right now, and why, was like attempting to scale Everest barefoot and without oxygen: impossible.

She straightened up in her seat a little as the next thought trickled through. Maybe she should start thinking like Lisa would – put herself in her sister's shoes rather than force her own thoughts on the situation. Okay. Marie got shot. Lisa had banked Connie's cash and *run away*. Why hadn't she called the police? Apprehension formed a knot in her windpipe and she had to swallow several times before it dissipated. Were the cops involved somehow?

And what about Marie? Had she come to persuade Lisa to patent MEG or to steal it? The fact she'd emailed Lisa regularly, and then stayed with her, meant Lisa considered her a friend, but that still didn't answer the question why Marie had come all the way to Lake's Edge. Was it because Lisa felt safer there? And what about Peter Santoni, the disgruntled scientist? Where was he?

Her thoughts evaporated when she realised Connie was going to take the next corner far too fast.

'Connie, slow up, will you? There might be ice on the road!'

'You are so uptight!' Connie exclaimed, but Abby was glad when she dropped her speed a fraction and took the corner without mishap. 'You're worse than Scott, and that's saying something. None of my other husbands minded my driving.'

'Husbands?' Abby tried not to sound surprised.

'Just the two before I met the love of my life,' Connie said drily. 'Third time lucky, that's what I always say.'

They passed a row of mailboxes next to a turning, but Abby couldn't see any houses. What people did in the middle of miles of open tundra, she couldn't think. Hunt, like Malone? Pick berries?

'Lucky you,' Abby said.

'Some days I still can't believe it.' Connie sighed dreamily. 'It was embarrassing at first, I could barely admit I'd fallen for my boss, but that's what happened.'

Abby knew all about clichés of the heart after Cal, and gave a sympathetic grimace.

'We both play hockey, that's how it started. I whacked him one before shooting a goal.' She gave a chuckle. 'Talk about getting his undivided attention, the poor man couldn't walk for a week.'

Abby couldn't think of anything she'd done to get Cal's attention. She had, she recalled, simply stood there and looked into his eyes. Talk about getting whacked by physical chemistry.

Connie had speeded up again, and seemed oblivious of the corner approaching. 'Can you slow down? Please?'

'Are we nearly at the haul road yet?'

Abby checked the map. 'We've a couple of miles–'

She swallowed her words when suddenly, Connie rammed both feet on the brake pedal, yelling, 'Shit!'

A tractor and trailer sat in the middle of the road, blocking their path. Brief snapshot of a guy watching them from a snow bank and then they were skidding straight for it, Connie and Abby yelling, and Abby was bracing herself for impact when the car slid to a halt just a couple of yards short of the trailer's rear tyre.

'Jesus,' said Abby.

'That *stupid* man,' gasped Connie. 'I nearly hit it, I damned nearly hit it. Holy hell, Abby. Are you all right?'

'Yes, but no thanks to you! Could you slow down a bit from now on? Like brake before a corner rather than right in the middle of it?'

'Okay okay, I'm sorry,' muttered Connie.

Abby was trembling all over and could have done with yelling some more to release her tension, but Connie was huddled in her seat looking so contrite she wrestled her temper under control and snapped off her seat belt, intending to climb outside and shake herself down, to try and regain her equilibrium.

She had her hand on the door handle when a shadow appeared at her window. It was the guy who'd been standing on the snow bank and he flung the door open and the next second he was hauling her outside, yelling, 'Get in the car! The SUV behind you! Do it now!'

170

Eighteen

Abby fought off the hands grabbing the collar of her parka, her elbows. 'What the hell...? Get off me!'

The next instant she was face down in snow, a man lying across her legs, another on her shoulders. Her arms were yanked behind her back, and she was bucking and lurching wildly but they were too heavy. Her hands were bound together.

'Fatso!' Another yell. 'Open the hood!'

Spitting snow, Abby twisted her head round to see a man pointing a pistol at Connie. Connie released the bonnet of her car and then he was leaning inside and ripping out a handful of wires from the engine. Disabling the vehicle.

'You're the lucky one,' he told Connie. 'You get to walk back to town.'

Horror flooded Abby. They were going to leave Connie, which meant they were going to kidnap her.

She kicked at one of the men, felt it connect, heard his grunt, and kicked again and again, but the other man had her by the scruff of her parka and was yanking her upright, and then they were dragging her to the rear of the white SUV. She twisted her head, trying to bite them, anything to stop them, if only for an instant, but they were stronger and with her hands tied she was unbalanced. Still she fought every inch, yelling.

171

'Shut the fuck up!'

Abby screamed back incoherently, and suddenly, the hands dropped away. She lurched sideways, trying to get her balance and make a run for it, when a fist landed on the side of her jaw.

Her head snapped back and she toppled to the ground. Vision distorted, ears ringing, her mouth was taped, then her eyes, and she was trying to struggle as the men lifted her upright, half-carrying, half-dragging her, but she could barely breathe against the tape and her limbs were unsteady and without much effort, the men heaved her into the back of the SUV. Abby scrambled to set her shoulders against the rear seats and thrust her feet blindly outwards and as soon as they connected against the door she shoved as hard as she could.

'Fuck,' one of the men said, and then the pressure was returned at double strength, and she knew both men were putting their shoulders to the door and although Abby put her best effort into it, head pounding and throbbing, the gap closed slowly and inexorably until it shut with a small click. She heard them lock it.

Nostrils wide, breathing fast, sweat pouring, Abby scraped her face against the rough carpet, trying to dislodge the tape across her eyes and mouth. She could hear Connie's shouts as the SUV's doors were opened and then slammed shut, but she couldn't see anything.

She rubbed desperately but the tape refused to peel off. The car started up and pulled away. Curled on her side she was sobbing with frustration and fear, trying to wrench her hands free, when one of the men said, 'Shut the fuck up, lady, or you'll get another thumping.'

Abby immediately fell quiet.

'Which one you want?' the same man said.

'No. No, and ... yup. That'll do.'

A handful of seconds later music flooded the car. A bluesy, laid-back tune with a tenor sax that was reminiscent of a smoky nightclub. She'd have expected them to play heavy metal or rock.

At the end of the fifth song, the car slowed, paused, then swung left and accelerated hard, gravel churning beneath the tyres. On to the haul road, she assumed. The Dalton Highway. Oh God, where were they taking her? There weren't any towns along the road for at least three hundred miles, until you came to the polar bears prowling the Arctic coast, the dendritic web of pipelines that were the start of the oil's six-day journey south to Valdez.

Eventually the blues came to a close, and the men picked another CD. Some sort of country band with a rollicking female singer. Come the third track, Abby finally gave up trying to scrape the tape free from her face. They'd obviously used duct tape, one of the hardiest, toughest tapes on the market that Abby used to appreciate. Right now she wished it had never been invented.

Her arms were aching, her jaw sore, and she shuffled around trying to get comfortable, but it was impossible with her arms tied behind her back. The car would bounce from time to time, jarring her spine and hips, wrenching her elbows, and she knew she'd be covered in bruises when they got to wherever they were going.

When the CD finished, the men didn't put on any more music, they just drove in silence. Abby dozed fitfully, coming to with a fearful jerk when the car dipped or swayed on the buckled permafrost road, convinced they were going to crash.

'Here,' said one of the men.

The car slowed and turned on to a rough surface, sliding and rolling. Abby realised they were on a track – a snowy, icy track from the motion of the vehicle. Abby tried to guess how far they'd come, but it was difficult to tell without any CDs playing. It felt as though they'd been driving for half the day, but she reckoned on two, maybe three hours – they must be at least a hundred miles from Lake's Edge.

'There it is.' His voice held the satisfaction of a journey's end, like a man talking to a colleague when he sights home after a long commute.

She made a last desperate attempt to free herself. What were they going to do with her? What did they want? Who were they?

The car came to a stop. She heard the men climb out and crunch round to the back. She wanted to charge them to try and run for it, but there was no point if she couldn't see. She might sprint straight into a tree. The door opened and a flood of ice-cold air rushed inside.

'Out,' said a voice.

Abby twisted round and swung her feet out of the car. A hand grabbed her elbow and hauled her to her feet. Her boots scrunched into stiff, ice-capped snow.

'Over here.' The same hand pulled and pushed her, stumbling and swaying, through the snow until her shin banged against something with a hollow knock. 'Get in.'

Get in what? Tentatively she raised her foot, and he added, 'It's a fucking sled, okay?' He yanked her forward but with her hands tied behind her back, she couldn't feel for the sled and couldn't picture where to climb.

'Jesus.' He gave her a shove that had her sprawling forward. Her knees smacked into plastic, making her yelp behind the tape. She dragged herself awkwardly into the sled. Hands tugged her boots until they rested against a plastic lip, about six inches high. 'You try and get out,' he warned, 'you'll fall a thousand fucking feet, okay?'

She nodded.

Footsteps crunched away, and then with a clattering roar, an engine started. She felt a moment of sheer terror. A snow machine? They were going to drag her behind them? Oh God, where were they taking her?

All thoughts fled as the engine engaged gear and the sled lurched forward, slowly at first and then gradually picking up speed. Abby braced her feet as hard as she could, feeling the plastic rim of the sled dig into her bound wrists in the small of her back.

Almost immediately the sled dived to the left.

Instinctively she leaned right, straightening it.

The sled then bounced, flinging her into the air. She shouted behind the tape, praying she wasn't going to fly out and plunge to her death down a cliff face, but then she slammed back into the sled.

Clumps of ice and snow hit her neck and face, kicked up from the snow machine, and she tried to duck her head down, but then the sled would hit another mound, snapping her neck back and jerking her upright.

Jesus. No helmet. She had to pray no rocks or stones would follow.

Another impact. Harder this time. The sled veered sideways.

She tried to keep the sled straight and steady, but it was no use. Unable to see, unable to grip the sides of the sled with her hands tied, she found herself just trying to remain on board.

Ice-cold air blasted her, cutting to the bone, and it didn't take long before she began to freeze up. The effort to keep herself braced, locked into the sled with sluggish muscles, gradually took its toll, and she found her body rolling more and more, and then suddenly another impact hit her and the sled jolted further to the left, almost spilling her out.

The engine note abruptly changed, dropped from a shriek to a roar. The sled lost its wild veering and eased into an unsteady rocking motion. Thank God, they'd slowed. Her wrists were numb, her breathing coming hard and fast through her nostrils. Her whole body was stiffening with cold. Minutes later her weight was pushed hard to the back of the sled and she knew they were climbing.

Her senses knew nothing but the blue cold smell of the snow, the occasional blasting stench of exhaust, the fear riding her muscles, and when they slowed to a stop and shut off the engine, her ears rang loud as a rock band playing at 150 decibels.

'Out.'

Abby tried to bring her feet up and over the lip of the sled but they refused to function properly. She was just about frozen where she sat.

Hands heaved her upright. She staggered and was surprised when they didn't let her fall. Probably because they didn't want to have to pick her up again.

The two men took up position on either side of her, hands gripping her upper arms, and walked her forward, uphill, through snow that was deep and dragged at her feet. The hill steepened, making the muscles in the backs of her calves tighten. The gradient was too extreme for the snow machine. Each time she got bogged down, the men caught her and held her upright.

They came to a halt. One of the men kept a firm grip on her while the other scrunched ahead and fiddled with something metallic, then a small click followed the sound of bolts being shot. A creaking sound of wood scraping on wood. A tug on her elbow and she fumbled ahead.

'In you go.'

The air was suddenly colder, and smelled dense and musty.

'Okay. Keep still.' She felt hands on her wrists and then the tape was loose and she was bringing her arms round when a hand planted itself between her shoulder blades and gave her a hearty shove. Abby fell to her knees and she was ripping off the tape over her eyes and mouth and as she swung round she heard the door being slammed behind her, bolts being shot into place.

Abby leaped for the door and grabbed the handle, put her shoulder against it, but it was locked from outside and didn't budge.

'Let me out! I can pay you, I swear! Don't leave me here, please!'

She hammered and pounded, her arms burning as the blood rushed to her hands, but the door was solid wood, absorbing the blows of her fists. 'Please!' she shouted. 'I've got lots of money! I won't tell anyone what you did if you let me go!'

She pressed her head against the rough wood of the door, but she couldn't hear anything above the pulse roaring in her ears. Abby continued to thump and yell, just in case the men were there, but then she heard the distinctive roar of the snow machine.

She listened to it engage gear, and move off. Abby kept listening as it faded away, swallowed into the sound of nothing.

Trembling all over, she rubbed her arms, and then her face, which was stinging. All she could hear was the deafening thud of her heart, the rasping of her breath, the blood hammering through her veins.

Gradually she gained control and at last, looked around in the gloom to see she was in a single-room wilderness cabin. There were no windows, just four walls of sturdy, snug-fitting logs. There was a waist-high stack of wood along one wall, a wood stove, a wooden shelf for a bed, a ten-gallon container of water, and half a dozen boxes of canned food. There was a bucket in the corner with a pack of loo rolls next to it.

Abby stared and stared at the supplies, dread filling her heart.

She wasn't expected to leave for some time.

Nineteen

Lisa pulled up Roscoe and searched the country with her binoculars. She noticed that since she'd crossed Beaver Mountain and out of King's territory, deer and other animals were more numerous. The moose and deer were living on the dormant buds and young twigs, while the goats and sheep foraged on dried grass or moss wherever the wind had swept some of the snow from the mountainsides.

In some places the sun had melted the snow only to re-freeze it at night, and she caught sight of a snowshoe rabbit running across the equivalent of an ice rink at top speed. She smiled, thinking of Malone, who would have had the animal in his pot come the morning.

A good man, Malone, who'd proved all the rumours about him to be quite untrue, thank God. And he'd been willing enough to go into town to give her message to Abby. Except he hadn't given it directly to Abby as she'd asked. He'd stopped for a beer and spoken to practically the whole town as far as she knew, including Big Joe and Billy Bob, Hank, and some woman he'd taken a fancy to. And one of them had talked to someone else, and that someone else had come straight to Malone's cabin.

Luckily, she'd been prepared, and was tucked up with Roscoe at the top of the hill behind

Malone's cabin, ready to flee if needs be. Sheltered by the forest, she'd been impossible to spot from the air, but when the faint buzz of an engine reached her, it still took an immense effort not to break into a blind run.

The buzz grew louder, and with a lurch she recognised it as the continuous clatter of a helicopter's rotors.

She quickly fished in her sled and loaded her rifle, double-checked the safety was on before resting it across her knees. She brought Roscoe close, feeling safer with him alongside and the rifle ready to fire.

As the machine approached, Lisa instinctively hunkered down. Flying low, the chopper was following the wilderness trail to the cabin. The forest seemed to shudder as the clatter increased.

God, it was close! About two hundred feet up, it was banking sharply, circling over Malone's cabin, rising into the air and hanging over it like a great noisy hornet.

Cautiously she raised her binoculars and peered at the chopper's windscreen but the sun was bouncing off the glass and she couldn't see who was inside.

The helicopter descended until it seemed to be almost brushing the tops of the spruce trees and then it banked a little, then a little more, and continued inching around the cabin until she realised whoever was inside was scrutinising the area minutely. For tracks. For small woman-sized footprints that might indicate she was here.

She congratulated herself on reading them so well. She'd swept her tracks clean, leaving

Malone's as best she could. Unless they walked the area, they'd never know she'd been here. And there was nowhere for them to land, not for at least a mile, and by the time they got here, she'd be long gone.

The helicopter continued its tortuously slow scrutiny until suddenly it rose straight up into the sky, pushed its nose down, and accelerated away.

Now, she had finally reached her destination, and was by the back door, shovelling snow aside. The last time she'd been here it had been late summer, when she and Saffron had joined a group of friends picking cranberries. Those contented days of wading through the bush with the sun hot on her back felt light years away now, as though they belonged to someone else.

She took a crowbar and levered off the bear shutter. Some folk left tin cans hanging down, filled with bug spray and baited by fat, but the simple piece of plywood with its nails pointing out appeared to be just as effective a deterrent.

Inside the air was cold and smelled faintly of smoke, even though the fireplace wouldn't have been used for months. She headed straight for the kitchen, where she knew the radios were stored. Short-wave, long-wave, a ham radio as well. Radios for all eventualities.

'Bravo Jericho? You read? This is the King.'

Big Joe must have been hovering over the radio because he answered almost immediately. 'King, we've been worried.'

'Yeah, sorry about that. How's that new bitch of yours? Alpha, weren't it?'

'Alpha's gone. I think someone's got her,

doesn't want to let her go. Everyone's telling me she's been stolen.'

Lisa felt as though she was in a ski-lift whose cable just snapped. Her greatest fear had just been realised. Abby had been kidnapped.

Even through the radio Lisa could hear the concern in Big Joe's voice. 'How are we going to get her back?'

'I've got some ideas. But only if you don't mind being the intermediary.'

They quickly hammered out a rough plan of action, which involved far too much risk for Lisa's liking, but she had no choice. She could no more leave Abby in danger than she could cut off her own hand.

If it was the last thing she did, she would get her big sister back.

Twenty

Abby was shivering. It was probably from shock, but her bones were aching with cold, so she quickly turned her mind to practical things. Heat was a priority. She had to fire up the wood stove.

There were two boxes of firestarters, a pile of kindling and two boxes of matches, and after Abby had lit the stove, she explored further to find candles, more matches, a can opener, a small saucepan and a tin spoon, and a down sleeping bag. So long as she kept the wood stove burning and kept herself warm, she could survive here for... Abby sank on the wooden sleeping shelf as she worked it out ... two weeks at least.

Lighting a candle, she inspected her prison. Could she dig her way out? The floorboards were solid as granite and the ground frozen beneath, and the roof fitted perfectly to the tops of the walls. What little light there was leaked through tiny cracks around the door, otherwise the structure could have been hermetically sealed.

Abby pushed the tin spoon into a minute fissure by the door and pressured it gently. The spoon immediately buckled. She double-checked the supplies, searching for a knife, a piece of glass, anything she could use to chip away at the wood, but the only thing sturdy enough was the can opener, and she daren't break it or she wouldn't be able to eat.

Still shivering, Abby checked her parka pockets to find tissues and a tube of lip moisturiser; nothing of any use. She brought the sleeping bag to the wood stove and huddled inside it, trying to get warm. At least whoever had organised her kidnap didn't seem to want her to die of cold, hunger or thirst.

She could have done with a cigarette to settle her nerves, but since they'd been in her day pack, she'd have to do without. She'd given up before, she could do it again. Abby gave a grim little smile. It wasn't as though she had a choice.

Resolutely, she turned her mind to Connie.

You're the lucky one. You get to walk back to town.

Had Connie reached Lake's Edge yet? Alerted the police? Were they now searching for her? Her body gave a violent shudder as she thought over the kidnappers' motives, their plans. Was she being held to be tortured, to give them information about MEG? A whimper fluttered in her throat. Nobody would hear her screams out here, or witness the gunshot when they dispatched her.

Don't think about it, you'll only go crazy.

Abby wondered if Lisa was hiding out in a wilderness lodge like this one, or if she was already across the border and heading for anonymity in one of the big cities. She hoped it was the latter, and that she was spending some of her $123,000 on a plush hotel.

Suddenly a wild clamour broke out, making Abby's heart jump. She swung to stare at the door. Then the noise stopped. Absolute quiet lasted for a minute or two, then the baying began again, clear-cut in the night air. She stared at the door as though waiting for the wolf-pack to burst inside, they sounded so close.

Gradually the wolf voices died down to one or two, tonguing only occasionally. Then a deep individual note joined in, and a wild chorus broke out. The hair stood straight up on the nape of her neck; she'd never heard such a terror-inducing sound.

Abby hurriedly fed another couple of logs on to the fire, but they didn't take well. They were damp. She went to the log pile and checked the rest to find they were in the same state. Christ, if she couldn't keep warm she'd die of hypo-thermia.

The wolf's deep call broke out again, filling the cabin. It sounded huge. She imagined the Hound of the Baskervilles galloping at the door and breaking it down. Then the baying stopped. Silence.

Huddled by the wood stove she kept an eye on the logs, terrified the fire would go out. Would Julia know what had happened? She hoped not, she'd go mad with worry, which in turn would make her sick, and she'd end up in hospital. Damn Lisa. It was all her fault, running away, hiding wherever she was. If it wasn't for her bloody sister, she would be safely tucked up at home with nothing more to concern her than which channel to watch on TV.

Tears filled her eyes and she scrubbed them away. She mustn't get depressed, mustn't give up. She had to keep her spirits high and prepare herself for an escape.

There was not a sound from the wolves. She hoped they'd gone away but for some reason she didn't think so. She could almost feel their presence closing in. She wished she had the length of thick fur that was Moke cuddled beside her, to help her keep warm and comfort her.

Abby was too cold to sleep, but she managed to drop into a light doze, trying to ignore her aching limbs and the way her face stung from where she'd ripped off the duct tape. She jerked awake when a solitary bark burst outside the cabin. It sounded like a command. Abby strained her ears. Gently a sound reached her, the barely audible padding of animals trotting on soft snow.

Abby hunkered closer to her pathetic fire, eyes fixed on the door. She told herself they couldn't break in but she still trembled.

Another piercing bark, so close she felt she could

185

have touched the animal. The candle finally splut-
tered out. The only light came from an ember the
size of a walnut glowing in the wood stove. Shuffling upright, teeth chattering and hands shaking,
Abby teased the ember into a one-inch flame and
fed it some kindling. She desperately tried to
remember what Cal had told her about wolves.

He had a lot of respect for the animals with their
intelligence and their affectionate family units.
Wolves, she recalled, rarely attacked humans
unless they were snared, when they would –
understandably – lash out.

She closed her eyes as she visualised Cal building up the camp fire each evening. He'd use hairy
lichen and punk for kindling: dried decayed wood
that smoulders when ignited. Then he'd carefully
add some birch bark for its resinous oil which
burned fast, and gradually built up the fire with
small twigs and branches before adding the larger
logs.

Hoping her memory was accurate, she picked
out a big log, soggy and soft, and kicked and
knocked away the outer portions until she got to
the inside and the flaky, dry and rotted parts that
was punk. Then she built a nest of bark, lichens
and punk beneath the logs, added a tissue from
her parka pocket and a couple of pine knots, and
lit the thing.

Twenty minutes later, it was crackling and spitting and Abby carefully banked it up with green
branches and decayed punky log to make sure it
didn't burn too fast. She hadn't realised she'd remembered so much from the expedition until
now, when she needed it. At some point she fell

asleep, she didn't know for how long, but when she awoke it was pitch dark, save for the fire, which was glowing deep and hard and red. No light leached from the crack in the door. Night had fallen.

She didn't need to add any more logs to the fire; without any windows, the small cabin had warmed enough for her to shed the sleeping bag and her parka. It would turn into a sauna if she wasn't careful. She was glad someone had installed a chimney, otherwise the cabin would have filled with smoke and suffocated her. She spent the night keeping an eye on her fire and listening to the wolves pad around the cabin.

The next day was spent trying to chip her way to freedom, working at the biggest crack at the corner of the door, but with only the edge of an aluminium can to help, she made little headway. For lunch she heated a tin of chicken soup and afterwards, arranged the cans in alphabetical order. Then she placed every item exactly around the cabin so she could put her hands on whatever she might need in the dark.

She pored over what she knew of Marie Guillemote's murder. She spent a lot of time considering MEG, which would replace the jet engine, and wondered what sort of fuel it might use. For some reason she kept hearing Lisa ranting about the oil industry. How short-sighted they were, how the world was going to run out of oil soon, how for every four barrels of oil consumed, just one barrel was found. Lisa was convinced that the energy crisis was well under way, but due to the fat oil-cats in their fancy houses having their heads buried in the sand, few people were doing anything about it.

Abby puzzled over this for quite a while. Lisa was passionate about the environment, why invent yet another engine?

Steadfastly, she refused to think about the fact the kidnappers might not return, that they'd crashed their snow machine and been tipped off the mountain, because she knew if she did, she'd go mad with fear. She scraped at the crack by the door, longing for a knife, and promised to buy herself one the second she was free so she'd never be stuck without a weapon or a set of decent tools.

Her nicotine cravings dropped dramatically the next day, and she noticed how much cleaner and nicer her mouth tasted, even though she hadn't got a toothbrush. Running her tongue appreciatively around her mouth, she promised herself that if she got out of here, she'd give up again. Permanently.

She thought quite a bit about Cal, and wondered – not for the first time – why he didn't wear a wedding ring. Some men hated jewellery, some men hated being pigeonholed, while others pretended they were single. Cal appeared to be the latter. He'd been hanging around Lake's Edge since she'd got there and hadn't mentioned Saffron once. Nor the fact that they might have had kids by now. And what did Saffron think of his lengthy absence? Did she take it all in her stride or was she at her wits' end?

And what about Lisa's husband? Who the hell

was he? Did he have anything to do with all this? Abby was still worrying over Lisa's elusive husband the following afternoon. She had just finished a mid-afternoon snack of warmed beans when she thought she heard something. Going to the door she pushed her ear against it, wondering if the men were returning. She couldn't hear the snow machine's engine and she pressed her ear closer, frowning in concentration. Eventually there was a faint crunching of snow, and then a snuffling sound followed by heavy breathing, and then the door gave an almighty shudder.

Abby sprang back, a shriek on her lips.

A snort and a growl followed. The door shook beneath another almighty pounding.

It wasn't a wolf or a human, she realised. It had to be a bear.

'Go home, bear!' she yelled. 'This food's mine! Go home!'

The bear gave a grunt, and started to circle the cabin.

She promptly recalled Cal telling her to store food so that bears couldn't smell or reach it. And not to keep food in her tent, not even a pack of mints, or toothpaste.

Abby hurriedly rinsed out the saucepan and can, but she knew it was too late. The animal would be hungry after its long hibernation.

She could hear the bear circling the cabin, stopping occasionally to thump the wooden walls. Abby prayed whoever built the cabin had made it sturdy and strong enough to withstand an attack. Oh, God. She remembered Connie's story about her friend in her wilderness cabin.

One day a bear tore the door off...

Her mouth dried up at the next thought. What if it broke the door down?

Abby hurriedly placed her empty cans, the tin spoon and saucepan to hand. Cal had told her that sometimes if you gave a bear a fright, facing it with something new that it might consider dangerous, it was possible it would turn tail and flee. She hoped her idea of chucking the tin cans at it and banging the spoon against the saucepan would work. Otherwise, she'd be bear meat.

More scrunching of snow, and the door shuddered again. 'Go away!' Abby shouted frantically. 'Leave me alone!'

The bear huffed and grunted.

She pictured its little piggy eyes searching for a fissure in the wood, where it could hook its four-inch claws and wrench open the door. Humans and bears, Cal said, had roughly the same eyesight, and bears were at least as intelligent as dogs. If a bear was determined to break into a car, or a cabin, it would find a way.

The door creaked and shook under another attack, and then suddenly, for no reason, silence fell.

Heart pounding, clutching her tin saucepan and spoon, Abby stared at the door. Maybe the bear was coming up with another plan. Maybe it was going to get a run-up and put its shoulder down, and charge at the door. Maybe...

She flinched at the grunting and thumping scrunch of snow. Trembling, sweat pouring, Abby listened to it diminish. It sounded as though the bear was departing, and in its place...

190

Her heart skipped a beat.

...was the clatter of the snow machine. She couldn't believe it. Barely thirty-eight hours after snatching her, the men were back. They had scared the bear away.

She waited until the snow machine stopped, and counted the seconds. Ten, twenty ... sixty... Three minutes passed before she heard footsteps crunching in snow.

Immediately she started thumping the door and yelling. 'Let me out! Please, I'll do whatever you want, just let me out!'

'Fucking calm down, will you? You don't, we leave you here.'

'I'm calm!' she assured them, glad she wasn't strapped to a lie detector. She'd never been less calm in her life.

'Holy crap,' the other man said. 'Will you look at these prints? They're big as a fucking elephant's!'

'Shut it.'

'Christ,' the man muttered. 'I'm fucking freezing out here even with the fucking suit. I look like a fucking astronaut. Next time I want to work in Miami. Never fucking snows there.'

'Since it was your idea to take this job, shut the fuck up and cover the door. I don't want her breaking loose.'

Abby heard the bolts being shot back, and then he barked, 'In the back of the room, hands up! We're armed, and if you try and make a break for it, we'll shoot you!'

'I'm right at the back, okay?'

Gradually the door inched open, flooding the

cabin with a bright, white light. Narrowing her eyes against the glare, she watched a man step inside, pistol in hand. He made a choking sound and raised his other hand to his nose.

'Jesus,' he said.

'Sorry,' Abby said. 'But there isn't a loo in here. Just a bucket.'

Abby was blinking, trying to adjust her vision to the light, but she could discern the outline that was the other guy a couple of yards from the doorway, and the shape of what she took to be a gun in his hand.

'Turn around. Hands on the wall.'

Abby complied.

'You move a fucking muscle, you get one in the leg. It won't kill you, but it'll sure hurt.'

'I won't move,' she promised, latching on to the fact he didn't want to be seen, and that maybe this meant he'd let her go because she wouldn't be able to identify him later. Aside from his height, which forced him to duck through the door, making him six foot or so, she hadn't a clue what he looked like.

She let him tie a cloth around her eyes and head. The relief it wasn't duct tape was immeasurable.

'Sit on the bed,' he commanded.

Abby sat. She heard him walk away. Then he said, 'Make the call.'

She was about to ask what call, when she realised he must be talking to his pal. Her thoughts went wild. She was being ransomed?

Nothing happened for the next ten minutes. She smelled cigarette smoke and heard the odd crunch of snow as the men waited. Then a phone rang. 'Yeah. Right, okay.'

Boots rang against the cabin floor. Something pressed against the side of her head. For a second she thought it was a mobile, but then realised it was much larger; a satellite phone.

'Say, hello,' he told her.

'Hello?'

'Abby?'

Abby felt as though she'd been thrown out of the door of a space shuttle and into freefall.

It was Lisa.

'Abby, are you okay? Are you all right? Oh, *fuck,* Abby, are you there?'

'Yes.' She had to struggle to stop herself from shouting. 'Yes, Lisa. It's me. I'm here.'

'They haven't hurt you, have they? God, please tell me–'

'I'm fine, I promise–'

'I'll get you back, okay?' Lisa was talking fast. 'Where are you?'

The phone was suddenly snatched away and Abby lunged after it, yelling, 'The mountains! I'm north up the haul road in the mountains!'

A hand shoved her shoulder and she sprawled to one side, still shouting, but then an arm went around her neck, a hand over her mouth, and she stilled.

'Shut the fuck up.'

Abby lay trembling, breath coming fast, hands clenching and unclenching.

'Yeah,' he said, and she assumed he was talking to Lisa. 'Fiveways, like we said. Six o'clock. Be there or we'll start messing with her like we said.'

193

There was a brief silence, then he said briskly, 'Get up.'

Abby rose.

'We'll do it like we did before. You fuck us around, we shoot you. Got it?'

'Okay. But can I put on my parka and scarf? They're on a hook on the back of the door.'

Boots clumped on the floor and when he shoved them at her she quickly put them on. Hand on her elbow, he pushed her outside.

Abby inhaled the tart, cold air. There was no sound except the murmur of wind in the topmost boughs. It felt like heaven being outside and away from the fug of wood smoke and human waste.

This time, her hands weren't tied and it was just the one guy who gripped her arm as she stumbled down the steep slope. Her boots crunched through a layer of frosty ice before sinking down deep, and she realised the mountain had been melting gradually during the day as the temperatures warmed, but froze again at night.

They hadn't gone far when over the rustle of branches came a high-pitched wail, like an injured animal.

'Fuck is that?' he said. All three of them came to a halt. Silence enveloped them.

'Christ knows,' said the other. 'But let's get the hell out. This place gives me the creeps.'

Again the creature wailed, and then came a snuffling grunt that Abby recognised. It was the bear. A blade of pure terror sliced through her. If the wail was what she thought it was, they were in deep trouble. Mother bears were fiercely protective and wouldn't hesitate to kill to defend their cubs. If the grizzly attacked, she had to make an instant choice. Pull up, back away, or do nothing.

'It's a bear,' Abby told the men, her voice high-pitched with fear. 'For Chrissakes don't move.' She scrabbled at her blindfold, waiting for one of the men to cosh her, but they didn't and it fell free.

Brief glimpse of two guys, one with a beard, one without. Neither were looking at her. They were staring at a grizzly no more than twenty yards away, a huge goddamn mother bear on all fours, who was staring back.

Mother bear looked as though she might be the world's biggest grizzly. Her coat was glossy and thick after her hibernation, but her rib cage protruded. Years of fighting had scarred her face. She must have weighed around 800 pounds.

From their left came the bawl of a cub.

'Don't move,' Abby pleaded, 'just don't move.'

'Fuck that,' the guy with the beard said, and raised his gun.

The bear immediately raised herself on her hind legs and stood there, immense. Slowly she peeled back her lips revealing two-inch-long teeth.

'Don't, please don't,' Abby begged, 'just keep still and she'll move on. We don't want to provoke her.'

Abby began inching backwards, judging how far she'd have to run to gain the cover of the trees, praying the men wouldn't do anything stupid, that the bear wouldn't see them as a threat. They weren't between the mother and the cub, she was certain, but if they weren't careful the bear might attack.

The bear snapped her teeth together. It sounded like an oven door slamming shut.

'Shit,' the man said. And, to Abby's horror, he fired his gun.

The bear didn't hesitate. She dropped down to all fours and charged.

Twenty-one

The bear came for them spraying snow on either side. She was fast. Her huge, chunky body moved with more fluidity and speed than a greyhound.

Abby forgot all about standing still and sprinted for the trees. She didn't look behind her as she ran, she put every ounce of effort into her race.

Several shots rang out, followed by the outraged bellowing of the bear, and a scream lodged in Abby's throat as she plunged across the slope, the snow dragging her, slowing her down.

Another bellow. The bawling of a terrified cub.

She risked a quick glance over her shoulder to see one of the men firing wildly as he ran, the other pelting in her footsteps, the bear right behind him, mouth foaming.

Christ, the bear was so close!

Gasping, adrenalin pumping, Abby pounded as hard as she could. No time to stop and look behind her. *She had to get to the trees. Try and hide.*

Another shot, and then she was in the shelter of the forest, fighting through the undergrowth, branches snatching and tearing at her clothes and hair, fingers and knuckles split and bleeding, and then she heard the man scream.

'Shoot it!' he shrieked. 'For Chrissakes, shoot it!'

Through the brush she saw a blur of limbs and fur. The bear was all over the man, dwarfing him. Another blast of gunfire, but the bear wasn't stopping. It grabbed the man's right arm and with a sickening, wrenching sound, plucked the limb clear of his body.

Abby stood paralysed with horror as the bear threw the man's arm aside and plunged on top of him, burying him deep in the snow beneath its massive weight, battering him with giant paws, snarling and roaring, going for his head, blood flying.

Finally the bear dropped its prey and looked around, blood dripping from its jaws. Abby didn't think she'd moved, didn't even blink, but to her horror the bear snapped its head to the forest and looked directly into her eyes. They were no more than ten feet apart.

Abby remained motionless.

If she ran, the bear would attack. If she climbed a tree, the bear would climb after her. If she waved her arms and made herself bigger like Cal suggested, she had no doubt it would kill her.

The bear's eyes were locked on Abby. Slowly, Abby let her gaze drop. A lowered gaze was less threatening.

'Keith! Keith, you okay?'

The tenuous truce between her and the bear was broken. The bear dropped her head, and came for her.

Abby felt a moment's disbelief, and then her

wits kicked in.

Play dead! Cal yelled in her mind.

The bear was crunching and thumping and nearly upon her.

Abby closed her eyes and flopped to the ground.

The grizzly thundered right up to her and stopped, huffing.

Abby's throat tightened. Her limbs went numb.

She felt the warmth of the bear's breath on the side of her cheek. It smelled of rotting, maggot-infested meat, but she didn't flinch, not even when she felt something warm dripping on her face.

I am dead, she told herself. *I am loose and floppy as a week-old corpse. I am as dead as one of Malone's fox pelts.*

The bear shoved her, making her tumble on to her side. Its strength was enormous. She felt as though she'd been pushed by an earth mover. The bear shoved her again, and then she heard it sniffing her face, and Abby knew it was trying to sense her breathing, to see if she was alive and still a threat, so she tumbled herself further and buried her face in the snow. Prayed the bear wouldn't see through her little ruse.

More sniffing. Another almighty shove. Her throat ached from trying not to scream. From somewhere came a wail from the cub. The bear stilled. Then it growled and whacked Abby's shoulder with a skillet-sized paw, making the air rush from her lungs. She was bracing herself for a full attack, her scream building, when the cub wailed again.

198

Huffing and grunting, the bear moved away.

Abby lay there, trembling, until she couldn't hear the bear any more. Cautiously, she raised her head and peered around. Nothing. She clambered to all fours. Her veins felt filled with water, her legs like strands of cotton and she had to use the trunk of a spruce to get herself upright.

She couldn't believe what had just happened.

Her face felt wet and she wiped it. Her fingers came away coated in bloody spittle.

She looked around again, and that's when she glimpsed a second grizzly in the brush. Smaller than mother bear, this one had a coat as blond as a haystack and was far swifter. It was silently creeping in the direction of the cabin.

Her eyes widened in dismay. How many more bears were out here? Abby urged herself to get the hell out. Moving as fast as she could she slipped through the trees until she came to the edge of the forest. She peeked out. She could see neither the grizzly nor the bearded man. But way down at the bottom of an almost vertical slope she spotted the snow machine.

Arms wide and flailing to keep her balance, she galloped straight for it, praying they'd left the keys in the ignition, praying she wouldn't meet another grizzly who would rip her apart as easily as tearing the drumsticks off a well-roasted chicken.

Crashing against the snow machine she gave a yelp of relief when she saw the keys were there. Jumping astride, she flinched when she heard another shot ring out above.

The bearded man was piling down the mountainside after her, yelling and brandishing his gun.

He was moving fast. Very fast.

Turning the key barely halfway, the engine roared into life. Abby accelerated cautiously, not wanting to get thrown off the machine as she U-turned to head back down the mountain.

The man was just ten yards away, running hard and fast, pistol held low.

Clamping her thighs around the seat she increased the throttle and the machine surged forward, spraying snow, and she was leaning into the first part of her turn when he brought up his pistol and aimed it straight at her.

'Stop,' he yelled, 'or I'll shoot you!'

A split-second image of him taping Lisa's eyes and mouth with duct tape seared her vision and she swung the machine back, straightened the handlebars and opened the throttle to the max. She accelerated straight for him.

'Stop!' he screamed.

Abby ducked as low as she could, engine howling, cold air blasting past, snow billowing.

Crack!

He hadn't hit her, thank God, and the snow machine was bouncing and leaping and she was aiming straight for him, his body standing firm, both arms outstretched, one hand cupping the other as he aimed his gun.

Shoot me, shoot me, she yelled at him in her mind, because if you don't I'm going to run you down.

Crack, crack!

She heard a metallic clank and she was nearly on top of him when he bunched his body and sprang

200

to his left, arms reaching, mouth stretched in a soundless yell.

He was too late.

The snow machine hit him squarely in the pelvis and flipped him into the air. His arms were spread-eagled, his legs twisted behind. His face was round with shock. He seemed to hang for a second and then he was plummeting on top of her.

Abby let go of the handlebars and flailed to one side, desperate to fling herself free of the snow machine but it was bouncing into the air and slamming into the snow and the next thing she knew they were airborne again and driving back down and then there was a long shuddering thump. Then silence.

Her breath returned with a rush. Gulping cold air she tried to get up but something was on her legs. Slowly she raised her head and looked around. The man was lying across her. He was face down in the snow, motionless. The snow machine was on its side, both skis facing her, engine stalled.

Abby carefully tested her legs to see if they were broken, but aside from an aching knee and a dull throbbing in her forearm, she'd come through pretty unscathed. Steadily she wriggled herself free, heaving at the man's shoulders and pushing with her feet until she was on her hands and knees beside him, gasping.

She studied the man for a few seconds. She didn't want to touch him in case he rose up and attacked her, but she couldn't leave him as he was. He hadn't been particularly good to her, but he hadn't been particularly bad, either. He hadn't beaten her senseless, or raped her. She was peculiarly grateful for that.

His hair wasn't long enough to grab into a fistful so she dug through the snow and found his chin and levered his head up until it was free. It was heavy, like hefting a bowling ball. A cut on his forehead bled down his face and across his beard. His eyes were shut. She hadn't a clue whether he was alive or not and carefully scooped an area of snow aside so his face wasn't buried in the stuff and he could breathe. She wasn't going to do anything else for him. He could take his own chances out here, along with his friend.

She glanced up the mountain, listening. Everything was quiet and still. Time to get the hell out.

Abby tried to right the snow machine, leaning her whole weight on the upper ski, but it barely moved. It was buried in the snow.

Briefly she contemplated heading back to the cabin for supplies, but just as quickly abandoned the idea. She didn't want to meet mother bear or her sidekick a second time. Boots crunching, Abby began to follow the snow machine's tracks down the mountainside.

It took a while before she regained control of her breathing, the trembling of her legs and hands. Her jeans were wet with snow, her shirt drenched in sweat. The trees and mountains seemed to glow with an extraordinary clarity around her, and she wasn't sure whether it was because she'd been locked up in the dark for two days or if it was her body's reaction to cheating death.

The track snaked down the edge of the mountain with thick forest on one side and a sheer drop on the other. Deep blue skies stretched as far as she could see, icy peaks all around, frozen streams spilling out of the snow-covered forests, their surfaces gleaming wet as they began to melt. She thought of Lisa and the panic in her voice.

Was Lisa headed to Fiveways, preparing herself to meet the kidnappers? Or was she working with the authorities and setting a trap for them?

No, Lisa would be doing this alone.

She tried to remember how long they'd driven up the mountain, and thought it might have been around an hour or so – which meant she had roughly thirty miles to go before she hit the snowy track, and then another mile or so before she reached the haul road. She checked her watch – three forty-five – and it was only then that she took in her predicament.

The sun would start setting around eight o'clock and the temperature would plummet to below freezing. She would have to walk through the night, maybe even jog, to try and keep warm. If she had a knife she could make a nest out of snow and spruce branches and shelter inside. But she didn't have a goddamn knife. And what about the wolves? It was all very well Cal saying they rarely attacked humans, but from the quantity of padding paws outside her cabin, the pack sounded *huge*. They might gang up on her for an easy meal. She didn't dare think about bears, or she'd remain rooted to the spot.

Abby sped up. She'd cross each bridge when she came to it. Meantime, she had to get some miles under her belt. She might come across another wilderness cabin where she could hide up for the night.

She walked for an hour without seeing any evidence of humankind. If it wasn't for the ski tracks in the snow, she'd have thought nobody had ever been here. It was clean and pristine and beautiful, and terrifying.

The mountains seemed to loom closer as the sun began to slide for their tips, taking on strange, menacing shapes, as though they wanted to crush her. Abby banged her gloved hands together and wrapped her scarf around her head, but her fingertips were cold, the tips of her ears freezing.

Slowly, darkness fell, and she was praying it would cloud over for the night, give her an extra couple of degrees in her favour, and that was when it happened.

She saw it out of the corner of her eye, and thought it was a jet contrail, maybe a lone cloud, until she looked up. Her breath caught in her throat.

A great arc of translucent pale, whitish green light flowed right across the sky. Unfurling into a broad, weightless curtain of silk, it rippled gracefully, delicate as gossamer, through the air. Abby forgot all about the cold, the wolves and bears, and she stopped and stared, completely absorbed. The aurora borealis. Northern lights. She'd thought she would never see it. And here she was, with the best seat in town.

She hadn't realised it moved. It was like watching a ballet dancer in slow motion. She reached up a hand. She felt as though she could touch it, it appeared so close. The curtain undulated gently as though it had felt the warmth from her hand, and folded back on itself before unfurling again, creating huge scythe-like shapes.

Abby felt a sense of awe seep into her, and with it, an immense feeling of being connected to the land, the sky, the world. A deep sense of peace filled her.

It was a moment of epiphany. She found herself making promises as she watched the miracle curl and fluctuate. I will reunite myself with Lisa and not force her to be someone I want her to be. I will let Cal say his piece and forgive him once and for all. I will have everyone over for Christmas lunch this year, and I will go to midnight mass and thank whoever you are for letting me live and see this miracle.

She was thinking about Cal and wondering if she'd be able to keep that particular promise, when she heard a shushing, scraping sound coming up the mountain, reminding her of skates on ice, and then she heard wood creaking, and the jingling of small bells. She immediately thought of Father Christmas on his sleigh, and wondered if she was hallucinating.

'Haw, George, haw!' A man's voice cracked through the still air.

He was terrifyingly close, just around the corner from the sound of it, and Abby was about to bolt for the cover of the forest when eight dogs came pelting around the corner. The man was standing on a sled behind them, headlamp blazing as he urged them forward, but the second he saw Abby, he cried to his team and the dogs immediately slowed to a stop. He fiddled with something briefly near his knees then came racing toward her, broad face anxious.

'I heard shots,' he panted. 'Are you okay? I saw the grizzly. I've git some binoculars, I was over there,' he waved a hand across the valley, 'training my team. I've been going like hell to get here, but I got chucked off when we came across a moose, took me ages to track down the damned dogs, nothing they like better than chasing moose.'

Abby didn't think she'd ever been so glad to see anyone before, and had to stop herself from hugging him.

'I'm Walter,' he added.

Walter was as wrinkled as a dried fig. Caverns and furrows were scored deep on his face, burned into the skin by the cold, the winds, and the sun. Like Big Joe, he was a Native, with almond eyes and black hair, but apart from that, he looked as western as herself with his big down jacket and fleece-lined boots.

'You are a *star*, Walter!' she exclaimed. 'I thought I was going to have to walk through the night!'

'Where's your vehicle?'

'Stuck.' Abby told him about her chase off the mountain, and backtracked to include the grizzly's attack, and her kidnap.

Walter's mouth dropped open revealing a couple of missing teeth along with some very dodgy dentistry. 'You're the woman they grabbed outside Lake's Edge?'

'That's me.'

'Well, holy heck!' He looked delighted. 'My friends won't believe my luck! Everyone's been looking for you – you're all over the TV, radio, newspapers. They've been going crazy.' Walter shook his head, grinning. 'And I get to be the hero who rescues you.'

Twenty-two

Walter turned the dogs around, a difficult process given the narrowness of the track, and involving a lot of untangling of traces and heaving of his sled. Then he bundled Abby in front of him, wrapping her legs in a length of lightweight caribou skin, with its hair facing inward.

'Traps air for added warmth this way,' he told her briskly before giving her his enormous fur hat with ear flaps the size of dustbin lids. 'Should keep the cold out.'

Standing behind her he urged the dogs down the mountain. 'It'll only take us a couple of hours if we take a short cut,' he told her. 'Then we can radio the troopers.'

He went on to tell her his village was called Raven's Creek, and that he was the only Native in the village who still kept a team of dogs.

'Everyone uses snow machines. Soon as they appeared, all the trails vanished. My father had a fit when he saw our way of life was just about over.'

They sped down the track. She could hear the patter of the dogs' feet on the frosty snow and their steady panting as they pulled them ahead. Unlike the plastic sled the kidnappers had used, this one was made out of wood and was sturdy and strong. The motion was incredibly soothing, along with the hiss of the runners on snow. Clouds of steam rose from the dogs' mouths, evaporating above their ruffs. Like Moke, the dogs were heavily coated and powerful, and from the way their tails waved, they appeared to be enjoying the run.

'Can't be doing with those snow machines,' Walter continued, 'not if you're serious about heading into the wilderness. They weigh a ton, they're impossible to manoeuvre over ravines and creeks, and as soon as it hits twenty below, the engine gets real cranky. And weak ice... Don't get me started. You try and free up one of them things once they're icebound.'

When they reached the valley the team veered sharply to the left, away from the kidnappers' ski tracks. The sled picked up speed. High above the endless spires of mountains and spruce, the stars shone with cold brilliance. Soon they were approaching a large, frozen river, about the width of two motorways, side by side.

'Short cut,' Walter informed her. 'Go round it, we'll be here all night.'

Nervously she asked if it would hold their weight.

Walter gave a chuckle. 'I learned how to read the colour of ice when I was knee high. But the best guides are the dogs. When they stray off course, it's because their paws feel changes in the moisture on the surface. A snow machine can't do that.'

As the sled bounced and slid across ribs of frozen water, he told her how to detect thin ice, how dark spots were to be avoided, and that she should steer clear of smooth patches and go for the large lumpy, heavy-looking peaks that were thick enough to support a 7-ton truck.

'Narrow valleys in between can crack under-foot,' he finished. River-crossing safely behind them, they raced toward Raven's Creek, the dogs barely skimming the surface of snow. They moved effortlessly, their gait smooth and elegant, all their tug lines taut.

The first sign they were nearing town was when they passed a gritty airstrip, banks of snow piled on either side. Drifts of fog were closing in, blanketing the stars and covering the mountain tops with pale gauze. Stray dogs darted up to the team, barking and nipping their heels. The team barked back, the sled bouncing and the bells jingling as they careered down the main street. A couple of people opened doors from rough-hewn log homes and yellow light spilled out on to the snow, looking warm and welcoming.

As they neared the end of the street, Walter shouted a command and the dogs veered left and slowed to a stop outside another log cabin, iden-tical to its neighbours aside from the ten dog kennels set among the spruce trees on the western side. Four huskies were pulling against their chains and yipping and baying, and the team happily joined in, creating a doggy cacophony that had her ears ringing.

She saw a satellite dish bracketed to Walter's front wall and as she looked further, she saw just about every cabin had one, which meant everyone had electricity and, given the telegraph poles, phones as well.

'Get yourself indoors,' Walter told her, plucking her out of the sled as though she was as light as a strip of balsa wood. 'Get warm.'

Setting the sled hook, Walter commanded the dogs to stay put, and quickly ushered her inside. The first thing that hit her was the smell: stale clothing, unwashed bodies, meat stew, urine, and just as she thought she recognised the distinctive odour of a butcher's, she took in the fresh moose skin hanging on the wall, still seeping blood, and the huge sections of carcass lying on the floor.

Walter introduced her to his wife, Kathy, and his five children, who all stared at her as though she'd landed from Mars. The cabin seemed far too small to house them all, and as she quickly scanned the room, she realised the kids shared one bed, while their parents had the other. A honey bucket stood in the corner and a colour TV blared out some game show.

There was no kitchen to speak of, just a container of water on a counter, and a wood stove, which had a pot of some kind of meat simmering on its top. For a second she couldn't put it all together. There was no fridge, no running water, no toilet, not even an outhouse, but they had satellite TV.

'Kathy, this is Abby. She'll be hungry.' Walter thumped to the phone in the corner. 'I'm calling the troopers.'

Abby stood by Walter as he made his call, stirring her bowl of watery-looking stew, wondering whether it was safe to eat or not. Kathy was making urgent eating motions with her hands, so Abby took a tentative bite. The meat was stringy and

210

tough, but to her relief tasted okay. She continued to eat while Walter got connected to Sergeant Pegati and explained he'd rescued Abby, and that yes, she was right here with him, looking just fine.

'No, we're a fly-in village... No. Fog is coming in...' He listened a bit longer, then said, 'Okay. Yeah, right,' and passed the phone to Abby. 'He wants a word.'

Walter went and started hauling sections of meat outside, letting vapours of cold air drift through the cabin while Abby spoke to Victor. He wanted descriptions of her kidnappers, where exactly she'd been held, where on the mountain the grizzly had attacked them – which involved Walter getting out a map and taking over the phone for quite a while – details of the white SUV, and how, precisely, she'd got away.

Finally Abby managed to get her own question across. 'Have you heard from Lisa?'

'She called to tell us she was in contact with the kidnappers and not to mess things up.'

'How did she–'

'Through an intermediary. And don't ask, we don't know who they are. We think they're using ham radios to keep in contact. It's the only way, aside from that radio station that broadcasts messages from village to village, which they'd find far too public.'

Abby's grip tightened on the phone. Who was this intermediary? Could it be Lisa's husband or was it someone else? And why hadn't they told her they were in touch with Lisa?

'Now, Abby, we need to know where the rendez-vous was meant to take place. We're hoping the third man might be there, waiting for an ex-change.'

Her mind started galloping. What about Lisa? Wouldn't she still be at Fiveways? She wouldn't know Abby was safe. Abby bit her lip. She wanted the police to arrest her kidnappers, but she didn't want them to arrest Lisa if they found her there.

A memory crashed through of Lisa waiting for her at the railway station in Oxford when she'd come down to visit from Leeds. Neither of them had mobiles then, and Abby had missed her train and was over three hours late. But Lisa hadn't gone home. She'd settled herself on a bench with a book, and waited.

'I don't know,' she lied.

She thought she heard a muffled curse, then the sounds of him talking to someone else. Walter came over, saying, 'Tell him visibility's over a mile, but I wouldn't risk it if I was him. I'd wait till morning.'

Abby gave Victor the flight report, to which he said, 'We'll send our chopper as soon as we can, okay?'

'What about the kidnappers? Won't they get away?'

'We've already got a vehicle on its way to see if they're still on the mountain. From Walter's description, we should find the cabin where you were held pretty easily once it's light.'

'Do you know where Connie is?' she asked. 'Is she all right?'

'Mrs Bauchmann is just fine,' he said, and for the first time she could hear the exhaustion in his voice. 'Although she's still shaken up about the attack, of course, along with having to walk over fifteen miles to get help.'

Abby could imagine Connie's verbal out-pouring. She'd dine off the story for years.

'She'll be glad to hear you're okay. She's been ... ah, quite persistent in keeping herself informed of events.'

Connie had, Victor went on to say, been abandoned by the third man the instant the kidnappers had driven off with Abby. He'd taken Connie's phone and gone off in the tractor, leaving her standing on the road alone with a disabled car. They'd found the tractor on the haul road where he'd either left a vehicle or been picked up.

'Quite a slick operation,' he remarked. 'Well organised. Three or four guys. All to swap you for your sister.'

'What do you mean, swap us?'

'Well, that's what we believe the kidnappers wanted. Your sister. Her research is pretty valuable, apparently. Which is why you were snatched. To draw her out.'

Abby felt a wave of dizziness. She'd been right. The kidnappers were after MEG.

'I know I asked you this before,' Victor said, 'but are you sure you don't know what Lisa was working on?'

'Sorry, no,' she lied, and hurriedly wound up the conversation. She was tired and might let something slip.

After she'd hung up, Abby turned to Walter and Kathy. 'Can I call my mother? I'll pay you. She's in England.'

Walter told her to go ahead, and went to put his

213

dogs to bed. She checked her watch to see it was early afternoon in Oxford. Perfect. The instant she heard her mother's voice, Abby's throat closed up. Julia was saying, Hello? Hello? and was about to hang up when Abby managed to force out the words, 'Mum, it's me, I'm okay, I got away and I'm safe.'

Julia promptly burst into tears. Surging wildly between relief, fright and worry, she fired questions at Abby, mostly about how she was, whether she'd been hurt at all, until finally, she began to calm.

'Abby, I am so relieved. I can't tell you... Yes, she's fine,' she said to someone else, obviously in the room with her. 'She's okay, she escaped, can you believe it?'

Abby heard Ralph's voice respond.

'He sends you loads and loads of love, he's beaming like a Cheshire cat.'

More reassurances all round, then Abby gave them a blow-by-blow report. When she finished, Julia sounded wary, almost hesitant.

'Don't you think you should come home?'

'I can't until I find Lisa.'

Small pause, then, 'I don't want to lose you both.'

'I know, Mum.'

A rush of cold air drifted over her as Walter came back into the cabin and took off his boots.

'You're very brave,' said Julia.

'I'm anything but that,' Abby replied on a sigh. 'I'm the biggest coward around.'

'No, you're not.' Her mother's voice strengthened. 'And I love you so very much... Please, darling, will you try and be careful?'

'I promise.'

Abby hung up, filled with admiration for Julia for swallowing her desire to have Abby home. She was one hell of a woman, her mum.

'All right?' asked Walter, and when she saw the concern in his deep brown gaze, she suddenly felt the strength rush out of her. She was, she realised, close to collapse.

'Sleep,' she said faintly. 'I'll be fine once I get some sleep.'

Kathy started bustling about, and despite Abby's protests, began preparing the kids' bed for her. 'They can sleep on the floor,' Walter said. 'They're used to it.'

The children didn't look at all perturbed, just continued to stare at her where they sat in a semi-circle in front of the TV, eyes wide and obviously fascinated by a six-foot Nordic-looking peasant dropping into their home. Kathy spooned Abby into the kids' bed, which was a nest of rancid blankets and animal skins with a huge dip in its middle. She didn't care how smelly it was, she was safe at last, and warm.

She lay with her head on a wolf pelt and drifted into an unsettled sleep, waking occasionally to hear Walter calling his buddies to come over and grab a hunk of moose, turn it into stew and 'eat the evidence' before the cops arrived. Moose, Abby realised, weren't meant to be shot at this time of year.

After Walter's mates had happily carted off the illegally procured meat, he settled into a chair with his ham radio, telling everyone across what

215

sounded like the whole of Alaska what a hero he was. It wasn't until his rescue began to take on epic proportions when she finally slid into unconsciousness.

'Flares!' Walter suddenly yelled, making Abby jackknife up in bed, hair in tufts, blinking wildly. 'Get the flares!'

The TV was still blaring, the lights still on. The kids scattered across the floor as Walter continued to shout. 'It's the middle of the night! What kind of crazy...? I can't believe it! Kathy, bolt the door and get the gun ready.' He shot a look at Abby. 'Just in case.'

Then he was gone.

'What's going on?' she asked Kathy, but Kathy was busy doing as her husband had told her, bolting the door and loading a shotgun, which she then held in both hands, facing the door.

'Kathy?'

'Airplane,' the woman replied. 'Here, nobody lands in the dark.' She shot the kids a look that had the eldest switching off the TV before scurrying with the rest of them for their parents' bed.

'Walter, he go light the strip. Help pilot to land.' This time Kathy looked at Abby as she spoke.

'He not sure if good man or bad man.'

216

Twenty-three

Abby tuned in to the faint buzz of an airplane. Oh, God. Was it the kidnappers? Had they seen the sled's runners in the snow and guessed where Walter had taken her, then somehow got hold of a plane? Abby leaped out of bed and went to the window. She saw several guys at the end of the street, running full tilt behind Walter. Each of them carried a shotgun or rifle. If it was the kidnappers, they'd have one hell of a welcome.

For the next twenty minutes Abby stood by the window, every sense fixed on the street. She thought she'd heard the distinctive sound of an engine throttling back as the plane landed, but couldn't be sure. All she knew was that she couldn't hear it any more. Kathy stood with infinite patience beside her, shotgun loaded, safety catch on.

Eventually they saw a group of men appear at the end of the street, walking easily, not rushing. Their shotguns and rifles were held loosely in one hand or strung across a shoulder. As they kept walking, individuals peeled away to enter their homes, leaving Walter and a tall guy with a shotgun crooked in his elbow, to walk on alone.

As they neared, Abby blinked and blinked, wondering if she was imagining things. The man with Walter was Cal Pegati.

She heard both men stamp their boots of snow

217

on the porch. Then the door swung open and Walter stepped inside with Cal on his heels. Cal propped his shotgun against the wall and didn't meet her eyes.

'What in God's name are you doing here?' she asked him.

'Nice to see you too, Abby.'

'But nobody flies in the dark!'

'Believe me, I wouldn't have done either, but for some obscure reason that I find hard to fathom, people are worried about you. I was in the area, I was told to get here. End of story.'

'I can't believe you risked your airplane like that,' grumbled Walter. 'You crazy?'

Cal's jaw tightened. 'Not when you take in the fact that Raven's Creek is a remote village, and that it won't take the kidnappers long to find the place, along with Abby. And since some people,' he loaded the word 'some people' with heavy emphasis as he looked straight at Walter, 'have been chatting like chimps on ham radios about her rescue, there's every chance they're already on their way.'

Walter hung his head while Abby stared at Cal. 'You came out here to protect me?'

'Have you heard from your sister?' he parried.

'You thought she'd be here?'

Cal sent her a narrowed look. 'Anything's possible.'

'Well, she's not,' Abby snapped. 'So you may as well leave, now you've checked.'

'I doubt if Lake's Edge is reachable under VFR any more.'

She asked the question by raising her eyebrows.

'Visual Flight Rules. I'll only leave when I've received clearance, and when I do, you're coming with me.'

'Your dad sent you, didn't he?'

Cal didn't respond, just stood there with his arms crossed, looking fed up. She glanced across at Kathy, who had been busying herself, tidying the stacks of smelly covers on Abby's bed, and now Kathy looked across at them.

'You two,' she said, 'you share. Big bed. No problem.'

Abby lay clinging to the edge of the bed, keeping as far from Cal as possible. She'd rather have slept outside in one of Walter's dog kennels, and although she knew she'd be insulting Walter and Kathy's generosity, at that moment she hadn't cared.

It was Cal who inadvertently made her change her mind.

'Don't worry,' his face cracked into a grin, 'I'll keep my clothes on, but only if you want me to.'

'Since I find you as attractive as a week-old codfish,' she snapped, 'sharing a bed won't be a problem.'

Famous last words, she now thought. She had perched herself right on the edge, fighting not to fall back into the dip in the middle, but she could still feel the heat of him rolling over her like waves, smell the odour of adrenalin and dried sweat from what must have been a fairly hair-raising flight.

She knew he was wide awake because he hadn't moved a muscle since he'd climbed in next to her. He'd lain like a felled tree without his usual

219

wriggling or tugging at the blanket. She guessed he was staring at the ceiling and, like her, wishing he was a million miles away.

Could he smell her above the reek of the cabin? She hadn't dared use the water while she'd been incarcerated for anything but drinking, just in case the men didn't return, and she knew she stank. Then she remembered their sharing a tent on the expedition. She hadn't bathed for two days, and was coated in sweat and dirt, but he hadn't minded.

Abby could feel the heat rise through her body at the memory, and she wanted to shift her position to disperse it, but she didn't dare. She didn't want Cal to think he was keeping her awake. She wanted him to think she didn't give a fig for him and was fast asleep.

A log shifted in the wood stove, flaring orange as sparks flew. She wondered about Saffron, and what excuse Cal had given for being here. What would Saffron do if she heard they'd shared a bed? Hit him over the head with a rolling pin? She certainly would. And she wouldn't believe him if he said 'nothing happened', not considering what had gone on before.

She peeped at the kids. Three of them had joined Walter and Kathy in their bed, and when Abby had offered to share with the remaining two, they'd looked so horrified, she'd given up trying to persuade them. The eldest and youngest were snuggled in a pile of skins and hides and blankets by the wood stove, and all she could see of them was one small, pale hand peeking out from beneath a wolf skin, and the shine of the eldest boy's jet-black hair.

She couldn't believe Cal was here. Had Victor really sent him to protect her? Then she remembered him asking about Lisa. He knew Lisa was alive, so why was he still looking for her? Did he need to present her in person to his insurance retainers or something? Whatever his reasons, she felt strangely glad he'd come. Probably because of the nice big handgun he'd pushed beneath his pillow. At least if the kidnappers arrived he'd be ready for them.

Eventually she closed her eyes and tried not to think about the way Cal used to cup her breast in his hand when he fell asleep. Without realising it, she sighed.

'Can't sleep?' Cal whispered.

Her skin tightened all over. Her muscles went rigid.

'Neither can I.' His voice was rueful. 'I wonder why.'

Abby concentrated on breathing evenly and deeply, even though her heart was banging away like a big bass drum.

'Sweet dreams, Abby.'

He rolled over and although she felt fingers of icy air dart over her neck and shoulders, she didn't move.

She had no idea how long she lay there when she heard Cal's breathing turn deep and regular. She'd forgotten how quietly he slept.

Twenty-four

The sun had disappeared behind the horizon and it was getting colder, re-freezing as the heat left the tundra. Roscoe had curled himself into a ball and tucked his tail over his nose to keep warm. Lisa wished she could do the same, but she couldn't relax, not yet.

She'd arrived at Fiveways an hour early and scouted the area before choosing her vantage point: a small rise where she could easily see the track from the haul road as well as the rendezvous site. There were no trees or shrubs to impede her view. The whole area as far as the eye could see was flat and featureless and covered in snow.

She checked her watch again to see three hours had passed since the deadline. A blue Ford Expedition had turned up on time, but nobody stopped the engine, and nobody climbed out.

As far as she could tell there was only one guy inside. Short-cropped military-style hair, white-winter camouflage suit; one of the guys who'd shot Marie. She made a mental note of the number plate and tried to ignore the anxiety rolling through her.

Where was Abby? Why wasn't the man bringing her out for the exchange? Why was there only one guy?

She wondered if she should shoot him if he got out of the car. She could shoot rabbits, deer and moose; could she shoot a man? She could try and wound him, get him to talk. She thought this over for quite a while, but although she was a fairly good shot it still carried risks, like he might move at the last second and she could hit a major artery. No, she decided. She wouldn't let it come to that. Not yet, anyway.

The man sat in his car for exactly forty minutes and twenty seconds before he climbed out. He was holding an assault rifle. She ducked low as he skirted the area. He didn't move far from his vehicle. Sensible man. He knew she'd be watching him, and that she'd probably be armed.

Finally, he left. She listened to the engine fading and then it was silent. Nothing but acres of still, cold white.

She wanted to scream with frustration, bang her fists on the ice, but she kept her anger and fear tight inside. Ranting and raving wouldn't help Abby, but a clear mind might.

Rummaging through her pack she pulled out a high-energy bar. Thank God for Big Joe. When they'd met up on the haul road, the first thing he'd asked was if she was hungry, and handed her a box of goodies. She hadn't had anything sweet for ages, and it tasted fantastic.

While she ate, she thought over everything that had happened. She wasn't pressed for time. She could sit here all night if she wanted. She'd come fully prepared and had the means to build a fire. She had food and ammunition, her big caribou skin and fur hat and gloves.

Lighting a cigarette, Lisa ran through every 'what if' scenario she could think of, including

Abby getting injured, Abby being tortured, Abby dying, but ever the optimist ended up with, 'what if Abby escaped'.

Her sister had never been the sharpest pencil in the box as far as Lisa was concerned, but she was tenacious and determined, and had a dependable strength that could move mountains.

If Abby knew about the rendezvous, if she thought there was the remotest possibility Lisa was at Fiveways, nothing would stop her until she got here.

Lisa decided to wait for her. For as long as it took.

Twenty-five

Cal had his elbow crooked over her ribs, his arm resting between her breasts. She could feel the warmth of his breath against her neck. Moment-arily confused, Abby wondered if she was dream-ing, but then she saw a pair of sombre brown eyes staring at her, just inches away.

One of Walter's children.

She glanced down to see she was holding Cal's hand in both of hers, tucked beneath her chin. Abby shot out of bed like a scalded cat, and Cal reared upright, hair askew, eyes bleary, and the next instant he had his gun in his hand. 'What is it?' he demanded.

'Nothing.' Abby tried to appear insouciant. 'Just need to go...' She looked at the honey bucket and amended it to, 'get some fresh air.'

'Not alone, you're not.' Cal scrambled out of bed and pushed his feet into his boots. The gun went into his waistband.

'Do you have a permit for that thing?'

He looked puzzled. 'Who says I need one?'

'Are you telling me anyone can carry a concealed weapon out here?'

'Sure. I mean there are rules, like you already have permission to legally carry a firearm, and you have to inform peace officers you're carrying, and not take a gun into a bar or school yard. Oh, and you have to be over twenty-one and not a convicted felon. You think I qualify?'

'Apart from the felon part,' she muttered, pulling on her boots.

'Please, Abby,' he groaned. 'Will you stop busting my balls?'

'You put them in the vice.'

'Jesus.' He stalked outside.

Abby followed him past the dog kennels, her muscles aching and groaning. She felt as though she'd run a marathon the day before. As soon as the dogs saw them, they barked and whined and leaped over and around their kennels, chains clanking, their tails going like crazy. She paused to pat one of the dogs and when it collapsed to its side, forepaws tucked against its chest, gave its tummy a rub.

'Wish you were Moke,' she told it. 'He's lovely, my boy.'

Except he wasn't her dog, he was Lisa's. And since Lisa never gave up anything she owned without a monumental fight, he would stay Lisa's until the day he turned up his hairy-padded toes. She would, she thought with a pang, miss him dreadfully when she went back to England.

Cal ushered her into a clump of poplars and, as he'd done when they were on the expedition, took a tree well away from her, giving her loads of privacy. She shivered as she pulled down her trousers, baring her behind to the chill air. Past the tree trunks she could see strings of fog clinging to the village, but just off the horizon a brightening haze indicated the sun was trying to break through.

Back in the cabin she let Kathy give her a cup of coffee and she took it outside and away from the thick smell of sleeping bodies, and worse.

'What happened?' Cal was standing beside her, gesturing at her forehead.

'What?'

Before she could move he'd reached up and was brushing her eyebrows gently with his forefinger.

'What's wrong?' She felt alarmed.

'Ah.' He let his hand drop, looking uncomfortable. 'You haven't looked in a mirror lately.'

'What's *wrong*, dammit?'

'Your eyebrows ... well, they're not quite as they used to be.'

She remembered ripping the duct tape from her face and the stinging sensation that had haunted her the first night. 'Are you telling me I haven't any?'

'No, no,' he reassured her. 'You've some. Just not as many as before.'

Promising herself not to look in the mirror until they'd grown back, Abby told him about the duct tape. She didn't add anything further, like how terrified she'd felt being locked up alone in the cabin, in case her voice trembled and she gave herself away. She didn't want his sympathy, and he seemed to sense that, because he turned his gaze to the sky.

'It'll be clear in an hour or so,' he said. 'I'll let the cops know I'll be flying you back.'

Abby turned her tin mug around in her hands. 'Would you fly me somewhere first?'

'Not until the ABI have debriefed you.'

'What if I told you I know where Lisa is? Would you take me there?'

There was a long silence while he studied her. 'It depends.'

Abby decided to go for broke. She told him about the rendezvous the kidnappers had arranged, and how she didn't want the cops to arrest Lisa if she was still there. 'Do you know where Fiveways is?' she finished.

'Yes.' He gazed down the street, his expression unreadable.

'So you'll take me?'

'Fiveways isn't a town or village,' he said. 'It's where five trails meet just south of Glacier. I can't see anyone spending the night out there. It's cold, remote and bleak as hell.'

Abby thought of Lisa's skijoring and how she'd camp out between wilderness cabins, and said, 'She's there. I know it.'

Cal gave her a disbelieving look.

'Come on, Cal. At least let's check the place out.'

'It won't make us particularly popular.

Especially with my father. Not only have you lied to the cops, but we could be messing up a crime scene.'

Abby waited while Cal frowned, obviously weighing up the pros and cons. Now the fog was lifting she could see several children heading for a tiny school, built, like the rest of the town's dwellings, out of rough logs. Walter was, she'd learned, the only teacher in the one-room school, but he didn't mind working alone since Alaskan teachers were generally some of the highest paid in the United States.

'Okay,' Cal said eventually. 'But you owe me.'

She turned to go back inside the cabin but stopped when he put a hand on her arm. 'I'd like to talk about what happened on the expedition.'

'Later, Cal.'

'Why not now?'

'Because we've got to radio the ABI.'

She went back inside the cabin but not before she caught the look of frustration on his face. She almost felt sorry for him, but mistrust had hardened her to a point where she found it easier to push him away. Sadly, the forgiving, beatific feeling she'd experienced when she'd seen the aurora borealis had vapourised, just like the magnetic cloud itself.

Demarco agreed to meet Abby at the strip when Cal landed.

'ETA Lake's Edge two p.m...' Cal glanced at his watch. 'Yes, I know it only takes an hour, but our ETA remains the same... No, I'm not...Yes...' Cal looked harassed. 'Our ETA Lake's Edge is two

228

p.m,' he repeated firmly and put the still squawking receiver down.

'Christ.' He ran a hand down his face. 'She's going ballistic – wants to know why it's going to take us so long to get there.'

'But you didn't tell her.'

'No.'

She went to him and touched his arm. 'Thank you.'

He looked at her hand. 'Fat lot of good that's going to be when I'm stuck behind bars.'

By the time they arrived at Fiveways, it was just after midday. Cal had flown them in his Cessna to Glacier, where he'd managed to cajole one of the locals into loaning them his four-wheeler for fifty bucks.

They hadn't spoken much after they'd left Walter's, and she was surprised when Cal talked her through the pre-flight routine, explaining each step in non-technical terms. Interest piqued, she found herself asking questions, and when they rolled to the end of the icy runway, he paused before take-off to explain what he was planning, when he would add power, waiting for the plane to gain speed, at which point he would pull back on the controls.

He did exactly as he said he would and although she still clutched the sides of her seat in white-knuckled fear, Abby was ready for the swoop as they lifted into the air. Cal's hands were strong and steady on the yoke, his demeanour calm and capable, and as he flew, he pointed out key flight instruments, so she gained a basic

229

understanding of what they were telling her. She still couldn't relax but she did, amazingly, feel a fraction safer. Just a fraction, mind you; she doubted she'd ever feel comfortable flying the equivalent of an aeronautical mini across the sky.

'Thank you,' she said when he'd finally come to a stop at Glacier. 'That wasn't as scary as it could have been.'

'I thought I'd try the kid-glove approach.' He grinned. 'Dad told me about Mac flying you guys to his cabin. I heard you screamed.'

'No, I didn't!'

'Well, a muffled squawk, then. But he gave you top marks for not panicking big time.' Cal stopped grinning and put his head on one side, looking at her appreciatively. 'You're a brave woman, Abby McCall. I like that.'

Flushing, feeling awkward, she looked at her knees. 'And I'd like you to get me to Fiveways. If it's not too much trouble, that is.'

'Before we go, can we stop for a few minutes so I can say what I want to say?' His tone was light but she knew he was pushing for The Talk About Us.

'Can't it wait? I want to see if Lisa's there.'

'Okay. Let's talk about it on the return flight.'

Abby unclipped her harness and cranked open the door. God, the man was persistent.

Forty miles from Lake's Edge, Fiveways was just half a mile from the haul road and, as Cal had said, cold and bleak as hell. Miles of open snow-clad tundra stretched beneath a hazy white sky and the air smelled clean and pure as iced water.

There was nowhere to hide out here that she could see, no trees or bushes or piles of boulders, and Abby felt her spirits sag. It was the perfect place for a rendezvous; you could see a vehicle approaching from any direction for at least two miles. Had Lisa turned up and been snatched by the kidnappers?

Head down, Cal started walking the area, studying various tracks and footprints, and Abby trudged to the point where the five tracks converged, but the snow was unmarked. She looked around, trying to think what might have happened.

'Abby,' Cal called her over. 'See this?' He was standing next to a set of vehicle tracks that stopped twenty yards short of the junction. 'They sat here a while with their heater running.' He pointed out several icy patches in the snow where drips of hot water had fallen from the exhaust. 'They got out, though, had a look around, but didn't go far.'

He looked into the sky then back at her. 'Let's split up, cover more ground. See if we can find any evidence Lisa was here.'

Abby crunched across the tundra. The whole area was covered in muskeg, thick clumps of grass more than a foot high, which had been eroded around the base. It was impossible to set a measured pace, or take even two steps without looking where she put her feet. There were rocks and holes to traverse and the last thing she needed was a sprained ankle. Halting every five yards or so, she scanned around, searching for tracks, but the place was pristine. The silence was

231

cold and thick as whipped cream and she could hear her pulse humming in her ears.

An hour passed before she heard Cal yell out to her. She turned to see she'd walked further than she'd thought, and that he was well west of their four-wheeler, partly hidden by a small rise. He was waving an arm and beckoning her over.

When she got there, he didn't say anything, just pointed at the ground where the snow had been compressed in a large circle. Cigarette butts littered the area. Marlboro. Lisa must have smoked a whole pack sitting here.

'She chose a good place, considering,' remarked Cal. 'One, she's behind them, and two, if she ducked down she was far enough away that only someone twisting round and looking at her at precisely that moment would have been able to see her. And even then, if she ducked quick enough, they'd be hard pushed to believe they weren't imagining things.'

'The tracks look fresh,' Abby remarked.

'She could have left two minutes ago, or two hours,' Cal said. 'But my guess is she left at sunup. She'd have been freezing.'

He looked at where their loaned four-wheeler sat near the tracks they'd followed. 'Whoever was in that car either got a call saying you'd escaped or left after you didn't turn up at the prearranged time. There's only one set of prints leading to and from this hideout, so it's a pretty safe bet Lisa wasn't seen and got away okay.'

Abby swung her gaze around the area, almost in hope that Lisa might pop up from behind a tussock, but nothing moved.

Abby spent the short journey back to Glacier in silence. Part of her felt immeasurably relieved Lisa was alive and obviously okay, but the other felt small and scared. Where was Lisa now? Did she have MEG and the lab books? She worried over Lisa's intermediary, then Lisa's husband, trying to think who they might be, until her head started to ache.

Soon, they were airborne again, clattering across a gleaming swathe of white. Abby craned to look through the window, checking the state of the break-up. Everywhere was still covered in snow, but the dark cracks at the edges of the lakes and rivers had broadened and she could see shades of light grey that Walter had warned her about, where the ice had thinned.

She recognised Coldfoot from her flight with Mac, and knew they were only twenty minutes from Lake's Edge and a hot bath. God, she couldn't wait to smell like a human being again rather than a dead moose.

'Abby,' Cal spoke to her through her head-phones, 'I want to talk about us. Look, something happened when we were on that expedition... I thought it was . . . well, just sexual attraction, but it was something more...'

She turned her head to look at the side of his face. He was staring straight ahead.

'How's your wife, Cal?' she asked him.

He closed his eyes briefly.

'Dead,' he said.

Twenty-six

Lisa accelerated up the haul road, cursing at her own stupidity. Hadn't she learned anything over the past four years? Jesus. There she'd been, hunched in her shallow little hidey-hole, when Abby had rocked up. With Cal. She couldn't believe she'd made such a basic mistake.

She hadn't put herself in Abby's shoes to see how she'd be feeling, let alone what she might be thinking. She had assumed Abby would get someone to show her where Fiveways was on a map and come to the rendezvous alone, because that's what she would have done.

Of course Abby would bring someone. She didn't know the area, and she certainly didn't feel comfortable in the wilderness. She may have enjoyed her little expedition in the Brooks Range, but only because there was a permanent camp with its luxuries, and a full-time guide with a rifle in his hand to protect her.

Thank God she hadn't reacted instinctively when she'd seen Abby. For a second she'd nearly leaped to her feet, her throat swelling with a shout of joy, but then she saw the tell-tale lump at the rear of Cal's jeans. He was carrying a gun.

Gravel spat beneath her tyres as Lisa accelerated around the next corner. She didn't think Cal had seen her, but she couldn't be sure; he had the eyes of a hawk. She hadn't dared leave a message for Abby. She couldn't be sure Cal hadn't been corrupted. MEG was worth such a lot of money, even friends could turn on their own.

She would have to find another way of contacting Abby. And soon.

Time was running out.

Twenty-seven

Abby stared dead ahead through the aircraft's windscreen. She could think of nothing to say.

'Saffron died six months after you left Alaska. I wrote and told you, but like all my letters, that one came winging its way back unopened.'

A jet of horror as Lisa's voice echoed through her mind.

Saffron will die *if she hears about this.*

'She knew?' Abby managed.

'No.' Cal shook his head. 'Why didn't you answer my calls, Abby? I went mad when you left.'

'I'm not a home wrecker,' she said. She wondered how the woman who'd been his childhood sweetheart, and a friend to Lisa and Diane, had died, but hurriedly turned her mind away from that train of thought. She'd done the best she could for Saffron by leaving the country and refusing Cal's attempts to contact her, and although she felt unsettled and off-balance that the woman had died, she knew it wasn't her fault.

Cal glanced at the instruments then across at her. 'Abby, you have to believe I had no intention

235

of having an affair. It never crossed my mind, not once, but when we met I found myself doing something I thought I'd never do...'

He paused and Abby rolled her head back. A tidal wave of exhaustion washed over her. She didn't have the strength to lift a toothpick let alone fight with him. 'Oh, go on, then,' she told him irritably, 'get it over with.'

He glanced at the aircraft's roof as though choosing his words before he spoke, then did some lengthy throat clearing.

'Saffron came from the Yukon-Kuskokwim delta–'

'She was a Native?'

'Yup. I won't say I didn't love her, because I did.'

His tone wasn't defensive or hesitant. He was simply stating the facts.

'But the thing is, and I'm not making excuses... Well, I guess I am, but... Shit... She was sick as a young kid. Really sick. Chronic coughing, asthma, respiratory problems, but when her parents moved her away from the area, she got better. When we met, she was fine. But then she got sick again. She was ill for six years before she died. We were only married for eight.'

She felt him glance at her but she kept her gaze firmly on the horizon.

'It was...' He took a breath. 'Awful. The doctors couldn't help, nor the hospitals... I looked after her as best I could, but there was nothing I could do. I remember picking up a colleague from the airport one day, and I went to the Alaska Airlines desk and nearly bought a ticket to L.A. I didn't want to go home, to see her like that, someone who'd been so wilful, so *strong*, struggling for breath, day after day...'

He closed his eyes briefly.

'And then I met you.'

'Yes.' Her voice surprised her. It was gentle and understanding. Well, it would be. She knew what he must have been going through having cared for her mother. She'd hit that same breaking point, and not just once, but several times.

'I made a mistake.' His voice went flat. 'It was the first time in three years I'd spent time with people who didn't know about Saffron, people who didn't ask after her all the time or look at me with pity. I felt as though I had my life back, but of course I didn't. I pretended I did, though. I buried myself in that expedition without any thought of the consequences. I hadn't felt so released, so *alive* in so long... I didn't care that I hadn't been ah, entirely truthful. Until the day we came back. Then I realised what I'd done.'

Neither of them said anything for a few minutes. The airplane gave a little lurch starboard, but quickly resumed its smooth ride.

'You left before I could explain,' Cal said.

'So I'm the one to blame?'

'No, I am. But if you hadn't stormed off and frozen us out...' He gave a long sigh, and fell silent.

Abby considered what might have happened if she'd confronted him instead of fleeing the country, but she didn't see that it would have made any difference, no matter how strongly he felt. It came back to the same old thing. He'd been *married*.

'I wrote to you,' Cal said.

237

Three letters, which she'd sent back, unopened. There had been nothing more until two years later, when he'd sent one letter a month for almost a year. She now realised this must have been well after Saffron's death, when he'd finished grieving. She hadn't had the courage to read them. No matter what he had to say, she knew it would hurt too much to relive the past, so she'd sent those back too. Finally, he'd given up. Despite the whole sorry mess, she couldn't say he hadn't tried to make amends.

'So,' he said, 'can you forgive me?'

She twisted her fingers together, wanting to forgive him, unable to. She didn't respond, and Cal didn't push her.

They spent the remainder of the flight in uneasy silence.

Demarco and Victor were waiting for them when they landed. While Cal scribbled in a book, recording the flight, Abby went to meet them.

'Glad to see you're okay,' Demarco said, and shook her hand.

'Me too,' Abby responded with feeling.

'You did good to get away. Real brave.' Demarco gave her a couple of affirming nods. 'We're real proud of you.'

Victor looked as though he wasn't sure how to greet her and settled on clearing his throat before shaking her hand. 'You've got grit in you, girl,' he said. 'Nice going.'

Demarco escorted her to the Ford Explorer while Victor went and had words with Cal. Buckled up in the back, she couldn't hear what they were saying, but from their body language she could see they weren't happy with each other. Victor was making stabbing motions with his hands, Cal staring dead ahead and not looking his father in the eye.

Abby studied the aircraft parking area. When Mac had flown her in it had been empty aside from the AST helicopter, but now there were two more choppers: a Bell 205 and a red and white Astar 350B with OASIS OIL decals on its doors.

'Here, I brought this for you.'

To her amazement, Demarco brought out her day pack. Inside were her purse, mascara, lighter and cigarettes. Nothing was missing as far as she could tell.

'They left it behind. Lucky for you.' Demarco turned and yelled at Victor to hurry up, which made Victor stab a finger at Cal's nose before sprinting for the car.

Victor sat with Abby in the back while Demarco drove. Behind them, Cal tagged along in his black Dodge Ram. When Demarco cracked open a window, tilting her head to catch some fresh air, Abby cringed. She had no doubt she smelled as bad as Malone. 'Sorry,' she said. 'I'll be fine after a bath, I promise.'

Demarco looked at her in her rear-view mirror, her features softening. 'It must have been tough. Can't be sure how I'd have reacted in the same position. Being alone, not knowing exactly what was going on... If you need to talk to a counsellor at some point, we can put you in touch with the right authority.'

Abby didn't think any amount of talking would

make her believe what had happened. Already it felt like a bad dream; distant, as though it had happened to someone else.

'We'd like to discuss exactly what happened at HQ,' Victor said. 'Do you feel up to it? We don't want to add to your trauma.'

She didn't feel traumatised, just absolutely and totally exhausted. Maybe she'd turn quietly insane once she'd caught up on sleep, but right this minute she felt perfectly normal.

Victor studied Abby carefully. 'Would a debriefing be okay? I don't want to be pushy, but we find the fresher the experience, the better.'

'Sure. If you can stand the smell.'

His eyes crinkled at the corners. 'That's great.' The crinkly eyes stretched into a smile. He nodded several times, then turned his head to look out of the window.

She studied Victor cautiously, wondering if she trusted this new cuddly persona. She wasn't sure if she preferred the grey-stubbled antagonistic hunter; at least she knew where she stood.

Demarco turned right at a T-junction to head into town, shuddering over a set of potholes that made Abby's teeth rattle along with a set of keys dangling from Victor's belt.

'I spent a lot of time thinking in the cabin,' Abby ventured after the vehicle had stopped bouncing. 'You want to know what I think?'

Victor widened his eyes slightly and the sudden resemblance to Cal made it hard to look at him, so she fixed her gaze outside.

'I think Peter Santoni's behind all this. He's the disgruntled scientist Thomas and Lisa shut out of their research. He was very bitter about being chucked off the project, especially since he'd worked on it for so long.'

'So we heard,' Victor was nodding.

Abby blinked in surprise. He was actually *sharing* something with her?

'Do you know what the project was?' Victor asked. 'We're having trouble finding out anything about it. Both Thomas and your sister were obsessively secretive.'

Abby wanted to tell him about MEG, but didn't dare after Connie's warnings. She couldn't risk betraying Lisa's dream, at least not yet. Prudently, she gave a shrug and muttered, 'No, sorry,' keeping her gaze firmly outside. She'd never been very good at lying and Victor would see right through her.

The car made another turn, slush spraying with wet, slapping sounds up its sides.

'Santoni went to the same university as your sister,' Victor said. 'We thought he might have something to do with that professor your sister accused of murder, but it's no go. He'd left way before all that happened.'

'You've found Crowe?'

He shook his head.

They hit a patch of permafrost and Abby grabbed the door handle, bracing her knees against the back of Demarco's seat as the vehicle rocked and bounced.

'Sorry,' said Demarco, glancing at Abby in her rear-view mirror.

Abby gave a quick smile to say it was okay, and decided to take advantage of this newly cooperative atmosphere.

'Did you find the men who kidnapped me?'

'They'd gone by the time we arrived,' Victor said, 'but one turned up at Fairbanks hospital at dawn this morning, mauled by a grizzly. He lost an arm in the attack.'

'He's alive?' She was astonished.

'His friend obviously had some training. We're thinking maybe military. He would have died otherwise.'

'What about the bear? Is it okay?'

Abby didn't want mother bear dead, even if she had nearly killed her. She'd only been protecting her cub, and the mountains were, after all, her territory.

'The park ranger we sent up believes it didn't even get hit. A bear's a big target, but when you're running away, it could be the size of a barn and you can miss it out of sheer terror.'

'What about the other guy? The one I hit with the snow machine?'

'We believe he rang the third man to collect them from the mountain. They dumped their pal outside the hospital, and vanished.'

'At least you've got one of them,' she said, thinking it over. 'Will he talk?'

'Oh, yes,' Victor said, and she took gratification from the steely determination set on his face.

It didn't take long until they came to the scattering of homes that were the outskirts of Lake's Edge, and Abby smiled at the town's sign. Four planks of roughly sawn wood were nailed on to a sturdy wooden pole, the white letters tilting unsteadily on each plank as though painted by someone who'd been drinking at the Moose for a week.

Welcome. To beautiful. Downtown. Lake's Edge.

She felt a rush of affection for the place. Probably, she thought ruefully, because she was traumatised.

As Demarco approached the school she stuck her foot on the brake. 'Ah, shit,' she said. 'How the hell did this happen? It's like a goddamn circus out there! I thought you said nobody knew we were bringing her in!'

Victor rebuked the trooper with a look. 'We had as much hope of keeping Abby's arrival a secret as flying to the moon, you know that. So don't take it out on me, okay?'

'Sorry,' Demarco grunted. 'Shall I go round the back?'

Abby saw the school's steps were crowded with people. She recognised Big Joe, Connie, Diane, even Mac the pilot was there. For a second she thought she didn't recognise the others, but as she looked closer, she began to realise that although she hadn't spoken to them, she knew most of them by sight. They were the people who'd searched for Lisa on the mountain and who had, according to Cal, searched relentlessly for her when Connie had finally staggered into town. Their community spirit was incredible, and she was suffused with affection for them.

'Back it is. Let's give her some time before–

'No,' Abby interrupted. 'I want to go in the front. They're my friends.'

Victor cut her a sideways look and shrugged. 'Your call.'

When Abby stepped out of the car, the crowd gave a cheer. Demarco and Victor struggled to keep Abby from being swept away as people greeted her. Surrounded by grins and smiles, her back was clapped, her hand shaken. Connie swept her into an embrace. It was like being hugged by a giant goose-down pillow.

'Dearest, I've been so *worried.*'

'You're okay?'

'Aside from the fact my feet are simply *covered* in blisters, I'm in the peak of health...'

Then Diane was there, hugging her tightly and kissing her cheek. 'I'm sorry,' Diane said. She was on the verge of tears. 'I just found it hard, you know, with Saffron ... but when those men got you, I realised what a bitch I've been. Lisa would have me strung up if she knew.'

Abby didn't have time to reply because the next second Mac had her in a bear hug that lifted her to the tips of her toes. 'Thought we'd arrange a welcome. Diane's doing a bit of a party for you later. Celebration.'

'Thank you all so much,' she told them, impossibly moved, voice thick with tears. 'You're all wonderful, you really are.'

A man with a microcassette recorder appeared in front of her, eyes glittering with excitement. 'Do you know who kidnapped you? Were you scared?'

'Oh, shut up, Frank,' said Mac. 'Go interview your ass.'

Frank, it transpired, was the only representative from the media in town, and he wasn't going to give up that easily. The recorder was about an inch beneath her nose.

'Are you happy to be back?'

The crowd began shouting Frank down but Abby held up two hands, halting the cacophony. 'I'm *very* happy to be back,' she said into the recorder. 'And although it wasn't the best experience in the world, I'm in extremely good shape. I just need a decent meal, and lots of sleep, then I'll start searching for Lisa again. She's out there somewhere, and I'm going to find her.'

Everyone nodded gravely, and Abby looked across the crowd at Big Joe. 'How's Moke?' she mouthed.

He gave her one of his enigmatic nods, which she took to mean the dog was just peachy.

When they eventually fell inside the school corridor, it was like falling into an empty church it felt so quiet.

'Now, what can we get you?' asked Demarco. 'Are you hungry? Thirsty?'

'A biscuit or something would be good,' Abby said. 'I missed breakfast.'

While Demarco trotted off, she followed Victor to the briefing room. The same white board was there but, like last time, it was turned away so she couldn't see how the three scenarios were going. Victor sank into his usual place behind the desk, she took the chair opposite.

'The white SUV,' Victor prompted, and ran through her description of the car, what the men looked like, only pausing when Demarco arrived with a bag of freshly baked cookies. Abby ate two. They were still warm.

Victor scowled when the phone rang. 'Sorry,' he said as he picked it up. He barked, 'Pegati.'

Demarco helped herself to a cookie. She ate with her eyes on Victor, who was staring dead ahead, phone clamped to his ear. Her crunching filled the room, but she seemed unaware.

Victor closed his eyes. A low groan escaped his lips.

Demarco stopped crunching. Abby's fingertips tingled.

He said, 'I'll be there in two hours.'

Slowly Victor hung up. He waited a couple of breaths. His face was grey with apprehension.

Alarmed, Abby said, 'What's wrong?'

Victor looked at Demarco and Abby in turn, then fixed his gaze between them.

'Bad news, I'm afraid.'

He picked up a manila folder, put it down.

'Sir?' Demarco was staring at him. 'What is it, sir?'

'Thomas Claire's body was identified yesterday. He was found inside a burned-out car in a remote area on the outskirts of Anchorage.'

Abby heard the words, but they were having trouble getting to her brain. The room suddenly felt overly hot and cramped. She could barely breathe.

'Lisa and Thomas left Fairbanks the same day.' Victor was talking to Demarco. 'Friday, second of April. They travelled separately in opposite directions. Lisa headed north to Lake's Edge, Thomas south to Anchorage. Apparently Thomas had someone called Meg with him.'

Abby tried not to start. Thomas had taken MEG to Anchorage? Did that mean his murderer now had the prototype?

'I'll chase it,' Demarco said.

Victor was staring out of the window but he didn't seem to be looking at anything. The seconds ticked by, turning into minutes.

'Sergeant?' Demarco prompted him.

He shook himself, turned to Abby. 'How well did you know Thomas Claire?'

'I met him a few times. At UAF, and at dinner. His place.'

He had, she remembered, barbecued fresh-caught salmon and potatoes and when the entire lot went up in flames, including his beard, he'd thought it immensely funny. Abby and Lisa had smothered his scalded cheeks with lotion, ordered home-delivered pizzas and beer, and laughed themselves ill as they tried to trim his blackened, scorched beard with a pair of nail scissors.

'I liked him a lot.' Abby's voice was husky. She had more than liked him; she'd been enormously fond of him, not just because he'd almost adopted her difficult sister, but because he was one of life's gems, full of kindness and generosity. Like Ralph, he had a big heart.

Victor glanced at her, saw the tears hovering, and pinched the bridge of his nose between his fingers. 'I'm sorry... I wish you could be spared, but I'd rather you hear this from me, now, than find out through the media.'

He took a breath, exhaled. 'Someone set fire to Thomas to make sure he wouldn't be identified easily. There's no evidence to show he was killed before he was burned. No trauma to the head or the skeleton. He'd been chained to the steering wheel.'

247

Victor's jaw clenched briefly. 'The forensic department believe he was burned alive.'

Horror coiled itself around her heart.

'Jesus Christ,' said Demarco, and closed her eyes.

'Are you sure it's Thomas?' Abby's scalp had tightened, making her eyes feel as though they were bulging.

'The dental forensics are one hundred per cent conclusive.'

'They'd have to be mad to do that to him, crazy, some sort of lunatic...' She was gabbling, unable to get to grips with what he'd told her.

'You haven't heard from your sister, have you?' Victor asked. 'By radio perhaps? We need to know where she is, make sure she's safe.'

She leaned forward, suddenly eager. 'Do you still think she killed Marie?'

Victor fixed her with a gaze. She didn't recognise the emotion there. Compassion, perhaps? Empathy? Whatever it was, it was world-weary and tinged with not a little exhaustion. 'We're withholding judgement at the moment, but it's imperative we speak to her. Her scientific project is at the heart of this investigation.'

'So the warrant for her arrest still stands.'

He spread his hands in a conciliatory gesture. 'In all honesty we don't think your sister killed Marie. They were friends, working towards the same goal: to patent whatever technology she and Thomas had cooked up.'

Victor got to his feet. 'Look, I'm sorry to have to cut you short, but I need to talk with Trooper Demarco before I go.' He went and pulled down a jacket from a hook on the back of the door and shrugged it on.

'Wait.' Abby jumped up. 'What about Peter Santoni? The scientist Lisa and Thomas shut out?'

'We're looking for him.'

Abby stared at Victor without blinking. 'Are you saying you don't know where he is?'

He didn't reply, which she took to mean 'yes'.

'Santoni's vanished?'

Going back to the desk, he grabbed three manila folders and stuffed them in a battered-looking briefcase. 'Unfortunately, he went to Juneau last week and we're having trouble tracing him.'

'Don't you find that suspicious?'

'Extremely.' Victor withdrew one of the manila folders and presented Abby with a handful of photographs.

'Do you recognise any of these men?'

Abby shuffled through them but none of them looked like her kidnappers. After she'd given them back, Victor plucked one out and asked her to think carefully before she responded. She studied the stern-looking man in his fifties, the neat iron-grey beard, the broad, hooked nose and narrow mouth, and shook her head.

'Sorry,' she said. 'Who is he?'

'That's Peter Santoni.'

She studied the photo again but she'd never seen the man before in her life.

Twenty-eight

Abby sat on the sleeping shelf in her cabin, her mind a jumble of memories: Thomas in his lab coat, computers chattering and spewing out multitudes of calculations, metal boxes with wires running everywhere, the smell of chocolate on her sister's breath.

How had it come to this? Marie and Thomas murdered, her sister on the run. Had the same person killed Marie and Thomas? Had they found Lisa, and killed her too?

She didn't react when someone rapped on the door. Didn't move when it opened.

'In,' she heard a man say irritably. 'For Chrissakes, will you just do as I say and go *in?*'

There was a brief patter of toenails and then a grey-and-white form catapulted against her legs, tail waving and tongue lolling.

Her lips felt stiff. She only knew that because they'd lengthened fractionally, into a smile.

Moke wriggled and squirmed, burying his head in her lap, then he reared back and did a little prance before flinging himself at her thighs again. He was groaning in his throat.

'Friends reunited,' Cal said. 'I heard the news. Thought you could do with cheering up.'

Abby pushed her fingers into Moke's thick ruff and shook his head gently from side to side. 'Thanks,' she said. The stiffness in her mouth began to ease as her smile broadened. 'Hey, boy, how are you?' Moke responded by wiping his tongue across her cheek. She could have hugged Cal at that moment. Moke was the best therapy she could have had.

'Mind if I come in?'

Belatedly she realised Cal was hovering in the doorway. She got to her feet. 'I'll put some coffee on.'

They didn't speak while the kettle boiled, just stood shoulder to shoulder looking outside. The boardwalks were still icy, the trails snowbound, but the street was melting, glistening with slush. Break-up was well on its way.

Abby spooned coffee into mugs and poured the hot water. She sniffed the milk in her fridge. Amazingly, it smelled okay. Had she only been gone three nights? It felt more like three months.

'You still have sugar?' she asked Cal.

He shook his head. 'Dad told me about Thomas. I'm sorry.'

'Me too.' She concentrated on stirring her coffee to prevent the tears rising. 'He was a lovely guy. He made me laugh.'

Moke was nuzzling her thigh as though he couldn't believe she was there. Cal looked at the dog. 'Don't forget you've a job to do.'

'What job?' she asked.

'To look out for you.' He ran a hand over his face. She could hear the rasp of his stubble against his palm. 'Demarco would love to have a team of cops protecting you against another kidnap, but since Trooper Weiding's returned to Coldfoot and Dad's flown to Anchorage... It's just her up here.'

The hair on Abby's forearms rose. She hadn't thought the men might come back for her.

'You'll keep him with you?' Cal said. 'Twenty-four-seven, no matter what?'

It wasn't a difficult request to accept. 'Sure.'

He nodded, took a sip of coffee. Stared out over the lake.

'Abby.' His tone was cautious.

'Yes, Cal.'

'Do you know what Lisa was working on?'

She turned away and rested her hands on the worktop, looking outside. 'She never said. Not to Mum, not to anybody.'

'Hmm,' said Cal. 'So how come you know?'

'I don't.'

'Hmm,' he said again, obviously not believing a word.

'I don't,' she repeated stubbornly.

'Be careful, Abby.'

There was something in his tone that made her shiver inside, and she wasn't sure whether it was because he sounded as though he cared about her, or because of the warning it held.

'God,' she said ruefully, 'you're as bad as Michael Flint with the prophecy of doom.'

'Flint?' Cal repeated. There was a peculiar look on his face. 'How do you know Flint?'

'He's my landlord.'

'Jesus, that man...' He shook his head. 'He seems to get everywhere. Be careful of him, would you?'

Abby stiffened. 'Why?'

'Dad pulled Lisa's phone records, both here and at her office in Fairbanks. Flint called her a

252

lot over the past year.'

'So?'

'You don't know?' He cocked a sceptical eyebrow.

'No, Cal, I don't, which is why you're going to tell me.'

Cal sighed, took a gulp of coffee. 'His family own Oasis Oil. He's top of the pile – rich as hell and wants to get richer.'

She immediately recalled the red and white helicopter with OASIS OIL decals on its doors, parked by the airstrip.

'You know that Alaska's economy is hitting the rocks?' Cal asked.

Abby was surprised. She'd assumed since Alaska didn't have any state taxes it was doing okay. 'But wouldn't the government enforce income or sales tax if it was that bad?'

'Both appear inevitable,' he agreed, 'but meantime oil is still our best hope for economic recovery. Unfortunately, Prudhoe Bay is drying up. Production is less than fifty per cent of what it was fifteen years ago and the mineral royalties have slumped too, down to a third in the same period...' He dragged a hand over his head. 'The thing is, Michael Flint is heading the national debate about opening up the coastal plain of the ANWR, the Arctic National Wildlife Refuge, to oil drilling.'

Her mind started to flail, fighting against the sudden current. 'I thought he was a friend of Lisa's.'

Cal looked astonished. 'Whoever told you that?'

'Diane.'

'Why on earth would she say that? Everyone

knows how much Flint and Lisa hate each other...' He was frowning. 'I don't get it.'

Abby was sinking, plunging over the edge of the falls.

'Why was he ringing her?' she asked.

'He insists they were settling their differences. Having "spirited discussions" was how he put it. But we're not so sure. We think he might have been badgering her about what she was working on with Thomas...'

He slowed as though a thought had just struck him.

'Abby, if you know what Lisa was working on, don't tell Flint, will you?'

Flint already knew, but Abby didn't react. In the distance she heard a snow machine's roar. She put down her coffee mug. She hadn't taken a single sip.

'Thanks for filling me in,' she said calmly.

Cal nodded, and downed the last of his coffee with one long swallow. 'I'll see you at the Moose later?' he asked. 'They're having a bit of a celebration for you, don't forget.'

Abby lay in the bath, water as hot as she could stand it. Moke lay on the bath mat beside her, and each time she looked across he raised his head and thumped his tail. The little bathroom looked remarkably unchanged from when she last saw it. Same board walls and tin roof, same soap and toiletries racked between the taps.

So much had happened in the past few days. She'd been under tension since she'd arrived and a sense of unreality pervaded everything. She felt as though she was moving through fog and although she knew it was exhaustion, knowing the fact didn't help. She needed a week of R & R, preferably somewhere nice and safe and warm, and a thousand miles from here. Like Hawaii.

She let her eyes travel over the ceiling, the spiders' webs in the corners, trying to make sense of everything she knew.

Why had Diane lied about Flint being a friend of Lisa's? She couldn't figure it out. And poor Thomas, burned alive in some car outside Anchorage. Shuddering, Abby ducked down so the water came to her chin. She ran over what Victor had said, that Thomas had gone to Anchorage with MEG the same day Lisa headed for Lake's Edge.

Then she remembered the money in Lisa's account. Had she planned to disappear? Abby's stomach hollowed as she thought further. What if Thomas's trip to Anchorage with MEG had been a ruse, to decoy the killer away from Lisa? This would give Lisa ample time to leg it to remote Lake's Edge and give MEG to Marie and then disappear. And when MEG was safely in Arlington, Virginia, she could come out of hiding, since there'd be no point in killing her; the technology now being in the public domain.

But given that Marie was dead, and that the men were still hunting for Lisa, she had to assume Lisa never managed to hand MEG to Marie. She'd bet her last dollar Lisa had MEG.

Hair still dripping, Abby tore back through the snow to the cabin and got dressed – warm padded trousers, stretchy shirt, thick socks and boots; it may be relatively warm during the day, but at night the temperature plummeted.

She just about leaped a foot in the air when Moke launched himself at the door, barking fit to burst.

'Jesus, Moke!'

She peered through the window. Two men in dark suits and ties stood on her doorstep. Both were around the same height, five ten or so, but where one was in his early thirties and carrying a couple of stone extra weight, mostly around his middle, the other had to be twenty years older and looked twenty times fitter. A rush of relief flooded her that neither were her kidnappers.

Abby tapped on the window pane, calling, 'Can I help you?'

Both men came over and studied her with serious, unsmiling expressions. They reminded her of undertakers. The fatter one pushed their badged ID cards to the window. Her skin tightened. NASA. National Aeronautics and Space Administration.

'We'd like a word regarding your sister,' he called.

Abby opened the door and had to grab Moke to prevent him from making a lunge for one of the guys' knees. 'Leave, Moke. *Leave.*'

'Nice dog,' said the fat one, but his voice was scratchy with fear.

'Sorry, he's a bit overprotective.' She shifted Moke aside with her thigh. 'Inside, Moke.'

Moke gave the men a final long look, then turned around and disappeared.

'You're Abigail McCall?'

'Yes.'

'I'm Ben Elisson,' he said, 'this is Felix Karella.' Elisson not only had the spare tyre, but a raggedy-clipped black beard that was attempting to follow his jaw line. He appeared to have dropped what looked like tomato ketchup on his tie and as she looked further, she saw he was as dishevelled as his colleague was immaculate.

'I understand you've undergone a fair amount of stress this week, but we won't keep you long.' Elisson's smile was sympathetic and warmed his eyes to molten treacle. 'It's very important we speak with you. Any chance of a cup of coffee?'

Abby wasn't sure whether to invite them inside or not. What could they do? Chloroform her and cart of her off in their car? She was still dithering when Felix Karella gripped her upper arm and without seeming to force or push her in any way, managed to twist her neatly around and the next second she knew they were all in her cabin with the door shut behind them.

Moke sprang to her side and started to growl.

'Nice doggy,' Elisson said. He started to put a hand out to Moke but Karella knocked his arm aside.

'I wouldn't,' he said. He flicked his eyes to Abby. 'Call him off.'

She could, she supposed, put Moke into attack mode again if she wanted. He seemed to have taken on the role of guard dog with extreme enthusiasm, thank God.

'Moke, leave,' she said.

The dog's shoulders seemed to slump in

disappointment, but he didn't move from her side.

'Good boy,' she said, her heart thudding.

'Shall we sit?' Elisson hitched up his trousers and smiled at her. She didn't smile back.

'Sure.'

Neither of them, it transpired, actually wanted coffee.

Karella fetched a stool from the kitchenette and put it in front of the TV. Elisson sat on the stool with Karella standing at his shoulder, arms crossed. Abby took the sofa. Instantly she realised her disadvantage; she was looking up at them.

'We're sorry about Lisa, what's been happening,' Elisson said. He folded his hands in his lap. 'We like her enormously. She's a nice lady. Sparky.'

To her relief Moke came over and plonked himself on the rug between her and the two men. Doggy barrier armed with nice sharp teeth.

'You've met her?'

'Oh, yes. Several times.'

Abby didn't like this. She didn't like their smooth insinuation into her cabin or the fact they knew Lisa.

'You know about MEG?' Elisson asked.

She made a little frown between her eyes. 'I've heard the name,' she said. Better to stick as close to the truth as possible.

'Hmm,' he said. 'Well, as you probably know, MEG is incredibly important. The implications for industry are immense, and as far as space travel goes ... it's mind-boggling what we could achieve. We might have mankind travelling outside our solar system within the next few decades. Exploring planets we'd thought were beyond our reach.' A dreamy look came into his eye and he blinked several times as though bringing himself back to earth. 'We are, however, extremely worried about the safety of MEG's technology. Not only have the two scientists who've had the most input into MEG disappeared, but all their research has disappeared too.'

Did they know Thomas had been murdered? She decided not to mention it.

'No lab books. No computers or discs. We haven't found a single piece of paper. Their lab was stripped bare aside from a coffee maker, a broken printer and a handful of electrical wires.'

'Their lab was robbed?'

Elisson looked amused. 'A lab? More like a broom cupboard.'

'I don't suppose they get the endless funding you guys do,' she responded, stung on Lisa and Thomas's behalf.

'Point taken.' He smiled some more. Abby wished Moke would leap up and bite him just to wipe the smile off his face.

Karella fixed her with a laser-like gaze. 'What can you tell us about Marie Guillemote?'

She didn't know where this was going and weighed her answer before speaking. 'Not much. She's a friend of Lisa's, the cops tell me. She hates flying in small aircraft, which is why she rented a car–'

'And she works for the patent office,' Karella cut in, 'which you're aware of, right?'

Abby gulped. Gave a nod.

'We heard Thomas and Lisa created a prototype machine. Guillemote's parents say she came over here to collect something.' Karella looked at his partner. 'In this case two and two, for us, made a perfect four.'

She stared at the tomato ketchup on Elisson's tie. She'd been right. Marie had come to take MEG to safety. Another question that had been bothering her popped into her mind. When Lisa and Thomas had split from Fairbanks, why hadn't Lisa flown MEG out of the state? Met Marie in Virginia? Was she worried she might be picked up at the airport? Maybe by these guys? Would they have stolen MEG from her?

'Marie Guillemote came to collect Lisa's technology,' said Karella, looking hard at Abby. 'Agreed?'

She managed a nod.

'And whoever killed her wanted it for themselves. What we don't know is where the technology is at the moment – if Guillemote stashed it, or whether Lisa has it. If your sister hid it, would you have any ideas where it might be?'

Abby shook her head. 'No idea. Sorry.'

Elisson was tapping his thigh as he thought. 'We really need to get our hands on the prototype.'

'It could be anywhere,' said Karella, looking frustrated. 'Especially since it can't be that big or that heavy if Guillemote was going to haul it back to Arlington with her.'

Abby's mind boggled. Jesus Christ. She hadn't given any thought to what the prototype might look like. A jet engine, surely the thing had to be *huge*. Or had they created a miniature version?

Something you could pop in your backpack? She leaned back and rubbed her temples. Her head was aching. Everything was just so *complicated.*

'How come you know about MEG?' Abby asked. 'Nobody else does, not even the cops.'

A hungry gleam came into Karella's eye that made her regret what she'd said. He said, 'Let's hope it stays that way.'

Elisson cut an annoyed look at Karella, who sank back.

'It's no secret,' Elisson said. 'Lisa met with one of our own scientists, Perry Torgeson, three years back, at a conference. Perry worked on our Breakthrough Propulsion Project. They bandied ideas and theories about, helped one another as work colleagues do. Eventually, we got to hear what she was working on...' Elisson scratched his scruffy beard with a forefinger. 'We, er ... approached Thomas Claire, but he wouldn't see us. Your sister, however, was more approachable. We offered Lisa an extremely generous sum for the technology, but she turned us down.'

'Did she give you a reason?' asked Abby. Lisa would have been looking for an investor back then; Connie had only appeared on the scene six months ago.

Elisson glanced at Karella, looking amused. 'You want to take this one?'

Karella looked dead ahead as though he was on military parade. His tone was stiff. 'She said she didn't want her work to benefit anything that wasn't humanitarian.'

'I see,' said Abby.

Nobody spoke as Moke, lying between Abby

261

and the men on the sofa, half rose to scratch an ear vigorously with his hind leg.

'The offer we made to your sister,' said Karella, 'is still open.'

'We are still very keen to invest in Lisa's work,' Elisson added for good measure.

'Gentlemen,' Abby said. She got to her feet, but neither man moved. 'I'm sorry, but you're wasting your time. I can't help you.'

'What if you found MEG?' Karella asked. The hungry gleam was back. 'Found her technology? The lab books?'

Abby paused. 'I doubt that's going to happen.'

'What would you do with it?' he insisted.

'I don't have it, so what's the point in–'

'The point,' Elisson cut in smoothly, 'is that the offer we made to Lisa would, of course, be redirected to yourself.'

Her mouth turned dry.

'Okay,' she said lightly, 'if I should fall on MEG or the lab books, which I very much doubt, how generous a sum are we talking here?'

Karella gave her an eight figure number that made her feel instantly dizzy.

'Excuse me,' she managed.

Abby walked to the kitchenette on legs that didn't feel as though they belonged. She felt numb and peculiarly detached. No wonder people were getting killed. The stakes were astronomically high. She heard Karella saying her name, voice insistent, but Elisson overrode him. Her skin was cold, as though she was standing naked in a snow drift.

'Abby.'

It was Elisson. She felt his hand on her arm and she flinched. 'Don't touch me.'

She had an urge to howl and weep. People didn't care about Lisa. They just wanted her damned technology, and if they found it, they might kill for it.

'Look at me, Abby,' Elisson said softly.

She managed to hold eye contact but only with difficulty.

'That much money can go a long way. You can help charities, save the whales, buy a château in France, take your mother on trips around the world. I bet she wouldn't say no to some of that money. You could design her a custom-built home by the sea, have round-the-clock nursing, which would free you up–'

'Get out.' Her voice was low and dangerous.

'Hey, don't be hasty here. I'm just telling you how it is–'

'Moke!' she yelled. The dog sprang to his feet, watching her. She pointed at Elisson, and Moke immediately fastened his eyes on him and drew back his lips into a snarl.

Elisson blanched, stuck his hands in the air. 'Jesus Christ. Don't sic him on me, for God's sakes.'

She swept her hand at Karella who was standing stock still in front of the TV. Moke turned his head between the two men and began to growl. Karella's nostrils flared. He looked like a bull that wanted to charge but had its nose ring pulled tight.

Moke put his head low and took a step towards Elisson's knees.

'Okay, okay.' Elisson's breathing was uneven. 'We're going. We're cool, okay?' He inched his way to the door and opened it. Karella followed.

Abby watched them scoot outside. When the door closed behind them, Moke came over and nuzzled her thigh. 'Good boy,' she said, her voice trembling. She was shivering head to toe.

'You see them again, you bite them.'

Twenty-nine

A stiff and cold breeze had risen, swirling grains of snow through the air and stinging Lisa's cheeks. She trotted Roscoe back into the cabin and closed the door. Opened a carton of long-life milk and put it on the stove to warm.

Hands tucked beneath her armpits she stood by the window and looked outside. All she could see was forest, snow and granite peaks rising in the distance. The sun was hidden behind thick clouds, the temperature hovering just below freezing. She couldn't remember when it had last been this cold in April. The average date of break-up was eight days earlier than it was in the 1920s, and although most Alaskans appreciated having one less week of winter, Lisa bitterly resented it because it was caused by global warming.

Checking the milk, she wished the cabin had a phone or radio. She also wished it had a TV, library, sauna and masseuse, but it was the lack of human contact that was getting to her. She could spend weeks without talking to anyone, but when she decided she'd had enough time out, if she didn't sit down and share a bottle of wine with a friend, she went nuts.

And she was going nuts now. She wanted to know how Abby was. She knew that she was back in Lake's Edge, but was she really okay? Didn't kidnap victims need hours of counselling afterwards? And what about post traumatic stress syndrome?

Lisa poured hot milk over her powdered chocolate and gave the mug a stir. Tears began to prick the backs of her eyes so she hurriedly turned her mind from Abby, wondering whether Thomas had managed to deliver the lab books as they'd arranged. She had to pray he'd succeeded, because if someone patented MEG tomorrow, she'd never be able to contest the application without them. Were they safe? Or had they been copied or forged, then destroyed?

Oh, God. Everything was her fault. If it wasn't for her, MEG would still be safe and Abby wouldn't be in danger. Thomas had told her to keep MEG quiet a while longer, but she hadn't been able to resist bragging to Santoni how far they'd come without him. And Santoni, who'd been trying to get NASA interested in one of his pathetic little projects, had obviously told the space admin guys about MEG, because that was when Perry called and warned her they'd come asking about her.

Perry worked for NASA on their BBP project, Breakthrough Propulsion Physics, and they'd met at a conference in Salt Lake City a couple of years ago. Perry was tall, with floppy blond hair and a wicked sense of humour that matched hers. They'd had a glorious fling filled with practical jokes and laughter, and if he hadn't been based in Huntsville, Alabama, it might have developed into something more serious. As it was, neither wanted to move and, luckily, they parted good friends.

Lisa finished her chocolate, looking at the frozen white forest outside.

If she hadn't boasted to Santoni, Abby would be safe.

Roscoe pushed his nose against her thigh, body wriggling close, and she dropped to her knees and hugged him, burying her face into the warmth of his fur for comfort.

God dammit. It was all her fault.

Thirty

The bar was three deep when Abby arrived. All the tables were full, and the floor was jumping with men and women dancing to music that thumped from two enormous speakers opposite the bar. It appeared everyone wanted to give her a hug and buy her a drink, and, spirits buoyed, feeling as though she'd returned to the bosom of a family, she hugged them back.

The first beer went straight to her head, and Abby felt something loosen inside, like a piece of wire stretched to breaking point had been cut. She wolfed down a steak, a bowl of fries, had two more beers, and she was dancing with Mac, feeling care-free and slightly crazy that she was *here,* and not locked in a wilderness cabin trying to keep hold of her sanity, when Connie arrived at a gallop.

'Dearest!' she shouted. She was beaming from ear to ear, eyes shining.

Connie obviously hadn't heard about Thomas's murder. It seemed nobody had, except the cops, herself and Cal. She decided to keep it that way.

Hugging her back, Abby spotted a large, smooth-haired man hovering to one side. He had ironed creases down the front of his jeans and a pair of Gucci glasses perched on his head. Although he was smiling, he looked distinctly ill-at-ease.

'This is Scott,' said Connie, beaming, 'my hus-band.'

Scott put out his hand and Abby shook it. He glanced around at the bedlam, then back at Connie.

'It's not really his thing,' Connie told Abby, 'but I wanted you guys to meet before we grabbed something to eat. He flew out the second he heard about our little escapade. He's real glad you got out.'

Abby smiled at Scott, who smiled back, then he raised his eyebrows at his wife. 'Tomorrow!' Con-nie called over the sound of the Dixie Chicks belt-ing out full blast. 'I'll come round in the morning!'

Abby nodded and let Mac take her hand and twirl her in an unsteady circle. Cal had been skulking in the background ever since she'd arrived, and she wasn't sure if she found his presence an annoyance or a comfort. Most of the time he was scowling, especially when Mac put his hand on her behind and gave it a squeeze.

Happily drunk, Abby finally collapsed on a stool at the bar and mopped her forehead. Diane poured her another beer and yelled, 'On the house!' Abby raised the glass in thanks, and when she nearly dropped it, set it carefully back down on the bar, deciding she'd probably had enough.

Mac sank on the stool beside her and started telling her about his latest passenger, who'd been so crazy he'd had to be tranquillised and tied up by the arresting officers. Unfortunately halfway through the flight his passenger recovered from his stupor and started thrashing about and, not wanting to shoot him, Mac had been forced to land on a lake, cut his passenger's lashings and throw him overboard. The 700-pound brown bear had hauled himself ashore and disappeared without any seeming ill effects.

They talked bears for a while, affection versus sheer terror, then a pretty girl with green eyes came and whisked Mac away to dance. A guy moved into Mac's place, said, 'Hi.'

In his twenties, like most of the guys he wore jeans and workshirt, and had a face browned by the cold, the winds and the sun. He looked as strong and muscular as a mountain lion.

'Hi,' she said. She didn't recognise him, but he obviously recognised her. Well, who wouldn't? she thought with a sigh. She was a local celebrity, a face everyone knew around town, and not just because of her kidnap or her sister's disappearance. She had enough history here to sink a battleship if she wanted.

'You wanna drink? I owe your sister several, maybe you could drink them for her.'

'I think I've probably had enough, but thanks.'

'Miss her, you know.' He peered into his beer. 'We had a big bust-up twelve months or so back. God, what a wildcat. She kicked me out barefoot in the middle of winter, the rotten cow. Nearly gave me a heart attack. Thought I'd get frostbite and lose all my toes.'

Abby blinked. 'You're Jack? Jack Molvar?'

'That's me.' He grinned. 'Luckily my bunny boots came sailing out a minute later or we wouldn't have stayed friends.'

Abby wished she hadn't had so much to drink. She'd loads of questions for Lisa's ex-boyfriend but right now she couldn't think of a single one.

'She always said you didn't look alike, but I had no idea,' he grinned. 'She is such a short-ass, whereas you ... well, you're a goddess.'

Abby pointed ruefully at his beer. 'I think you've had enough too.'

'Hey, Abby.' A hand rested lightly on her shoulder. She glanced up to see Michael Flint looking cool and crisp in a blue shirt and jeans. His eyes were warm. 'Boy, is it good to see you.' He ducked his head and kissed her cheek. 'I can't believe you got the better of those bastards. Well done you.'

'If you don't mind,' Jack Molvar said, an edge to his voice, 'we were talking.'

Flint turned to give Jack a cool look. 'And you are?'

'Jack Molvar.'

Flint looked the younger guy up and down. His gaze came to rest on the man's boots. He didn't

269

say a word, but the atmosphere became tense.

'You gotta problem?' Jack growled.

'No problem.' Flint gave a sigh. 'I'll catch you later, Abby. Okay?'

'Piece of shit,' Jack muttered as Flint vanished into the crowd.

'He seems nice enough to me,' Abby said, hoping to prompt Jack into spilling some beans. 'I like him.'

'Your sister didn't.'

'How come?' She hooked her elbows on the bar. At the far end she spotted Connie's husband, cigarette in hand as he perused the single-page, plastic menu with a resigned expression.

'Because she's a greenie and he's a fucking oil...' Jack paused, began digging in his pockets as a barmaid came over. 'Yeah, Doreen ... a beer thanks...'

'At each other's throats they were,' a man interjected from Abby's left. He had a set of whiskers the colour of wet ash and a foamy rim of beer around his lips. 'Lisa wantin' to protect the environment, Mister Flint Almighty trying to destroy it. It got real personal – a lot of mud slinging. Press loved it.'

'When was this?'

'A year or so ago. All died down in the end.' The man scrutinised her at length through a pair of rheumy eyes. 'You and Cal an item yet?'

'Certainly not.' She was indignant.

'Don't go all hoity-toity on me. Only askin'. I know there's others all disapprovin' of what you two got up to, but I thought it was the best thing for the guy. He needed cheerin' up, and you sure did that.'

Abby looked at him blankly.

'You know,' he went on, 'what with his wife being ill and all. My Shiralee got real sick before she died, and I could've done with you brightenin' up my day, believe me.' He was shaking his head. 'It's not right for a guy to get married then have his wife fall sick the rest of the time. Broke your heart to see her go like that. A real beauty too, all eaten up by illness. She used to be such a sparky lass. Independent as hell. She always knew what she wanted. She had a bit of a temper on her, but she was soft as butter inside.' He looked wistful. 'Tough too, even though she only came up to here.' He put a hand to his chest, which made Saffron around the same height as Lisa.

So what if Saffron had been a real beauty? She was also a dwarf, Abby thought, feeling suddenly uncharitable.

'She could butcher a moose, fix an engine, service her truck, make cranberry jam, the best sourdough you could want. Good shot too, that gal, and not a bad fisher, either.'

What in the world Cal had seen in her compared to this parody of self-sufficiency, Abby couldn't think. She was as useful as a paper napkin here.

'Shame she was so ill, it sounds awful,' Abby muttered into her beer, trying not to feel jealous. How childish was she being? The poor cow was dead, for God's sakes.

The barmaid, a handsome woman with a black braid and a dusting of dark hair on her upper lip, suddenly cut in with a sneer. 'Don't tell me you cared.'

'Hey,' Abby reared back, 'hang on a second–'

'You outsiders are all the same. See one of our men and it don't matter if he's married or not. You want him, you just have him and high-tail it home without a care in the world about any diseases you've given him that he's gonna pass on to his wife.'

'Doreen,' the old guy said, 'butt out, I was talking–'

'She took one look at Cal and set her sights on him. Poor bastard didn't stand a chance–'

'Shut up, Doreen.' Diane arrived at a trot. 'I've already told you it wasn't like that.'

'And you're the expert,' Doreen hissed.

'Yes, I am, because Cal told Lisa and Lisa told me.'

'She's a man eater. Everyone says so. Like a praying mantis, and she bites their heads off once she's mated.'

The room suddenly went quiet: no music belting out, no people yelling. Nothing. All Abby's senses were focused on the barmaid – her jowls, her broad cheekbones, her small mouth and mean dark eyes. Slowly, she stood up, said quietly, 'You say another word, and you'll regret it.'

'Ooh,' a man shouted behind her. 'Cat fight!'

The next second she was surrounded by guys yelling and shouting and egging her on. 'Go on, give her one, Abby!'

'Let's see your right hook, darlin'!'

Someone gripped her upper arm and she shook it free.

'Abby, it's me!' She turned to see Flint clutching her parka in one hand and beckoning frantically with the other. 'Let's get out of here!'

She waded for him like a drowning surfer, gasping and gulping. He grabbed her wrist and tugged her after him.

They were nearing the door when Abby heard the barmaid yell, 'Not him as well! Can't you keep your hands to yourself for once?'

Abby tried to turn around to yell back at her but Flint's grip was like steel and the next instant she was outside.

'Definitely time you went home,' he said.

'Jesus,' she gasped. 'What the hell happened in there?'

'You were about to lose your rag.' Flint was eyeing her warily. 'Not without good cause after what you've been through, but on top of all that beer...'

'Oh, God.' She cringed. She was so drunk she'd nearly slapped the barmaid! It was definitely time for a couple of pints of water and bed.

'I'll walk you home,' Flint said. 'Make sure you get there unscathed.'

The cold clean air cleared her head a little, but not her legs, which were behaving as though they weren't connected to her body. Without a word, Flint tucked her arm in his, and slowly walked her down the icy boardwalk as though he did it every day.

'You're as bad as your sister,' he remarked, but he didn't make it sound like a bad thing. Affection threaded his voice.

'She bad,' Abby said, 'me good.'

'Yes, I know.' He looked across at her, waiting until she met his gaze. 'Lisa's not married, you know. In case you're still trawling through the White Pages.'

'How d'you know?'

'She made it up to gain Malone's sympathy. My guess is she told him her husband was abusing her, and that she was hiding from him. That kind of situation's not uncommon around here. Which is why whenever a man calls in a woman as "missing", the cops don't leap into action until they've concrete evidence she hasn't just run away from him.'

She remembered the hunger in Malone's eyes. *I'll deal with him. Scum.*

'He was going to shoot you,' Abby said. 'Malone thought you were Lisa's husband.'

'I don't know about that, but whatever she told him, it worked. Clever old Lisa.' He looked pleased. 'She knew how to get him onside.'

Abby was still uncertain. 'But she might have got married. Especially to a pilot. She loves flying.'

'You don't believe me.' He said it very flat.

Abby didn't know what she believed. Her emotions were all over the place and not just because of her kidnap. Hearing about Saffron, Superwoman of the Bush, made her feel as though she'd been slugged with a sandbag.

Flint gave a sigh as he parked her by her front door. He asked if she'd be okay. Abby nodded and fumbled in her pocket for her keys. She tried to fit the key in the hole, but it kept slipping. Flint took the key from her and slotted it in first time, but as he turned the lock and made to open the door, she grabbed his arm.

'No, no,' she said. 'Dog is in there.'

She could hear Moke scrabbling and whining on the other side. Flint seemed unperturbed

274

about the dog and turned to face her.

'Go home, Abby,' he told her gently. 'You're in over your head, and you're going to get hurt if you're not careful.'

Confusion swept over her. One part of her wanted to trust him, but the other insisted on caution. Peering blearily at him, she desperately tried to kick her alcohol-sodden brain into gear. 'I've heard you and Lisa had a bit of a ... set-to. Her trying to protect the environment, you trying to destroy it.'

A flash of amusement crossed his face. 'It certainly spiced up my day.'

She could imagine their rows, Flint keeping his cool and inflaming Lisa's volatile temper, the fur flying.

'But we got through that, became friends.' He flapped a hand vaguely. 'Business acquaintances.'

'She doesn't like you, does she?'

Something slid at the back of his eyes as he looked at her. 'You know about MEG.'

Abby took a step back. 'No,' she managed, 'not really.'

He considered her at length. Then he looked up and down the street as though checking for anyone watching. 'Look, there's something you should know.' Stepping close, he lowered his voice. 'But you can't tell anyone. It'll put you in danger. And me. Promise you'll keep it secret?'

Trying to hide her unease at this sudden switch to co-conspirator, she sketched an unsteady cross over her heart.

'I've filed an application with the USTPO on Lisa's behalf.'

Abby felt her mouth slacken.

'The patent office has an electronic filing system. Lisa's now got a customer number and a digital certificate. All she needs to do is get the prototype to them, fully disclose it along with the lab books, and the technology will be officially registered.'

'They wouldn't let you do that for her,' she protested. 'She'd have to do it herself.'

'What if I told you I have Power of Attorney?'

Abby froze as if he'd just slapped her.

'If you know where the prototype is, we can take it to the USTPO. Get the killers off our backs.'

'We?' she croaked.

'You and me.' He raised a hand, let it fall. 'Abby, where is it?'

'I don't know.'

'And even if you did know, you wouldn't tell me, am I right? You don't trust me.' His jaw flexed. 'Jesus Christ, Abby, why don't you just go home and stop making everything so difficult?'

Fear crawling through her, she took several steps back but he was already spinning on his heel and walking away, his long coat flapping behind him like crow wings.

Thirty-one

Abby let Moke out for his pre-sleep amble and stood watching him sniff various clumps of grass. She was drinking a glass of water in the faint hope it might help rehydrate her, so she could try

276

and make sense of what Flint had said.

Had he really filed a patent application for Lisa or was it just a ruse so he could get his hands on MEG? And if he really was a friend of Lisa's, or business acquaintance or whatever he was, wouldn't he know where Lisa and her technology were?

Swaying slightly, Abby considered Flint and her sister. He was, she admitted, an extremely attractive guy. But his business was an insurmountable problem. She could remember Lisa going out with a fellow student she really liked, and dumping him the second she learned his father owned an industrial refuse incinerator. Lisa was black and white about environmental issues, and anyone remotely involved in anything she disapproved of always got short shrift. Abby couldn't honestly see Lisa befriending a man involved in the oil industry, no matter how personable or good looking.

She was attempting to recall exactly what Flint had said about the patent office when a shadow materialised just yards away. *Bear!* her mind yelled and she tried to turn and run, call for Moke, but her mind and body were clogged by alcohol and all she did was drop the glass, trip over her feet and end up sprawled on the boardwalk.

'Jesus.' Cal bent over her and plucked her skywards. 'Talk about wasted.'

Abby peered round to see Moke watching him. No hackles or bared teeth that she could see.

Cal carted her bodily inside the cabin and dumped her on the bed. Then he unpicked her laces and slid her feet free from her boots. She wanted to run her fingers through his thick, springy hair and had to look away before she gave in to the urge.

He went and fetched her glass, luckily unbroken, rinsed it out and refilled it, put it by her bed. 'Have a nice walk with Michael Flint?' His tone was acerbic.

She blinked a couple of times. 'Yup.'

'I thought I told you to be careful, Abby...' She heard him give an irritated sigh. 'Have you a spare blanket?'

She blinked a couple of times. 'What?'

'I'm taking the couch.' He pulled out his pistol and pushed it beneath a cushion. 'I have no intention of sitting outside, freezing my butt off in my car, keeping an eye out for a bunch of potential kidnappers.'

Abby started to shake her head, but when the room began to spin she stopped. God, she hoped she wasn't going to throw up.

'You want a bucket?' He was surveying her with a frown.

Her reply was to crawl beneath the covers and close her eyes. The last thing she heard was Cal filling Moke's water bowl.

After Cal left the next morning, Abby sat on the deck. Moke lay next to her. Cal had been making toast when she'd finally crawled awake, and to her relief he hadn't crowed over her condition, just solemnly passed her a glass of water and two double-strength painkillers and agreed some fresh air might help.

It didn't seem to be working. Her head throbbed, her mouth felt as though it had been packed with sand, and she could have been sitting in a fridge filled with cotton wool her senses were so numbed. She hadn't had such a horrendous hangover since she graduated from Leeds.

She felt hot and sweaty and wasn't sure if it was another symptom of too much beer or if the weather really had warmed up that much. The street was now clear of snow, the sun blazing down, and she could hear the steady drip-dripping of melting snow from roofs and trees. A soft thump made her heart jump, but it wasn't a grizzly, just a chunk of snow that had fallen from a branch on to a four-wheeler below.

She should never have drunk so much, but she had been so anxious about Lisa, so wound up after NASA's visit, she hadn't been thinking of the consequences.

At her side Moke stiffened and started to growl.

She glanced at the figure approaching. 'Leave, Moke,' she told him and the dog fell silent.

'Dear Abby, how are you?'

Abby watched Connie glide towards her with more than a tinge of envy. Despite her bulk, her feet were as sure as a speed skater's on the icy boardwalk.

'You were drinking for England the last time I saw you. You must be feeling awful. Look, I brought you some Tylenol and Coca Cola, they're the only cure, you know.'

Abby struggled up as Connie clumped on to the deck and kissed her cheek. 'That's kind of you.'

'I can't blame you for letting your hair down. It must have been such a *relief*. I simply can't imagine how you coped, I'd have gone quite mad. I'm not terribly good on my own, as you can imagine, but you, you're a tower of strength, a positive tour de force.'

Abby led the way into the cabin, shut the door behind them.

'Thank heavens for Scott, if he hadn't come over I'd have crumpled, but he held my hand and helped me be strong. He's gone back home today.' Connie unwound several scarves and draped them over the back of a stool. Dropped her carpetbag to the floor. 'And I saw Michael Flint took you home. I know he's a nice-looking man but don't you think you ought to be a bit more careful?'

'He just walked me to my door.' Abby heard the edge to her voice at Connie's uncalled-for advice, and tried to temper it. 'That's all.'

'He didn't mention MEG, did he?' Connie looked anxious.

Abby busied herself in the kitchenette. Should she break her promise to Flint and tell Connie about what he'd said about applying for MEG's patent? Abby chewed the inside of her lip. Connie was Thomas and Lisa's investor, and if Flint had been lying...

'Abby,' said Connie. Her tone was sombre. 'Look at me.'

Abby turned and looked at the soft ruddy hair, the bangles and big, tawny eyes.

'I've something to tell you. It's an apology really. Because I haven't been absolutely upfront with you about MEG.'

'What do you mean?'

'You see, I thought if you didn't know exactly

280

what MEG was, you'd be safe. But I was wrong. They kidnapped you anyway.' She put a hand to her forehead. 'I can't believe how stupid I was.'

Abby stared at Connie. 'You lied to me?'

'Yes, I did. And for nothing. It didn't protect you. I'm sorry.'

Her mind was swarming, trying to make sense of it. 'Are you saying that MEG isn't a jet engine after all?'

'I made that up. I've been such a fool.' Tears glistened in Connie's eyes. Her lips trembled. 'Can you forgive me?'

Abby briefly closed her eyes.

'Abby?' Connie's tone was anxious.

'Tell me what MEG really is.'

Connie pulled a stool towards her and hitched herself on top, letting her plump legs dangle. Late-morning sun flowed through the windows, lighting dust motes drifting through the air. The fridge clicked in and started a low-pitched hum that clashed with the hangover ringing in Abby's head.

'MEG stands for Magnetic Energy Generator. Basically, it converts magnetic energy into electricity.' Connie leaned forward, expression earnest. 'Which means we will no longer need to rely on diesel, oil, gas or electricity to power our world. And not only is it unbelievably cheap, it's fueless and carbon-free, and meets both energy and propulsion needs with incredible efficiency... We all know the environmental impact of using fuel for energy.

'In Alaska alone the temperatures have climbed seven degrees and the sea ice, they tell me, is forty per cent thinner than it was twenty years ago. But

MEG,' Connie spread her hands, her face slowly lighting with excitement, 'is going to solve both the pollution and global warming problems for the world. There's no onboard energy source needed, just a small starter motor. It'll power our cars and trucks, airplanes, even our space rockets, without harming the earth's environment. And what it's going to do for the Third World... You know Lisa's dishes on her roof?'

Abby nodded numbly.

'Well, they collect magnetic energy when the sun's not out. There will be no more electric cables running to places like this. Lake's Edge won't need a town generator, every house will have their own little MEG, which will provide heating as well as light, and energy for cooking, your TV, whatever you want.'

Connie's face split into a beam. 'Lisa even believes it will recycle free energy to repair our environment, can you believe it?'

Amazingly, she could. Lisa's involvement in creating something that would help the environment made far more sense than her producing another jet engine.

'The oil industry will go bust,' she said faintly.

'Eventually,' Connie agreed. 'There are an awful lot of people who don't want this to happen, which is why Lisa's in such a lot of trouble.'

Abby thought of Elisson and Karella and NASA's eight-figure offer. 'There are also a lot of people who *want* it to happen,' she said.

'Whichever camp they're from,' Connie said glumly, 'they've all got the same goal: find MEG and either destroy it or steal it to make them-

282

selves richer than Croesus.'

Abby wrapped her arms around herself. She felt cold and shaky. Connie had, she realised, been very clever about the whole thing. She'd realised that Marie had been murdered because she'd known what MEG was, and by creating the jet-engine story for Abby, bullshitting the cops about Brightlite investing in EVals, she'd kept herself and Abby as safe as she could.

'Abby dearest, I heard a rumour yesterday. I was wondering if you knew anything about it.'

'What is it?'

'That Flint and your sister were sleeping together.'

Abby stared at her, speechless.

'You don't think it's true?'

'No.'

Connie pursed her lips. 'You sound very definite.'

'I just can't see it. Oil magnate and environmentalist...' Abby bit her lip.

'Then why has he been going to his lodge?'

'What do you mean?'

Hopping off the stool, Connie bent over and pulled a map out of her carpetbag, and unfolded it on the kitchenette counter.

'See this?' She planted a fat forefinger on a circle with a U inside it on the side of a mountain standing 4,053 feet high.

'Unverified landing area,' said Abby.

'Which belongs to Clear Creek Lodge,' said Connie. 'And do you know who the lodge belongs to?'

Abby stared at Connie.

'Michael Flint,' Connie supplied with a flourish. 'I think that's where Lisa is hiding. At his place.'

Abby ran her tongue over her lips. Why would Lisa be hiding there?

'You see,' Connie went on, 'Flint has never, not once, gone to his lodge before the first of June. He employs local people to get it ready in the spring, carry out maintenance and so on, and breezes in when the weather's fine. But it seems he's been up there rather a lot lately.'

Abby concentrated on the map. As the crow flew, Flint's lodge was around forty miles from Malone's cabin. Could Lisa have made it with just one dog in her weakened state? 'Wouldn't it be inaccessible at this time of year?' she asked. 'The strip would be under snow, surely? The trails blocked?'

'My point exactly. It would be a tough journey in, then out. It would have to be for something important.' Connie held Abby's gaze. 'What if they *are* sleeping together?'

Abby began to shake her head, then remembered Flint's absolute certainty that Lisa wasn't married.

'Come *on*, Abby, don't dismiss it out of hand... Flint may have gone to his lodge to check if Lisa went there.' Connie pointed out the lodge on the map, then the ridge where Malone lived.

Suddenly all the hairs on her body were standing upright.

She could see Diane's smile playing on her lips. *I remember Lisa staying there once. She did it for kicks... She ate his cupboards bare, slept in his bed...*

284

Lisa, playing hide and seek. Lisa, who always won.

Best place is always close to the enemy, she could hear her sister telling her. *They never think of looking under their noses.*

Holy cow. She'd bet her last pair of knickers that Connie was right. Lisa was hiding at Flint's place, but not for the reasons Connie thought.

'It's impossible,' Abby said. She made her tone brisk to cover the fact she was lying. What had Ralph always told her? Be strong and firm, even aggressive, and you'll bluff anyone. 'Malone said she was really weak, there's no way she'd manage such a trip.'

'Not even with that innate stubbornness that drives us completely *mad?*' Connie was frowning.

Abby shook her head. 'In fine weather and with two dogs, it might be possible for someone in peak condition to make it, but let's also remember where they are... They'd have to break their own trail as well as detour for miles around dangerous canyons and rivers.' She paused and gave a dramatic sigh. 'The entire area is covered in deep snow. She wouldn't have had the strength.'

'So where did she go?'

'If I knew that,' Abby made her tone irritable, 'I wouldn't be here, would I?'

Connie's shoulders slumped. 'I will throttle her when I see her.'

'Me too,' Abby said, and although she sounded cross she was gazing at the map in disbelief, almost wonder. Clever Lisa. She should have known her sister would have found the perfect hiding place.

Now all she had to worry about was Michael Flint.

Was he Lisa's enemy or her friend?

Thirty-two

Abby headed for the Moose to collect Diane's SUV. She'd rung her after Connie left to ask where she could hire or borrow a car and Diane had immediately offered her own vehicle and wouldn't hear of being paid.

'Just fill up the tank when you've finished with it.'

Since fuel cost a fraction of what it did in the UK, it was a bargain.

While Abby walked, she made a mental list. She'd fill up Diane's SUV tonight, and prepare an emergency pack – make sure she had a torch, some matches, lots of warm clothing. Some chocolate bars. The next time Lisa got into trouble, she hoped she'd do it somewhere less inhospitable, like Dorset.

Flint's hunting lodge sat roughly thirty miles north of Lake's Edge and twenty miles west of the haul road. Driving would take ages longer than it would to fly, not just because you'd have to drive three sides of a box, but the track was forced to wind its way tortuously around a variety of rivers, forests and hills. There was also a lake to skirt. The track headed north for roughly two miles before it came to a bridge spread over the lake's mouth, and then you had two miles south. No wonder Flint had an airstrip.

She was already tense at the thought of driving out there, but she was determined not to be a wuss and to go alone. Lisa wouldn't want anyone else turning up. Her note from Malone had said, *Don't tell anyone*, and she assumed nothing had changed. Besides which, she reckoned they could both do without Connie's verbal and emotional outpourings. When they were finally reunited, she wanted Lisa entirely to herself.

To her surprise, as she neared the Moose, she saw two souvenir shops had opened and that the café two doors down had unlatched its shutters and put some tables outside. Spring was here and welcoming the first visitors before the summer rush: mountain climbers.

She was passing a group of people buying postcards when she heard her name being called. Turning, she saw Demarco striding her way.

'Abby? Can I have a word?'

The tourists stopped what they were doing. All eyes went from the uniformed trooper to Abby, and she felt herself flush, as though she was guilty of something.

'Of course.'

Demarco walked a little further down the boardwalk and out of earshot from the tourists.

'The sergeant wanted me to tell you that we've managed to talk to the man in Fairbanks hospital. He's taken the deal we offered. We've names and addresses for the other two guys, and we're chasing them up as I speak. We'll have them tomorrow latest. They were hired to kidnap

287

you. They've done this kind of thing before. That's why they were reasonably experienced. They knew what they were doing.'

Demarco took a breath. 'They were also hired to kill Lisa. They didn't know about Marie when they got to Lake's Edge... They thought Marie was Lisa. There was no research for them to steal – the cabin had already been cleared.'

Abby said, 'And Lisa burned what she couldn't take with her.'

'It looks that way.'

The trooper's intelligent eyes fixed on Abby's. 'All communication was by email. Payment by wire transfer. Difficult to track down, but with our bird singing we're piecing it together.'

'Who hired them?'

'The email address belongs to Peter Santoni.'

As if she hadn't guessed.

'And have you arrested him yet?'

'Not exactly.'

'What do you mean by that? *Not exactly.*'

'It means we've found him...' Demarco averted her eyes to look past Abby's shoulder. 'But he's dead. The cops finally managed to identify him this morning.'

'He's *what?*'

Demarco kept her gaze resolutely to one side and didn't repeat herself; she knew Abby had heard the first time.

Abby was shaking her head in disbelief. 'How did he die?'

'He was chained to the steering wheel of a car just outside Juneau. Doused with gasoline and burned to death.'

Abby closed her eyes. 'Oh, God.'

'Which is why it took the cops so long to ID him. Burned bodies give few clues and at first they didn't even know what sex he was. It was only because of the way Thomas Claire was murdered that the cops looked at colleagues of his who might be missing.'

Abby's mind was scrambling. 'When was he murdered?'

'They're having trouble pinning it down exactly, but they think it was before Thomas's murder. Around the first, second of this month.'

Abby shivered. Santoni had been killed while Thomas headed for Anchorage, Lisa for Lake's Edge. 'Are you saying Santoni wasn't behind this after all?'

'For what it's worth,' Demarco said, 'we're finding it hard to take in too. And I'm sure you'll understand it when I tell you we urgently need to talk to your sister. Without her input we're working in a quagmire. There's a lot we don't understand and she'll help fill in the gaps.'

There was a long silence while Demarco looked at Abby and Abby stared down the street.

'You'll let us know should she contact you?' Demarco asked.

'Sure,' she said and gave the trooper a smile, making sure she injected it with warmth and creased her eyes at the corners. She had no intention of turning Lisa over to the cops until those gaps had been filled, preferably with double-strength concrete. 'Haven't you any other suspects?'

'We're considering one or two.'

'Michael Flint?' Abby suggested.

Demarco started. 'What do you know about him?'

'I heard he and Lisa were enemies.'

Demarco leaned forward a little, her expression turning more intense. 'A word of warning?'

Abby stared, alarm bells ringing. 'Sure.'

'Cal says he's been trying to keep tabs on you, but if he's not around ... eyes in the back of your head, okay?'

'Flint's behind this?' Abby asked.

Demarco looked hesitant, then seemed to come to an internal decision and added, 'All we have is that Michael Flint was seen on the UAF campus the day Lisa and Thomas split. He says he was meeting with a professor of geology, and the professor confirms this.'

'But you're not sure?'

'I think you'd better talk to the sergeant. He's due up here later today.'

Demarco scrubbed her face with her hands, then said, 'Look, there's something else. Through a public appeal, we spoke to a truck driver who was on the haul road at the time of the kidnappers' rendezvous at Fiveways. He spotted a vehicle parked in the area. He remembers it because he wants one just like it. A white Dodge Ram pickup.'

If Big Joe was surprised to see her, she would never have known it. His broad, weather-beaten face perused her with its usual impassive expression, followed by a grunt that could have meant he thought she looked okay or reckoned she could do with a pair of false eyebrows.

'Coffee?' he offered.

'Love some.'

Before she sat down, she went to the window to check on Moke. He'd upgraded himself from the back of Diane's ketchup-red SUV and was sitting in the driver's seat, peering through the window.

Abby settled herself on one of the upended logs in the kitchen. There was a sink, an oil stove for cooking, and the usual wood stove for warmth. A couple of caribou antlers by the door had fur parkas and jackets hanging from them. The floor was strewn with shoes, socks, sweaters and toys, and she could hear the kids outside, playing with their mother in the sunshine.

The coffee was strong and gave her heart a solid jolt. 'That's good,' she told him.

Big Joe leaned against the wall, cradling his mug against his chest. 'They know who grabbed you?'

'They were professionals. Paid by a scientist, Thomas and Lisa used to work with – Peter Santoni.'

Big Joe nodded.

'You know the guy?'

He shook his head.

'Good thing, since he's dead.'

If she'd expected the Native to react, she'd been fooling herself. Not a single muscle on the man's face moved. She decided on a different tactic. 'Joe, why was your car parked near Fiveways at the time of the kidnappers' rendezvous?'

Again, no response.

Abby put her mug down and rested her arms on the table. A relentless thudding echoed behind her eyes. She remembered him giving her whiskey to drink after she'd heard about Marie's murder, and his quiet confidence that Lisa was alive. 'You've been helping Lisa, haven't you?'

Big Joe fixed his dark gaze on her and gave a nod.

She went and stood in front of him. 'Jesus, Joe, why didn't you tell me? And don't say because I didn't ask or I'll hit you!'

'We were trying...' He seemed to struggle for words. 'To protect you.'

'Jesus,' she said again. 'Do you know where Lisa is?'

He shook his head.

'How do you keep in touch?'

'We don't.' He said it very flat. 'She's only called me a couple of times.'

'The cabins,' she said, breathing coming fast. 'You put the M & Ms and necklace there to put everyone off the scent, along with the dog harness.'

'No. Someone else did that.'

'Who?'

For the first time since she'd known him, his face held an emotion. He was, she realised with a start, worried. 'I don't know.'

'Did you know about Marie's murder?'

He shook his head. 'I knew something was up, though, because Lisa entrusted something to me for safekeeping. When she didn't collect it like she said that Saturday, I went to her place but she'd gone. That's when I hit the panic button and got the search started.'

She stared at him in astonishment. 'You've got MEG?'

'Not any more. I met Lisa on the haul road and gave it to her for the Fiveways deal. She still has it.'

Thunderstruck, Abby managed to make it back to her log seat. She tried to steady herself by taking a gulp of coffee, but her blood was popping, her mind galloping.

'Joe, I wish you'd told me this before.'

He looked away and scratched the back of his head. 'Lisa told me not to. She believes whoever's after it will kill anyone who knows what the thing really is... So when they patent it, there's no one to go against them.'

'Why tell me now?'

Big Joe shuffled his feet. 'Because I think you should know. In case Lisa... I'd help you. Goes without saying.' More shuffling, and she realised Big Joe was trying to tell her that if Lisa died, he wanted her to join him in taking up Lisa's cause.

Abby pushed her head in her hands, praying the killers never found out she and Big Joe knew what MEG really was.

'Joe, how long did you have MEG for?'

He thought it over a bit, then said, 'A couple of weeks. They thought someone was after it, so Lisa brought it up here. Gave it to me.'

'And while Lisa got Marie to come and collect MEG,' Abby thought out loud, 'Thomas went to Anchorage as a decoy, to draw anyone interested away. But their plan went wrong. Marie was killed before Lisa had a chance to give her MEG, which left Lisa running for her life while you had MEG stashed here.'

'Got it in one.'

'Where's Lisa now?'

'She didn't say.'

'Okay, which direction did she go after the rendezvous?'

'North.'

'Up the haul road?'

'Yup.'

She hadn't needed confirmation where Lisa was, but it didn't hinder either. Flint's place was north, up the haul road.

'And she was okay?'

'Bit of frost nip here and there, but pretty good.'

'What's she planning to do?'

Big Joe sighed, expanding his chest to its full capacity and letting out a rush of air like a belch from the funnel of a steam train. 'She's waiting to see if the cops find the killer. Then she might be safe to show herself and get MEG to the patent office.'

'What about the lab books? Does she have them too? I gather they're almost as important as MEG itself.'

The worry returned. 'She never said.'

Abby ran her hand over the polished wood table, wondering whether to keep Flint's supposed secret or not, and just as quickly decided: not. 'Michael Flint says he's already filed an application at USTPO on Lisa's behalf.'

There was long silence while Big Joe studied the space above her shoulder.

'I heard he and Lisa might be having an affair.'

Big Joe sighed again. 'If you believe everything you heard, she'd be having an affair with me too.'

Abby sat motionless and gazed at a small, red

shoe with a white daisy buckle lying on the floor. Everything was upside-down and inside-out. She felt shaky and disembodied ... unsure of anything.

She dragged her mind over what Flint had told her and was struck with an idea. 'What if I took MEG to the patent office? The kidnappers knew I didn't have it, so why would they take any interest in me?' The more she thought about it, the more her excitement grew. 'I could pretend to be flying back to England. I'd buy a ticket from Anchorage to Seattle and on to Heathrow, but I'd jump ship in Seattle and fly to Arlington, and patent it and we'd beat them!'

Big Joe considered her. 'Good plan,' he said. 'But first, you've got to find your sister.'

Abby's face split into a grin. 'Don't worry, Joe. I know where she is.'

Thirty-three

Just after midnight, Abby decided it was time. She got out of bed in the darkness and reached for her clothes. Moke came over and when she hushed him, went and sat by the door, expectant.

The night silence was thick, almost palpable. She checked she had her car keys and purse, then she pulled on her parka. She propped the brief note she'd written earlier by the kettle; a precaution should she get into trouble. She doubted anyone would read it for twenty-four hours but it was better than nothing.

295

Day pack at her feet, she did a last-minute check. She didn't have a shotgun, but she had her new penknife. Not that she had any intention of stabbing a grizzly with it, but having it strapped to her ankle felt immensely comforting.

She opened the front door and stepped outside, the dog at her side. Total silence. The sky was as clear as glass and there was no moon. Stars shone hard and bright in the cold, still air. She pulled the door gently behind her and walked for Diane's SUV.

With Moke in the back, Abby started the car and drove slowly out of town.

A couple of years ago Abby thought she might forget what Lisa looked like but now her mind was crowded with memories. Lisa's dark cap of curly hair, her energetic movements, never at rest unless she was in the thick of sleep. She brought Lisa's face into focus, recalling the shape of her jaw, strong and determined, the small scar on her forehead caused by crashing her go-cart into a wall, her straight black brows and wide, smiling mouth.

How she'd come to turn her back on Lisa now seemed irrelevant and insignificant against the last couple of weeks. She could see now what she couldn't before, that she'd spent her entire life wanting Lisa to be someone she wasn't, desperate to have a little sister with whom she could share secrets, a sister she could rely on, a sister to whom she could relate.

She swung left when she came to the haul road and powered the SUV north on the gravel road, stones clicking the bodywork, the headlights cutting through the darkness.

She remembered the emails Lisa had written, the ones she'd deleted with a click of her mouse, unread. She was a coward, she realised. She'd held on to her anger for so long, she was as bad as Lisa.

It was time to ask Lisa to forgive her for what she'd done.

Abby drove straight past the turn-off without realising it. She'd been keeping an eye on her odometer and when it clocked forty miles, she slowed and did a U-turn. Backtracking at half the speed, she searched the darkness for wheel ruts, tyre tracks in the snow at the side of the road, anything to give her a clue where it was. Again, she passed it and, nearly screaming with frustration, forced herself to turn around and retrace her route at 30 mph.

'We mustn't rush,' she told Moke, 'or we'll be driving back and forth all night.'

There was no response from the dog, and when she glanced round, she saw he was sprawled full-length across the back seat, fast asleep.

This time, she spotted an area of snowy slush and stones without any trouble. Driving cautiously off the highway, she placed her SUV's tyres exactly where the previous vehicle had driven; Michael Flint's tracks.

It felt strange following his route, but since he was – like most Alaskans – experienced in driving through snow, she felt confident he'd have taken the best and easiest course.

From time to time the car would slip and her heart would jump into overdrive, until the wheels gripped and hauled her forwards. All she could see was snow and the occasional patch where it had melted, showing limp brown grasses and grey stones, shiny with ice.

By three o'clock her eyes were beginning to burn.

Eventually the track swung north. On her left was a four- or five-foot drop to the frozen lake, on her right planes of flat snow. She wanted to drive further away from the drop but didn't dare leave Flint's tracks. He knew the terrain. She didn't.

She was wondering if Lisa had grown her hair or if it was still cropped short, when she approached the northern-most end of the lake, and a bridge finally came in to view. Thank God. She was over halfway there.

Carefully she drove over the planks, hearing them rattle and creak under the tyres, headlights cutting to the corner ahead. A sharp bend up an icy slope meant she'd have to get a run-up to it or she'd slide straight back downhill.

Abby pressured the accelerator, changed up a gear, and she was doing around 20 mph, turning the car into the corner, driving cautiously but as boldly as she dared, when suddenly the wheels lost their grip and the SUV went into a graceful, slow-motion slide, straight towards the drop to the lake. A frozen lake that was cracked and weeping at the edges, and would buckle immediately, plunging the vehicle straight to the bottom.

Thirty-four

Horrified, she realised she was on a frozen stream, sheet ice all the way to the lip of the lake. Don't panic, *don't panic*, you're right in Flint's tracks and he came home, so will you.

Heart in her mouth, Abby turned the steering wheel, trying to get a tyre to grab on a chunk of snow, a rock, anything, but there was nothing to grip but sheer ice. To her disbelief the car kept sliding.

'Nooo,' she wailed. She felt more than saw Moke sit up and take notice.

She tried the hand brake, then tried slowing the engine speed. No response. The weight of the car was making it glide inexorably, appallingly slowly, towards the edge of the lake.

Her mind was a blur of panicked thoughts. Should she get out? The vehicle was travelling slowly enough. What about Flint? How had he survived this?

The lake's bank began to near.

She was about to turn to open Moke's door, to let the dog out before she too leaped from the car, when she spotted several dark patches on the ice, like scattered ash. She turned the steering wheel for the first patch and the instant the tyres brushed it, they gripped. The car immediately stopped sliding. She had full traction.

Abby drove past the treacherous corner until

she was safe, and pulled up.

'You stay, boy,' she told the dog.

Opening the door she climbed out, gasping, her breath clouding the air. On unsteady legs she walked back. Studied the patches of grit and gravel Flint must have shovelled across the ice.

Sweet Jesus. If she'd been going any faster the car would have sailed right over them and plunged into the lake. Had that been his intention? Not to grit the whole corner in order to trap the unwary?

A surge of anger helped steady her. She wouldn't be trapped when she returned. No way. Crunching up the bank, Abby grabbed some boughs, covered in dry needles. Lugged them back and laid them across the ice. Then she went back and lugged some more. Moke was watching her through the window, eyebrows creased, but she didn't stop until she'd made the corner as safe as she could.

When she climbed back inside her car her trembling had ceased. Clever bastard, she thought, easing the car forward. Letting me follow your tracks like that. Well now I'm ready for you, you tricky son-of-a-bitch, I won't get caught out like that again.

She was surprised there were no more death-traps as she drove down the other side of the lake, no icy corners as the track wound around the river, then the forest. Abby reached the hunting lodge in faint amazement she'd made it in one piece.

The stars were beginning to fade and the deep blue-black of the sky had softened into grey. Dawn was approaching. She climbed out into the freezing air and looked around. The lodge was one big main house with five smaller cabins set in a semi-circle opposite. All had pitched roofs and were built out of logs and looked impossibly romantic in their snowy setting. An open-ended building sat at the end of a snowed-over airstrip with two four-wheelers and a snow machine to take care of year-round transportation. There were cottonwoods and spruce, creeks and rivers. In summer it would be thick with game; grizzlies, moose, eagles and salmon.

She let Moke out. He took a handful of paces, sniffed the air briefly, then rushed at her, bouncing joyfully across the snow before darting away and running for the lodge.

She'd forgotten Moke knew the area. His owner used to look after Flint's lodge in summertime, and being here again must have felt like a kind of homecoming. Moke bounded ahead as she brought out her torch and crunched her way to the lodge. She peered through the windows to see a kitchen the size of the British Museum with granite worktops, a living room with a fireplace for roasting whole oxen, lots of animal hides and heads on the walls, rugs and throws everywhere. It was rustic and masculine and nobody was living there that she could see.

Abby walked to each cabin and had a look.

No Lisa, but she was here, somewhere. She knew it.

Abby crunched around to the rear of the lodge, backed against the edge of a forest. Everything was very still. No breeze stirred the topmost branches. No birds called or cawed into the silence. She could hear her breathing loud as a hurricane, her footsteps like gunshots.

A bear shutter was propped against the wall. Someone had levered it off recently; the marks on the wood were still fresh. Abby tried the door and to her amazement, found it was unlocked. She shone her torch around. Her heart jumped.

Fresh snow-machine tracks led straight from the lodge and into the forest. As easy to follow as a lighted highway.

She could hear Diane's voice. *He's got some wilderness cabins through the forest. She uses them like they're hers.*

If Lisa was hiding in the forest, did this mean she'd been forced to raid Flint's lodge for supplies? But wouldn't he have seen the tracks? Not necessarily, if they'd been made recently. First, she'd better check the lodge, to make sure Lisa wasn't hiding there. No point in heading into the forest if she was.

Her footsteps echoed on tiles, then wooden boards. Her breath poured clouds into the freezing air. No way would Lisa be able to hide in this cold, but she'd better check. Speeding up her pace, Abby swept through the ground floor. The evocative scent of wood smoke still lingered on the air even though the fire hadn't burned for a while. A frying-pan, saucepan, single plate and knife and fork were draining in the kitchen. She pounded upstairs, checking bedrooms and bathrooms, barely seeing the richly coloured rooms, the designer touches, the life-sized bronzes of wolves and eagles on the landings.

She found herself looking in wardrobes and

behind doors, and in the back of her mind she could hear Lisa shrieking, *Found you!*

Lisa always won hide and seek.

Abby heard Moke pattering on the wooden boards downstairs as she sped into the master bedroom. The bed was rumpled, and a red towel had fallen to the floor in the shower room. She had a vision of eight-year-old Lisa crouched in the attic, stifling her giggles while Flint pottered around below, and glanced up at the ceiling. No moveable panels that she could see.

Downstairs she found Moke checking out the mud room. Fishing rods and nets, waders, boots, mosquito netting, fridges and chest freezers – all silent – and an empty gun cabinet. As she ran her eyes around something niggled at her. Something small was knocking her memory. Carefully she looked again at the stacks of maps on the window-sill, the waterproofs and walking sticks, and then she remembered the broken lock on the mud-room door in Lisa's cabin, the coats and scarves pulled to the floor, the freezer door left wide open.

The freezers.

All three had locks. Whether this was to prevent people nicking a tender haunch of moose or a side of a fifty-pound salmon in summertime, Abby didn't know, but what had caught her eye was that where two of the freezers had keys in their locks, the third didn't. Also, its plug wasn't in the wall socket like the others, but lying on the floor.

Abby tried to open the freezer. It was locked. Why would someone lock an empty freezer? She opened all the others to find them empty. She looked at the one that was locked. It was bound to be empty too, the fact it was locked an accident. Someone had probably lost the key.

Moke's bright blue eyes watched her, curious.

'I've got to open it,' she told him. 'Sorry.'

Abby put down her mittens and hunted around until she found a screwdriver and a hammer. Pushing the screwdriver into the lock, she whacked it with the hammer until it snapped.

With a rubber sucking pop, she opened the lid. Peered down.

Four cardboard cartons stared back at her.

Kershaw's Wholegrain Kibble provides all the goodness a healthy dog needs.

'Shit,' she said. Michael Flint had obviously taken the precaution of sealing the dog food inside the freezer to prevent a grizzly smelling it and breaking into the lodge for a free feed. Like a kid who'd been given a present she didn't like and was hoping it might be something better in disguise, Abby ripped open one of the carton lids.

'Shit,' she said again.

Instead of dog food were stacks of zip discs. She picked one up and read the label: *Sir John Ross Institute.*

She felt her legs weaken. 'Shit.'

She opened the next box to find piles of ring binders. She pulled one out. Had a look.

Monthly reports. Notes. Experiments. Results.

Each page had been dated and signed by a witness.

Each page was headed: MEG.

She'd found the lab books.

With Moke trotting ahead, Abby started walking

into the forest, following the snow machine's tracks. Had Lisa hidden the lab books at Flint's? If so, it was a very daring, very dangerous move. Typically Lisa. But then she remembered what Demarco had said.

Michael Flint was seen on the UAF campus the day Lisa and Thomas split.

Had Flint stolen the lab books then gone after Thomas, believing he had MEG? Abby shuddered as she thought of how she'd put her arms around Flint's waist on the snow-machine ride, how he'd warned her off MEG. He had told her to go home.

As she crunched through the forest she called out, 'Go home, bear,' every few paces but still her skin was tight with fear. She'd rather face a band of kidnappers any day than a startled grizzly.

Abby dug in her pocket for her mittens, but only found one. She stopped and shone her torch backward but couldn't see the other. She'd live, she decided. Hand in her pocket, she walked on.

The tenuous dawn light dimmed as the tracks wound through the forest. Trees loomed close on every side and her ears strained to register even the slightest sound. Dread was flooding through her veins like a drug. Her breath came out in short gasps.

'Moke,' she commanded, tapping her thigh, 'stay close. Close.'

The dog paused and looked at her over his shoulder, puzzled, then trotted briskly forward. He obviously couldn't smell any bears about, but there wasn't any breeze to smell them on. For all she knew there was an almighty grizzly having a nap just yards away.

Abby kept walking steadily, as confidently as she could, still calling out to warn bears of her presence. Just below the surface of her skin she could feel a scream building up. *I shouldn't be here!*

She became aware the sky was lightening, but there was no dawn chorus to herald the rising of the sun. Not like in Oxford when blackbirds, robins and sparrows burst into song the second they thought night might be over. It could have been the last dawn on earth it was so silent.

Suddenly Moke stopped. Stiff-legged, he took two paces forward, tail flat, and stopped again. His hackles rose.

Oh, fuck.

He gave a low growl.

To her horror, she heard an answering growl. It seemed to come from directly in front of Moke.

'Go home, bear!' she yelled. 'Leave us alone!'

The growl erupted into a roar and Moke responded with a series of barks that had his forefeet clearing the ground, his hackles erect, teeth bared.

'Leave, Moke. LEAVE!'

There was another roar and then a shadow burst from behind the trees, going straight for Moke.

She heard the soft *thump* as the two bodies collided. A blur of fur and teeth and snarling and Abby was backing up, tensing her muscles to sprint behind a tree, when suddenly, it was all over. The animals had separated and were standing opposite one another, touching noses.

It wasn't a bear. It was a goddamn *dog*.

Weak with relief, Abby watched the two animals

sniff each other all over; ears, crotches, bottoms, and then Moke gave a lunge and barked, a deep *woof!* that Abby knew was a greeting and the other dog obviously knew too because the next instant they were running alongside one another, biting each other's ruffs, tails waving, tumbling in the snow, tongues lolling happily.

'Roscoe?' she called hesitantly.

Both dogs immediately stopped their play and stood looking at her.

'Moke,' she commanded. 'Roscoe.'

They trotted over. Moke leaned against her legs, looking up at her while Roscoe did the head-to-toe doggy inspection. Lots of sniffs and half-wags but he didn't seem convinced and moved away each time she tried to pat him.

'Well, boys,' she told them, 'lead on. We've another reunion to be getting—'

She never finished her words because there was a rush of air behind her and something crashed into the backs of her knees and she went down like a felled tree. She twisted, lashing out with her boots, trying to struggle up but something lay across her chest, pinning her down. She was about to call for Moke when she took in the gun.

A double-barrelled shotgun. And although it wasn't pointed directly at her, it wasn't broken either, and she had no doubt it was loaded and ready to fire.

'Abby?'

A wave of relief crashed so hard over her she wanted to cry.

'Lisa?'

'Who's with you?'

'No one. It's just me,' she gasped. 'I came *alone.*'

She could see her sister's face now. She'd lost a lot of weight and her features had hollowed, making it gaunt. There were charcoal marks on her cheekbones but she couldn't think what they were, with Lisa straddled across her chest and clutching a shotgun.

Lisa glanced around. 'You're kidding me. Abby shit-for-brains actually worked out where I was?'

Abby promptly lost all control.

'Fuck you!' she yelled, and as she yelled it was as though a dam had broken. 'You think you're so fucking smart but I fucking found you! So how fucking intelligent are you if Abby shit-for-brains is right here under your fucking nose, you FUCK?'

In a single movement Abby knocked the shotgun away and heaved her sister aside. It was like pushing a bundle of dried leaves aside she was so light. With a small *oof* Lisa landed in the snow and Abby was on top of her but Lisa wriggled free and they were grabbing each other and hitting and yanking and pushing, and Abby had snow in her face and down her neck and she was kicking Lisa's legs from beneath her and pushing her head into a snow drift, and it was as though they were ten years old again, scrapping in the snow.

Abby sat astride Lisa, panting heavily.

'Give up?'

'Never.'

'You are nothing but a pain in the ass,' Abby said. 'I do my best and all I get is a gun stuck in my face.'

'Don't exaggerate. It wasn't in your face.'

'Damn nearly.'

Small silence.

'Sorry.'

'You're always sorry,' Abby said. 'But nothing ever changes, does it?'

'Is that a rhetorical question? Because if it is, can I get up? You're squashing me.'

'No.'

'Okay.' There was a small pause, then Lisa said, 'It's good to see you.'

Abby didn't respond. She could feel Lisa's chest rise and fall beneath her, see her breath clouding the air. She felt as though she were fainting. She struggled with the sense of vertigo. Lisa was speaking, but she couldn't hear a word. Her sister's face was open, trusting, the same as always. As though she didn't give a damn that Abby was twice her size and sitting on top of her. The same as always. Fearless and in command and not in the least bit apologetic. She was lying in the snow, waiting for Abby to come to her senses. Then they'd laugh and joke over what had happened. Put it behind them.

'Not this time,' said Abby.

'No,' Lisa agreed. 'It's gone too far for that.'

Abby blinked. 'Did you just read my mind?'

'Come on, Abby. I've known you since I was born, remember? My first memory is of you peeking down at me in my pram. The next is you trying to feed me spinach–'

'You hate spinach.'

'Which is why I filled my mouth with the stuff then went to the loo and spat it all out.'

'Dad went ballistic,' Abby recalled.

'Not at you,' Lisa sighed. 'At me. Everyone's always angry at me.'

An explosion erupted inside her head and Abby suddenly found herself in Lisa's place. Four years old, six, ten, seeing their father yelling at her, face swollen red with apoplectic fury, veins popping around his nose and across his forehead, sending her to her room again and again. Dad had never been angry with her. Only at Lisa.

'Oh, God,' she said.

'Yeah.' Lisa's voice was smiling. 'He never got it. That I'm me. Different from him.'

'Different from me, too.'

'Not so different.'

Abby heard the words but didn't believe them.

'You and me,' Lisa said. 'We're a couple of stubborn old cows, don't you think? Believing we're absolutely right all the time? How I ever thought you'd have a fling with Cal if you knew he was married defies belief. I know how goddamn puritanical you are. I just had my head up my ass, as usual.'

'Is that an apology?'

'The second you left I knew I'd fucked up. I'd said too much in the heat of the moment, stuff I didn't mean ... but you'd bloody well left the country before I could explain. Jesus, Abby, you are such a pain in the bum sometimes.'

'You too.' She sighed. 'You never *listen.*'

'It's a failing, I know. But you shouldn't have left like that.'

'I couldn't bear it. I liked him *so much.*'

'Yeah, so I gathered.'

Roscoe nudged Lisa's shoulder and whined.

'It's all right, boy,' Lisa told him, then raised an eyebrow at Abby. 'Can I get up now? I'm freezing my ass off down here.'

Abby levered herself off and took Lisa's hand and lifted her to her feet.

'I'd forgotten,' Lisa said, sounding surprised.

'Forgotten what?'

'How strong you are.' She patted the snow off her thighs, dusted her jacket down. 'I always envied that. God, I hate being short and puny. I used to dream of being you, tall and confident and calm and not needing to be the centre of attention...' She broke off suddenly and looked away. Abby saw the tears welling up.

'Fuck. How I wanted to be you.'

Abby swallowed, a hard knot in her throat. Carefully she picked up the shotgun and broke it, resting it across her elbow, like she'd seen Malone do.

'I hated you,' Lisa said, voice rasping.

'I hated you too.'

Lisa turned and looked up at her, eyes wet, her mouth curved in a sad smile. 'Well, at least we have something in common.'

Thirty-five

Lisa's cabin was almost a replica of the wilderness cabin Abby had been incarcerated inside. It had a sleeping shelf in one corner, a simple kitchenette in the other, and a wood stove churning out heat in the middle. But instead of a bucket there was an outhouse, so there was no stench of human waste, just the smell of wood smoke. To her relief, there were no rows of canned food to mock her.

Kerosene lamps licked warm yellow light over an overstuffed armchair, two hand-hewn stools, faded curtains at the windows, farm hooks and rings hammered into the walls, and a big tree stump for a table, which had been ground and polished until its top gleamed like oil. A feather-plumped duvet and four pillows lay on the sleeping shelf.

'Five star,' said Abby, impressed.

'Says the expert.'

Abby froze, stiffening up at the familiar dismissiveness in Lisa's voice.

'Fuck.' Lisa was scrubbing her face with both hands. 'I'm sorry. I thought we'd be hugging each other to death when we finally got together. You know, all is forgiven, I love you, blah, blah, blah. But it's not that simple, is it?'

'No.'

'Bugger it.' Lisa went to the wood stove, fed some logs inside. 'And you know what really pisses me off?'

Abby looked down at her sister's strong small body, seemingly indefatigable, and suddenly felt exhausted. 'No.'

'That bloody dog of yours.'

Startled, Abby put her hand on Moke's ruff. 'He's not my dog. He's yours.'

'So why hasn't he moved an inch from you the past half-hour?'

Abby hadn't noticed Moke's presence and

reckoned it was because she must be used to it.

'I feed him, I guess.'

'I fed him too.'

'He likes spaghetti.' Abby yawned and Moke looked up, mouth stretching wide in unison so she could see right down his throat.

'Oh for God's sakes,' Lisa said, half-laughing. 'He even mimics you.'

Abby shrugged, jiggling the ejected shells from the shotgun in her pocket.

'Coffee?' Lisa offered. 'I've chocolate if you prefer.'

'Chocolate, please.'

Abby took a stool at the tree stump. Moke flopped at her feet while Roscoe took prime position next to the wood stove. Her eyes moved over Lisa's face while she brought out mugs, opened a carton of long-life milk and put a pan on top of the stove. The smears on her cheekbones had to be frostbite. If she hadn't known that, she might have thought Lisa had used an unusual shade of blusher. She looked strangely Gothic.

'Nothing a cosmetic surgeon can't fix,' Lisa said brightly.

'Does it hurt?'

'Like buggery at first. But I was lucky. It's not frostbite as much as frost nip. I keep it smothered in Camomile lotion. Seems to do the trick.'

Once the milk was hot, Lisa poured it over the chocolate, stirred it vigorously and passed it over. Then she went to the window and looked outside before returning to the kitchenette and lighting a cigarette. Abby held out a hand. 'Mind if I pinch one?'

313

'So long as it's not your first,' Lisa said. 'I don't want to be responsible for you taking up smoking again.'

'You already are.'

'Ah, shit.' Lisa chucked the pack over.

Abby lit up. She hadn't had a cigarette since the day of the kidnap and the nicotine hit her system fast and made her feel giddy.

Upending an old mayonnaise lid, Lisa put it on the table, flicked a length of ash inside. 'Some predicament I got us into, huh?'

'Just a bit.' Abby rolled her cigarette between her fingers. 'Any ideas on what we should do next?'

'I've one or two,' Lisa hedged.

'Joe told me you've got MEG,' Abby said.

Lisa didn't say anything, but Abby saw the mention of MEG had made her eyes cloud.

'You know about Thomas?' Abby ventured gently.

Lisa looked away. 'Yeah. Big Joe told me. I radioed him last night from the lodge.'

'I'm sorry.'

'Me too.' Lisa was brittle, holding herself together. 'He was… Like a father to me.'

'I know.'

'How's Mum?'

'How do you think?'

'That bad?'

'For goodness' sake, Lisa, did you think she'd be doing cartwheels over this?'

Her sister looked away. 'Sorry.'

Abby took a deep breath. 'She's actually doing okay. Still at home. No hospitals or anything.

314

Ralph's been amazing, looking after her all this time.'

'And she's okay with that?'

'Seems to be.'

Lisa gave a smile. 'Maybe he'll get that date he's always wanted.'

'And maybe pigs will fly.'

Lisa flicked some more ash into the mayonnaise lid. 'You've sorted things with Cal yet? Big Joe told me he's been hanging around you quite a bit.'

'What's to sort? He lied to me.'

'Yeah, so he said.' Lisa took a sip of coffee. 'Poor bugger.'

Abby put down her mug too hard, making chocolate slop over her wrist, but she barely felt it. 'He let me believe he was free and available and he wasn't. I'm not sure I can forgive that.'

'Judge and jury, are you?' Lisa took a pull on her cigarette and exhaled a stream of blue smoke.

Abby stared at her sister, skin prickling. 'What he did to me was unforgivable. And what about Saffron? Even you said she would have been devastated if she'd found out.'

Lisa took a long drag of her cigarette. 'Don't tell me you were never tempted to jump on a train and never return when Mum was sick.'

'That's *different*. I didn't lie to anyone!'

'Come on, Abby, can't you see the guy made a mistake?'

'No way, he crossed a line that should never–'

'And he's been paying for it ever since. He was devastated when you left, he knew he'd fucked up, but would you listen? Oh, no, you just–'

'He was devastated?' Abby gave a hysterical laugh. 'Give me a break.'

'SHUT UP!' Lisa roared, making Abby and both dogs jump. 'Will you fucking listen for a minute? I've spent the last four years working out what the hell went wrong and I won't have you start this crap all over again!'

Abby's heart was jumping like a firecracker.

'I condemned you that day.' Lisa stared at her, eyes challenging. 'And you condemned me. And Cal. Did you ever think you might have been a teeny bit precipitate?'

Her cigarette had burned down to the filter, but she didn't notice.

'You lost two people who loved you in a single day because you were too damned stubborn, too *self-centred* to think of anyone but yourself.'

Abby loosened her tongue where it seemed stuck to the roof of her mouth. 'Talk about the pot calling the kettle black.'

'Exactly,' Lisa said, looking satisfied. 'You ever wonder about the things you hate about me? Why you hate them so much?'

She kept still, eyes fixed on her sister.

'Because they're the same traits you have in yourself. The ones you hate about yourself. They're the same ones I hate about me too.' Lisa ground her cigarette out on the side of the sink, lit another. 'Took me ages to work it out.'

'I'm not like you,' Abby said stiffly.

'No. You're not.' She gave a long, heavy sigh. 'But there's bits that you can't deny.'

Lisa finished her cigarette in silence. Abby's mind was crashing, going over Lisa's words.

316

You condemned me.

'I'm sorry.' She heard the words come out of her mouth as if they didn't belong to her.

Lisa came over and tucked a strand of hair behind her ear, a gesture she remembered from her teens, when she had long hair. 'It's okay,' she murmured. 'I forgave you ages ago. All you have to do now is forgive yourself for being such a complete and utter prat.'

Abby felt her throat start to tighten.

Lisa opened her arms. 'Come here, big sis.'

Lisa felt fragile and light as a sparrow but her grip was fierce. Her hair smelled of wood smoke. Abby's eyes began to fill. She hugged Lisa tightly, her eyes closed, every sense concentrated on the feeling of her little sister in her arms.

'So what's next?' asked Abby a little later, blowing her nose and wiping her eyes. She hadn't cried all the time Lisa was missing, and now she'd started, she was finding it hard to stop.

'We've got to get MEG to the patent office. It's the only way to get the killers off our backs.'

Abby outlined the plan she'd made with Big Joe. Lisa immediately brightened. 'You'd do that for me? Really?'

'You'd trust me with MEG? Really?'

Lisa looked startled for a second, and then she laughed. A joyous laugh that filled her belly and stretched her mouth wide. Abby found herself laughing too. She'd forgotten how infectious Lisa's laughter was.

'Yeah,' said Lisa, still chuckling. 'I'd trust you with MEG.'

Suddenly Abby was dying to see the invention that had caused so much mayhem, but she knew better than to ask. She busied herself wiping the remaining tears from her face and throwing the tissues into the bin.

'Join me?' Lisa asked. She was putting on her bunny boots and preparing to go outside.

'Sure.'

Together they walked to the back of the cabin. Lisa grabbed a shovel leaning against the rear wall and gave it to Abby. Then she pointed past the outhouse at an enormous jack pine.

'You want to see MEG, you've got to dig.'

MEG's prototype was about the size of a shoebox, and weighed just over two kilos.

'It doesn't need any maintenance,' Lisa was telling her proudly, 'and it produces all the energy you need to run your home. Larger ones will eventually be used to run factories and cars. One day even airplanes. It doesn't have an engine, just uses the earth's magnetic energy.'

They were crunching back to the cabin, Moke and Roscoe mock-wrestling in the snow as though celebrating their reunion. Lisa was cradling MEG in her arms, as she would a baby.

'And it doesn't produce any waste products or pollution, nor contribute to any negative environmental impacts.' Lisa gave the machine a pat. 'Thomas's baby.'

'And Peter Santoni's,' Abby added.

'Hardly,' Lisa snorted. 'Santoni Craponi. The God of EVals indeed. The God of shite, more like. Imagine naming your invention after someone's cat. The Curtis Cluster, huh. Thomas just about cracked a rib laughing.'

Lisa kicked her boots of snow and walked into the cabin, put MEG on the polished tree trunk. Abby went and ran her fingers lightly over MEG's cool metal.

'Santoni's dead,' Abby said. 'He was murdered.'

Lisa swung round. 'You're kidding.'

'He was burned alive. The cops say whoever did it didn't want him to be identified.'

'Jesus. They caught who did it? They should do, with the other deaths having the same MO.'

Abby was opening her mouth to tell Lisa about her last conversation with Demarco when Moke started barking.

The sisters spun around to face the door.

He kept barking, a deep warning shout that Abby recognised.

Lisa and Abby looked at each other in dismay.

Then Roscoe joined in.

'Fuck,' said Lisa, eyes wild. 'They've bailed something up.'

Grabbing MEG, Lisa shoved it inside a backpack by the door. Tied it up tight and bundled it beneath her sleeping shelf. She put her finger to her lips and tiptoed to the window. Abby crept to the other. She looked at their twin sets of tracks leading from the forest, the compacted snow that led to the outhouse round the back. She scanned the forest, peering past the tree trunks, trying to spot some movement, praying whatever the huskies were yelling at was nothing but a wild animal, maybe a wolf.

Suddenly the barks turned into a hysterical

baying. Moke was barking so hard his voice was cracking.

Abby gestured they should lock the door. Lisa shook her head, mouthing, *wilderness cabin*. Shit. That meant it was permanently open in case anyone was in need of shelter and was probably only lockable from the outside.

Suddenly, there was a *crack!* and the barking abruptly stopped. Then a terrible scream ripped through the air that had the hair on Abby's neck standing bolt upright. 'Roscoe!' said Lisa, at the same time Abby said, 'Moke!'

They held each other's eyes, paralysed with horror as the screaming went on and on until there was another *crack!* and everything fell silent.

Abby brought her hand to her mouth and bit her knuckles, trying to stop the tears.

'Abby,' Lisa hissed, pointing at the door.

Abby's heart flipped. The door was opening.

'Quick, *hide*.'

She scurried behind the wood stove while Lisa took up position behind the door.

Gradually it inched wider.

The man was standing well back but she could see his face. And his gun. The same matt black pistol she'd seen tucked under his pillow at Walter's was cocked and ready to fire.

It was then she realised she'd made a monumental mistake. She'd left the shotgun on the porch.

Thirty-six

'Abby?' Cal called urgently. 'You in there?'

Lisa shook her head violently, telling her not to answer. She had her legs spread wide and was clutching a sturdy log in both hands. She looked as though she was holding a baseball bat, ready to strike.

Cal pushed the door open a little more, took a tentative step inside.

'Abby? Lisa? Are you okay?'

Another tentative step, then another, gun held firmly in both hands. Then he saw Abby. His face started to relax, but he didn't put down the gun.

'Abby, what are you–' he started to say when Lisa stepped forward, swinging the log with both hands, aiming it for the back of his head. Her face was tight and Abby knew she was putting all her force behind the blow.

Abby didn't move or say anything to protect Cal.

He'd shot one of the dogs.

Cal seemed unaware of Lisa but at the last second, he must have heard something because he started to turn.

Abby shouted, 'Here, Cal! Over here!'

Immediately he swung back and Lisa struck. Abby heard the almighty *thunk* as the log connected with his skull. His head jolted forward, his mouth opened, almost as if in surprise, and then

321

his eyes rolled back and he folded to the floor with a dull thud, like a sack of sand. His pistol was buried beneath him.

Abby stared at the way his head lolled to one side, the blood seeping from the wound beneath his hair. Thick, springy hair that she used to comb with her fingers before curling them at the nape of his neck. She kneeled beside him and tentatively touched his hair. It felt just as she remembered, soft and sleek as a seal's pelt.

'What the fuck is he doing here?' Lisa was staring down at him. Abby remembered Cal's relentless hunt for Lisa, his warning her to be careful. He'd known that she knew what MEG was.

'I don't believe this,' Lisa said, and then she was belting around the cabin, flinging belongings on top of MEG and into her backpack. Abby remained crouched next to Cal, stroking his hair, her mind numb.

'He followed you, dammit,' Lisa was panting. 'You think you're so smart... Jesus, what did I do to deserve you? Who's with him, do you know? Christ, we've got to get out of here... Abby! For Chrissakes, *move.*'

Lisa had her backpack over one shoulder. She grabbed Abby's arm and tried to heave her upright, but it was like a mouse trying to shift a dead bear for all the effect she had. Abby didn't want to move. She felt as though her heart was breaking all over again.

'If you don't come with me, they'll *kill you.* You know what MEG is, we've got to fucking *get going.*'

At last a trickle of thought permeated her brain. She didn't want to die. Not really. Not even of a broken heart.

Slowly, she struggled up.

'Put your parka on. I've a snow machine hidden round the back, ready to go. Wrap up tight, it's going to be cold.'

Abby did as Lisa said, watching her race across the room and grab an oilskin parcel from a shelf that Abby knew she'd prepared for this moment, and that it would contain emergency supplies, matches and kindling and rations. Lisa was shovelling it inside her parka pocket when Abby heard a wet metallic click. Someone had just primed their gun.

Her skin went cold. She stood paralysed for a moment. Then she looked at the doorway, and almost fainted with relief.

'It's okay, he's okay,' she gabbled. 'I mean he's not, since Lisa clubbed him with a log. But he hasn't moved. He might be dead.'

'Oh, thank goodness,' said Connie and stepped inside the cabin. She kept the gun in both hands, and although it wasn't pointing at her and Lisa, it wasn't exactly pointing at the ground either. Remembering the woman's appalling driving, Abby backed off. She didn't want to get shot by accident.

'You can probably put it down now,' suggested Abby.

'All in good time.'

'He shot Moke,' Abby went on. 'Or Roscoe. I must go and see if they're okay–'

'I shot the dog,' said Connie calmly, 'and if you move an inch, I'll shoot your sister.'

Abby stared at Connie. Her gun wasn't pointed

aimlessly any more, it was trained slap bang on Lisa. Lisa was white as bone and looked as though she was going to be sick.

'What the...'

'I mean it,' snapped Connie. 'You twitch your eyelid and I'll blow a hole the size of a truck tyre through her chest.'

It was like looking through the wrong end of a pair of binoculars – the horror flooding through her, narrowing her vision, making her dizzy.

Lisa was staring at Connie. 'You,' she said. Just the one word, but Abby heard the emotions behind it: recognition, contempt, and hatred.

'Oh, yes,' said Connie, smiling. 'It's me all right. But this time, I get to win. Where's MEG?'

'My goodness, what on earth happened to your figure?' said Lisa, her voice gaining strength. 'You used to be slim, but now you're incredibly fat. Almost obese. What happened? Too many donuts while you creep around stealing other people's ideas?'

'If you think insulting me is going to help you, you're wrong. Now, where's MEG?'

'I'll never give it to you,' Lisa said fiercely. 'I'd rather die first.'

Abby could hear their voices echoing through her ears, but she couldn't make sense of it.

'But Connie's your investor,' Abby said.

Lisa gave a hollow laugh. 'I see you haven't lost your touch,' she said to Connie. 'You always were the consummate liar.'

Abby looked between Connie and Lisa, desperately trying to make sense of what was happening.

'Brightlite,' managed Abby, 'they gave you all

324

that money.'

Lisa looked startled. 'Brightlite's Santoni's investor. For EVals, the Curtis Cluster. Which is how this piece of shit learned about MEG. Through Santoni.'

'Brightlite lied to the cops?' Abby said, then she remembered Scott, Connie's husband and her boss, covering for her, working with her to get hold of MEG. Her mind's eye pictured Scott smoking at the bar, and she remembered what Julia had said about the man who'd asked all those questions about Lisa.

Quite a big man. Brown hair, brown eyes. Mid forties. No distinguishing features, but he did wear a pair of designer glasses. Tinted too…

Scott's Gucci glasses had been tinted. It had to have been Scott who had gone to the UK. And Santoni had given him all the details he needed to make him sound like a genuine friend. Which left one last thing she didn't understand. 'So who's your investor if it's not Connie?'

Lisa sent her a venomous look and Abby shrank inside. Of course. Lisa wouldn't want Connie knowing, or she'd kill them too.

'I already know the answer to that one,' Connie said. 'It's so obvious a child could have guessed. I'm not stupid.'

'Yes you are,' Lisa glared. 'You're so thick, you couldn't recognise a charge cluster if it jumped up and bit you on the nose. You haven't had an original idea in your life, you've sponged off others, cheating, manipulating, bribing, *murdering* a fellow student for their Ph.D. thesis–'

'Who cares?' Connie said. 'Jared's dead. And

325

you will be too if you don't give me MEG.'

Abby was less than three feet from Connie. Could she knock the gun out of her hand before she fired off a shot?

'So kill me,' spat Lisa, 'Professor fucking Crowe. See if I care. I'm more clever than you.'

Abby's whole body jerked. Sweet Jesus. Connie was Lisa's old enemy, whom she'd accused of murder when she'd been at University. For a moment she was so stunned she could hardly take it in, and had to force herself to concentrate. She had to *do something*.

'You'll never find MEG,' Lisa was saying. 'I've hidden it, hidden the lab books, hidden everything where you'll never think of looking with your pathetic little brain. So get used to the fact you'll never be famous, never get the glory you've always wanted. You'll die fat and alone and unknown just as you should.'

Abby's pulse was rocketing and she was tensing her muscles, readying herself to leap and knock Connie to the ground, when Connie spun, fast as a cat, and Abby was putting up her hands, trying to defend herself but something thudded against her skull. Pain blasted through her like a furnace and her head was roaring and she was trying to stop her knees buckling but they didn't belong to her any more and the next thing she knew she was lying on the floor, and Lisa was screaming and Connie shouting, and through her blurred vision she saw Lisa fly at Connie.

She wanted to shout, *No*, and then Connie pulled the trigger.

There was a terrible pause and then Lisa fell to

the ground. Teeth bared, she was clutching her stomach and groaning, her legs kicking.

Abby was trying to ignore the waves of nausea passing over her. She tried to get up, but a dark cloud began to encroach on the corners of her vision.

The last thing she saw was Connie pushing her gun back into her waistband.

Thirty-seven

Abby thought she was suffocating.

There was something against her mouth and nose and although she was sucking as hard as she could she wasn't getting enough air.

'Calm down, Abby.' She heard Connie's voice. 'If you stop struggling, you'll find you can breathe.'

Abby turned her head and at the same time became aware of the rope tied tightly around her neck. When she tried to move, she felt her shoulders spasm. It took her a moment to realise she was on the floor, her feet tied in front of her, her hands tied behind her and to the wall.

Immediately she kicked out, panic mounting. She had some kind of hood over her head. She couldn't fill her lungs. She was going to asphyxiate.

'Abby, do as she says,' called Lisa. Her voice quavered, threaded with pain. 'You've had the pillowcase on for the last five minutes and you were able to breathe, okay?'

Gasping, sucking cloth against her mouth and nose, Abby tried to calm herself but the sensation of being smothered just made her struggle all the more.

'I'll take it off if you tell me where MEG is.'

'Outhouse!' Abby yelled, muffled.

'What? It's *here?*' Connie sounded astonished.

'Yes, yes!' Abby shouted.

'Is it buried in the snow? Or is it at the bottom of the drop? I do hope not. I really don't fancy having to face more of Lisa's shit.'

'Off!' shouted Abby, fighting for air. 'I told you. Take it off!'

'Not until you tell me *exactly.*'

'No!' Lisa called. 'Abby, don't!'

'Bottom of the drop!' Abby was panting, dragging the pillowcase into her mouth, blowing it out. 'Under the lime!'

She heard Connie's quick footsteps on the boards, heading outside.

'Take it off!' she yelled.

Connie didn't answer. She'd gone.

Abby wrenched and thrashed on the floor but her bonds were tight and didn't give.

'Abby, calm down,' Lisa told her urgently. 'You're just making it worse.'

Panting against the pillowcase, Abby lunged against whatever was holding her, hoping her strength might break it, pull it loose.

'You're tied to a ring in the wall. It's been there twenty years, according to Mike. I doubt if you'll be able to pull it out.'

'Mike?' she repeated, hauling against the ring

just the same.

'Michael Flint. Mike's my investor.' Lisa gave a moan that made Abby's heart clench.

'Where are you hurt?'

'My tummy.'

Oh God, Connie's bullet could have perforated Lisa's stomach, her kidneys, liver or spleen or the whole damned lot for all she knew.

'Mike's my secret investor,' Lisa went on. 'He didn't want his industry, or his family ... knowing just yet. I didn't know how you felt about Cal until I met Mike. Made me realise why you went so berserk. We're going to get ... married. Soon as I get out of here.'

Abby remembered Michael Flint crunching around Malone's cabin, searching for Lisa, the shadows around his eyes, his exhaustion.

'Thomas was going to give Mike ... lab books. Don't know if he managed it.'

'They're at the lodge,' Abby assured her. Then she turned her mind hurriedly to Flint, and whether he might rescue them. 'Does Mike know you're here?'

'No. I didn't want him anywhere near me or MEG in case he got hurt. It was the only way I could think to keep him safe.'

It'd worked. Connie had known it was odd that the oil-man was hanging around Lake's Edge, but hadn't known exactly why until she'd heard the rumour that he and Lisa were sleeping together.

'Cal,' Abby gasped against the hot cloth. 'He okay?'

'Hasn't moved a muscle since I whacked him.'

'Lisa, can you get over here? Untie me?'

'Sorry, she's got me strapped to the wood stove.'

'Knots? Try and unpick them.'

'Try it yourself. She's used duct tape.'

Shit, shit, shit. There had to be a way. And then, like a light bulb popping inside her head, she remembered her knife. She couldn't believe she'd forgotten it. She scraped her ankle against the floor, but couldn't feel the familiar bump of leather. Dragging her hands as far down as she could, she twisted her legs backwards, raising her feet, but she couldn't reach her ankle.

'What are you doing?' Lisa's voice was losing strength. She'd be losing blood, maybe starting an infection or whatever happened when you'd been shot in the stomach.

'Had a knife. By my ankle.'

'She took it,' Lisa said quietly, 'sorry.'

Enraged, Abby started pulling and yanking against the ring in the wall, using her whole strength, but it held fast. Gradually she felt the exertion draining her of any oxygen and she had to slow down to stop herself being suffocated.

Abby lay quietly, pulling hot wet cloth into her mouth, letting it out, until she felt her heartbeat settle, her lungs ease into a less frantic gasp.

I won't give up, I won't.

'Cal,' she said. 'He tied up?'

'Just his hands.'

'His gun? He fell on it...'

'Still there.'

'Cal,' she called. 'Wake up, will you? Come *on*, you can hear me. *Wake up.*'

Nothing.

'Door's open?' she asked Lisa.

'Yes.'

'Moke!' she yelled. 'Roscoe! For Chrissakes, Cal! One of you, fucking help us!'

Abby kept shouting. Sucking in the pillowcase long and deep before letting a holler rip. She shouted for the dogs, for Cal, until her throat started to ache but she didn't stop. Not until she felt a large, furry body brush against her.

'Moke,' she breathed, and put her head down. 'Pull it off, will you? Pull, boy, pull!'

Moke pressed against her, whining.

'Here, boy,' Lisa called. 'I'll show you what she wants.'

But Moke wouldn't leave Abby. He pawed at her legs and butted her shoulder as though telling her to get up.

Then Abby heard the familiar quick steps on the porch. Moke growled.

'Good boy,' she encouraged him. 'Good boy!'

His growl grew to a subdued roar.

'Good boy! Now go sic her. GO!'

She heard his nails clattering as he bolted for the door. Connie gave a startled yell.

Bang!

A single gunshot, but there was no yelping or howling, no scuffle. Abby held her breath.

'That bloody dog,' Connie said. She was panting. 'When I get my hands on it, I'll slit its guts wide open.'

Connie had missed, Abby realised. She hadn't shot Moke. Thank God, thank God ... her skin tightened as she heard Connie walk over to her.

'You lied to me, Abby.'

She could smell the stench of human faeces on

Connie, and while part of her mind thrilled that she'd sent Lisa's enemy to dig around in her loo the other was quietly petrified.

'No, no,' she muffled. 'Lisa told me it was there.'

'Hmm.' She could almost see Connie looking around the cabin, evaluating, calculating. 'I think it's buried somewhere outside in the snow, don't you?'

'I don't know.' Her voice trembled.

Suddenly she felt a hand on her face and she jerked aside but Connie had her nose pinched between her fingers and was trying to force something in her mouth.

Lisa was shouting as Abby felt a metal bar mashing against her lips and teeth and she wasn't going to let it in, no matter what, but she couldn't *breathe* dammit.

'Open wide, Abby.'

No matter how much she struggled, Connie never lessened her pincer-grip on her nose. Abby made gulping sounds at the back of her throat, lungs screaming, determined she would pass out before she opened her mouth, but her body had other ideas.

Against her will Abby took a huge gulp of air and at the same time the barrel of a pistol was pushed inside her mouth.

She went perfectly still. The metal was grating on her lower teeth, and although her tongue tried to push the barrel away, it felt as though it was touching her tonsils.

She wanted to be as strong, as tough as Lisa, but she couldn't help the trickle of urine escaping. The whimper that fluttered from her throat.

'Lisa.' Connie's voice was conversational. 'Tell me where MEG is, or your sister's brains will be splattered over this wall. I don't care if Abby lives or dies, but if I leave with MEG intact, I'll let her live. I'm not saying I'll let *you* live, because that would be pushing things too far, and you'd never believe that, not in a million years. But I've grown quite fond of Abby. And although she's gutsy in her own way, I can't really believe she'll have the strength to fight me once I get to Arlington. She'll be like a fish out of water.'

Connie chuckled her deep fat chuckle. 'Can you imagine her trying to persuade the patent office that she knows about MEG? There are countless web sites proclaiming magnetic energy devices, she could have pulled her information from any one of them. She doesn't know how it works, doesn't have a clue. She's no threat.'

Abby knew Connie was bluffing. She'd never let her live, and she bet Lisa knew that too.

Cal! she yelled inside, the taste of metal and gun oil in her mouth.

'So, Lisa, what's it to be?'

'Unhood her,' Lisa said. 'Untie her.'

'No.'

The gun moved in Abby's mouth, scraping against her teeth. 'Then that's it,' Lisa said. 'You shoot her, and you know you're stuffed. You've already said I'm not leaving here alive. So what's the point in telling you where MEG is if Abby's dead?'

There was a long silence while Abby tried to keep still. Sweat trickled down her face, down her neck and back, soaking her waistband.

'I won't tell you where MEG is until she's free.

We are sisters, remember. Oh, I'm sorry, I forgot...' Lisa's voice turned sarcastic. 'Of course you don't know anything about siblings, do you, being a spoiled only child. You couldn't understand what it means to feel close to someone you share the same blood with.'

Abby kept as still as she could, feeling the shameful wetness in her padded trousers, the pulse roaring in her ears. She knew what Lisa was doing. She wanted Connie to free her so she could go for Cal's gun.

'No.' Connie's voice went flat.

Silence stretched. Abby found herself listening for Cal's breathing, but she couldn't hear anything aside from the roaring in her ears; her pulse and heartbeat gone mad.

'Sweetheart, Abby,' Lisa's voice was soft, 'I'm sorry. I really am. It's not that I don't love you...' Her voice cracked. 'Because I do. Desperately. But we've reached a stalemate.'

She heard Lisa gulp, then her voice rang out, hard and strong.

'So shoot her, Professor Crowe. Shoot my sister.'

Thirty-eight

Without warning the pistol was removed from her mouth so fast it knocked against her upper front teeth. Abby ran her tongue around her gums, trying to work saliva into her mouth. She felt Connie working at the rope around her neck

334

and suddenly, it loosened. Then the pillowcase was pulled off. Blinking furiously, Abby gulped in lungfuls of blissfully cool air.

She saw her sister bent double by the wood stove, a dark bloody stain the size of a soup bowl across her shirt and seeping into her jeans. Her gaze flew to Cal, who lay motionless. She blinked some more. His hands were tied behind his back, but hadn't his legs been spread-eagled when he fell? Was he conscious? He didn't look it. She couldn't even see him breathing.

'Untie her,' Lisa said.

'I don't think so,' Connie replied and, to her surprise, she left the cabin.

'You okay?' Abby asked Lisa urgently.

She didn't reply for a couple of seconds, but then she rallied. 'I've been better.' Her tone was trembling but Abby's heart twisted as she heard the attempt at humour.

Abby turned her attention to Cal. 'Wake up, Cal Pegati, or we'll be dead meat! You're lying on your gun ... for God's sake, Cal, WAKE UP!'

She thought she saw his fingers twitch but it must have been wishful thinking. She wrenched against the iron ring, forcing her aching muscles to keep fighting until they burned white-hot, scorching with pain, but Cal didn't move. She paused when Connie returned.

She was lugging a Jerry can with her.

Abby's insides abruptly turned liquid.

Uncapping the can, Connie went to Lisa and poured gasoline over her head, her shoulders, drenching her entire body. Lisa was choking and gasping and kicking.

335

'Don't tell her,' Lisa panted to Abby. 'Promise me. *Don't tell her.*'

Connie stood back and took out a box of matches. She opened it and withdrew a single match, raised her hands high. The match was poised to strike.

'It's your turn, Abby. Tell me where MEG is or Lisa burns alive. It won't be very pretty, but it won't take long. She'll be in her own little hell, screaming just like Thomas did when I tossed the match into his car.'

'No,' Abby pleaded. 'Please, *no.*'

'You've five seconds, Abby.'

'Don't tell her,' Lisa begged.

'Four,' said Connie, 'three, two–'

'Okay, okay!' Abby broke in. 'Put the match away, please...'

Horror pumped through her as Connie scraped the match gently against the sandpaper.

'It's under the sleeping shelf,' Abby blurted.

'I don't believe you,' Connie said.

'It is, go and see,' Abby pleaded. 'It's in the backpack.'

Lisa slumped against the wood stove. She was sobbing quietly.

Abby concentrated on Cal, railing at him in her mind: Wake up, for God's sakes, WAKE UP!

Connie returned with the backpack and emptied the contents on to the floor next to Cal. She picked up MEG and turned it around in her hands, almost in reverence. 'At last,' she breathed.

Abby's breath caught. This time she was sure she'd seen Cal's fingers move! Get up, she yelled at him, get up and shoot the bitch!

'Dearest, Abby,' Connie said, stroking MEG like she would a cat, 'I didn't realise what a little sleuth you'd turn out to be. Thank you for leading me to the lab books.' She gave Abby a broad smile. 'I'd never have looked past the kibble if it hadn't been for you dropping a mitten.'

The look on Lisa's face was more than Abby could bear and she turned her head aside. Tears leaked out of her eyes and down her cheeks. A knife twisted in her heart. She'd failed her sister. One hundred per cent, she'd failed her.

With MEG under her arm, Connie walked outside but within a handful of seconds, she returned and picked up the can. She splashed gasoline around the cabin, soaking the rugs, the bedding on the sleeping shelf. The acrid stench made Abby's nose burn, her eyes water.

'Who's the clever one now?' Connie said, putting the can down.

'Please, Connie,' Abby began to plead, but then she stopped. Cal's shoulders had moved, and also his arms. Oh, please God make him shoot Connie.

'Just think. I'll be in Virginia tomorrow. Once I've taken care of Michael Flint, that is. He hasn't a clue, poor man. It'll be like shooting a sitting duck.'

CAL! yelled Abby in her mind. For Chrissakes, HELP US!

Connie went to Lisa and poured the last of the gasoline over her head. Then she brought out the box of matches and with an awful horror Abby knew what was going to happen next.

Abby was screaming when Connie dropped the lit match into Lisa's lap.

Thirty-nine

When Abby came round, she was still screaming.

She never knew if she fainted from the shock of knowing her sister was going to burn to death, or whether her body reacted to her all-encompassing panic and had simply shut down, but by the time she regained consciousness the sleeping shelf was ablaze, crackling and roaring, devouring the pillows, sending clouds of thick black smoke through the cabin. A cupboard in the kitchenette dropped with a crash, the curtains flared like rockets, sending flames shooting across the ceiling. The heat was so intense her skin felt as though it was blistering. An orange wave of flames began rolling down the shelf to the floor, licking the rug at her feet.

She was choking and gasping. She looked for Lisa through the billowing smoke, but she'd gone.

She stared in disbelief at Cal crawling toward her on all fours. His head was hanging. His clothes were burned, his face bloody and smeared with ash. He was clutching a knife in his hand.

She felt a surge of wild hope.

Had he saved Lisa?

Part of the sleeping shelf dropped in a shower of embers. A torrent of smoke and flame belched across the room, knocking him sideways.

'Hurry, Cal!' she croaked. 'For God's sake, hurry!'

338

Cal sawed through the tape at her feet, and then he turned aside and she was yelling at him not to stop when his shoulders spasmed and he vomited.

The rug was burning fast, a jagged line of flames edging towards them.

'Cal! Quick!'

He struggled to cut the tape around her hands. The instant she was free she sprang to her feet. Crouching low, she headed for the door.

She took a quick glance over her shoulder at Cal. He'd slumped to the floor. His boots were on fire, flames licking his ankles. Coughing, eyes streaming, Abby tore off her parka and dodged around a wall of fire that used to be the kitchenette counter and raced for the sink. She dumped her parka inside, turned on the taps full blast and left them open. With soaked coat in hand she swerved back to Cal and threw it over his feet and legs. Then she grabbed his wrists and pulled. It was like trying to shift a buffalo.

Legs braced, she gathered all her strength and began dragging Cal for the door, six inches at a time.

She was yelling at him, coughing and choking, smoke searing her throat, flames licking all around.

'I will not let you die on me, you bastard!'

Another six inches. Then another. Sweat poured down her face. She braced herself again. Pulled another six inches. And again.

She saw his shoulders heave. Then he dry retched. A trail of spittle hung from his mouth.

'Get up! It's not far!' She put her arms beneath his and let him push against her until he was on his knees. 'Come on, move!'

With Cal on all fours, she cajoled and yelled, pushing and pulling him until at last, they were on the porch and outside in cold clear air. It was like breathing champagne. Cal managed to get to his feet briefly but he only took six paces before he folded to his knees.

'Doggy style is fine,' she panted, 'just keep going.'

She made sure he was well clear of the cabin before she told him it was okay. Immediately he slumped into the snow.

'Cal?' She bent over and looked into his eyes. His pupils were pin dots. He was concussed.

A soft crunching sound from the edge of the forest made her spring into a crouch, fear rocketing that Connie had returned, but it was only Moke.

BOOM!

The cabin was a fireball. The roof had caved in, sending a column of black smoke into the sky. The radiant heat seared her face like sunburn and she scrambled to her feet, turning her head away, gagging at a terrible smell hanging in the air, like scorched flesh.

Then she saw Lisa.

She was lying in the snow where Cal had carried her.

She had no hair. Her face was raw and bloody, like a piece of uncooked steak. Her clothes had melted into her skin, charred into blackened threads all over her neck and shoulders and arms.

Abby fell to her knees. She felt as though she was losing her mind.

Lisa couldn't be dead. She was indestructible.

She'd survived trying to fly with an umbrella from the roof of the house. Survived nearly blowing herself up in the school's physics lab. Survived rock-climbing, gliding and skydiving.

All that adventurous spirit had nothing to do with the obscene crimson-black bundle of flesh and bones weeping blood and ash on to the snow.

'Abby.'

It was a croak.

'Chrissakes … Abby.'

Abby scrambled over. 'Lisa? *Lisa?*'

'Yeah.'

She could barely believe it. 'You're alive.' She started to shudder. 'Oh, Jesus. You're *alive*… Christ, hang on, Lisa… We'll get you to a hospital, fix you up…' Abby looked around desperately, unsure what she was looking for … her mind was filled with images of bandages, nurses and saline sheets but all she saw was a cabin being devoured by flames, and Cal kneeling in the snow, retching.

'Abby…'

'I'll get the snow machine.' Abby stumbled to her feet. Her heart thudded against her rib cage. Her knees trembled. 'Ride to the lodge. Radio for help.'

'Wait…' Lisa reached out a hand. It was dripping blood. 'Need you … do something … first.'

'No time, Lisa.' Her mind was shrieking *get help!* repeatedly, loud as an ambulance siren. Her sister couldn't survive much longer without a team of medics to hand. 'I've got to go *now*.'

'Please.' Lisa's eyes implored.

Abby paused, tried to fight down her panic.

341

'You must ... stop Connie.'

'Lisa, there's no *time*...'

'All time ... in the world. Do *not* think ... of me. Or Mike.' Lisa bared her teeth with the effort of speaking. 'Abby, think of Thomas ... our dream. We want to give MEG ... to the world. For free.'

Lisa tried to shuffle herself upright but fell back with a groan. She pressed her bloody hands to her wound.

Abby dived to her side. 'Don't move,' she begged. 'Please, little sis...'

'MEG more important ... than me,' gritted Lisa. 'You must see that ... everyone needs MEG. The world–'

'No, no...' Abby's eyes flooded. 'You can't ask me to do this. *I won't leave you to die.*'

'You must.' Lisa tried a smile but it vanished beneath a groan of agony.

'I can't.' Abby started to pour sweat.

'You don't stop Connie ... I swear I will never ... speak to you again.' Lisa closed her eyes. 'I will hate you... Always. You gave her ... the lab books.'

'No,' bleated Abby.

'Yes,' said Lisa.

'Oh, God...' Abby's emotions climbed from her pelvis, past her ribs and to her heart. Red and raw, they clawed their way upwards, through her throat, and into her eyes. 'I don't want to leave you.'

'You owe me.'

She held her sister's gaze. Her eyes were filled with blood but they seemed to look right through her and into her soul. She couldn't stop the keening sound deep in her throat. 'Please... Oh,

Christ. Lisa, only you could do this to me...'

Lisa's scorched and blackened lips twisted into a smile. 'You'll do it?'

Abby nodded.

'Cross your heart?'

Abby crossed her heart. Tears were pouring down her cheeks.

'And hope to die.'

Forty

There was no way to estimate how long it took her to find Lisa's snow machine, bundle Cal behind her, and head to the lodge.

Her lungs kept spasming in the cold air, making her cough over and over, and she could feel the shock entering her body, weakening her limbs, but she forced herself to concentrate, yelling at herself not to give in.

She had wrapped Lisa as best as she could in Cal's parka before they'd left. They hadn't dared move her. Cal was going to return to Lisa once a medivac crew was on its way. Abby just had to pray she'd survive that long.

She followed the tracks back through the forest; hers, Cal's and Connie's. All of them had driven to Flint's, she realised, then followed the person before them on foot until, one by one, they came to Lisa's wilderness cabin.

Abby brought the snow machine to a halt at the front of Flint's hunting lodge and turned off the ignition. For the first time she became aware that the wind had picked up and that the trees were swaying and snapping, pieces of ice thunking on to the snowy roof. To the right of the front door a window was hanging wide open, its glass broken. It hadn't been broken when she'd been here earlier, she was sure of it. She took in the woman's prints in the snow. Connie.

Abby saved time hunting for keys by jogging for the open window. She was about to pull herself through when Moke arrived in a rush. He'd fallen behind as she'd snaked the snow machine through the forest, and was greeting her as though he hadn't seen her for a year.

'Stay,' she rasped, and levered herself on to the sill, cautious of the broken glass. She then dropped inside and raced for the front door, her boots clattering on the polished boards.

She pulled back the bolts on the door, yanked it open. Cal had the hood of his car up and was looking inside.

'I'm going to find a radio!' she yelled. 'Get help!'

Without turning, he gave her the thumbs up.

Moke's claws clicked behind her as she ran through the living room and into a den. No radio. She raced into the hallway, then the kitchen. There was a granite worktop covered in smashed pieces of plastic. More broken plastic lay on the floor and the kitchen table, the remnants of a ham radio intermingling with a variety of handsets and transmitters.

Connie had covered all the bases.

Abby felt a wail building in her lungs. Lisa

344

would die if she didn't get help soon. She tore through the rest of the lodge, Moke hot on her heels. Tears scalding her throat, she belted outside to Cal, who'd abandoned their vehicles and was in the lean-to, fiddling with a snow machine and its electrics.

'Cal, she's broken them. No way will any of them work.'

'Shit,' said Cal, but he didn't stop what he was doing. He dropped the pliers and began twisting some wires. His tongue was protruding with the effort of concentration. 'She's taken the alternators from our cars, and sabotaged this lot. I should be able to get this one going. Then I can go get help.'

'Are you sure you're up to it?'

'Yes,' he said.

She put her fingers on his jaw and brought his head round so she could look into his eyes. His pupils were still shrunken into pin points.

'You've got concussion.'

'I've had worse, Abby. I'll make it.'

Belatedly she looked past his scorched clothing, past the blood on his face, to see the burns beneath. She looked at his hands. They were also burned.

A new panic seized her. 'You're hurt.'

'I'll be fine,' he insisted, and turned back to the snow machine. Abby forced her anxiety aside. 'Okay, tough guy,' she said, trying to keep upbeat, 'have it your way.'

He gave a grunt.

'Cal, what time did you get to Lisa's cabin?'

'Seven forty-five.'

345

She checked his watch. Eight forty-three. Ice shivered through her veins. She was losing time. She had to get moving. She needed a map. Abby bolted for the mud room.

The chest freezer that had held the lab books gaped open, mocking her.

'Don't you worry,' she told it, 'I'm getting them back.'

She pulled on a scarf, grabbed some gloves and a fur hat with earflaps, and climbed into a snow suit. It was big enough for her and Cal together, but she didn't care what she looked like, so long as it kept her warm.

She hurriedly put an emergency pack together. Matches from the kitchen wrapped in plastic, a handful of kindling from the basket beside the fireplace. A knife, some chocolate bars, a packet of dried fruit.

Unfolding the map she ran her eyes over the winding track that led to the haul road. She focused on the time, trying to choreograph the last couple of hours. She couldn't be that far behind Connie. Connie had walked to Lisa's, and walked back, but Abby had saved a lot of time by using Lisa's snow machine. She studied the map, trying to work it out. If she was right, Connie would be approaching the forest. She'd have to traverse it a couple of miles north, come all the way down, and do the same for the river and then the lake.

Abby pelted back to Cal. The wind was like frozen needles on her face and smelled of snow.

'I'm going after Connie,' she told him. 'Will you be okay?'

He swung round. Took in her snow suit. His eyes filled with alarm. 'No,' he said.

'I promised Lisa.'

Something in her expression must have told him she wasn't going to be deterred. Horror flooded his face. 'But she'll be alone.'

Abby's throat closed. She looked away. 'I know.'

'Jesus, Abby, if I'm going...' he flapped a hand south, to where Lake's Edge lay, 'you can't possibly leave her. I could be *hours*...'

'I know.'

She lifted her eyes to his. They stared at each other.

'Oh, God.' He closed his eyes briefly. His face spasmed. 'I can't believe this is happening.'

'Me neither.'

'If I only came round sooner... I tried...' His voice broke. 'I'm so, so sorry.'

She brought up her hand but she didn't dare touch his burned and bloody cheek. 'I know.'

'I had no idea Connie had followed me.' He swallowed. 'I wish I hadn't reacted without thinking, but I was worried about you. I found your note. Rang Big Joe. He got worried too.'

'You give him a time you'd return?'

'Tonight.'

Cal would arrive before Big Joe rang the emergency bells. Would Lisa survive until then? She turned her mind away from that avenue of thought before it started to splinter her emotions into a thousand pieces.

Cal put his hand over hers. Cupped her fingers. 'I wish it were yesterday so we could start again.'

'Me too.'

She looked at the pain in his eyes, felt the warmth of his hand in hers, and knew her life had changed irrevocably. Whether Lisa lived or died, nothing could ever be the same again. And as she recognised this, she felt a silence enclose her, a silence that reached a hand into her consciousness without warning, cutting off that restless, flickering part of her brain that processed everything – colours, images, feelings – leaving her thoughts distilled and cold.

Lisa's survival was now in the lap of the gods.

It was time for her to fulfil her promise.

Forty-one

Abby had gone two miles before she realised Moke was following. She'd cut across a bend, trying to save time, and had automatically checked over her shoulder as she would in a car – to make sure there wasn't any traffic – when she caught sight of a small grey dot bobbing behind her.

She felt no twinge of regret as she turned her back on him and throttled down the edge of the next hillside. Her heart was as cold and hard as if it had been buried in a freezer.

From time to time she clattered over the track, but most of the time she was on snow and moving much faster than she had when she'd driven the SUV.

Ahead of her, the wind was growing stronger, the gusts more frequent. She checked the horizon

348

to see it was piled with angry grey clouds. A storm was brewing. Yesterday she would have felt scared, but today the cold part of her wondered how she could use it to her advantage.

Eventually she came to the river bank and paused, studying the smooth stretches of ice and the mass of boulder-like sculptures. She drove the snow machine to a messy jumble of ice above a waterfall. Lumpy ice like this, Walter had told her, could support a 7-ton truck.

Slowly she eased the machine on to the ice. It tilted and rocked and slid over the rough terrain but the ice didn't creak or crack, didn't break up and drop her into the freezing water below, and she was moving steadily forward. She couldn't see any water seepage anywhere, just solid white peaks of ice, and as she pressed on, her confidence grew. Every few seconds Abby glanced for Connie's car heading south down the riverside, but she didn't see it.

The river crossing only took ten minutes. She'd saved more time than she'd envisaged, and by going over the next hillside and through the forest instead of traversing it, she'd save another twenty minutes and, God willing, would drop ahead of Connie.

Abby accelerated up the slope, snow spraying, dodging drifts of snow and trees, the odd boulder flashing past.

The snow got deeper as she worked her way up the hill, the treads fighting hard to grip. The trees thinned as she climbed, and then they were behind her and she scrambled the snow machine higher, until she came to the top. The wind howled unimpeded, knocking and punching her as she scanned the track below.

Moke came into her mind, but there was no grey dot in the distance that she could see, but then she spotted a movement way below. Her skin tautened. It wasn't Moke. It was Connie.

For a second she couldn't believe it. Connie was *behind her.* She was halfway along the riverside and she still had to traverse the hill Abby was on. Would she see her ski tracks? She doubted it. But if she did, and stopped to look, it would give her even more time.

A surge of triumph made her want to shout, but she bottled the energy inside, storing it, keeping it in reserve. Taking the hillside at an angle, she powered over the snow towards the plank bridge and the treacherous bend.

She was going so fast she didn't see the hillside fall away behind a lip of ice and snow and, the next instant, she was airborne.

A moment of weightlessness. Abby could see the lake below, the swathes of spruce trees like skirts at the base of the mountains, the dirty grey sky. She felt a moment of sheer disbelief that she was flying.

Engine shrieking, the snow machine plunged down. Instinctively she leaned back, trying to keep the nose up so they wouldn't plough head first and there was a *thud* that had her spine snapping and the snow machine spinning wildly to one side. Abby clung on for dear life as it veered again. Another almighty thud and the snow machine straightened before it continued bouncing down the sheer slope.

350

Another sense of weightlessness as they were flung into space again, and then a long shuddering thump and the ground levelled and she was still astride the machine, and she wanted to stop to get her breath back but she couldn't, not with Connie just behind her.

Abby had to force herself not to lessen her speed. She had to be bold, be as brave as Lisa. And keep her eyes peeled for any more sheer drops. She risked a glance behind her, down at the track, and saw Connie was less than a mile away. Time was running out.

She pushed the snow machine hard, pointing it directly for the bridge. If I fly over another drop, I'll grow wings, she told herself. But come hell or high water I'm going to stop her.

Praying Connie wouldn't spot her, Abby belted down the hillside, bouncing and sliding, engine roaring, and the track was getting closer and closer, and finally she decelerated and eased the snow machine over the lip of the bank and on to the track. She'd made it. She was gasping with relief as she bumped the snow machine to the bend that led down to the bridge. She parked it just before the apex, where Connie would only see it at the last second, and she hoped she'd act on instinct as she'd done before, and ram both feet on the brake.

The wind was increasing as Abby jogged back up the track to see if the snow machine was visible in the approach. Shit, she could just see the handlebars, which meant Connie, sitting higher in her car, would see it too.

Cursing, Abby tore back. She was gasping for

351

air. Her boots slipped on the ice and she crashed on to her hip. Lay there stunned.

Get up, she told herself. Stop being such a useless piece of shit and get moving. Connie's nearly here.

She got back to her feet. Repositioned the snow machine further into the bend, side on, almost filling the track. Pocketing the snow machine's keys, she raced to collect the boughs and branches she'd laid there earlier. She pushed them down the riverbank. The frozen stream re-emerged, slippery grey. She could hear an engine approaching. No time now. She had to get out of sight.

She looked frantically around. The engine grew louder, closing every second. It was too late to cross the track and hide in the trees. Abby plunged down the side of the lake, haring for a pile of logs twenty yards away. She mustn't be seen, she *mustn't*.

She made a final, desperate charge for a tree stump and scurried behind it on all fours. Her heart was pumping so hard she thought it might explode from her chest. Cautiously she peered round the tree stump, past a broken branch and some frosted twigs, to see Connie's car flash past, powering for the bend. Breathless, she waited for the engine note to change and kick down a gear as Connie saw the snow machine in her path and braked, but it maintained its same smooth level.

Abby scrambled up the slope, peeked over a crest of snow and down the track.

Connie entered the bend far too fast. Just as Abby had hoped. She saw the brake lights come on, saw the car fishtailing for the snow machine.

Watched it slam into the snow machine's flank. The snow machine spun wildly to one side. The SUV veered to the other, tail end spinning. She could see the front tyres were pointing left. Away from the drop to the lake. Bad move. Always steer into a skid.

The brake lights were still on but the tyres weren't gripping. The SUV did a full circle, graceful as a dancer, and then dropped its rear end over the lip of the lake. Engine rumbling, it sat there, both rear tyres suspended in mid-air.

Seconds ticked past. Eventually the engine was turned off. The driver's window buzzed down, and she could see Connie peering outside, looking at her predicament. It looked more scary than it was. With the weight of the engine in the front, the car wouldn't tumble into the lake, not unless it was given an almighty great shove by an earth mover. But Connie wouldn't know that.

Abby could see the fear on her face, but she didn't feel any satisfaction or concern with her emotions suspended in dry-ice. Carefully Connie opened her door, as though she expected the movement to plunge the car into the lake. Then she inched out, moving her bulk carefully around the door until she was standing in front of the bonnet, feet placed firmly on the track. She had her gun, Abby saw, but not MEG. MEG and the lab books were still inside the car.

Connie looked around. Abby slid to the bottom of the bank and crouched as low as she could, stumbling over rocks and boulders, praying Connie wouldn't see her before she'd got enough distance between her and her gun. Then she could break cover and run for it. She knew she'd outrun Connie easily.

'Who are you?' Connie shouted. 'What do you want?'

Abby detoured a fallen log, then another pile of boulders, and all she could hear was the rising wind, a *pock-pock* as little chunks of snow and ice hit her snow suit. Faster, she told herself. You've got to go faster.

Images intensified. A frozen leaf, its veins laced white. The shine of ice on the rocks, gleaming, melting, flowing. The crunch and scrape of her boots against rocks.

It started to snow, thin hard flakes that stung her face. Connie was running after her, just twenty yards away. She held her gun low at her side.

The chill in Abby's veins deepened.

How to stop Connie?

Abby studied the lake, water shining on its surface, the dark fissures that were cracks in the ice, then she looked back at Connie.

Could she draw Connie on to the lake? Trap her into stepping on to thin ice? Would Connie dare come out here, weighing as much a bison?

Abby pushed a boot on to the ice. There was an ominous cracking and her boot was suddenly ankle deep in icy water.

Oh, Jesus.

Quick glance behind her.

Connie was barely twenty yards away and was slowing, bringing up her gun.

Lisa's voice. *Cross your heart?*

And hope to die.

Abby launched herself on to the lake.

354

Forty-two

She leaped for a patch of lumpy white that indicated the ice was thick enough to take her weight. It felt as solid as tarmac, as solid as the path to the post box at the end of her mother's garden. She kept moving. She had to put enough distance between herself and Connie to avoid getting a bullet in the back of her head.

'ABBY!' It was a roar of rage. Connie could have been yelling into her ear she sounded so close. The wind had carried her voice, distorted it from where she was running full tilt along the track.

Wind tugging her snow suit, snowflakes pinging her cheeks, Abby kept sliding one foot in front of the other, watching for dark patches of ice, light patches, reading every nuance she could remember from Walter.

Crack! Crack!

The shots sounded oddly tinny, as though the oncoming storm had swallowed them in two quick gulps. Skin tight across her shoulder blades Abby looked back to see Connie was on the edge of the lake, squinting against the swirling snow.

'Where's Lisa?' shouted Connie.

'You killed her!' yelled Abby. 'You killed Cal! I hate you!'

She didn't want Connie returning to the lodge and shooting Cal. She had to make Connie believe she was the last thing between her and

355

monumental fame and glory.

'I'm going to the cops!' she shouted. 'Get you locked up for life!'

Connie didn't move as Abby inched backwards. 'See you in jail, Connie!'

Abby turned and continued sliding. Snow pellets blew on to the ice with a tat, tat sound that began to grow in volume. The trees near the track had offered some shelter, but out here there was little protection from the wind, and the temperature was several degrees colder.

Hunching her shoulders, Abby looked ahead and saw a long patch of dark ice, thin and unstable. Carefully she skirted it and glanced over her shoulder. For a second, she couldn't believe her eyes. Connie was on the lake. She was following her route, gliding gracefully, almost effortlessly, across the ice, as though she had a pair of skates strapped to her feet. She was moving at twice Abby's speed.

A moment of disbelieving horror.

We both play hockey, that's how it started, Connie's voice echoed in her mind. *I whacked him one before shooting a goal.*

Connie hadn't just played hockey, she'd played *ice hockey.*

Connie swooped past the long patch of dark ice Abby had skirted so carefully with barely a glance.

She was closing in fast.

Abby urged herself on. You've got to try and skate like Connie and keep out of range!

Connie fired off three rounds in quick succession, and Abby heard a *whap* and at the same time she felt something stroke the hair just above her ear.

Abby broke into a shuffling, stumbling run, a scream lodged in her throat. She couldn't die yet, *not yet*.

The wind's direction suddenly shifted. It was now blowing from the north-east and getting stronger, driving snow into her eyes.

Another *crack!* and then she heard a metallic and repetitive clicking over and over again. She prayed Connie didn't have a spare clip. Didn't have pocketfuls of bullets.

She tried to read the ice through the flurries but the flakes of snow were settling fast, forming a tentative blanket. She kept sliding forward, trying to head for patches of white, but it became more and more difficult to discern colour. Blindly, she increased her speed. Jesus God, she panted, don't let me fall through the ice.

She risked a glance behind her. Her heart kicked. Connie was barely ten yards behind her. She had what looked like a flensing knife in her right hand. She was skating fast like a professional, her expression concentrated, gaining with every pace.

Eyes stinging, Abby broke into a wild, shambolic gallop, trying not to slip and fall, desperately dodging patches of weeping ice as she came to them. She was going too fast to see a dark shadow, black as a thundercloud beneath its cape of snow, until it was too late.

She felt the ice beneath her begin to bend and break. For an instant she nearly stopped but her mind shouted instructions at her, like a drill sergeant, to bloody well keep moving!

Abby spread her legs to distribute her weight and edged forward with both feet on the surface.

There was a deadly creaking sound beneath her and she immediately dropped down, stretched out her arms and legs, and started to shimmy for safer ground. Water spurted up through a crack and the ice heaved.

Her hand found a block of ice ahead and she grabbed it, pulling her body over it and on to a ridged and lumpy area. Lumps were good. Lumps meant thick ice. She was scrambling up when Connie gave a shout.

Abby turned to see Connie was just three yards away and right in the middle of the icy thundercloud. She wasn't on all fours, distributing her weight on the thin ice. She wasn't even shuffling forward with both feet on the surface. She'd stopped dead.

'Abby!' she called, panicky. 'It's moving, it's going to collapse, oh, no, please...' She dropped the knife. Both hands were outstretched.

Abby stared at her through the driving snow. An ice pick buried itself in her heart.

Connie began to ease herself to her knees. Looking like an oversized starfish, she started a slow-motion breast stroke for Abby.

The ice gave a deep groan and Abby felt it reverberate through her boots. Then came a ripping sound, like a yard of silk splitting.

Connie's face widened into terror, her eyes huge. Abby kept quite still.

Connie rose briefly and flung herself towards Abby. There was a terrifying grinding noise as the

358

ice finally collapsed.

A soft explosion as Connie's body hit the water.

Connie was thrashing and churning, trying to climb out but the ice kept crumbling, breaking up around her, driving her back into the freezing water.

'Abby,' she gasped, 'get me out.'

The ice pick shifted deeper, sliding into her entrails.

Connie was choking and sobbing, but it didn't take long before her thrashing gradually slowed. Barely a minute, maybe ninety seconds later, her legs began to drop lower in the water.

'Abby.' Connie's movements were already becoming sluggish, her voice weakening as the cold black water penetrated her bones. 'Help me. *Please.* I'll p-pay y-you ... w-whatever you w-want...'

Abby stood quietly, snow drifting over her, and watched Connie die.

Connie said *please* three more times but after that she fell silent. Her limbs stopped moving. Soon, her head fell backwards, and water lapped the corners of her mouth. She'd fallen into a state of hypothermia, where her core was freezing, shutting down, sending her to sleep.

Abby didn't wait any longer. The wind was whistling across the lake. The storm could well land full force on her within the next couple of hours. She had to get back to shore, finish what she had started.

It was only when she looked around to get her bearings that she realised her predicament. She could barely see five yards ahead. Cloud had enveloped the entire lake.

Lisa's voice echoed through her head. *My God, Abby. You're more stupid than I thought.*

The one thing she hadn't put in her emergency pack, was a compass.

Forty-three

Abby skirted the treacherous ice hole and tried to pick up her and Connie's tracks. There! A distinct footprint. Cautiously Abby followed it to the next print, and the next, and then there weren't any more. The ice was covered in a thin layer of snow.

Wind driving against the side of her face, Abby studied the way the fresh snow lay, to see if there was any way it indicated a footprint, but she wasn't a Native, brought up to read such signs. The entire area looked uniform, pristine.

She decided that if she kept the wind on her right cheek, she'd be heading west and would eventually hit the shore. So long as the wind didn't change direction, like it had earlier. The mountains made the weather do strange things, she just had to pray that this time the wind would stay in the same direction.

She checked her watch. Ten-thirty. Mid morning and it felt as dark as night. Okay. If she didn't reach the shoreline by midday... Well, she'd think about that when the time came.

Slowly she shuffled forward, trying not to be overcautious. She couldn't stay out here for long, despite her snow suit she was already bitterly cold, and unless she warmed up she would start becoming hypothermic.

Abby flapped and swung her arms to try and keep herself warm. She wished she could stamp her feet, break into a jog, but since that might break up the ice beneath her, she settled on a rhythmic slide, keeping both feet on the ice at the same time, her weight distributed, senses alert for the warning sound of creaking ice.

Her world became a blur of swirling ash-coloured cloud, her snowsuit rattling as the wind hurtled pellets of snow down the lake. Her lungs ached with cold. She rubbed her face but it was numb. Would she get frost nip, like her sister?

She was shivering. That was good. It meant she was still producing heat faster than she lost it.

For a sudden, blissful second, the wind paused as though taking a breath, and she looked ahead, searching for the shoreline. Nothing but thick cloud. Then the wind returned, full strength. The temperature began to drop further.

Abby continued trudging and when she came across a dark patch of ice she glanced at her watch. Nearly twelve o'clock. It felt as though she'd been walking far longer, like half the day. Pray God she was nearly there. Then she could shelter in the forest, build a fire with her emergency supplies, and wait out the storm.

Carefully she skirted the thin ice, and then she saw a gaping black hole of water with clumps of ice floating on its surface, and a great hump of something shiny jammed in one corner.

Abby stared and stared.

It was Connie's body.

She'd come full circle.

She fell to her knees. 'DAMMIT!' she yelled. 'Oh, dammit. I'm going to fucking die out here.'

She couldn't think what to do next. The wind had obviously shifted. Without a compass she could walk in circles until her body froze solid. She raised her head to the sky but the cloud was all around her. In every direction all she could see was grey.

She couldn't work out how it had come to this: her sister lying bleeding to death in the snow while she sat in the middle of a gigantic lake and froze slowly to death.

'Shit,' she said. 'Shit, shit, SHIT!'

She didn't want to die sitting next to Connie's floating corpse. She didn't want to die, not until she'd finished what she'd set out to do.

Abby had just clambered to her feet when she thought she heard something through the blasting wind. It sounded like someone had coughed. She cocked her head, concentrating, but didn't hear it again. It was probably her imagination, playing tricks, the cold making her hallucinate.

She studied the shape of the hole where Connie lay, and tried to work out which way west was. She heard the coughing sound again. It was much closer. And it was real. And no way would it be a bear. They were far too sensible to be out on a crumbling lake in this weather.

'Hello?' she shouted. 'Hello?'

To her astonishment, a shadow materialised right in front of her and launched itself at her thighs.

'Moke? *Moke?*'

She collapsed on to the ice and the dog leaped into her embrace, groaning and puffing, tail wagging furiously, body squirming against hers. She pushed her numb fingers into his ruff and shook him from side to side.

'My God, you followed me all the way here. I don't believe it. You crazy dog, what on earth possessed you?'

His tongue slurped across her face.

'Yeah, I love you too, but you're mad, do you hear? Now, are you going to show me the way back? Walter told me dogs are best at this sort of thing. So come on.'

Abby stood and waited for Moke to move off, to lead her away, but he didn't. He stood right next to her, looking up into her eyes, tail waving at half mast. She began walking west. He didn't move. She tried heading north, but he just stood there, ears pricked, looking at her as though trying to read her mind.

She started walking south. Immediately he trotted past her and took the lead. Maybe it wasn't south, she thought. He obviously knew something she didn't. At least she hoped so.

Moke led her through the whistling, shrieking cloud, sometimes trotting, but as soon as she dropped behind he'd wait, head over his shoulder and watching her, until she caught up. Then off he'd go again, striding confidently ahead.

It was like following a meandering stream as it tried to find its way to the coast. She was sure they were walking in circles, but since they hadn't come across any treacherous or thin ice she put her trust in the dog. Suddenly Moke made a sharp turn. Abby followed his tracks to see he'd avoided some overflow, which occurs when water bursts through the surface and seeps over the top of the ice creating a fragile shell.

Abby could feel her toes growing numb. She couldn't feel her fingers. She went back to windmilling her arms and trying to pump her fingers to bring the blood to them but it didn't seem to be paying off. She felt as though she was slowly freezing to death.

Moke paused and looked back at her as though trying to communicate with her.

'What is it, boy?'

He turned and immediately broke into a canter, then he bunched his hindquarters and leaped into the air, landing awkwardly, half rolling, and then he was upright and looking back at her expectantly.

Abby hurried over to see a yard-wide fissure in the ice, and that on the other side, Moke was standing on a bank with boulders and rocks and brush and sedges. The edge of the lake.

She couldn't leap as far as Moke and started skirting to her right. The dog went ahead. Then he stopped and walked towards her. The ice went all the way to a boulder that came up to her waist. It was surrounded with frosted tufts of grass, flattened by the wind.

As soon as Abby felt her feet sink into soft snow she put every effort into scrambling up the bank, wanting to get away from the lake, put distance between her and all that treacherous, deadly ice, and when the ground levelled out, she saw they were on a track and that there were trees on the other side.

She looked up and down the track but didn't recognise any of it. She frowned. She'd have thought Moke would have followed his own scent, and hers, to the plank bridge, but she couldn't see it anywhere.

Where the hell was she? Where the hell was Connie's car, and MEG and the lab books?

Moke started down the track, steps purposeful, tail high, as though he knew precisely where he was going. She had no choice but to follow.

After two hours she was struggling to put one foot in front of the other. Despite eating the last of her chocolate bars, her legs were like lead, her heartbeat sluggish, and although she knew the dog was leading her to safety, well – at least what *he* considered safety – she didn't know how long she could keep going.

The wind had been dropping, and there were snatches of blue in the sky, but it didn't lift her spirits. She was exhausted, and felt adrift and vulnerable in the endless expanse of the white-grey world.

She came to a halt. Looked around. All she could see was white and a few snatches of black where the snow had melted. Moke came up to her and snibbed her glove between his teeth. Darted away. Came back and barked. Darted away again.

Abby rallied her failing strength and trailed after the dog.

It was three p.m. when she heard a distant rumble, like a train approaching. In the cold, every sound reverberated between the warmer air above and the heavy, cold air below, so she didn't expect a locomotive to appear any second.

But she knew an engine when she heard one.

The roar increased and then it began to diminish into the distance. It was as though she was in her bedroom in Oxford, listening to the traffic pass.

My God, she thought. It's a truck, a goddamn truck. She broke into a stumbling run and immediately Moke sprinted ahead.

She was gasping and panting when the track became a mess of churned snow and gravel. Abby slowed to a walk as she came to a T-junction.

Moke was standing slap bang in the middle of a road, a gritty road of stones and gravel with snow banked on either side, and buckled by permafrost.

Abby stared at the grey and white dog who was looking at her, eyebrows creased, tongue lolling.

He'd only led her straight to the haul road.

Forty-four

The truck driver who picked them up stank of overripe cheese and rotting meat and although Abby knew it was because she'd smelled nothing but snow and ice the past six hours, she couldn't help but crack her window open and try and stick her nose outside.

Moke sat between them on the bench seat,

looking through the windscreen, expression alert as though making sure the driver was taking him in the right direction.

The truck driver – call me Jerry – had bundled her quickly into his truck at her story of her snow machine turning over on top of her friend.

'Nearest place is Lake's Edge,' he said. 'They'll help.'

'Don't you have a radio?' she asked him.

'Sorry, it's bust. Can't take this rig down there either or we'd never get out.'

Grinding through the gears fast as he could, Jerry gave her his thermos of coffee and a stack of sandwiches, but it was the coffee that revived her. Hot liquid warming her core. After a while she unzipped her snow suit and shrugged off her scarf and hat. She was glad Jerry was concentrating on driving his truck close to its limit and left her alone. She didn't want to talk. She felt peculiarly numb inside, her emotions flat, her body drained.

Finally he roared into the village, and with a hiss of air brakes came to a jerky stop outside the Moose. She clambered outside, wanting to run into the bar but her body refused to co-operate, barely managing a shambling trot.

She fell inside to see the fire roaring, the worn wood floor freshly mopped. The place was empty aside from a big Native guy drinking coffee at the bar and a woman opposite him, talking.

Big Joe and Diane turned and stared.

'Your head,' Diane said, alarmed. 'Abby, there's blood...'

Abby touched the side of her scalp where

Connie had hit her with the butt of her gun. The hair was matted with old blood. Almost immediately it started to ache. The cold must have anaesthetised it, along with a good dose of mind-over-matter.

She dropped her hat and scarf to the floor. 'Cal here?'

Big Joe was on his feet. 'He's meant to be with you.'

'He hasn't made it?' Horror coursed through her, bundling her nerves into knots. 'Oh, God... We need to get help to him. And Lisa... Cal had concussion, he might have lost consciousness, got lost ... and Lisa's in a really bad way. They're at Flint's lodge...'

The story came tumbling out, and as she spoke, tears filled her eyes and ran down her face, into the corners of her mouth, but she wasn't crying or sobbing. She kept talking while Diane made phone calls, Big Joe holding her hands gently in his.

'Joe,' Abby said, 'I've something I want you to do for me. Straight away, and before the cops get to know I'm here.'

She told him what she wanted and he gave a nod, strode outside. She desperately wanted to collapse into the armchair by the fire and sleep, but she had to keep moving. She had to hold on.

She tied Moke to the bar's foot rail with her scarf and walked outside. She crossed the slush-filled car park and headed down the main street, for the southern end of town. The snow was melting fast and her boots slipped and skidded on wet ice, then gripped on the gravel, reminding her of when she nearly lost Diane's SUV into the lake after crossing the plank bridge.

She paused when she reached the dirt airstrip. A snow machine buzzed in the distance, a raven cawed above her, but otherwise it was quiet. Nobody seemed to be around.

Abby settled herself on a flaking oil drum. The sun was warm and she unzipped her snow suit down to her waist, wondering how long Big Joe would take.

Half an hour later her skin tightened. She could hear an engine being pushed hard, hear the scrunch of stones and splash of slush. She edged off the drum. A four-wheeler was bouncing wildly towards her. With a squirt of gravel it lurched to a stop. The man jumped off and ran for her, face bleached white with anxiety.

'Is she all right?' he asked.

'I don't know.'

He raised his head to the sky. His fists were clenched.

Abby walked to Michael Flint and wrapped him in her arms. His grip was fierce, like that of a drowning man. He was shuddering.

She held him tight. Told him what they had to do.

'I thought you hated flying,' he said.

'I do.'

Flint prepped his aircraft in three minutes flat. He didn't check the weather, nor did he announce his departure. Abby doubted his helicopter had taken off as fast before, or accelerated as hard.

She kept her gaze outside, desperately searching for Cal, a snow machine caught in a drift or toppled down a ravine, but as they roared north all she saw were blankets of white interspersed with patches of dead grasses and shiny rocks.

Soon, the lake came into view, with the plank bridge at the far end. Moke had, she saw, led her straight across the lake; the shortest route to the haul road. When she got back, she was going to give him a can of spaghetti bolognese. It was the least he deserved.

Flint dropped altitude. The closest he could land was at the southern end of the lake, on a gravel beach. Abby stayed in the helicopter while he jogged away. Her reserves of energy had been used up. She rested her head against the fuselage as she watched him go. It took him forty minutes to collect MEG and the first few lab books, but it felt like forty days.

They arrived at his lodge in a flurry of snow and ice. Two guys had brought Lisa out of the forest on a stretcher and were loading her on board the AST chopper. Cal stood to one side, head hanging.

Abby ran across.

'It wouldn't start,' Cal kept saying over and over to his father. He sounded close to tears. 'The snow machine wouldn't bloody start...'

Victor had an arm around Cal's shoulders. 'You did the best you could, son. You did the best you could...'

Abby spun for Lisa.

'We're flying her straight to Fairbanks hospital,' Demarco was saying briskly. 'They're standing by.'

Flint was nodding as though he was listening to the trooper but Abby knew he wasn't hearing a word. Every cell of his being appeared concentrated on Lisa.

Lisa was covered in gauze. Face, neck, shoulders and hands ... only the tips of her fingers showed.

'Hey, sis,' Abby said softly, 'it's me. And Mike's here too. Don't talk... We've brought something for you...'

Abby brought up the smooth metal box and brushed it against Lisa's fingertips.

Lisa made a gasping sound.

'I stopped Connie,' Abby said. 'I kept my promise.'

Forty-five

Abby loped down the street, ignoring rush-hour stares. The pavement was damp and dirty, her bare feet filthy, but she didn't care. She should have thrown out those bloody shoes when she'd first been tempted.

When she came to the rubbish bin by the bus stop she flung the high-heeled pumps inside. No way could she give them to charity to torture some other poor soul.

Five minutes later she was padding into the house, yelling, 'I'm home!'

'See you when you're ready!' her mother called.

'Red or white?' asked Ralph from the kitchen.

371

'White, thanks.' Abby gulped down half the glass before her equanimity began to resurface.

'Bad day?' Ralph squinted in sympathy. He didn't remark on her bare feet.

'Too many meetings.' She took another glug of wine. 'I'm not supposed to be locked up inside, I'm supposed to be *outside* doing my job.'

'You poor thing,' he commiserated. 'I'll make some fresh pesto to cheer you up. Spaghetti and pesto do you?'

'Lovely.' She turned so he couldn't see her face. Whenever anyone mentioned spaghetti she thought of Moke, and when she thought of Moke she wanted to cry. She'd only looked after the damned dog for a few weeks but she missed him dreadfully.

'Go and see your mother then,' Ralph told her. 'Supper in half an hour.'

Abby trailed down the corridor, hearing the familiar rumble of traffic outside, breathing the odour of sweet peas and beeswax. Normally she'd relish the feeling of an evening at home, but since she'd returned from Alaska she'd felt cramped and claustrophobic, unable to settle in one place for more than thirty minutes.

'Hi, Mum.'

'Darling.'

She went and kissed her cheek. Julia, as usual, was working, her half-moon glasses perched on her nose. 'Ralph looking after you?'

'Always.'

'You don't have to move out, you know. He loves having you here.'

'Mum,' she protested, 'of course I have to move

out. Three's a crowd, remember?'

Julia snorted. 'It's not as though we're getting married or anything...'

'But you're living together,' Abby said for the hundredth time, 'which means you can't cavort naked if I'm hanging around like a bad smell.'

Julia burst out laughing. 'Now, there's a thought.'

'Anyway, I've found somewhere nice.'

'Just nice?'

Abby thought about the apartment she'd seen, a great lofty space with tall windows, but it still didn't feel big enough.

'It's perfect,' she lied.

She turned to head upstairs for a shower, but Julia held up a hand.

'Lisa rang.'

'How is she?'

'Doing as well as can be expected.' Julia took off her glasses and pinched the bridge of her nose. 'She'd like you to go over for a couple of weeks. Nothing urgent. She thought you could do with a holiday. Help her with a bit of R & R. She's horribly bored.'

Abby felt a little hop of excitement. 'I can't. I'm swamped at work.'

'That's what I told her.'

'I've got three private gardens to design by the weekend, and there's Lord and Lady Cunich's estate—'

'I told her you'd be too busy to go.' Julia had pushed her glasses back and was peering at a computer printout.

'Yes, well,' Abby huffed, 'it's impossible.'

Forty-six

Mac flew low over the dirt runway and studied a wind sock in an alder.

'Looks good to me.'

At the end of the strip was a Cessna and a Piper Super Cub, and despite Abby telling herself that if they'd landed safely, so would Mac, her knuckles were white. She'd forgotten how much she hated flying, and right this instant wished she'd never left Oxford.

Mac made a wide turn, and dropped altitude. The plane skimmed a bluff and kissed the gravel, roared towards the parked aircraft, and swung around with ten feet to spare.

Abby unbuckled her harness and hopped outside. Resisting the urge to kiss the ground, she shuffled her boots in the gravel instead, glad to have the earth beneath her feet again.

Mac brought out her bag and looked around appreciatively. 'Nice place,' he said.

When she'd last been here, she hadn't seen the beauty of Michael Flint's hunting lodge. Running on fear and adrenalin, she'd taken in the basics, and that was all her memory had retained: a monochrome picture of one big main house with five smaller cabins opposite, and a lean-to housing the four-wheelers and snow machines.

The reality in the soft September sunshine was quite different. The logs glowed honey-warm and the trees were luminous in capes of golds and reds and greens. Shiny globes of red berries clustered everywhere she looked. It was so still she could hear the buzz of a wasp near by, and the sound of water tumbling over rocks. A pair of eagles soared above the cottonwood trees.

'Abby,' Mac's voice was a whisper, 'over there.'

A female moose was foraging at the edge of the forest. It looked as though she was after the leaves and roots of a saxifrage plant. Suddenly the moose flung up her head as a large grey form burst from behind the lodge. The moose took one look, and fled. Abby was tempted to do the same. Facing a husky headed full speed for you wasn't for the faint hearted.

Moke knocked her straight off her feet. Sprawled in the grass she was half-laughing, half-protesting as he nipped and slurped and made that doggy groaning sound deep in his throat.

'Told you he was your dog.'

Abby scrambled up to greet her sister. The last time she'd seen Lisa was in Los Angeles in July, just before her first round of plastic surgery. Mike Flint had told Abby it had gone well, but she hadn't realised how well until now. Lisa was no longer wrapped in gauze, nor was she wearing the oversized plastic gloves that used to protect her hands. Her skin still looked raw and was covered in lumps and caverns – deeply, irrevocably scarred – but her dark eyes sparkled.

'Like it?' she asked.

Abby studied the bright pink wig. 'Suits you.'

'Yeah, so Mike said.' Lisa turned to Mac. 'Fancy a coffee?'

'Nah. Got a pick-up in Lake's Edge I can't be late for. Good to see ya, though. Lookin' good as usual.'

Lisa chuckled. 'Sure, Mac. Sure.'

Abby stood with Lisa, stroking Moke, and watched Mac take off. The sun warmed her skin, burrowing under her T-shirt and the denim of her jeans.

'See that?' Lisa said, waving at the Cessna at the end of the strip.

Abby nodded.

'Damned man landed without permission this morning, without a word of warning...'

'Was he in trouble?'

Lisa studied her. 'No, but he might be.'

'Why? Who is he?'

'Cal Pegati.'

'For God's sake, Lisa, I thought I asked you–'

'Take your fingers out of your ears, will you? I didn't tell him you were here. He would have heard from Diane. Or Victor or Mac or any one of that lot. You know what it's like out here.'

'Shit.'

'Yeah, well. I'm going to pick some cranberries while you go see him. Sort yourselves out.' Lisa gave Abby a stern look. 'Just remember, *it wasn't his fault.*'

Part of her knew Lisa was right, but the other couldn't forgive Cal for not regaining consciousness sooner. She'd seen his fingers twitch barely a minute before Connie had splashed the last of the fuel over Lisa. She kept replaying the scene, wishing with every fibre of her being that Cal had risen with his gun and shot Connie dead. But he hadn't, and now she didn't think she could ever look at him without reliving what her sister had gone through.

When Cal stepped out of the lodge and walked her way, her heartbeat went into overdrive. She wasn't sure whether it was nerves, or simply because he looked so damned good. Moke bowled over and greeted him with a lolling tongue and waving tail. 'Hey, boy.' Cal patted the dog. 'She going to talk to us, you think?'

His shirtsleeves were bunched at his elbows, his shirt open at the neck, showing skin lean and tanned from the summer. He didn't look as though he had an ounce of spare fat on him. His burns had healed, and she had to stop herself from reaching up and touching the blemishes on his cheeks.

'I won't take up much of your time,' he said.

She shrugged.

'You left before I could say goodbye,' Cal said. 'Again.'

Abby averted her eyes. 'Sorry.'

'I'd like to say goodbye now. Properly.'

Startled, her gaze flew to meet his.

'I won't badger you again. I know how you feel about me. I also know how I feel about you, and probably always will.'

He put his fingers on her jaw and gently raised her head. Pressed a kiss against her lips. His mouth cupped hers with easy familiarity. Warm and soft and tender. His eyes were closed.

She felt his lower lip catch hers, and she was about to part her lips, kiss him back, God, *how she wanted to*, when he pulled away. Looked her straight in the eye.

'Goodbye, Abby.'

Stunned, she watched him head for his Cessna. She wasn't sure what she felt, but she wasn't sure she wanted him to leave, either. Moke trotted after Cal, paused to look back at her, then stood undecided.

Cal hopped inside his aircraft, and she was wondering if she had the courage to go over, when he started the engine, leaned outside. He yelled, 'Moke!'

The husky looked between them. His tail was down. Abby suddenly realised that Cal must have been looking after Moke all this time, that he'd adopted the dog when she'd left.

'Your call!' he shouted.

With a final glance at Abby, Moke burst into a gallop straight for the Cessna and sprang inside.

Abby took a step forward, hesitated. Cal still had to do his pre-flight check, she had a couple of minutes to think...

To her horror, the Cessna sprang forward. Cal wasn't hanging around. He was taxiing for take-off.

Abby broke into a run. Please God, let him see me, make him stop. Breath hot in her throat, she raced after the airplane, bouncing along the strip. He'd see her when he turned. He couldn't miss her, surely.

She was halfway along the strip when Cal turned, and without pausing, pushed the throttle. He was glancing at his instruments, then glancing forward through the windscreen, then down at his instruments...

Abby was running and yelling. 'Stop, wait, Cal. Wait!'

The aircraft got enough air under its wings and he pulled back and began to soar. At the last second, Cal saw her. He smiled and gave her a wave.

Then he was gone.

Forty-seven

Supper was buttered salmon steaks and salad, followed by warm pecan pie and whipped cream. Abby's favourite food, except she found it hard to eat. She kept touching her lips, thunderstruck that a single kiss could elicit such fierce emotion in her, and scared that it was just her body's response to not having sex in over a year.

'It doesn't have to be over, *over*, just because he wanted closure or whatever he came here for,' Michael Flint remarked.

'You should go and see him,' Lisa added for the hundredth time. 'He's crazy about you, you're crazy about him, what the hell's the problem? I mean we all know he loved Saffron and she loved him back, but it's been nearly four years...' Lisa swallowed, then gave a wobbly smile. 'Sorry. I miss her sometimes. I've even been known to go and talk to her when I'm in Fairbanks. She's buried there, so she's not too far away.'

'She sounded like an amazing woman,' Abby ventured.

'She was. But then, so are you.' Lisa smiled.

'I can't skin a moose.'

'Oh dear. That is an insurmountable problem. Cal won't look at you twice until you master that particular art.'

Lisa finished her second helping of pie, then got to her feet. 'Look, let's forget about Cal a minute,' she said. 'Mike and I have a proposal for you. Come next door?'

Next door had a blazing fire in the enormous hearth that kept the autumnal chill at bay. There were heads of caribou and moose on the walls, a bear skin on the floor. Thick rugs and paintings gave splashes of colour.

Lisa went to the big table by the window, where a model village was displayed. Log cabins with thatched roofs, a stream and a pond with ducks, a church, fields of crops and horses grazing. It was picturesque and bucolic and Abby had looked at it earlier – when she'd first arrived – and almost immediately, had forgotten it.

'This is Bearpaw,' said Lisa. 'The first fully sustainable ecovillage in Alaska.'

Abby raised her eyebrows.

'It hasn't been built yet, but we've got the land, and the permission.' Lisa's face was alight, and there was a gleam in Mike's eyes too.

'It's just north of Fairbanks, so it's not as if it's in the middle of nowhere. It'll be a sustainable community. It's got fresh running water, a good variety of agricultural and natural resources... And you can guess where the power will come from.'

'MEG,' said Abby.

'Too damn right.'

While Lisa had been fighting for her life in hospital, Mike Flint had flown MEG to Arlington, Virginia. Using Lisa's Power of Attorney, he had registered the technology for patent. The patent had been approved two months ago, and hadn't been contested.

Connie's husband, Scott, had protested his innocence, but was being held in jail without bail until his trial in October. He was, the court had decided, a serious flight risk.

'We're going to make sure it works a hundred per cent before releasing it to the world,' Lisa added. 'And what better way to show MEG off than by using an ecovillage.'

She took a breath. 'We do, however, need some advice about stuff we're not that great at. I mean, I'm a scientist, Mike's an executive... We need someone who knows plants and what grows and what doesn't, and what's feasible and what's not...'

'You need an environmental architect.'

Lisa swung to Flint. 'See?'

'Fine by me.' He nodded.

'Are you going totally green?' asked Abby, now curious. 'Using organic paints and glues and stuff? Clay tiles for the roofs...' She glanced at the model village. 'How many people are you planning to have live here? You'll need some sort of social contract for them, or social management plan.'

Abby sent them both a sharp look. 'Are you sure you've thought this through?'

'Oh, yes.' Lisa looked cheerful. 'But it's rather dependent on whether a certain person will work with us or not – someone we can trust to do a good job and not to rip us off.'

Abby stared at her sister, then at Flint. Both were grinning.

'You can't mean me.'

'And why not?' said Lisa archly. 'We'd pay you well, and I mean *really* well. And you'd love it. You'd be outdoors and not stuck in an office. You'd be striding about overseeing the building, the planting, re-routing the stream...'

It was amazing and incredible and fantastic and Abby couldn't quite believe it. 'I'm not sure.'

'Oh, come on. You said yourself you missed the place, the space, the *bigness* of it.'

'At least, think about it,' Flint told her.

'Sure.' She stared at the ecovillage model, completely lost for words.

Through the hallway came the squawk of a radio. It sounded like, 'Hike, hum in,' which Abby took to mean, 'Mike, come in.'

He vanished, to return a handful of seconds later. 'It's for you,' he told Abby.

'What?' She couldn't think of anybody in Alaska who would want to radio her.

Lisa glanced at Flint, and smiled. 'Perhaps it's Big Joe. He wanted to catch up. Maybe buy you a drink at the Moose when you're next down that way.'

Abby trotted into the kitchen. Picked up the receiver, pressed the button on the side. 'Hello?'

'Does your running after my aircraft mean you'll have dinner with Moke and me next week?'

This Large Print Book for the partially sighted, who cannot read normal print, is published under the auspices of

THE ULVERSCROFT FOUNDATION